To Mor:

It was a pleasure to meet you.

All the best,

Nancy Prud'homme

# Behind the Drapes

Nancy Prudhomme

authorHOUSE®

*AuthorHouse*™
*1663 Liberty Drive, Suite 200*
*Bloomington, IN 47403*
*www.authorhouse.com*
*Phone: 1-800-839-8640*

© *2009 Nancy Prudhomme. All rights reserved.*

*No part of this book may be reproduced, stored in a retrieval system, or transmitted by any means without the written permission of the author.*

*First published by AuthorHouse    2/27/2009*

*ISBN: 978-1-4389-5898-9 (sc)*
*ISBN: 978-1-4389-5899-6 (hc)*

*Printed in the United States of America*
*Bloomington, Indiana*

*This book is printed on acid-free paper.*

*I dedicate this book to my husband Michel. You always believed in me and your constant support and encouragement allowed me to accomplish my dream.*

## *Special Thanks*

To my dearest friend Juliann for always being there to listen and encourage me, I thank you.

To my sweet Samantha, your support and kind words during the publishing process of this book were invaluable to me.

# Chapter 1

Sheila sat at her desk and waited for the bell to go off. School was almost over, it was her birthday, and she was hoping for a pleasant evening. The bell started to ring, and Mrs. Morris reminded her class to have their permission slips in by Friday for the field trip the following week. Oh, how Sheila wished that for once she could go, but she dreaded asking her parents for money. Then again, since it was her birthday, maybe they would say yes.

Mrs. Morris stopped Sheila as she was leaving and wished her a happy birthday. Mrs. Morris cared for all her students, but there was something special about the beautiful little girl with the big, sad eyes. She knew Sheila was from a poor family, but almost all the children at West Central Public School were from poor families. Eighty percent of the students were from the project. Sheila was a small child with golden blonde hair, big blue eyes, and creamy white skin, but all the teacher could see were those sad eyes.

Sheila was always jumpy and nervous, and at times she seemed to drift away. Sometimes, a look of terror would come across her face that worried the experienced teacher, but it was the early 1970s, and no teacher had the right to interfere in family business based only on suspicion. Sheila would never tell of her life at home. She knew how dangerous that would be.

Sheila put her coat on and went outside to her tree—the big weeping willow just outside of school grounds—to wait for Joann, her little sister. Sheila loved that tree; she had spent many hours sitting under it with her back against the trunk, imagining that no one could see her. She felt safe as long as she was invisible. It was spring, and she knew it wouldn't be long before the tree's branches would grow to reach the ground. Then, she would have her safe place back. The thought filled her with a warm feeling. How rare it was for anyone in her family to feel safe. She would enjoy these moments, because they didn't come often.

Sheila was pulled from her thoughts as Joann came running over.

"Where have you been? You know we can't be late," snapped Sheila. Joann had the same complexion and hair color as Sheila, but her huge blue eyes did not yet show any sadness.

"I'm sorry, Sheila. Look what my teacher gave me—a gold star!" beamed Joann.

"Good for you, Joann. Now put that in your bag, and let's get going home before we are late," said Sheila. She grabbed Joann's hand, and they started home. Sheila looked down at Joann, and she knew she would always take care of her. Nobody would hurt Joann the way they hurt Sheila, not even him. Sheila didn't know how, but she was sure she would take care of her sister.

They passed through the fence and into the project, every house like the next, row after row of houses. It was an ugly sight: a four-foot-by-four-foot square of brown grass in front of each house, and around the grass, four white cement pillars linked by a thick black chain. The pillars reminded Sheila of headstones in a cemetery she had seen once in a picture at school.

The houses were all square boxes with white wood siding; the same roof seemed to cover the ten houses in each row. One row faced north-to-south, the other, east-to-west. Each house had two upstairs windows, one downstairs window, and two doors, front and back. The back door entered into a fenced yard that was six feet by six feet of grass. Like the front, this square seemed to be brown throughout spring, summer, and fall.

It was the only home Sheila had ever known. She had never been out of the project, so she assumed most people lived like this. Ironically, the project was called Golden Street. It was known to everyone in the city as a place where all the welfare bums and the dregs of society lived. Sheila Parks lived at 1966 Golden Street, unit 8.

Walking home, she remembered it was her birthday. Maybe, oh please God, she hoped, they would have a calm evening, but Sheila knew anything could happen. They reached the house in about eight minutes; their mother only allowed ten minutes for the trip. Joann chatted the whole way, so excited about her gold star. Sheila just smiled at her and listened. At seven, Joann was still relatively sheltered from most of the abuse. She did see her siblings get their share of beatings, but as the baby, she had yet to receive any pain at the hands of her parents. She seemed almost happy; however, she felt the tension when he was in the house, just like everyone else.

As they approached the front door, one of their older brothers, Rick, was there with some friends. Rick was fourteen and the apple of his father's eye, although this did nothing to shield him from his fair share of beatings—Joann seemed to be the only one to escape. Rick was the spitting image of his father. With his light brown hair, soft blue eyes, and lean build, all the girls in the project thought he was the most handsome boy they had ever seen. He knew his power with his father, and he used it to his advantage as often as he could. He was the golden boy in Sheila's house.

"Well look, it's the birthday girl," said Rick with a smile. "You better hurry in the house. You don't want her to start yelling already." He rolled his eyes, which set both the girls giggling.

As soon as they entered the house, they could hear her yelling at Pauline: "Did you hear what I said, you useless piece of crap? Wipe the table before you set it!". Their mother was a beautiful woman with light brown hair, deep brown eyes, and a body that stopped most men in their tracks. However, she had an ugly side that was mean and selfish. Her name was Hugette. She had met Bobby, Sheila's father, at the age of twelve. He'd been twenty at the time. By the time she was twenty-five years old, Hugette had borne five children.

Hugette was the youngest of twelve children; she was raised in a loving Christian home. She told her children often how she had been spoiled rotten by her father. He would buy her anything she wanted; she would only have to comment that she liked something, and it was hers. She told her children about the huge meals and her safe, comfortable upbringing. All the while, her children went hungry, were beaten often, and wore only old hand-me-downs from her family—the family that still spoke to her. She had been disowned for coming home pregnant at the age of sixteen. For this, she blamed her children, as if in some way it was their fault she had lost her father's love, respect, and money. The child whom Hugette blamed the most was Pauline, the result of her first pregnancy. However, that pregnancy had produced two children, and the other twin, a boy named Peter, was Hugette's favorite.

Pauline and Peter were fifteen years of age, and like most twins they had a special bond. Peter tried to comfort Pauline in her living hell, but his existence was no better, holding the position of his father's favorite punching bag. Pauline was of average build, with dirty blonde hair and the same blue eyes as the rest of the family. However, she wore glasses, something else her mother seemed to dislike about her. Pauline was Hugette's slave; she did all the cooking and cleaning in the house and had basically raised Sheila and Joann.

Hugette continued with her instructions for Pauline: "When you are finished setting the table, go get the girls out of their school clothes, and make sure the front hallway is cleared of shoes and clothes.... And stupid, make sure it's done right!" she demanded. Sheila walked into the plain, empty kitchen, not a picture on the wall or a clock, only a chrome table and seven chairs. As Sheila saw the table, she felt so sad; Pauline was only setting six places.

Sheila looked at her mother and asked a question she already knew the answer to. "Mom, could Pauline eat with us tonight since it's my birthday, please?"

Her mother turned to face her with such an evil look, Sheila felt herself stepping back. Hugette hissed, "You know she isn't part of our family anymore, and if you ask again, there will be no birthday, you hear me?" With tears filling her eyes, Sheila nodded yes and went to her bedroom.

About a year earlier, Hugette had announced that she had heard Pauline saying bad things about their family, so she was no longer a part of it. She was only permitted to leave her room for school and chores.

*Behind the Drapes*

Hugette never did say what was said, or to whom, but that didn't matter. They were children, and children didn't have any opinions in this house. The children were expected to do what they were told, and that was that. All the children living in this house knew their place, and would never dare question anything.

The house had four bedrooms: one for Hugette and Bobby, one for Peter and Rick, one for Pauline, and Sheila and Joann shared the last. Sheila's bedroom was just as empty as the other rooms in the house—bunk beds and one dresser for her and Joann to share. Not that sharing a dresser was a problem, since they didn't have many clothes.

Sheila sat on her bed and cried. Why did her mother have to be so mean to Pauline? Sheila loved Pauline. She had always been more of a mother to Sheila and Joann than Hugette had ever been. A moment later, Sheila could hear Joann excitedly talking about her gold star. Then the bedroom door opened, and Pauline and Joann entered. Pauline came over to Sheila and asked her to stop crying.

Sheila sobbed, "I want you to be part of the family and eat with us. I miss you."

"Me, too," cried Joann. Pauline smiled and held them close. She reminded them to be patient and wait for her to finish high school. Then she would get a job, and they could move out, the three of them. They said okay and got changed. Once Sheila and Joann's school clothes were hung up, Pauline went to the kitchen to finish making dinner. The girls followed her downstairs.

The girls came into the kitchen. "When is dinner, Mom?" asked Sheila.

"In an hour, as soon as Pauline gets it on the table. Go to the basement and play or watch television," replied Hugette. "Pauline, as soon as you get dinner finished, you get back to your room," she insisted.

"It will be ready in five minutes. I will put it in the oven on low to keep warm until Dad gets home," Pauline told her mother.

"Fine," Hugette snapped. The girls went into the living room, but the boys were watching the television, so they decided to go play in the basement.

It was damp and cold in the basement, but he never came downstairs, so they spent a lot of time here when he was home. It was an empty room. On one side was their mother's washer and drier, which was only used by Pauline. On the other was a small toy table with chairs that had been given to Sheila and Joann by their uncle Pierre. Pierre was Hugette's brother, the only person in her family to ever come by the house. He was the only one of their mother's family the children had ever met.

Sheila reached under the table to pull out a small box. In it were all the toys Sheila and Joann owned, mostly colouring books and crayons and a few puzzles. To the girls it was gold; they picked out a picture and started to colour the picture together. The crayons were starting to get very small, but they didn't mind. They had lots of fun, and they colored a very nice picture they were making for Pauline.

Peter came down into the basement a few minutes later. He was a sweet boy who had the weight of the world on his shoulders. He did not look like his twin. He had black hair with the same soft blue eyes as the rest of the children, but he had a stocky frame, unlike the thin build of the others.

"The show on TV that Rick and I were watching is over now if you want to watch some TV, before he gets home," announced Peter. The girls finished their picture and went to the living room to watch television.

The living room, like the other rooms, was sparsely furnished. A small table sat between the sofa and an armchair, and then there was Bobby's best friend, the television. The girls sat on the sofa and watched a cartoon. When the first commercial came on, Sheila told Joann to stay put and she would bring the picture to Pauline. They both knew if Sheila got caught, she would be in for a beating. Joann was willing to stay and watch TV if Sheila wanted to risk bringing the picture to Pauline. Sheila would make sure to let Pauline know the picture was from them both.

Just as she reached the stairs, she heard Hugette say, "Where are you going?" Sheila turned to see Hugette standing at the kitchen window, watching for Bobby.

"I have to go to the bathroom," replied Sheila.

"Be quick about it, and don't forget to wash your hands," responded Hugette. Sheila raced up the stairs. At the top of the stairs there were two bedrooms, the boys' and Pauline's, and then the bathroom. She stopped in front of Pauline's door and slipped the picture underneath. When she came out of the bathroom and headed for the stairs, she saw Pauline standing in her doorway, holding the picture with a big smile on her face. She winked at Sheila and closed the door very quietly. It was worth the risk, thought Sheila as she ran down the stairs.

When Sheila got to the bottom of the stairs, she saw Hugette closing the drapes of the kitchen window. All the hairs on her back and neck stood up. The closing of the drapes meant he was home. She raced past her mother and into the living room; she sat on the couch with Joann and whispered, "He's home." Both girls knew they now had to be very quiet. Children in their home were to be seen, not heard. It was the golden rule: you only speak when spoken to. They held hands and stared blindly at the television screen.

A few minutes later, Bobby entered the living room. He walked to the television, grabbed the TV guide, and looked through it. After deciding what to watch, he changed the channel and turned to look at the girls.

"Get off the sofa. I want to watch TV."

The girls jumped down without a word and left the room. Sheila turned to see him stretch out on the sofa; he was the most terrifying man on earth.

Bobby Parks was a handsome man. He had brown hair and those icy blue eyes that terrified his family. He was an only child who never knew his father; his mother, who was a nurse, raised him in an upper-middle-class home. She worked long hours, and therefore was not home very often. Bobby spent most of his childhood with babysitters who didn't care what he was up to, so long as he was out of their hair. He was constantly in trouble, and he dropped out of school at an early age.

When he met Hugette, she was the most beautiful girl he had ever seen. He had walked into the hockey arena and there she was, talking with a few girls. Bobby had walked right over to Hugette and introduced himself so confidently. He knew at that moment he would have her for life, and he spent the next four years trying to get her into bed and pregnant. He knew her family would never approve of him, but if she were pregnant, she would have to get married—and that's what happened. Now that she was his, he would do anything to keep her. If she wasn't with him, nobody would have her.

Sheila went into the kitchen to ask her mother if she and Joann could go out to play until dinner. "Dinner will be on the table in five minutes. Go wash up and I'll call you when it's ready," replied Hugette. Sheila brought Joann upstairs and made sure she washed her hands, then washed her own.

"Now, don't touch anything, Joann. You know what will happen if you get them dirty and she thinks we lied about washing them," warned Sheila. They went back downstairs into the living room. Rick was in the armchair, so Sheila and Joann sat on the floor with Peter. He smiled at them, gave them the don't-make-a-sound sign, and they nodded. They knew better.

Hugette hollered, "Dinner is ready!"

They didn't move a muscle until Bobby got up and left the room. Then, one by one, they went into the kitchen and took their places at the table. Sheila watched her mother serve dinner. Bobby was first, as always. He received a huge amount of mashed potatoes and corn with six sausages. Next was Hugette—four sausages and a large amount of potatoes and corn. Next were the boys—three sausages each, and a fair amount of potatoes and corn. Finally, Sheila, Pauline, and Joann were served. Their plates consisted of one sausage with a small spoonful of potatoes and corn.

Sheila and Joann's plates were placed in front of them, while Pauline's was placed on the counter for her to have after the family was finished. She always had a cold dinner, but, as she use to say, cold dinner was better than no dinner. They had all experienced no dinner from time to time.

Everyone sat and ate in silence. Finally, Hugette spoke. "Bobby, when I went to the store today to get some groceries, there was a sign outside of Simpson's Sears saying they were hiring. Do you think I could apply for some part-time work?"

"Are you crazy? You know I like my dinner on the table when I get home from work, and a clean house. How will you work and still have everything ready for me?" he responded.

"I've given this some thought. We both will agree, some extra money would be useful around here, but I can't let my duties slide, so the best solution that I have come up with is to take Pauline out of

*Behind the Drapes*

school. Then she can cook and clean and take care of the kids while I'm at work," continued Hugette.

"Hey, now that is a good idea. After all, she is a girl, and girls don't need an education. They only need to know how to diaper a baby and cook a meal. Okay, you can go see about a job tomorrow morning," Bobby said.

Bobby's mood seemed to improve with the thought of more money flowing into the house. He turned to Rick and asked, "How was school? Did you feel up any sluts? Let me smell your fingers."

Rick laughed and responded, "There is a new one in school I have my eye on, and I'll get my hands on her soon."

"That's my boy. Like father like son, you can have any woman you want," exclaimed Bobby.

Bobby turned then, and looked at Sheila. Sheila, noticing this, started to tremble. "So, it's your birthday today. Did you have a good day at school?" Bobby asked.

"Yes I did, Daddy," replied Sheila. At that moment, she threw caution to the wind and decided to ask about the field trip with Mrs. Morris. "Daddy, the teacher said today that we have a field trip next week. I need to get my permission slip signed, and it costs a dollar. Can I go? Please, Daddy?" As soon as the words were out of her mouth, she knew what a mistake it had been to ask.

"You must be kidding," Bobby snapped. "You expect me to spend money on school for a girl? Did you not just hear what I said about school and girls? I guess you must be deaf. Let me repeat it so there is no mistake. You are a girl and girls do not need an education. All they need to know is how to diaper a baby and cook. So the answer is no, and don't ask me another stupid question like that again. Do you hear me?" Sheila felt the tears sting her eyes, and she nodded yes to her father. "Now shut up and eat your dinner. I don't want to hear another word from you," Bobby barked.

Sheila wanted to cry, but she knew better. That would infuriate her father, and she did not want to face his wrath. Just then, Rick started to speak, which broke the tension for the moment. Sheila was so happy with Rick, until she heard what he was saying. "Hey Dad, Sheila just reminded me. I have a field trip with my school this Friday. It only costs five dollars. Can I go?"

"Well, of course you can, my boy. Remind me on Thursday and I'll give you the money," responded Bobby. Sheila felt the tears sting her eyes again, half for the trip and half at the thought of Pauline having to quit school. What would happen to her plan of getting a job and taking Joann and Sheila away from this place?

Everybody had finished their dinner when Bobby looked over at Sheila. "You have something on your face. Get upstairs and wash your face, and don't come down until it's clean!"

Sheila got up from the table and ran up the stairs, into the bathroom; she looked in the mirror, but could see nothing on her face. She grabbed the facecloth and soap, and started to scrub and scrub. She scrubbed until her face was red. When she was finished, she rinsed the facecloth and hung it up. Heaven forbid, if something was not in its place, there would be hell to pay.

When Sheila arrived back in the kitchen, Bobby called her over and demanded to see her face. "I thought I told you to wash your face, and it's still dirty. Do you want me to go up with you and wash it, because if you do I'll come up and wash it until you have no skin left. Now get up there and wash it right!" Bobby shouted. He held her face firmly with one hand, and as soon as he let it go, Sheila ran back to the bathroom.

Sheila stood in front of the mirror and stared. She could see no dirt. All she could see was Bobby's handprint. So she scrubbed and scrubbed; she would scrub until she was sure it was gone. After about five minutes of scrubbing, Peter appeared in the doorway. "Come downstairs now, Sheila," he said.

"I can't, I can't find the dirt, so I'm not sure I got it all. He will be mad and hit me. You heard him, Peter," sobbed Sheila.

"It's okay, Sheila. I just looked and it's gone," Peter said.

When Sheila entered the kitchen, Bobby called her over. "Let's see the face. You idiot, you scrubbed until you drew blood to the surface of your skin. You are so stupid. There was no dirt; we just needed you out of the room so we could put the candles on your birthday cake. Oh well, you took too long, so we started to eat the cake without you. Maybe next year you won't be so stupid. Now sit down and eat your cake." Without a word or a glance, Sheila went to her chair and sat down. This time, she could not hold back the tears. She cried and ate her cake.

*Behind the Drapes*

Bobby got up from the table to go watch TV. "Bobby, we haven't given Sheila her gift," remarked Hugette.

Bobby turned to look at Sheila. "Do you deserve a gift, Sheila?" Sheila looked at her father with her little face covered in tears, and before she could answer him, he threw her gift at her. "Well, you little baby, I don't think you deserve one, crying like a little baby. Here, catch!" A small box flew through the air, bounced off Sheila's face, and hit the floor. Without another word, Bobby left the room.

Sheila did not move a muscle until everyone had left the table. As she stared at her cake in front of her, she felt a small hand on hers. She looked up and saw Joann smiling at her. "Happy birthday, Sheila. Pauline and I made this birthday card for you. We love you."

Joann bent down, picked up Sheila's present, and handed it to her. Sheila heard somebody come back into the kitchen. She turned to see her mother.

"Sheila, eat your cake and you and Joann can go play for a while in the basement," instructed Hugette.

"Mom, I don't want any more cake. May I be excused now?" Sheila said.

"You don't want your cake? You want to waste it? Next year I won't waste my time making you a cake, you ungrateful little bitch! Get out of my sight!" screamed Hugette. Joann grabbed Sheila's gift, and the girls left the room.

Just as they were at the basement door, Hugette yelled to them, "Go tell Pauline she can come and clean the kitchen now." Sheila told Joann to go ahead into the basement, and she went upstairs to get Pauline. When she got to Pauline's door, she could hear her crying. She knocked and went inside. Pauline sat on her bed, and when she saw Sheila, she tried to hide her tears.

"What's wrong, Pauline?" Sheila said.

"What are you doing up here, Sheila?"

"Mom told me to come and get you. It's time to clean the kitchen and have your supper. I didn't eat my cake, so you can have some."

"Thank you, Sheila. Peter just told me about what Mom and Dad were talking about at dinner. I hope they don't make me quit school. I better get going before she starts to scream. Go play, and we will talk later, when I get you ready for bed." Pauline leaned forward and kissed Sheila on the cheek. Her lips were a salve to Sheila's raw skin.

Sheila went down into the basement. Joann was sitting at their little table. "Sheila, open your present now," pleaded Joann. Sheila sat down and looked at the package. She knew what it was—she and Joann always got the same thing for their birthdays. She peeled back the wrapping paper, and there was her birthday present: eight new crayons. Joann and Sheila squealed with delight.

"Let's try them out, Sheila. I picked out a picture while I was waiting for you. Do you like it, Sheila?" Joann asked.

"Sounds like a great plan, and I do like the picture," Sheila said. Sheila grabbed the crayon box and opened it. She pulled out a crayon, and at that moment, both smiles disappeared from their faces. All the crayons were broken from when Bobby had thrown them. Some pieces were even smaller than their old ones.

"They're all broken, Sheila. What will we do?" Joann cried.

"We are going to colour our picture, and we will use the pieces just like we did before," Sheila demanded. "Okay?" Joann nodded, and they started on their picture.

When they were just about finished, Hugette yelled down to them, "Sheila, Joann, put your toys away! Get up here!" Without wasting a second, the girls had everything put away. They ran up the stairs.

When the girls opened the basement door, they saw Bobby, Hugette, and Pauline sitting at the kitchen table. Pauline's face said it all. Tears were streaming down her face as she looked at Sheila and Joann, trying to smile. "Go get ready for bed and brush your teeth, and you can watch TV for half an hour before bed," demanded Hugette. They quickly ran to their bedroom and closed the door. They quietly changed and went to brush their teeth. Just as they were approaching the bathroom, Peter was coming out. He gave them the sign for *be quiet*, and pulled them into his bedroom.

"Why is Pauline crying, Peter?" asked Sheila.

"I guess she is not happy about leaving school. I don't blame her. I would be, too, if I was her. Sheila, I just wanted to check your face. He hit you pretty close to your eye. Does it hurt very much? Can you see alright?"

"It's okay, Peter. Don't worry," Sheila said. Peter told the girls to go downstairs and watch TV, and not to make a sound. They brushed their teeth and did exactly what they were told.

When they entered the living room, Rick was sitting on the sofa watching the television. They sat on the sofa next to him. "Sorry about your school trip. You know how it is, you being a girl and all. I can't stop having fun just because you can't have any," informed Rick with a smile. Sometimes, Sheila found it difficult to like Rick; he could be so much like their father.

"Do you have to rub it in, Rick?" Peter questioned as he entered the living room.

"Keep your nose out of it, Peter, if you know what's good for you," responded Rick. At that moment, Peter pounced on Rick. He pounded his fist on his Rick's face until blood appeared. There was a look on Peter's face that scared Sheila and Joann. They jumped down off the sofa just as Bobby entered the room.

He walked over to the boys and pulled Peter off Rick. "You want to fight, Peter? Well, let's go!" screamed Bobby as he threw Peter into the wall. Peter hit the wall with a loud thud and slid to the floor. Within a second, Bobby was on top of him, punching and punching as Peter tried to defend himself from the blows.

Just then, Hugette entered the room. Observing the commotion, she started to scream at Bobby to stop. He seemed to be in a trance; he just kept pounding on Peter until he went limp. Sheila looked at Rick. He had tears in his eyes. Rick looked at his sisters and ran from the room. Sheila was sure Peter was dead. Bobby got off him and instructed Hugette to get him out of the living room.

Bobby looked at Sheila and Joann cowering in the corner. "You two little bitches better get out of here before you're next!" hollered Bobby. Sheila and Joann ran to the doorway, but had to stop because Hugette was dragging Peter down the hall to the kitchen. While Joann stood trembling, Sheila bent down and helped drag Peter to the kitchen. Once they reached the kitchen, Pauline, in tears, came over with a wet cloth and applied it to Peter's battered face. After a few moments, Peter came round. He said he was fine and went to clean himself up.

Hugette looked at the two girls trembling in front of her. "Sheila and Joann, it's time for bed!" she yelled. "Pauline, go clean up the blood on the floor in the living room, and stupid, make sure you get it all or you will be the next one to be bleeding."

Everyone immediately did what they were told.

Sheila and Joann reached the top of the stairs to hear Rick telling Peter how sorry he was. "I don't want to hear it," snapped Peter. In a huff, Rick stormed out of the room.

"Are you okay, Peter?" Sheila asked.

"I'm fine, girls," Peter told them with a smile. "Now it's time for bed, so you had better get going." Sheila and Joann went to their room and climbed into their beds.

"Sheila, I'm scared. Can I sleep with you tonight?" Joann begged.

"It's not even dark outside yet, but I guess it's okay. But just for tonight," Sheila responded. With a squeal of delight, Joann jumped into Sheila's bed and went to sleep within a few minutes. As she did most nights, Sheila cried herself to sleep, worrying about Pauline, Peter, Joann, Rick and herself. *Would he kill them before they were old enough to escape?* Too much to worry about for anyone—especially a-nine-year-old.

# Chapter 2

Sheila awoke the next morning to a sweet, soft voice: "Time to get up, sleepy head," she heard, and she opened her eyes to see Pauline's face. "Come on, you two. Time to get up and get dressed," Pauline instructed. Pauline got out their school clothes and helped them get dressed. She brushed and put ponytails in both their hair. It was Pauline's favorite way for the girls to wear their hair. "How does your face feel, Sheila? You have a little black eye this morning," Pauline announced.

"I'm okay, Pauline," Sheila responded.

Pauline brought them to the bathroom, washed their faces, and told them to go down for breakfast. Pauline had to get ready for school herself. She prayed that when she went down, her mother would tell her that they'd changed their minds, and she didn't have to quit school.

Sheila and Joann were at the table having a piece of toast when Pauline entered the room and sat at the table. Sheila was horrified. *What is she doing here? She is not allowed to eat with us. Mom will beat her*, Sheila thought, panicked. Sheila looked around the table. Bobby had already left for work, and Peter had not come down yet, but Rick and Joann had the same looks on their faces as Sheila; it was obvious everyone was thinking the same thing.

"I have an announcement to make," Hugette informed them. "Pauline is now part of our family again. She has agreed to drop out of school to help around the house so I can get a job, so your father and I agreed, if she is willing to help the family, then she can be a part of it."

Sheila was so happy. She did not want Pauline to have to quit school, but her being a part of the family was the best birthday present Sheila could have hoped for.

"Joann and Sheila, finish your toast and go brush your teeth. Then you can watch cartoons until it's time for school," Hugette told them. "Pauline, when you are done with the breakfast dishes, get the girls ready for school. Once Sheila and Joann have left for school, you can go to school and bring back your books, and tell them you will not be back. I'll be leaving at the same time as the girls. You will be home before me, so you can start the laundry and clean the house and then start dinner. I should be home around three this afternoon." Hugette went upstairs to change. Pauline's eyes were full of tears, but she did not dare let Hugette see. This morning was bad enough without a beating.

Pauline came into the living room a little while later, and told Sheila and Joann it was time for school. Pauline was helping Joann with her coat as Peter and Rick were leaving for school. "I'm really sorry about school, although it's nice to have you back in the family," Rick said with a smile, and ran out the door to go to school. Sheila was bent over tying her shoe, and when she looked up and saw Peter's face, the shock of what she saw caused her to jump back so that she fell over.

Both of Peter's eyes were black, and his lips were all swollen. One side of his face was blue and puffy. He looked scary, and it frightened both the girls. They started to cry.

"Please, girls, you have to stop crying. It looks worse than it is. It doesn't even hurt," Peter assured them. He gave them a kiss and they stopped. Pauline and Peter were doing a lot of whispering, and for some reason it scared Sheila, but she didn't know why. All the children whispered. It was a way of life.

Hugette came down the stairs looking beautiful as usual. "You look pretty, Mommy," Joann commented.

Hugette smiled. "If you are lucky, Joann, you will grow up to look like me and not like Pauline," she snapped. Then she added, "Now come on, girls. I will walk you to school on my way to the bus stop. Pauline, you know what you have to do today, and Peter, I don't want you to go to school until your face heals a bit."

"Mom, I have a test today. I can't miss school," pleaded Peter.

"You heard me, Peter!" Hugette shouted. Peter threw his coat on the floor and marched up the stairs. "Hang up that coat, Pauline!" Hugette barked as she left with the girls.

When Sheila arrived at school, she reminded Joann to meet her at the willow tree right after school, and not to be late. Joann ran to play with her friends. Sheila went to find her friends and play before the bell rang. Sheila was having such fun playing with Kim and Lisa—they played double Dutch, a jump rope game they loved. Kim and Lisa both lived in the project, but on the other side. They lived too far for Sheila to play with them outside of school, but during school, they were the three musketeers.

Kim and Lisa didn't have fathers, and they thought Sheila was so lucky. However, Sheila thought them to be the lucky ones. "What happened to your eye?" Kim asked.

"My brother threw a ball, and I walked into the way. It doesn't hurt, looks worse than it is." She repeated Peter's words and felt like a grown-up. The school bell rang. Kim grabbed her rope, and they ran to the doors.

Mrs. Morris noticed Sheila's face immediately. "Good morning, class. I hope everyone remembered their permission slips and money for the field trip," she said. The teacher instructed those who had permission slips to bring them up to her desk. Sheila never moved. Mrs. Morris then asked her class to open their math books to page forty-seven, and to start working on the math problems.

"Sheila, could you please come up to my desk for a moment?" the teacher asked. Sheila started to tremble. She hated to be singled out; at home it could mean a beating. She slowly approached her teacher's desk. She was sure everyone was staring at her, and she wished she were invisible. "Sheila, here, sit in this chair. I want to talk to you. How was your birthday? Did you have a party?" Mrs. Morris questioned.

"Good. No, just my family," Sheila responded.

"I noticed you did not hand in your permission slip. Will you bring it tomorrow?" Mrs. Morris asked.

Sheila shook her head no. "I'm not allowed to go, Mrs. Morris."

"What happened to your cheeks and eye? Your cheeks are all raw and red, and your eye is blue," the teacher probed. Sheila repeated the same story she'd told Kim and Lisa, adding that she'd used a rough washcloth to wash her face that morning.

"Sweetie, your eye is scratched, and I don't think a ball would be sharp enough to cut skin, and I've never seen anyone hurt themselves washing their face. Are you sure that's what happened?" Mrs. Morris said.

"Yes, I'm sure, Mrs. Morris," Sheila replied.

"You can go back to your desk," the teacher instructed. Mrs. Morris knew there was more to the story, but what could she do? The child insisted on keeping everything inside. Just as always, she had an answer for every injury. The teacher decided to continue keeping a close eye on the child, and started to teach her math lesson to the class.

That afternoon, at second recess, Sheila was playing double Dutch with Kim and Lisa when she got the feeling someone was watching her. She stopped and looked around. Down by her willow tree, someone was standing there, and it looked like they were waving, but it was so far that Sheila wasn't sure, so she went back to her game. She looked again a few moments later, and nobody was there. The feeling was gone, so she just went back to playing with her friends. Then the bell rang, and they went back inside.

Sheila stood by the willow tree and waited for Joann. *She had better hurry*, she thought. *We can't be late.* A minute later, Joann came running over with a smile and another exciting tale about her day. Joann talked all the way to the gate and into the project and up to the front door. Sheila heard someone call her name and saw Rick next door at his friend's house. Rick told her and Joann to come over to Ralph's house for a minute. Sheila and Joann did as they were told, as always.

"There's something strange going on at home. I got home from school, and Mom yelled at me and told me to go and play," Rick warned. "You two better be on your best behavior tonight. Did either of you talk to Pauline or Peter this morning? Did they say they were going somewhere? I don't think they're in the house, and I can't find them in the project," Rick explained.

*Behind the Drapes*

"They didn't say anything to us, Rick. Mom told Peter this morning he couldn't go to school until his face healed. He seemed mad. We better go; we don't want to be late," Sheila responded.

As Sheila and Joann entered unit 8, the tension was thick enough to cut with a knife. Hugette flew around the corner from the kitchen, screaming, "Where have you been?" Sheila and Joann jumped back.

"We came straight home," both girls responded at the same time.

"Go change out of your school clothes, and then go watch TV. I don't want to hear a word from you!" Hugette bellowed.

Sheila hung up their jackets, and they started up the stairs. As an afterthought, Hugette called them into the kitchen. As they entered, Sheila thought how strange it was for Pauline not to be setting the table for dinner. Then she realized she didn't even smell anything cooking.

"Do either of you know were Peter and that ugly bitch Pauline are?" Hugette questioned. Both girls shook their heads no and did not make a sound. "Get out of my sight!" Hugette screamed. Sheila and Joann ran as fast as they could, without saying a word until they were in their bedroom.

"Where are Peter and Pauline, Sheila?" Joann asked with a terrified look on her face.

"Don't get upset, Joann. I don't know, but I'm sure they will be home soon. We have to change now and do what we are told," instructed Sheila. Sheila remembered the person waving at recess. *Could it have been Pauline?* she wondered. The girls changed, went into the living room, sat on the sofa, and watched the television.

A while later, Rick came into the house. The girls heard Hugette screaming at him and telling him that everything was his fault. He just walked away from her, came into the living room, sat on the armchair, and watched television with Sheila and Joann. Hugette followed him and continued screaming: "Wait until your father gets home from work! You will be in trouble then!" Finally, Hugette went back to the kitchen and stared out the window, to watch for Bobby so she could close the drapes. The children tried to enjoy the quiet. They knew it would not last long.

Bobby came home screaming; as soon as he walked into the house, he noticed the table was not set for dinner. He became very angry when he realized dinner was not even started. Hugette tried to explain, but

Bobby hit her hard across her face. "Once dinner is on the table and I've eaten, you can talk to me, not a second before! You hear me, woman?" Bobby growled. He started down the hall toward the living room; the children heard him, and the girls started to tremble.

Bobby entered the room and looked at the sofa. He didn't need to say a word; his look said it all. Sheila and Joann jumped off the sofa and ran from the room. Rick stayed, and watched television with his father. Sheila always thought Rick was so brave when he stayed with his father, especially when Bobby was in one of his moods.

The girls went into the kitchen and asked their mother if they could go out to play until dinner. Hugette turned to face the girls. She had tears streaming down her face, and her lip was cut and bleeding. "Sheila, it's your job to set the table now, so you get started on that, and Joann, you go watch television," Hugette announced. Joann looked terrified. She didn't go anywhere in the house without Sheila. Both girls realized at that moment, things would never be the same at unit 8.

Joann slowly went down the hall to the living room; her father was lying on the sofa, and Rick was in the armchair. She sat on the floor at the back of the room so as not to draw any attention to herself. Sheila set the table and tried not to let her thoughts go to what might come next. Where were Peter and Pauline? She was very worried. Where would they eat their dinner, and what about sleeping? Would they have a bed to sleep in tonight? What worried her most was, would she ever see them again? She also felt sorry for her mother. Bobby beat on Hugette just as often as he did the kids.

Sheila stared at the table. She had to be sure she had not forgotten anything. "Sheila, you forgot the salt and pepper," Hugette announced. "You have to learn how to do this properly. Pauline will not be coming home. All her chores are now yours and Joann's." Sheila almost fell to the floor. Pauline would never be coming home. She and Joann were all alone now. Sheila was about to cry, but then she realized she had to be strong for Joann; she was going to have to take Pauline's place and take care of her sister. Sheila placed the salt and pepper on the table and told her mother she and Joann would go wash for dinner.

Sheila quietly walked down the hall to the living room. When Joann saw her, she smiled, but the smile left her face quickly as she saw her sister's expression. Sheila grabbed her hand and turned to go down

*Behind the Drapes*

the hall. She almost wet her pants as she heard Bobby call her name. She told Joann to go to their room and ran back to her father. "Yes, Daddy?" she trembled.

"I want a soda. Get me one, and turn the channel to number thirteen," he said. Sheila quickly ran to the kitchen and got a soda. As she reached the end of the hallway, she dropped the soda. She felt a ripple of fear run through her body as she watched the soda roll over to the sofa in front of her father.

"You idiot, come here!" Bobby hollered. Sheila approached her father slowly; as soon as she was a foot away, she felt herself flying through the air. Sheila hit the floor and felt a tremendous pain in her jaw. Bobby had hit her across the face with all his force, lifting the child off her feet. "Pick that up and get me a new one," he barked. Without a sound, Sheila picked up the soda and brought it to the kitchen. Hugette, hearing everything in the kitchen, was standing there with a soda in her hand. She gave it to Sheila and told her to hurry, dinner would be ready in five minutes.

Sheila carefully walked down the hall, carrying the soda with both trembling hands, and handed Bobby his soda. Without saying a word, he ripped it from her hand. Sheila quickly turned and ran, but stopped quickly as Bobby reminded her to change the channel; Sheila changed the channel and ran from the room, up the stairs. The moment her bedroom door was closed behind her, she allowed the tears to flow. Joann came to her and tried to comfort her. "What took you so long, Sheila?" Joann asked.

Sheila responded with "Dad," which was all that needed to be said. "Mom told me that Pauline is not coming home," Sheila cried. Joann burst into tears.

"Who will take care of us, Sheila?" Joann pleaded.

"I will. You don't have to worry. Mom also said that we have to do all of Pauline's chores. I will do most of it, but you will have to help me, Joann. I promise everything will be okay. Now we have to dry our eyes and wash up for dinner," Sheila said. As they washed up, Sheila worried if she would be able to keep her promise to Joann.

When Sheila and Joann reached the bottom of the stairs, Bobby was coming down the hall with Rick following; the girls stopped dead in their tracks and waited for them to pass. Sheila and Joann took their seats and stared at the empty chairs. Just this morning, Sheila had thought Pauline would be eating dinner with them for the first time in over a year, and now she was gone for good. Sheila prayed for time to pass quickly until she was sixteen, so she could leave home like Pauline.

Bobby's screaming pulled Sheila from her thoughts. Hugette had just placed his dinner in front of him, and he was not impressed. "What is this shit? You call this dinner? Scrambled eggs, leftover sausage, and toast?" Bobby hollered. He picked up Hugette and threw her; she bounced off the wall and hit the floor. He calmly walked over to Hugette and picked her up. He started to beat her, punching and punching with a full fist. The children sat there with tears falling down their faces, without making a sound—they knew better. It seemed to go on forever. Finally, Hugette's body lay lifeless on the floor. Bobby stopped and spit on her. He turned, picked up his plate, and went into the living room.

Rick ran to his mother as Sheila and Joann sat trembling, frozen with fear. Sheila was sure he had killed her this time. After a few moments, Hugette started to moan. Within five minutes she was sitting up. Rick was trying to help her, but she ordered him to sit and eat. Hugette got up without a word, put food on the children's plates, instructed them to eat, and told Sheila to clean up the dishes. Then she went upstairs to clean herself up.

Sheila and Joann finished their dinner. Rick had already finished, so he went outside to see his friends. Sheila looked around the kitchen. *What a mess*, she thought. She had never done dishes before. It had always been Pauline's job. Sheila pulled a chair up to the sink and filled it with soap and water. She had Joann clear the plates, and she started to wash.

Hugette came into the kitchen. She didn't even look like herself, all swollen and bruised. She told Sheila to go and get Bobby's plate and see if he wanted a cup of tea. She was scared, but she also knew she had no choice. She walked down the hall slowly. When she reached the living room, Bobby lay spread out on the sofa, and his empty plate sat on the table beside him. Sheila picked up the plate, trembling, and asked Bobby if he wanted a cup of tea. Bobby looked at her.

*Behind the Drapes*

"Well, I guess you will be taking Pauline's place. You are much prettier," he commented with a smile. He stared at her in a way that made her very uncomfortable. "Yes, I want a cup of tea and some cookies, and tell your mother to bring it to me. We need to talk."

Sheila went back to the kitchen and told her mother that her father wanted Hugette to bring him tea and cookies. Sheila thought her mother looked scared. Hugette told Sheila and Joann to finish the dishes and go play in the basement, and to stay there until she told them otherwise. Hugette left the kitchen with Bobby's cup of tea and cookies. The girls finished the dishes and cleaned the kitchen. Sheila looked closely to make sure she had not forgotten anything. Once she was positive nothing had been overlooked, she and Joann went into the basement.

"Sheila, where do you think Peter and Pauline are? Do you think we will see them again?" Joann asked.

"I don't know where they are, but I know it has to be better than here. We just have to be good and stay out of his way, and when we are sixteen we can leave here forever, just like they did. Now let's colour a picture or two until Mom calls for us," Sheila instructed.

The girls were finishing their second picture when Hugette called for them. They put away their coloring book and crayons, and went upstairs. Hugette was waiting for them at the front door. "Sheila, I want you to go outside and find you brother. Joann, you go upstairs and change for bed. We need to have a family talk," Hugette told them. Joann looked at Sheila with a sad face and went up the stairs. Sheila looked outside.

"Mom, it's starting to get dark. Can you come with me?" Sheila pleaded.

"Would you like me to call your father and tell him you're not behaving, Sheila?" Hugette threatened. Sheila put on her coat and went outside without another word. The project always seemed different and scary at night. Lots of older kids were out playing music and screaming. Sheila looked around. She didn't see Rick anywhere, so she thought she would check next door at Ralph's house. Sheila walked up to the door. There was a lot of noise coming from inside the house. Ralph and his five brothers lived here with their grandmother. Both their parents were dead; their grandmother was very tiny and frail. She did her best with the boys, but mostly they were out of control. Ralph and his five brothers called her Ma Mère, and so did Rick. He loved her just as much, if not more, than her grandchildren.

Sheila knocked on the door. Ma Mère answered after a few moments. "What brings you out so late, my sweet child?" she inquired.

"My mother wants me to find Rick and bring him home. Is he here, Ma Mère?" Sheila asked, using the name she had heard the boys use so many times.

"I don't think he's here, but I will check for you. Wait a minute, my dear," she told Sheila with a big smile. A few minutes later, Rick came to the door. Sheila was very glad to see him. She needed to get back to Joann. Her sister was in the house all by herself.

"What do you want, Sheila?" Rick said.

"Mom wants you home now. She said we have to have a family talk," Sheila responded.

"Oh brother, I hate family talks. Okay, get going and tell her I'll be right home," Rick instructed.

Sheila walked into the house and told her mother what Rick had said. Hugette told her to go upstairs, get ready for bed, get Joann, and be back in the living room within five minutes. Four minutes later, Sheila and Joann entered the living room. Bobby was spread out on the sofa as usual, and Hugette sat on the armchair. Rick was not home yet.

The girls sat on the floor, holding hands and staring at the television, not making a sound. Sheila felt someone looking at her; she looked around and saw her father staring at her with that same look on his face as earlier, the one that made her feel uneasy. Rick walked in and sat on the end of the sofa by Bobby's feet. This pulled Bobby's attention away from Sheila, and she was very relieved.

Bobby broke the silence. "I'm sure by now you are all aware Peter and Pauline do not live here anymore. They are almost sixteen, so they are allowed to leave. Actually, I was thinking about throwing them out anyway. You see, that's the other thing about being sixteen. I can throw you out anytime I want. If you are behaving and helping the family, then you can stay. Otherwise, you have to leave on your sixteenth birthday. As I was saying, Peter and Pauline are gone, and they are never welcome back. I never want to hear their names mentioned in this house again. Is that understood?"

They all nodded, including Hugette. Sheila looked at Joann, and for the first time she saw sorrow in Joann's eyes. It was like looking in a mirror. They had broken her as well.

# Chapter 3

It was the last day of school before summer vacation. Sheila stood by her willow tree and waited for Joann. As soon as she arrived, they started on their way home. As they approached the fence, Joann spoke. "You know who has been in my thoughts today, Sheila?" Sheila knew instinctively. She had been thinking of Pauline all day as well. It had been well over a year and a half since they had seen her or Peter.

"I don't know, Joann. Who?" Sheila responded. Even though she could guess the answer, Sheila didn't want to say her name just in case she was wrong.

"Pauline. I don't know why. It's been so long since I've even thought of her or Peter."

"I miss them too but we shouldn't waste our time thinking about things we have no control over. Let's just get home and get dinner started before Mom gets home," Sheila suggested.

Hugette had recently taken a job at a grocery store, working as a cashier. She seemed to love it, and Bobby loved the money. However, it increased Sheila and Joann's workload considerably. It had been three weeks so far, and they had survived. This was one of the reasons Sheila was happy school was over. Between school and home, the workload

*Behind the Drapes*

was getting tough. Sheila was starting to get a lot of homework, and her parents didn't think school was important, so if she wanted it done she had to do it around her chores. She was just happy that she would now have two and a half months of not having to worry about it.

The girls arrived home and started dinner. Sheila was actually becoming a very good cook, something that irritated Hugette very much. Sometimes, Bobby would comment on dinner, and Hugette would be furious with Sheila. She had no idea how this attention terrified her daughter. Sheila cooked, and Joann set the table. When Rick came into the kitchen and started looking in the pots on the stove, Sheila smacked his hand, and he left the room giggling.

Rick wasn't around much these days. He was sixteen, and for some reason Sheila could never understand, he stayed. He had quit school. He had a job and at least ten girlfriends at any given time. He had quite a reputation in the project as well. Everybody knew Sheila and Joann were his little sisters, and nobody ever bothered them. He saw to it. Sheila and Joann looked up to him. He had matured in the last year and a half since Peter and Pauline had left.

Now that Rick worked, he spoiled the girls with candy and little presents as often as he could. The girls thought he was everything and more. Sheila yelled after him that dinner would be ready in an hour. She hoped he would like it; his opinion was so important to her. Sheila heard the front door, and her thoughts returned to the task at hand. Hugette came in from work, looking as beautiful as ever. She stopped in the kitchen to check on dinner, and then went upstairs to change.

Hugette came back into the kitchen a few minutes later and reminded Sheila to start the laundry right after dinner. "I was hoping to play outside for a little while after dinner. Could I start the laundry first thing in the morning? Please, Mom?" Sheila said.

"No, Sheila. You have housework in the morning. After dinner, you will start the laundry. Do you hear me?"

"Yes, Mom," said Sheila, and she continued preparing dinner. Hugette told Joann when she was finished setting the table to watch in the window for Bobby, and to close the drapes as soon as she saw him. Sheila could never understand Bobby's fear of someone seeing in their house, but she was not to understand it, only obey it. Hugette went to watch television as she waited for dinner.

Joann saw Bobby coming and closed the drapes, and after making sure it was okay with Sheila, she went to watch television with Hugette and Rick. Bobby came through the door in an unusually good mood. He was actually whistling, something Sheila never remembered hearing from him before. Hugette came to the door to greet him; Sheila and Bobby both knew she wanted something.

"How was your day?" Hugette inquired. He smiled and slapped her on her fanny. She smiled, giggled, and took Bobby's lunch box.

"I had a great day. I got a raise today—eight dollars a week! I guess the idiots I work for finally realized they have a smart man working for them," Bobby told her, beaming. Bobby was a truck driver for a local company. However, he never kept a job for long. Sheila did respect him for working; all her friends in the project's fathers (if they had one) or mothers were on welfare. Bobby hated welfare and always vowed to never be on it.

"Great, Bobby. Can I go to the bingo tonight, please?" Hugette pleaded.

"I knew you wanted something, but it's your lucky day. Sure, you can go, but you have to take the bus. I'm not driving you, and you are only getting ten dollars."

"Oh, thank you, Bobby," Hugette said excitedly, very much like a child. Bingo was Hugette's one passion. She would spend their last dollar on bingo and let the children go hungry if Bobby let her.

Hugette told Bobby to go into the living room, and she would get him a soda. She handed Sheila Bobby's lunch box and reminded her that Bobby was leaving at ten o'clock sharp to go fishing the next morning. She was to pack an extra-large lunch. "Get dinner on the table soon. I have to leave in an hour, for bingo," Hugette said. "Make sure all the laundry is done before I get home. I'm taking the bus, so I should be back by eleven o'clock. Sheila, don't forget, tomorrow is Saturday, and breakfast should be on the table at nine AM sharp."

*Great start to the summer*, Sheila thought. Grabbing a soda, Hugette left the room.

A few moments later, Joann came into the kitchen. "What's with Dad? I've never seen him like this," she commented.

*Behind the Drapes*

"Who knows? Let's just enjoy it," Sheila whispered, and they both giggled. Sheila had dinner on the table within ten minutes. She walked down the hall into the living room and announced dinner was ready.

"It's about time," Rick said with a smile. Everyone went down the hall to the kitchen, following Bobby. Sheila filled the plates, and Hugette placed them on the table, as if by doing so she had played some major role in the dinner itself. Bobby commented that it looked and smelled great, which caused Hugette to send Sheila a vicious stare. Bobby had never commented on Pauline's cooking and when he praised Sheila it infuriated Hugette.

Nobody talked during dinner. It was one of the most peaceful dinners Sheila could ever remember, and she was really enjoying it until she felt his stare. She looked up to see Bobby giving her that stare that made her so uncomfortable, but tonight he had a huge smile on his face. Sheila tried to ignore it and ate her dinner.

Bobby finished first and went back to stretch out on the sofa. Rick was next to finish. He announced he and Ralph had dates and got up from the table. "I won't be home tonight. I'm staying at Ralph's," Rick said, informing his mother, not asking. Hugette and Rick hated each other. It was so obvious to Sheila. Rick had more freedom than Hugette, and it infuriated her. Rick thought his mother the most selfish person on earth, and Sheila agreed. Hugette and Rick tolerated each other to avoid upsetting Bobby and risking a beating. Rick walked into the living room and said bye to his father.

"Enjoy your slut this evening," Bobby announced as his son left the room. Rick chuckled. *All class, my father*, he thought sarcastically. Everyone knew what a pig Bobby Parks was.

Hugette got up from the table. She left her plate where it was and went to get ready for bingo. Sheila and Joann finished up their dinner and chatted about the exciting summer that lay ahead. "Paula is going to meet us at noon tomorrow by the play structure. I told her we should be done with the housecleaning by then," Sheila said.

Paula was a girl Sheila and Joann had been playing with for years; she lived a couple of rows away from the girls in the project. Paula went to a different school, but on weekends they were always together. Paula had ten brothers and sisters, and she was the second youngest, just like Sheila. Her parents were on welfare, but Sheila decided to overlook that one small thing. Joann didn't care. She had fun with Paula, and that was all that mattered to her.

Hugette came into the kitchen and told them she was leaving. She yelled bye to Bobby, and she left the house with a smile. Sheila started the dishes. Joann cleared the table. "What do you want to do when we are finished cleaning the kitchen?" Joann asked.

"I have to start the laundry if you want to help me," Sheila replied. Just then, Bobby started hollering for the girls. They trembled and ran down the hall.

They stood in front of the sofa and waited for whatever might come next. Bobby told Sheila to turn the channel for him and asked the girls if they wanted a treat—candy or chips. Not sure what was about to happen, they both nodded yes. This was a side of Bobby they had never seen. He told Joann to go upstairs and get him a blanket, and told Sheila to go make him a cup of tea. Joann ran upstairs, got a blanket, and brought it to Bobby, while Sheila put the kettle on the stove for Bobby's cup of tea.

Joann came back into the kitchen and told Sheila that Bobby had given her two dollars and told her to find out what Sheila wanted, and go to the store. "Just wait until I bring Dad his tea, and then we can go together," Sheila suggested.

"No, Dad said I had to go alone while you made his tea," Joann said as tears filled her eyes.

"It's okay. You go, and I'll get the laundry started. Get me a Crispy Crunch," Sheila instructed. Joann knew she had to do what Bobby told her, so she left to go to the store. Sheila made Bobby's tea and brought it to him.

"Put my tea on the table, Sheila, and come closer. I want to tell you something," Bobby said. Sheila moved closer until she was inches away from him. He took her hand and smiled. "I want you to be my special girl. You are starting to look a lot like your mother did when I first met her. You are very sexy, Sheila. Do you know what that means?"

Sheila started to tremble and shook her head no.

"Sexy means that men like you, and want to be near you. I want you to lie down here with me, Sheila," Bobby instructed.

Sheila did as she was told. As Bobby lifted the blanket that was on him, Sheila climbed on the sofa with her back to him and lay down.

Sheila was terrified. She didn't know what was going to happen, but she instinctively knew it was bad. Bobby started to stroke her hair and kiss the back of her neck. All of a sudden, he put his hand around her neck and firmly turned her so she was lying with her back on the sofa, looking up at him. He held her down and stared at her. "This is going to be our little secret. You do not say a word to anyone about this or I will kill you. Do you understand, Sheila?" Bobby growled.

Sheila lay there without making a sound, staring at Bobby with tears flowing from her eyes. Bobby lifted her top and began to caress her breasts. Sheila could feel him against her side. He was getting hard, and he kept pressing against her. She closed her eyes and prayed it would end soon. Bobby then put his hands down her pants and roughly began to rub her between her legs.

"Open your legs, Sheila," Bobby demanded. Sheila did as she was told, and he penetrated her with his fingers. It really started to hurt, and she begged him to stop. "Shut your mouth, Sheila, and be a good girl to your daddy," Bobby demanded. He took her hand and placed it on his penis. He told her to rub him and she did. He encouraged her on, and he kept telling her to be a good girl and take care of her daddy.

Just then, they heard Joann come in from the store. He whispered in Sheila's ear, "Don't move or say a word." Sheila did not say a word or move a muscle. As Joann entered the living room, Bobby continued to fondle Sheila under the blanket. Sheila tried to hide her tears from her sister. "I decided I want a Popsicle as well, Joann. Go back to the store and buy me a red Popsicle. Now!" Bobby barked.

Joann turned without a word and went back to the store. "Now, where were we, my good girl. Oh yes, come on and rub Daddy some more," Bobby ordered. With a trembling hand, Sheila did as she was told. The pain was unbearable, and he was so rough with her, pounding between her legs with his fingers. "Open your legs wider," Bobby kept repeating.

After what seemed like hours, Bobby started to moan, and suddenly her hand was all wet. He lay there for a moment, motionless, and then bent over and kissed her forehead. "Good girl, Sheila. You took good care of your daddy. Now don't forget, if you tell anyone our secret, I will kill you. I want you to put this blanket and your clothes in the laundry, now. Do you understand!"

"Yes, Daddy," Sheila replied. She got up immediately and went to the bathroom. Her legs were covered with blood. She was scared. She didn't know where she was bleeding from. She washed away the blood and changed her clothes; she picked up the blanket and her clothes, and went to start the laundry, hoping she could wash away what had just happened to her. At that moment, Sheila made a promise to herself: she would survive the next five and a half years, and when she finally turned sixteen she would leave this hell, and no man would ever treat her badly again.

# Chapter 4

The next morning, Sheila awoke with the memory of the night before. For a moment, she tried to convince herself it was a dream, but the pain she felt between her legs told her it was real. She looked at Pauline's old clock on her dresser and panicked when she saw the time. It was eight thirty, and she had to have breakfast ready by nine. She jumped up, got dressed, and ran down the stairs to the kitchen.

She stopped dead in her tracks when she saw him sitting at the table. "Good morning, Sheila. How is my good girl this morning?" Bobby said.

"Fine," Sheila replied. "I am sorry I slept in, Dad. I'll have your breakfast on the table soon."

He grabbed her hand and looked her in the eye, "It's okay. You are my good girl, remember? Everything is okay now. Just make me coffee and toast, and get my lunch ready."

"I made your lunch last night, after I finished the laundry," Sheila informed him.

Bobby winked at her and slapped her bottom. "Okay, then, just coffee and toast."

While Sheila prepared Bobby's breakfast, he chatted away to her like they were old friends. Sheila was shocked by the way he was treating her. He'd never spoken to her before. Bobby only barked orders. Sheila was very confused. "Sheila," he said, "I've been thinking. You do too much work around this house. When I get home tonight, I'm going to have a talk with your mother. I think it's time she started acting more like a wife and mother, and started doing more around here." Sheila served him his coffee and toast, and tried to understand what her father was telling her.

Bobby finished his coffee and toast, and walked over to Sheila. "If anyone gives you a hard time today, including your mother, you just let me know when I get home and I will take care of them. Would you like me to buy you something while I'm out today, Sheila?" Bobby asked.

"No thank you, Daddy," Sheila responded, still confused. He handed her five dollars, told her it was hers to do anything she wanted, and left with a smile. Sheila was so baffled. What did his attitude change mean? Because of that terrible, ugly thing he did to her last night, he was going to start to be nice to her? How was this possible? She started to cry. She didn't want to do it again, and she prayed she wouldn't have to. Did all girls do this with their Daddy? As she thought of it again, she felt sick to her stomach. She ran up the stairs to the bathroom and threw up.

There was knocking on the bathroom door. It was Joann. Sheila didn't know how long she had been sitting there. She got up, rinsed out her mouth, and opened the door. "What were you doing, Sheila? I was banging for five minutes. I need the bathroom!" Joann said.

"Sorry, it's all yours. I'll go start our breakfast," Sheila said. She didn't want Joann to know; she didn't want anyone to know what her father had done to her. Sheila started breakfast, and Hugette came into the kitchen.

"Is your father already gone, Sheila?" Hugette inquired.

"Yes, he left about half an hour ago," Sheila replied.

"You didn't have breakfast ready before he left. I'll bet you got a good beating. Oh well, you know you are supposed to have breakfast ready. I reminded you last night, Sheila. You deserve whatever you got," Hugette insisted. Sheila realized her mother was right. Usually, not having his meal ready was enough for him to beat you. Were the

*Behind the Drapes*

beatings going to stop now that he wanted her to be his good girl? Sheila thought she would rather have the beatings.

Sheila served her mother and Joann breakfast. Sheila didn't have any appetite this morning; she just had a cup of tea and started to clean the kitchen. Hugette finished her breakfast and went upstairs. Joann reminded Sheila they were to meet Paula at the play structure at noon. They hurried and finished cleaning the kitchen. Just as they were done, Hugette walked into the kitchen wearing a bikini. She looked positively stunning.

"I'm going out back to get some sun in the yard. You two can start your housecleaning," Hugette instructed. Hugette had been a sun worshiper as long as Sheila could remember. She spent hours just lying there in the sun.

The girls went upstairs and got started on their chores. Sheila started on the bathroom while Joann dusted the upstairs. Once that was done, Joann swept each room as Sheila followed and washed the floor behind her. They had the upstairs done in one hour. They were making good time as they headed downstairs. They continued to clean downstairs, and had the downstairs almost finished when Hugette came in looking for lunch. Sheila went to prepare lunch as Joann continued with the cleaning.

The girls finished lunch and all the cleaning by noon. Sheila went out back and told her mother they were finished and going to play. Hugette reminded her to be home by four o'clock to start dinner. She came back in and grabbed her sister's hand, and they raced to meet Paula. As they arrived at the play structure, Paula was leaving. "I was just about to give up on you two," she said. "I thought your mother found more work for you."

"Not this time," Sheila replied. Sheila was trying hard to forget the night before. From time to time, as she played, the image raced back into her mind. She did her best to push it from her mind. The three girls sat on the swings and talked about what they would do when they grew up. Paula never talked much about her home life, but Sheila suspected it was much the same as her own. The three of them hated to be at home and loved to play together. They decided to go to the park down near Sheila and Joann's school. Sheila and Joann were not allowed that far away from home, but Sheila was feeling brave today, and Joann would follow her to the ends of the earth.

When they got to the park, they saw some of Rick and Ralph's friends. They asked Sheila where Rick was, they were waiting for him. She told them that he didn't come home last night because he had stayed at Ralph's house. No sooner had she got the words out than Rick was standing beside her. "What are you two up to? You know you are not supposed to be this far from home," he said.

"I know, but this park is so much better than the play structure in the project, Rick. Please let us stay and don't tell on us," Sheila pleaded.

"Okay, but stay out of trouble, and go play. I have to talk to my buddies in private."

"What do you think they are doing?" Paula asked, watching Rick and his friends. They could see Rick hand the boys money, and they gave him funny cigarettes in return. "I think it's drugs. My older brothers do it. We should try it," Paula continued. Joann was horrified at the thought, but to Sheila, it sounded like a great idea. "Does anyone have any money?" Paula said.

"I do," Sheila said, pulling out the five dollars her father had given her.

"Were did you get that, Sheila?" Joann asked nervously.

"Dad gave it to me," Sheila stated.

"What? Why would Dad give you money?" Joann pressed further.

"I don't know, maybe he fell on his head," Sheila answered curtly. "He gave it to me this morning and told me I could do whatever I wanted with it."

Paula and Sheila decided they were going to check on what the boys had bought. After Rick and Ralph had left, they walked over.

"I'm staying right here, Sheila!" Joann shouted.

"Suit yourself. We will be right back," responded Sheila. "How much?" Sheila inquired, trying to sound as old as she could. The two older boys looked at each other and smiled.

"Aren't you two a little young for this?" one of the boys asked.

"Fine, if you don't want to do business with us, I'll go see someone else. This project is full of this stuff," Paula said. They knew she was right, and they didn't want to lose the sale.

"Two dollars a joint," the other boy said. Sheila handed one of the boys her money and asked for one. He handed her a joint and her change, and they started to leave. One of the boys yelled back to them, "Don't tell your brother where you got it if you get caught." Sheila reassured them they wouldn't as she placed the joint in her sock, and walked back over to Joann.

"What do we do with it, Paula?" Sheila asked her friend.

"I think you smoke it like a cigarette," Paula said. Paula and Sheila had been experimenting with smoking cigarettes for at least a year; it made them feel grown-up.

"Well, we need a match. Let's go to the store and see if we can get matches, and I'll buy us a treat," Sheila suggested. They all agreed and headed to the store. They got their treat, but the man wouldn't sell them any matches. He said they were too young. They left the store and went to another one where Sheila bought cigarettes and matches, saying it was for her father. The clerk didn't even question her about it.

"What are you going to do with the cigarettes, Sheila?" Joann asked.

"I don't know. Maybe I'll smoke them, too," Sheila told her. Joann looked at her sister. Something was different about her today—she seemed almost angry at the world. Joann didn't know what it was, but it scared her. She loved her sister so much, and she didn't understand the change in her. Joann wondered what happened to Sheila. She knew something had happened to change her sister's attitude so much in one day. Sheila would tell her when she was ready. Sheila was her sister and her best friend, and that was all that mattered.

By the time the girls had got matches, it was almost time for Sheila to go home and start dinner, so they decided to save the joint until the next day. Tomorrow was Sunday, and all Sheila had to do was make breakfast and clean the kitchen before she was allowed out to play. They arranged to meet at the play structure the next morning at 10:00 AM. Sheila and Joann started home.

Sheila and Joann came in the house and found Hugette still in the backyard, sunbathing. Sheila went into the kitchen and asked Joann to start peeling potatoes. She put the chicken legs into a pan, added spice, and put them in the oven. When Joann was finished with the potatoes, Sheila asked her to set the table. Sheila went out back and told Hugette they were home and she had started dinner. Hugette got up and went upstairs to shower before Bobby came home. She reminded Sheila about the drapes before she left. *As if I could forget*, Sheila thought. It had been the same for the last ten and a half years: watch for Bobby, and close the drapes as soon as you see him coming.

Sheila went back to the kitchen and had Joann watch out the window while she put the potatoes on the stove. Joann closed the drapes, and the hair on Sheila's neck stood up. "I'm going to watch TV," Joann informed Sheila.

"*No!*" Sheila shouted. "Please, just stay here with me," she begged. Joann looked at her, puzzled. Yes, something had happened. Joann walked to the sink, pulled up the chair, and started to wash the few dishes. "Thank you," Sheila whispered.

Bobby came home from his day of fishing with three rainbow trout, all over four pounds. He was very pleased with his catch. "Look what I caught!" Bobby announced as he walked into the kitchen. Hugette walked into the kitchen, sporting a dark tan. "I see you had a tough day in the sun. Well, you can go clean these fish in the basement sink for me," Bobby said.

"What? Sheila can do that," Hugette responded bitterly.

"I said you can do it, Hugette. Sheila is cooking my dinner," Bobby growled. Hugette grabbed the fish, some newspaper, and a knife, and headed for the basement. Bobby smiled at Sheila and went upstairs for a shower.

"What was that about?" Joann said.

"Who knows, but did you see Mom's face?" Sheila replied, giggling.

"That's not what I was talking about, but that was strange, too. Why did you panic about being alone with Dad? Sheila, you have never acted like that before."

"It's nothing. Go watch television, Joann. Dinner will be ready as soon as Dad comes down from the shower," Sheila said. Bobby came down and yelled to Hugette to hurry with the fish and put supper on the table. He came into the kitchen and told Sheila to make him a cup of tea and bring it to him in the living room.

"Bring me a cup of tea." The words terrified her as she thought about the night before. Sheila started to tremble, but she put the kettle on.

*Behind the Drapes*

She tried to calm herself. When the tea was ready, she slowly walked down the hallway and stood in front of the sofa. Bobby looked at her and grabbed the cup of tea. "Change the channel to eight and go help your mother with the fish. I'm getting hungry," Bobby instructed.

"Can I help with anything, Mom?" Sheila inquired as she reached the bottom of the basement stairs.

"No, I'm just about finished cleaning the fish, but after you are done the dinner dishes, you and Joann come down here and clean out this sink," Hugette said.

Sheila looked into the sink. It was full of skin, bones, and slime, and it smelled horrible. Sheila reluctantly replied, "Okay, Mom, right after the dishes." Hugette handed Sheila the trout fillets and told her to bring them up to the freezer.

Dinner was a quiet event. Rick wasn't home, so it was just the girls and their parents. Sheila was lost in her thoughts and quite happy, when Hugette broke the silence. "What did you want to do tonight, Bobby?" she inquired, even thought she already new the answer.

"Well, I know what I'm doing. I'm going to relax and watch the television," Bobby replied.

"Bobby, could I go to the bingo tonight, please? Last night I won ten dollars, remember, so I don't need any more money, and I'll take the bus. Tomorrow is Sunday. I will spend the day baking for you. Please, honey?" Hugette pleaded.

Bobby looked at Sheila, and then at Hugette. "Okay, you can go," Bobby said, and Sheila started to tremble.

"As soon as you are done cleaning the dishes and the kitchen, you can go clean the basement sink out," Hugette told her daughters.

"You dirtied the sink cleaning the fish, Hugette, so you go clean the sink if you want to go to the bingo," Bobby said. "Sheila has to clean the dishes and the kitchen. You are the mother and wife in this house, and you will start acting like one. No more is Sheila your slave." Hearing this, Hugette got up from the table and gave her daughter a hatful stare, then went to clean the sink.

Bobby got up from the table and went into the living room. Joann and Sheila looked at each other and silently started clearing the table. Just as they were about finished with the dishes, Hugette came into the kitchen and told them she was leaving. Then she stormed out the front door. It was still light out, so the girls hoped to go play outside.

"Who's going to ask if we can go outside?" Joann asked nervously.

"We both will," Sheila said.

They walked down the hall together and stood by the sofa, waiting for Bobby to acknowledge them. Bobby turned to look at them, and Sheila asked if they could go outside to play. "Has you mother left?" he inquired.

"Yes, about five minutes ago," Sheila replied.

"Joann, you go out and play and Sheila will be out soon," Bobby told the girls. Joann looked at her sister and saw that Sheila was trembling uncontrollably. "I said go outside and play, Joann!" Bobby shouted, and Joann ran down the hall, out the front door.

"Go get me a blanket, Sheila," Bobby instructed with a smile. Sheila slowly went up the stairs, fearing what she suspected would happen next. She stood in front of the sofa, and Bobby took the blanket, telling her to lie down with him. "Be a good girl and take care of your daddy," Bobby told her, and Sheila did as she was told. She climbed onto the sofa with tears flowing down her face, and tried to think of being somewhere else. Bobby removed her pants and directed her hand as she held her eyes closed tight.

Finally, her hand was wet, and Sheila heard the words, "Go clean yourself up and wash the blanket." She ran up the stairs and into the bathroom, and threw up her dinner. After she had cleaned up and put the blanket into the washing machine, she slowly walked down the hall into the living room. She looked in, and there was Bobby sound asleep on the sofa. She burst into tears and ran out of the house. She didn't stop running until she reached the willow tree; she climbed under and sat with her back against the trunk. Sheila hugged her knees, and for the moment, she felt safe.

The next morning, after breakfast, Sheila started to clear the dishes, trying not to think about what happened. She was terrified. Was this to be a regular thing? She longed for the days of the beatings. She was dimly aware of an intense conversation going on at the table. Soon, she was pulled from her thoughts by the sound of her mother screaming, "What do you mean, Bobby, I have to do all the cooking and cleaning around this house?"

"That is what I said."

"How am I supposed to have dinner on the table when you get home from work? I don't finish my job until four o'clock. I'll never have enough time, Bobby!"

"That's the other thing. With my raise, we really don't need you to work full time, so tomorrow you will tell them you can only work part time from now on. You will start acting like my wife!"

"You two can go outside to play now," Bobby told his daughters. "Sheila, put down those plates and let your mother do it. Go out and play, and be home for dinner by five."

The girls were walking out the front door when Bobby walked up and gave Sheila ten dollars. "Your mother won at the bingo last night. Buy something for yourself and Joann," he said.

When they were outside, Joann flashed her sister a questioning look. "Did Dad get struck by lightning or something?" she asked.

Sheila returned her sister's look angrily. "Stop asking me questions, Joann. I don't know what the hell is going on. I don't have any answers," she snapped.

Joann never asked her again.

Sheila and Joann arrived at the play structure to meet Paula. They were an hour early. They decided to go to the store and get some pop. On the way to the store, they passed a man, and he looked at Sheila the way her father did. Sheila hadn't yet noticed how she had been starting to develop, but the men had. *They are all the same*, she thought. *Men are creepy people who like to do disgusting things to little girls.* Sheila hated them all.

When Paula arrived at the play structure, Sheila and Joann were sitting on the fence. "You're early. I can't believe it," Paula said.

"Don't ask," Sheila requested.

"Did you bring the joint?" Paula inquired. Sheila smiled, bent over to roll down her sock, and there it was. They giggled. They decided to go to the park near the school. It was far enough, and there was a big field with some bushes.

When they arrived, they sat down, and Sheila pulled out the joint. "I'm not having any," Joann told them.

"More for us," Paula responded. Sheila lit it, and she and Paula smoked it. Within five minutes, the two of them were rolling on the grass, laughing hysterically. Joann thought they looked stupid, and she went to play on the swings. Sheila and Paula spent the next three hours laughing for no reason and being silly. The entire time, Sheila had no bad thoughts or images flash through her mind. Sheila loved it, and she told Paula they needed to get some more.

Joann walked up to Sheila and Paula with a frown. "Are you two ready to do something, or are you just going to sit her all day?"

"Where have you been?" Sheila asked.

"I've been gone for hours, Sheila. I got bored, so I went to play with some girls in the project," Joann replied.

"I'm thirsty and hungry. Let's go to the store. I still have money," Sheila suggested. The three of them went to the store, and on the way back they saw the boys they had bought the drugs from the day before. Sheila bought two more joints.

# Chapter 5

Sheila ran out of the house. She was in a hurry to meet Paula. She got to the play structure, and Paula was there waiting. The girls were very excited because it was their last day of grade six. They didn't go to the same school, but next year they would both be starting junior high together. The thought thrilled Sheila. Sheila and Paula had become inseparable over the last year. Joann didn't spend much time with them anymore. Sheila and Joann were in different places mentally, but they still loved each other.

Sheila pulled a joint out of her sock, and the girls ran immediately to the field behind Sheila's school. They had decided they were going to skip school that day. Sheila would go into the school to get her report card and say she was sick. Sheila just needed the joint to numb her mind from last night's memories. Paula didn't worry about getting her report card; she could do anything she wanted because both her parents were always drunk. They only cared about their next drink, not their ten children.

Sheila and Paula smoked their joint and lay on the grass, silently staring at the sky and dreaming of their futures. "Sheila, you're going to be late for school," Sheila heard Joann saying. She looked up and saw her sister standing there.

"Yes, I'm coming," Sheila said. She sat up and watched Joann walk to school. She got up, and told Paula she would be back in twenty minutes.

Sheila walked onto the school grounds, looking for Kim and Lisa. Sheila had been playing with Kim and Lisa since they were in grade one, but only in school. They weren't her friends the way Paula was. She found them by the wall of the school. Kim was crying, and Lisa was trying to console her. "What's wrong, Kim?" Sheila asked.

"My mom is getting married, and we are moving out of the project. I just found out this morning, and we move next weekend. I won't be in junior high with you two," Kim cried.

"Poor baby, how will you survive with such a big problem," Sheila snapped. Sheila gave Kim an icy stare that startled both Kim and Lisa. Just then, the bell rang. They went inside.

Sheila sat in her classroom and watched her friend still crying. She felt sorry for Kim, but she also felt a little jealous. As soon as the teacher walked in the class, Sheila jumped out of her seat and ran out the door. She waited for a few minutes in the girls' bathroom. Sheila wet her face and eyes with water; her eyes were red from the joint. She went back to class and told the teacher in a whisper, "Miss Clark, I am really sick. I've been throwing up all morning. My mother wanted me to stay home, but I didn't want to miss the last day of school. I know now my mother was right. I have to go home."

"Oh, you poor dear. Here is your report card. You have a wonderful summer and a great time at your new school," Miss Clark told her fondly. The teacher had always liked Sheila, but she worried about the child who always had such a sad look in her eyes. Miss Clark would miss her. Sheila smiled at her teacher and waved to Kim and Lisa. Then, she walked out the door.

Paula was still lying on the grass, staring up at the sky when Sheila got back. Sheila kicked her softly with a chuckle. "Boy, that was too easy. Look, I passed everything," Sheila commented, waving her report card. Sheila always got As in every subject; she was very intelligent, but she didn't realize it. The girls got up and ran to the bus stop; they were

*Behind the Drapes*

off for an adventure. Sheila had two more joints and ten dollars in her pocket.

They got on the number 2 bus and went to the mall. Sheila thought she was so grown-up. In the last year, she had been out of the project over a dozen times. The first time Paula had ever suggested it, she had been terrified, but she went along. They had had such fun. Sheila was starting to realize not everyone lived the way she or Paula did in the project. There was a life outside of Golden Street, and the day Sheila turned sixteen she would leave the project, never to return.

The bus stopped, and the girls jumped off. The girls went first to the burger shop to get some soda and fries. Then they went into a clothing store. They were walking around, looking at all the pretty clothes. Sheila still wore only hand-me-downs, and it appeared Paula did as well. Paula picked up a pretty skirt and showed Sheila. "This would look great on you," Paula said. Sheila could not believe her eyes as Paula put the skirt under her top and started walking out of the store. Sheila followed her friend.

They reached the mall and started to laugh, just as a store clerk grabbed both of them by the arm. "What's under your shirt, little lady?" he asked Paula.

"Nothing, mister," Paula replied. He took them both into the store and told them he would have to contact their parents, because they were caught shoplifting. Sheila almost fainted—her father would kill her—and she started to tremble. He put them into an office, and Paula grabbed Sheila by the arm to get her attention. Smiling, she whispered, "Let me do the talking, Sheila."

The man asked the girls for their phone numbers. "We are sisters. I will call my father, and he will come and get us," Paula informed him. He handed her the phone. She dialed and started to talk. Sheila thought Paula was really calling her father. "Yes, Dad. Sheila and I are at the mall, and this man thinks we were trying to steal a skirt," Paula said. She told him what store they were at and hung up. "He will be here in a half an hour," Paula said to the clerk. She turned and winked at Sheila.

Forty minutes later, a tall, stocky man walked into the office. "What have my daughters been up to now?" the man asked as he looked at Paula, then at Sheila, and smiled. The store clerk told him what had happened, and the man apologized. He offered to pay for the skirt, saying it must have been a misunderstanding.

"That's not necessary, mister. I just thought their parents should know what they have been up to," the clerk said.

"I will have a firm talk with them when we get home," the man informed him. The man, Sheila, and Paula left the store and the mall.

They walked into the sunshine, and Paula started to laugh. "Thanks, Marty, or should I say Dad," she said as she continued laughing. Paula introduced Sheila to her uncle Marty. He was Paula's mother's youngest brother, and very handsome, Sheila thought. He was thirty-nine, and the tallest person Sheila had ever seen. He had soft blue eyes that danced when he smiled. Marty knew how hard Paula and her siblings had it at home, and he tried to help, in his own way, when he could.

They climbed into Marty's truck, which was parked in front of the mall. It was the nicest truck Sheila had ever seen, so shiny and red. Her father's vehicles were always falling apart and full of rust, just like everyone else in the project, if you had a vehicle. "Why aren't you in school?" Marty asked.

"We didn't feel like it today. Rough night last night," Paula answered.

He looked at her with a smile. "Well, it's only eleven thirty, and you don't have to be home until school's over. Let's go to my place," Marty suggested. They got to Marty's apartment, and Sheila loved it. She had never seen a place like this. The walls were covered with lots of pictures. Everywhere Sheila looked, there were pillows and bright colors. Marty saw her smile and asked her if she liked it. Sheila nodded yes and sat on a big fluffy red sofa. "What have you got to drink, Marty?" Paula inquired.

"Check the fridge and take what you want," Marty called to her as he stood staring at Sheila. Paula sat beside Sheila on the sofa and handed her a beer. Sheila looked at the beer. She had never drunk a beer before. "You don't have to drink beer if you don't want to, Sheila. I have wine and rum, if you want," Marty said.

"No, beer is fine, Marty," Sheila replied, trying to sound mature.

"Marty, Sheila has a joint," Paula announced. Marty smiled at Sheila and told her to light it, so she did. Marty started to laugh at Sheila, and she blushed with embarrassment. He explained to Sheila how you were supposed to wet the outside of the joint before you lit it. That way it burned longer. Marty took the joint from Sheila and wet it with his lips. He gave it back to Sheila. She took some puffs and gave it to Paula.

She felt so grow up, sitting here drinking beer and smoking pot with her friends. After the joint, Marty put on some music, came over to Paula, and whispered in her ear. She got up and left the room. A few moments later, Paula came back with some little glasses filled with a liquid and topped with a lemon slice. Marty explained to Sheila that it was called tequila, and it was from Mexico. He showed her how to drink it. It was strong, and Sheila choked on it.

Marty offered the girls a cigarette, which they both accepted. Marty got more tequila and told Sheila the second time was easier, handing her another drink. He was wrong; she choked again. Sheila was starting to feel a little woozy from the joint and the drinks, and so she put her cigarette out. Marty started to whisper to Paula. She smiled and sat really close to Sheila. Marty started to tell Sheila that if she ever needed help, he would help, and he would never hurt her. He came and sat on the other side of her, and she felt happy and safe.

Sheila closed her eyes, and a few moments later she felt her clothes being pulled from her body. She thought she must have been dreaming of her father, until she opened her eyes. There was Paula standing in front of her, naked, and Marty was pulling off Sheila's clothes. Sheila tried to protest, but they held her down. She couldn't believe what was happening to her. This was Paula she thought they were friends.

Marty was giving all the instructions to Paula. He told her to kiss Sheila while he got on top of Sheila and forced his way inside of her. Paula encouraged him on and told him what a bad boy he was; this only made him pound into her harder. Sheila cried. She still couldn't believe what was happening to her. Was there not one person on the planet who didn't want to hurt her this way? No one could be trusted. She saw that now. It was Sheila against the world.

When it was finally over, Marty went into the shower. Paula came over to Sheila and told her not to tell anyone, or Paula would say it was Sheila who attacked her. "You have been a great supply of joints for me, Sheila, and I hate to lose that. But I needed help today. I couldn't go to juvenile hall for stealing. The judge said one more time and I go. As a bonus, Marty pays me one hundred dollars for every girl I bring him, so I had to do it," Paula told the friend that she'd had since they were five years old. Paula, she had learned the lesson a long time ago: you have to fight to survive, and sometimes that means stepping on a friend.

Marty came out of the shower and asked the girls if they wanted a ride. Sheila shook her head no and ran from the apartment, into the hall. She had a terrible headache. *This is the last time that anyone hurts me again*, Sheila vowed. She walked out of the building, and, not sure where she was, Sheila walked until she saw a familiar street. After a long walk, she reached the project and walked to the house. As she approached her row, she wondered what time it was. Sheila reached unit 8, and she thought her heart would stop. The drapes were closed. He was home, and she was late.

Sheila opened the door, praying for it to be over quick. She could remember the time Peter wasn't home before the drapes were closed. Her father had beaten him severely. As soon as the door was all the way open, Sheila saw him. He pulled her in, slamming the door behind her. And the beating began.

"Why didn't you go to school today? Where were you? Who were you with, Sheila?" Bobby questioned, screaming as he struck her with blows of his closed fist. Miss Clark had called to see how Sheila was feeling. Sheila thought it was bad, until he smelled alcohol on her breath. Then he went crazy. He picked Sheila up, and, calling her a slut, he threw her across the room, into the wall. Everything went black as Sheila slumped to the floor.

When Sheila came to, Joann was mopping the blood off the wall and the floor. Hugette was serving the dinner plates, and Bobby, noticing she was awake, screamed at her to get up. "Sheila, I don't know who you were drinking with today, probably a man you little slut. You are not allowed out of this house until I tell you. You are no longer part of this family. If you see me in the hall or stairs, you are to turn and run the other way. You eat your meals in your bedroom; you are to stay in your room unless you are doing chores for your mother. Do you hear me, you little slut?" Bobby hollered, and before Sheila could nod yes, he hit her a few more times. "Hugette, you have your slave back. Now, you little slut, get to your room." Sheila climbed the stairs to her room.

Sheila reached her room and closed the door softly behind her. She walked to her bed and collapsed on it. What had happened? When she'd left this room only this morning, she'd thought she was off for an exciting adventure. She lay on her bed and cried herself to sleep. *Someday*, she thought, *my life will be different.*

The next morning, Sheila woke in so much pain. There was not a part of her body that wasn't sore. She was not permitted to leave her room until Bobby had gone to work. She was hungry; she'd never had dinner the night before. She got up, dressed, and sat on her bed, waiting to be told to come down for breakfast.

"How are you feeling, Sheila?" Joann asked as she came into Sheila's room.

"I'm fine," Sheila lied. Joann knew she was not fine. Sheila looked awful. Every inch of her was swollen and black-and-blue. It was one of the worst beatings Bobby had ever inflicted on Sheila. Joann knew Sheila had not seen herself in the mirror yet, too scared to meet Bobby in the hall.

"He's leaving in a few minutes; I'll let you know the second he leaves," Joann assured her, and she left the room.

When Sheila saw her face, she couldn't believe what she was seeing. For the first time, Sheila worried she wouldn't see her sixteenth birthday. She tried to brush her teeth, but her lips were too sore. She thought of Paula and Marty and started to cry. At that moment, Sheila thought she was going to have to toughen up if she was to survive. She wiped the tears from her eyes and the images from her mind, and she went down for breakfast.

Hugette was sitting at the table when Sheila came into the kitchen. She looked up and started to cry when she saw her daughter. "I'm just fine," Sheila informed her mother. Sheila put some bread in the toaster and filled the kettle with water for tea. Hugette got up and left the room. Joann started to clear the table as Sheila ate her breakfast. "I'll do it. Go out and play," Sheila told her sister. Joann was about to object when she saw Sheila's eyes. They weren't sad anymore, only angry. Joann put down the plates in her hand and went outside.

Sheila had just finished the breakfast dishes, and was on her way to her room when she heard the doorbell. She turned, and through the screen door she saw her uncle Pierre. Sheila smiled instantly. She loved her uncle. He was Hugette's older brother. Sheila's smile disappeared when she observed the look on her uncle's face.

When Pierre saw the child, his heart broke. Everyone in Hugette's family suspected Bobby beat Hugette and the children, but he never could have imagined it to be so bad.

"Sheila, come here," Pierre instructed. The child walked to the door and opened it. As her uncle came into the house, she noticed he had tears in his eyes. "Where are your mother and father?" Pierre asked.

"Dad's at work and Mom's out back, I think," Sheila replied, and she went up the stairs to her room. She could hear her uncle screaming for his sister.

Hugette came in the back door and, looking down the hall, saw her brother. As she got closer to him and saw the expression on his face, she knew he had seen Sheila.

"What happened to Sheila, Hugette?" Pierre said. Hugette was about to tell her brother the standard lie, when she realized that this time, he would not accept it. Hugette finally admitted to her brother what he had always known. Bobby had been beating her and the children for years, and their home was a virtual prison.

"You can't stay here another day, Hugette," Pierre told his sister.

"Where would I go and how would I live? Bobby made me quit my job a while back, after he beat me so bad I couldn't go to work for a few weeks until my face healed. How would I live, Pierre?" Hugette said.

"I have a big, empty house for now, and Hugette, there is welfare. I know you don't like it, but you have to think of your children. Please, Hugette, think of the children," Pierre pleaded. Pierre was divorced, and his ex-wife and daughter lived in Montreal, at least a six-hour drive away. He never saw them. He would be happy to have Hugette and the girls stay with him for a while. Finally, after a few minutes, Hugette agreed.

Pierre told her to pack all the clothes she could for her and the girls. He wrote a note for Bobby and one for Rick. He told Rick to phone him and left the number. He placed the note on Rick's bed. Bobby's note was not as short and sweet. He basically told Bobby his days of using his family as a punching bag were over. He wrote that Bobby had never taken care of the children, but Pierre would, and if Bobby tried to come near his sister or the children, he would kill him. Pierre was

*Behind the Drapes*

a large man, and he was not worried for a moment that Bobby would come looking for them. He placed the note on the table and went to help Hugette pack.

Hugette came into Sheila's room and told her to pack her clothes. *I'm not sixteen yet, you can't throw me out yet*, was the first thing that came to Sheila's mind. Hugette saw the fear in her daughter's eyes and explained they were leaving Bobby to go live with Uncle Pierre. Sheila couldn't believe her ears; they were leaving Bobby and the project, now. She jumped off her bed and started to pack, quickly, before her mother could change her mind.

Just then, they heard the front door close. Hugette and Sheila froze. "Keep packing," Pierre instructed and went downstairs. A few moments later, he returned with Joann on his shoulders. "I've found someone to help us pack," Pierre told them, and he put Joann down. Hugette explained to Joann what was happening. She grabbed a bag and ran to her dresser to pack, giggling all the way.

Pierre brought the five small bags to his car and put them in the trunk. *How sad it is for three people to have so few belongings*, he thought. He buckled the girls into the back seat, and he and Hugette climbed in the front. He started the car and drove away. Sheila and Joann turned and watched out the back window as the project got smaller and smaller, until it was gone. *Good-bye and good riddance to unit 8*, thought Sheila as she smiled and turned to sit properly in her seat.

# Chapter 6

The car rolled to a stop in the driveway of the biggest house Sheila had ever seen. She climbed out of the car and looked around. All the houses looked different, not like in the project. There was a driveway; in the project, there were a few large parking lots where everyone parked their vehicles, and you walked to your row, and then your house. At the end of the driveway was a two-vehicle garage; Sheila had only seen a garage on television.

Pierre opened the door, and they walked in. The house was beautiful. Hugette and the girls looked around in awe. Hugette had never been to her brother's home. Bobby wouldn't allow it. They came into a hall with a big closet and a bench. Pierre put the few bags of their belongings on the bench and told them to come in and make themselves at home. They walked into a big, beautiful kitchen and then a huge dining room, which led to a massive living room with two couches, three armchairs, and a fireplace.

Pierre brought the girls up to his daughter's room and told them, "You two can stay here and use anything you want. And there are toys in the basement." They looked around. There was a desk and hundreds of crayons, not pieces, but long crayons in big jars. There were paints,

*Behind the Drapes*

markers, and paper of all colors. The girls thought they had arrived in heaven. Sheila lost her excitement as she wondered what evil deed would be expected of her for this luxury. Her uncle had never done anything to Sheila, but she trusted no one, and he was a man. He would have to earn her trust.

That evening, they had a wonderful dinner: roast beef, mashed potatoes, and carrots. The girls had never seen so much food in their lives, and they were allowed to have a big glass of milk. They loved it; they only had milk in their tea at home. After dinner, Pierre made popcorn, and Sheila and Joann curled up on a sofa to watch television. That night, as they went to sleep, Sheila and Joann felt safe and secure for the first time in their lives.

When they woke the next morning, it was with smiles on their faces. As they came into the kitchen, they saw Hugette sitting at the table with a big smile. "Good morning, girls. How about pancakes for breakfast?" Hugette suggested. The girls nodded, and Sheila went looking for a frying pan. "Sheila, I will cook breakfast," Hugette told her. Then she grabbed them by the hand and took them into the living room, where she asked them to sit on the sofa, saying she wanted to talk to them while Pierre was at work.

Hugette started to cry, which got the girls crying as well. Hugette started to speak through her tears. "Sheila, Joann, I know life hasn't been easy for us, but I hope this is a new beginning, and I want us all to make the best of it. We might have to live on welfare for a while, just until we get settled. We will get a new house, and I want us to be a family, just the three of us. You can trust me and tell me everything, and we can make a new life for ourselves," Hugette promised her daughters. The three of them hugged and cried for a few moments.

Sheila pulled away first and looked at her mother. "I have something to tell you, Mom, and it's bad." She continued to tell her and Joann everything Bobby had done to her. Hugette listened to her daughter's story in horror, but all of a sudden, so much started to make sense—Bobby's attitude change toward Sheila. Joann realized what had turned Sheila so bitter. Now she understood her sister a little more.

Sheila asked her sister something she had always wanted to know. "Did he ever do anything to you, Joann?"

Joann stared at her mother and sister. She assured them both that for whatever reason, he had never touched her in any way. Hugette promised Sheila at that moment that she would never let Bobby hurt her again. "We will never have to live in the same house as that man ever again, I promise. I love you and I will show you how much. I will never let him hurt you again," Hugette said. Sheila wanted to believe her.

Within a few months, the welfare system had found them a small house in a different part of the city. It only had two bedrooms, so Sheila and Joann would have to share a room, but they didn't mind. Life had changed so much. They were happy and calm. Rick came to visit and told them Bobby had moved to an apartment, while Rick had moved in with Ralph and his family. How funny, Sheila thought, that Rick wanted to stay in that project. She was so happy to be away. Rick told the girls to call him if they needed anything, and he gave them a hug. But he still disliked his mother, and he left without even a smile toward her.

The months they had stayed with their uncle had given Sheila a little hope that some people were good. Her uncle had never let her down. He always treated Sheila and Joann with care and love. He never hurt them in any way, and Sheila loved him for it.

Pierre helped them move and gave Hugette some furniture. Bobby had taken all the furniture out of unit 8; even the children's bunk beds were gone. Between Pierre and the welfare system, their house had everything it needed. Hugette and the children were used to getting by on less than what they had now. The house was plain and small, but it was theirs, and they loved it. It was in a small project, only twenty-one houses, three small rows, not like the hundreds on Golden Street. It was government-owned and subsidized, so the rent was really cheap, based on income, just like Golden Street.

Pierre helped Hugette place the furniture where it belonged, and then he left, telling them he would be back soon. Hugette put on the radio, and the three of them danced around giggling; they were so excited to start a new life. Hugette had changed so much in the last few months. She was carefree and happy, and it reflected greatly on her parenting skills. She took care of her children now and enjoyed it.

Pierre returned a couple of hours later with bags and bags of groceries, and a big surprise for Sheila and Joann. He had bought them each a shiny new bicycle. They were thrilled and thanked him again and again. Neither had ever had a bike before. He took them to a restaurant for dinner. Sheila and Joann had never been to a restaurant until the last few months, and they loved it. They had had a long day, and it was dark when they returned to their new house. Pierre dropped them off and told them he would be back to check on them in a few days.

Sheila and Joann lay in their beds that night feeling safe and happy. Joann drifted to sleep quickly, but Sheila lay there for hours dreaming of her new life. No one knew her here, and nobody knew about Bobby. She had never used drugs since she had left the project, and she had no desire to use them again. She could be anyone she wanted here, and she fell asleep dreaming of the new Sheila.

The next morning, while having breakfast, Hugette told the girls they would have to register for school. The school year was beginning in two weeks. It was the first time Sheila and Joann would go to different schools—Sheila was starting junior high, and Joann was still in grade school. Hugette had a special treat for them to make the transition easier. The welfare system allowed $150 per child for school supplies and clothes. After they registered for school, they went shopping.

Hugette made a nice dinner that evening. Sheila asked her mother if she wanted the drapes closed. Hugette shook her head and said, "No," with a smile. They sat and ate their first meal in their new home. The girls chatted excitedly about their new cloths and new schools. They had never had new clothes before, and Hugette had allowed them to choose whatever they wanted. For once, the girls' clothes were their own.

They each received new running shoes, three pairs of pants, and five new tops. They even had enough money left over for new pajamas, socks, and panties. Sheila was visibly shaken when Hugette told her she had to start wearing a bra. Sheila was developing at alarming speed, and it appeared she was to inherit her mother's curvaceous figure. They picked up two training bras for Sheila, and, after she was over the shock, she felt more grown-up wearing one.

The next day, Sheila went outside feeling proud and happy. She and Joann were wearing new clothes, and they climbed onto their new bikes to go for a ride. Sheila looked across the small field of grass between the rows of houses. She saw a girl about her age. Sheila and Joann walked their new bikes over, and Sheila introduced herself and her sister. "Hi, my name is Chantal. I live two doors down from you. Do you want to play?" the girl asked.

Chantal had lived there her whole life. She was a chunky girl with dark hair, skin, and eyes. Chantal was the same age as Joann, and an only child. She lived with her mother and father. The girls nodded, and they played the whole afternoon. They rode their bikes, and Chantal showed them where the parks were. Sheila discovered while talking with Chantal that the three of them were the only children in the small project. However, there were many babies and toddlers. The project, unlike Golden Street, was full of poor, young working families, struggling families just starting out.

Chantal's father was in a wheelchair and on welfare. From what Sheila could gather, Chantal's and Sheila's families were the only ones on welfare, a fact that humiliated Sheila. She knew she would never let anyone know her family was on welfare, and she changed the subject when Chantal inquired if her mother worked. Sheila knew one thing: when she grew up she would never live off welfare. They played until dinnertime and arranged to meet after dinner.

Sheila and Joann ran into the house. Music was playing. Hugette was singing while she prepared dinner. They sat down to another enjoyable meal. When they were finished with dinner, Sheila and Joann cleared the table while Hugette started the dishes. There was a knock at the door, and it startled them. They were happy now, but it would take some time to heal from Bobby's terror.

Hugette went to the door, and a moment later, she called Sheila. Sheila walked to the door slowly. When she looked up, she saw a lady and a little girl. "This is Mrs. Wright and Cassandra," Hugette said. "Mrs. Wright would like you to watch Cassandra for her, Sheila, only if you would like to babysit?" Sheila still had trouble making decisions. She was used to things being decided for her, and it was taking a little time to adjust.

"I pay a dollar an hour, Sheila, and Cassandra is a good girl," Mrs. Wright explained. The term sent a chill down Sheila's spine, but as she looked at the cute little girl, she heard herself saying yes.

The next Friday night, Sheila and Joann left for Cassandra's house after dinner. "If you need anything, Sheila, you just call and I'll come right over," Hugette said.

"We'll be fine, Mom. Don't worry," Sheila said. Sheila and Joann where very excited, and Sheila felt so very grown-up to be asked. She had no intention of letting Mrs. Wright down. She wanted to save money for when she grew up, and she would need to do a lot of babysitting to make the amount of money she wanted.

They arrived at the door, and Mrs. Wright greeted them with a big smile. "Come in, girls. Cassandra is waiting for you in the living room. She is watching cartoons."

"My mother told me to tell you not to worry; she will be home all night if I need anything. She said to make sure to get a number where you will be," Sheila told her, trying to seem professional.

Mrs. Wright grinned and replied, "The number is on a pad by the phone. Cassandra has eaten her dinner, and she is to be in bed by eight o'clock. If she is being good, then you can give her a treat before bed, around seven." Mrs. Wright left then with a man who Sheila had a feeling was not her husband, but Sheila didn't care. She was happy to be making money.

Sheila walked into the living room and saw Joann and Cassandra sitting on the sofa. Cassandra was an adorable little girl. She was two and a half, with curly red hair and big green eyes. Her mother was right; she was easy to take care of. They played for hours, and then they had a snack. Then Sheila read Cassandra a bedtime story. Cassandra fell asleep by the second page, and Sheila quietly went downstairs. She cleaned the dishes from the snack, tidied up the living room, and put all of Cassandra's toys away.

Sheila and Joann were watching television when Mrs. Wright got home. When Mrs. Wright noticed how clean the place was, she was very pleased. She paid Sheila eight dollars and told her she would call her again. "I would be happy to babysit Cassandra anytime, Mrs. Wright," Sheila said. Sheila and Joann left quietly and went home. Sheila knew she'd just tapped into a gold mine.

Sheila and Joann entered the house, and Hugette yelled for them to lock the door from the living room. She was watching a movie on television. Joann said goodnight and went straight to bed. Sheila went to watch the movie with her mother. Sheila told her mother what a great time she had babysitting, and how much money she made.

"Thank you for letting me babysit tonight, Mom, and thank you for this new life. I feel happy," Sheila told her mother. She walked over, kissed her cheek, and then headed for bed. Sheila lay in bed that night thinking of her new school, the new friends she would meet, and her future. Not long ago, Sheila had dreaded her future, but now she looked forward to it.

# Chapter 7

Sheila was carrying too many books when she almost lost her footing and tumbled down the stairs. All her books went falling, and two boys almost started to fight trying to pick them up for her. One of them, the bigger one, Tony, managed to scoop them up and bring them over to Sheila. "Thank you, Tony," Sheila said politely, and she hurried down the stairs without looking back. She still felt nervous around boys, and she thought she always would.

Sheila had turned fourteen a few months back, and she still had no idea how beautiful she was. She had grown into a girl who could easily have passed for eighteen. Sheila had definitely inherited her mother's body. She had a full, curvy figure. Her hair was long and golden blonde, and she still had those beautiful blue eyes, only now they were sparkling instead of sad. Sheila Parks was absolutely stunning.

"Sheila, Sheila, wait up," Sandy was shouting. Sheila turned to see her friend running behind her. Sheila stopped and waited for her friend to catch up. Sandy and Sheila had become friends that very first day of junior high. Over the years, they had become very close, although Sheila never told Sandy about her past or Bobby. Sheila didn't trust anyone.

She told everyone her father was dead, and she never invited her school friends over to her house. Sandy had never even been there.

Her uncle Pierre had died six months after they had moved into their new house. He had been killed in a car accident. As far as Sheila was concerned, he was the closest thing she had to a real father, so she told everyone about Pierre, but in her stories he was her father. Hugette had taken Pierre's death very hard. He had been Hugette's social life, taking her to the bingo and out to movies. Hugette had dated a bit, but never found anyone she liked. She had been lonely ever since Pierre's death.

"When are we going to go shopping, to get our graduation dresses?" Sandy inquired. School was almost over, and next year Sheila and Sandy would be starting high school. They were very excited. Sheila had become very popular in school; the boys wanted to date her, and the girls wanted to be friends with her. Sheila always kept to herself, and that seemed to make people want to know her more. She was really enjoying school, and lately, Sheila had even been thinking about college. "I have to get my dress soon," Sandy insisted. Sheila got her calendar out of her school bag and opened it.

"Okay, I can't tonight. I'm babysitting Cassandra, and tomorrow I'm babysitting for the Scarfs, and on Friday night the Smiths, and on Saturday night Cassandra ... "

"All you ever do is babysit, Sheila," Sandy complained. They decided to go on Saturday afternoon, after Sheila finished studying for final exams. Sandy was right, though. Sheila was babysitting every chance she got, and she had saved just over three thousand dollars since that first time she babysat for Mrs. Wright all those years ago. Sheila had plans for that money. It was for her future.

As Sheila was walking home from school, she stopped at the corner store. Just as she was coming out of the store, Joann was going in.

"Hi there," Joann said. "Why don't you wait for me? I'll be out in a minute, and we can walk home together."

"I'll be waiting," Sheila said, assuring her little sister. Joann came out, and they started walking home together. They chatted about school. Joann was excited about junior high next year. Sheila was excited about graduation and buying a new dress.

*Behind the Drapes*

They were giggling about something as they turned the corner and started down their row. As they approached the house, the smiles left their faces. They were consumed with fear as they stopped dead in their tracks. They looked at each other in disbelief. The drapes were closed. They started to tremble, and Sheila was about to turn and run when the door opened, and there he was. Bobby was standing in the doorway with a large grin on his face. He opened the door and told them to come in.

They slowly walked up the walk and into the house. "Long time, no see," Bobby snickered. Sheila and Joann didn't know what to say or how to react, but they knew the devil had come for them. Bobby told them to go into the kitchen for a family talk. As they started for the kitchen, they wondered how he'd found them. Where was Hugette? Had he beaten her? The first thing Sheila noticed when she entered the kitchen was the flowers on the table. She had only seen flowers in her house once, and that was when Uncle Pierre had died. *Who died?* Sheila thought, and then she knew. Sheila felt the joy die in her at that moment.

Hugette sat there at the table with a big smile, and Sheila was disgusted when she saw her mother's neck—it was full of hickeys. Sheila felt her stomach turn. She was worried she would get sick any minute. Bobby looked at Sheila. "Boy, you sure have grown over the years," he commented. The look on his face made the hairs on her neck stand up. All Sheila could think at that moment was that she had to survive the next two years.

"When your mother called me this morning at work," Bobby started. Sheila and Joann looked at each other in disbelief. Hugette called him. She brought him here. How could she? She had promised. "I was surprised, but quite happy," Bobby continued. "Your mother and I have spent the day together, talking, and we have decided to get back together. We know things were rough before, but things will be different this time," Bobby announced.

Bobby informed the girls they would be moving and making a fresh start. Bobby felt the children had been running wild with too much freedom since he had been away, and that would have to change. Hugette let him do all the talking and just sat there with a stupid grin. Sheila hated her mother at that moment, more than she had ever hated

Bobby. Sheila knew if she could not even trust her mother, there was nobody on earth she could ever trust.

Bobby got up from the table then, and announced the meeting was over. He was going to watch television until dinner was ready, and he expected Sheila to have it on the table soon. He felt everything had been said. After all, in Bobby's opinion he was the king, and only his views were important. As soon as he left the room, the girls looked at their mother with a pleading stare. "I'm sorry, girls. I have to think of myself, and I *love* him. Things will be different. You'll see." Sheila thought her mother was the most selfish and stupid person on the planet. Things would be the same, and Sheila knew it.

When Sheila and Joann were finished with the dishes, Sheila went into the living room and told Hugette she was leaving to go babysitting, and Joann was coming. Her parents were curled up together on the sofa, and the scene only filled her with dread. "Your mother told me how often you're babysitting. You have quiet the little business going," Bobby commented.

"May I go now? I'm going to be late," Sheila pleaded. Bobby nodded, and she ran to the door. She and Joann escaped for a few hours.

When Mrs. Wright left with her gentleman friend, Sheila and Joann played with Cassandra until she was sleepy. While Sheila read her the first page of her story, she fell asleep. Sheila quietly left the room and went to join Joann on the sofa. They both started to cry uncontrollably as Sheila held her sister.

"Joann, we have to be strong and get through this. The second I turn sixteen, I'm gone. I have money put away. As soon as I get settled, I'll go to your school and let you know where I am. When you turn sixteen, you can join me. I'll always have room for you. We can and will do this," Sheila promised her sister.

That night, when Sheila and Joann returned home, Bobby was sitting at the kitchen table. He looked very pleased with himself. "Who would have thought you could make so much money babysitting?" Bobby snickered. He pulled all of Sheila's money out of his pocket and placed it on the table. Sheila felt as if someone had just kicked her in the stomach. "Sheila, from now on your mother and I feel you should start paying room and board, now that you are making your own money," Bobby said.

Sheila and Joann climbed the stairs to their bedroom crying, and when Sheila opened the door, she was crushed. Bobby had ripped Sheila's bedroom apart while he was looking for her money. There were clothes all thrown about. The mattress was on the floor, and all the drawers of the dresser were pulled out and overturned. Sheila bent down and started to clean up the mess. Joann had started to help when the door opened. "I'm sorry," Hugette whispered, and quickly closed the door. *Too little too late,* Sheila thought.

The next morning, when Sheila left for school with Joann, neither girl said a word. When Sheila arrived at her school, she went over to Jeff with a smile. Everyone in school knew Jeff sold drugs. He was in a couple of Sheila's classes, and, like all the boys, he thought she was beautiful. Sheila knew that with Bobby back, she needed something to numb her pain. She handed Jeff a ten-dollar bill. "What will that get me?" Sheila asked with a smile and a wink.

"Anything you want, sexy," Jeff responded, and he gave Sheila a large bag of pot. Sheila was sure he gave her a lot more than ten dollars' worth. It was enough to last a week. For the first time, Sheila had used her sex appeal to her advantage, and she made a mental note of how easy it could be to use men. She knew they were all dirty pigs at heart, and she hated them all. She waved bye to Jeff and headed off to smoke a joint before school.

When the lunch bell rang, Sheila ran out of the school. The only thing she had on her mind was to smoke another joint, and she almost ran into Sandy. "Sheila, what's with you today? You have been avoiding me all morning. Someone told me they saw you talking with Jeff this morning. Is that true? What do you need Jeff for?" Sandy started hitting her with questions. "Are we still going shopping on Saturday?" she continued.

Sheila turned on her friend with an evil stare. "Would you just shut up?" Sheila hollered at her stunned friend. "I can talk to who I want, when I want, about what I want. I'm not going shopping and I'm not going to the grad dance, so stop asking me about it and leave me alone!" Sheila ran from the school as Sandy stood there in shock. What had happened to her friend? She thought she would give Sheila some time to cool off. She would try and talk to her friend after school.

Sheila sat on the grass, fuming. She had to put up with Bobby, but there was nobody else on the planet she had to take any shit from. Sheila lit her joint and smoked it, and she calmed down. She thought about studying for her exams, but she didn't care about her marks or school anymore. For that matter, she didn't care about anything, except the day she turned sixteen.

On the last day of school, Sheila arrived with a black eye and bruises, and she was limping. It had only taken Bobby two weeks to go back to his old self. The night before, Sheila had burned the pork chops, and the result was a severe beating. When a teacher inquired about her injuries, she told her and everyone else she had been in a minor car accident. That morning, when she had looked in the mirror, she'd thought she looked like Uncle Pierre when she had seen him in the hospital after his car accident. Sheila could come up with a lie quickly. She'd had practice over the last fourteen years.

She limped over to Jeff and used his sympathy to get an even larger bag of pot. Bobby was still stealing her money when she babysat. However, she always managed to hide a little in her sock. Sheila told Jeff she was moving, and he told her he would find her a connection to buy from. Then he gave her his phone number. Sheila promised to call as soon as she knew where she would be living, and went to smoke her joint and forget the night before.

That day, at the end of school, Sheila passed Sandy in the hall as she was leaving. Sandy had tears in her eyes. When Sheila noticed, she stopped and went over to her.

"Sheila, are you okay?" Sandy inquired.

"I'm fine, really," Sheila assured her, but Sandy didn't believe her for a second. She had changed so much in the last two weeks. She was not the Sheila Sandy had know for all these years.

"Are you sure you won't change your mind about the grad dance? Please?" Sandy pleaded. Sheila shook her head no, and then regretted it as her head began to pound. Sheila told Sandy that she would be going to a different high school, and Sandy was crushed. Sandy wished her friend all the best, and as she watched Sheila limp away, she wondered what would happen to her. This was something Sheila wondered daily, ever since Bobby had come back.

*Behind the Drapes*

Six weeks later, they were living in a two-bedroom apartment, and Sheila hated it. Jeff had kept his promise, and as it turned out, his cousin Carl lived on the next street from Sheila. Carl was just as generous to Sheila as Jeff had been. One look at her, and he would have given her anything. Sheila did enjoy taking advantage of men in some way. She felt she deserved it because of what her father put her through.

Sheila and Joann had registered for school. Now that Bobby was back, there were no new school clothes, and with him stealing Sheila's money, she couldn't afford any school supplies. Sheila and Joann would make due just like they had in the past. *The new kid again*, Sheila thought. She didn't even care about making any new friends. Who knew how long she would be there, and she hated to answer the questions every time her father beat her. She would just put in time, and hopefully, time would pass quickly.

Sheila looked at the clock, and, seeing the time, she walked to the tiny kitchen to start dinner. Joann was not home yet, so she got dinner on the stove and started setting the table. Hugette came into the kitchen. Seeing that everything was started, she went back to the sofa. Sheila barely spoke to her mother these days, and neither did Joann. It didn't appear to bother Hugette. She didn't try to talk to them. They were so hurt by her decision to reunite with Bobby, and Hugette was also turning into her old self again. She only seemed to care about herself.

Joann arrived, breathless, not knowing if Bobby was home. She had run all the way up the stairs. "I'm sorry, Sheila," Joann told her sister as she entered the kitchen.

"It's okay. He's not here, and dinner is almost ready," Sheila replied, to Joann's relief. Just then, they heard the door slam. Bobby was home.

Bobby had a hearty appetite that evening, and he asked Hugette if there were any seconds. She happily got him another plate and asked him a question that shocked her daughters. "Bobby, do you mind if I go to the bingo tonight? I haven't went in so long. I'll take the bus, and you can stay here and relax and watch TV." Bobby looked at his wife, and then at Sheila, and he smiled.

"Sure you can go, Hugette," Bobby said, to the horror of his daughters.

65

All Sheila could hear in her head was Hugette's promise, the promise she had made to Sheila years before. "I love you and I will show you how much. I will never let him hurt you again," Hugette had told her daughters. Now she was leaving Sheila alone with him, and giving him the opportunity to do whatever he wanted. Sheila couldn't believe her mother. She knew Hugette didn't love her. Sheila tried to look at her mother, but Hugette would not make eye contact with her. Hugette got up from the table and told Bobby she was going to get ready for bingo.

Bobby finished his second plate, got up from the table, and went to the sofa. Sheila looked at Joann, horrified. "Don't worry, Sheila. I'll stay with you," Joann assured her sister. Joann knew what Sheila was worried about. She remembered what Sheila had told them, even if Hugette had forgotten. Hugette left, and the girls quietly finished the dishes.

Bobby came in and told Sheila to make him a tea. He turned to Joann then, and told her to go to the store and buy him cigarettes. "Now!" he yelled, and threw money at Joann. Trembling, she bent and picked it up, and left the room.

Joann left crying. When Sheila brought Bobby his cup of tea, he told her to put it down. Then he dragged Sheila to her bedroom, stopping only to lock the door. When they reached Sheila's room, he threw her on the bed and jumped on top of her. "It's been a long time, Sheila. You have really grown up, and I can't wait to have you. Be a good girl and take care of your daddy," Bobby instructed.

# Chapter 8

Sheila woke up the next morning in so much pain. Bobby had been especially rough with her the night before. She climbed out of bed and noticed her sister looking at her. "Don't say a word. There is nothing I want to talk about, Joann," Sheila snapped. Joann looked at her and started to cry. She felt such sorrow for her sister, but it did not compare to the anger they both felt for their mother.

Sheila showered for school, went to the kitchen, and made breakfast. Hugette came in smiling and announced she had won two hundred dollars at the bingo. Sheila looked at her mother with disgust in her eyes. Hugette tried to give Sheila some money, and she refused. What did Hugette want? To pay Sheila for the pain and suffering she had endured? Or was she trying to ease her guilt? Either way, Sheila wanted nothing from her mother.

Sheila and Joann took the bus together in silence; their new schools were right next to each other. The girls said good-bye and Sheila walked toward her school when she saw a familiar face. It was Kim. When Kim saw her, she ran over to Sheila. The girls hugged. Sheila looked at her old friend and was shocked at the changes in her. Kim was wearing about an inch thick of makeup, and her hair was long and curly. What shocked Sheila the most was her clothing. She had very tight jeans on, with a jean jacket sporting a crest on the back that read *sex, drugs, and rock and roll*. She didn't look like the little girl Sheila remembered from the project.

"What are you doing here, Kim?" Sheila said. Kim explained that her mother had just gotten remarried, and they had moved into the neighborhood. She was starting school today. Kim told Sheila how she had come to love her last stepfather, but despite that, her mother had divorced him and married this new man. Kim wasn't sure how she felt about the new man yet. Sheila told Kim about her parents breaking up and getting back together.

Sheila was surprised how happy she was to see someone from the project. Sheila hadn't wanted to make friends since losing Sandy, but when Sheila saw Kim, she felt herself longing for a friend. Sheila remembered how she and Kim had been such good friends in grade school, and she was excited to have that back. They arranged to meet up at lunch and catch up on things. Sheila told her old friend that she had to go somewhere, and Kim asked to come along.

Sheila looked at Kim and could only remember the little girl from the project. She wasn't sure how Kim would react to the drugs, despite her jacket. Sheila decided to be honest and told Kim she was going to smoke a joint before classes started. Kim squealed with delight. She had been smoking pot for years now. The two girls ran to the bush on the edge of the school grounds and shared a joint before school.

They didn't have any classes together that morning, and when the lunch bell rang, Sheila waited for Kim at the designated spot. The two girls talked, and Sheila was able to open up to Kim in a way she had never experienced before. Sheila hoped that she could trust her old friend. For the first time in her life, Sheila let it all out. She told her about the beating and the abuse, and how much she hated her mother for going back to Bobby. Sheila told her friend about her father stealing her money, and how the second she turned sixteen, she was leaving.

Kim hugged Sheila and promised to keep her secret safe. She told Sheila that she had always known about her father's beatings. Everyone in the project knew about Bobby. The children, except for Joann, were constantly bruised and swollen. Kim was shocked to find out about the sexual abuse, and Kim had to agree with her friend. Hugette was a bitch to have gone back with him and put her daughters in such danger.

Kim told Sheila a secret of her own. She had a boyfriend that her mother didn't approve of. He was a lot older than Kim, and her mother had forbidden her to see him, but Kim still saw Steve every chance she could. Steve was tall and handsome, and he had his own apartment, and Kim knew one day she would marry him. Kim insisted that she and Sheila promise each other to always keep their secrets, and not to tell. As Sheila agreed, she thought to herself how she wished she had such a simple secret.

Lunch was over, and they went back to class, both lost in their own thoughts. They both felt better having confessed their secrets to each other, and knowing they each had someone to confide in. When Sheila realized they both had art class right after lunch, she was thrilled. She was just happy to have someone on her side. It felt so warming to her.

When school was over, Sheila saw Kim talking with a tall man. He was leaning on a light orange Mustang; it was a beautiful car. Kim turned and saw Sheila. She called for her to come over. Sheila looked down at her watch and knew she didn't have time to talk. She had to get home and start dinner, but Sheila felt almost pulled towards her old friend. Sheila felt her feet moving, and she was walking over to them.

Kim introduced Sheila to her boyfriend, Steve. Sheila looked up at him and thought he was the most handsome man she had ever seen. She was shocked to be actually attracted to a man. Sheila had never dreamed she would see a man in this way. Steve stood up straight, and he was so tall at six foot three, with sandy blond hair, deep green eyes, and a beautiful smile. Sheila felt herself blush as he reached out to shake her hand.

Steve grabbed her hand and felt it trembling. He shook it gently. "It's very nice to meet you, Sheila. You are all Kim has been talking about since I pulled up five minutes ago," Steve said gingerly. He asked Sheila if she needed a ride home, and she felt so shy, it was hard to speak to him or look him in the eye. She shook her head no.

"I have to go home and start dinner, and I'm already running late, but thank you for the offer," Sheila responded, staring at the ground. Kim looked at her friend and smiled. "I'll see you in the morning, Kim. Bye, Steve," Sheila whispered as she turned to head home.

"Sheila, if you're running late, wouldn't you get home faster with us in the car instead of taking the bus?" Steve inquired. Sheila stopped and turned to look at Steve. He seemed so kind and gentle that she felt safe, and she nodded yes. Steve opened the door and pulled the front seat forward. Sheila climbed into the backseat of the car. She knew he was right. It would be faster. However, she asked to be dropped off around the corner. Sheila needed to be sure nobody would see her getting out of Steve's car. If her mother or father saw her getting out of a man's car, she was sure to get a beating.

"Not a problem, Sheila. Consider it done," Steve told her. Steve grabbed Kim's hand, kissed it, and helped her into the car. Then he jumped in, and the car sped away. Steve had her home with time to spare. Sheila jumped out and thanked them for the ride. Sheila started to walk away from the car. She turned to wave bye, and stopped when she saw them kissing. Sheila felt so lonely at that moment. Then she thought of Kim, and she was angry with herself for not just enjoying having a friend back in her life.

Sheila walked into the apartment with a smile, but it soon left her face when she heard her mother screaming and saw Bobby on top of her, pounding. Sheila gasped, and Bobby heard this. He turned to her, and, with an evil look, threw two more blows to her mother's face. Then, he spit on her.

"Bitch!" Bobby yelled as he got up and started walking toward Sheila. She started to tremble. He shoved Sheila into the wall with such force that the books from her backpack that she had slung over her shoulder went flying. She hit the wall and slid to the floor. Sheila immediately started to pick up the books on her hands and knees. Bobby came over, picked up a heavy textbook, and smashed Sheila on the back of her head with it.

"Clean this up and get dinner on the table now!" Bobby demanded, screaming. He left the room. Sheila didn't say a word to her mother as she finished picking up her books. Sheila felt it was Hugette who had brought them back to this living hell, and she deserved her fair share of the beatings. Sheila put everything back into her backpack, and then she washed her hands and started to peel potatoes.

Joann walked into the apartment just as Hugette was getting up off the floor. She put her books down and came over to Sheila, and started

*Behind the Drapes*

to peel potatoes. Sheila put down her knife and prepared the chicken legs for the oven. Hugette got up and went to the bathroom. Sheila nudged Joann and pointed to the blood. Joann looked at her sister with a pleading look. She was sick of cleaning up her mother's blood.

Sheila looked at her sister with an angry look and whispered, "You can clean up the blood or tell him when dinner's ready; you choose, Joann." Without a word, Joann put down her knife, and she cleaned up her mother's blood again. Sheila finished the potatoes and put them on the stove along with the peas; then she finished setting the table.

When everything was ready, Sheila told Joann to go and tell Hugette it was ready, and she started for the living room to tell her father. As Sheila reached the living room, she felt her body shaking. She walked up to her father and waited to be acknowledged. Sheila wasn't sure what was worse, the fear she had of her father or the hatred she felt toward him. Either way, she knew it was only a few more years and she would be free. Sheila had made it this far, and she would survive a couple more years.

Finally, Bobby turned to her with an ugly stare. "What do you want?" he barked.

"Dinner is ready," Sheila informed her father. She turned and went back to the kitchen. Joann was sitting at the table. She told her sister that Hugette had said she didn't want any dinner. Sheila sat beside her sister, not knowing if she should serve the food or wait for Hugette. The girls sat there without saying a word, looking down at their empty plates.

When Bobby came in, he looked around for Hugette. "Where is your useless mother?" Bobby asked to no one in particular. Sheila and Joann looked at each other, terrified of what might come next. Sheila spoke first, protecting Joann the best way she could.

"She said she doesn't want any dinner," Sheila told her father. Bobby turned and went to the bedroom, and within seconds they heard their mother scream. Bobby returned, pulling Hugette by the hair. He pushed her toward the stove and demanded she serve him dinner. Hugette picked up two plates, filled them high, and placed one in front of Bobby, one in front of herself as she sat down.

Sheila and Joann looked at each other, but didn't dare say one word. Finally, Bobby looked up. He took a moment to breathe while stuffing his mouth with food. Seeing their empty plates, he told them to go to their room if they weren't hungry. They got up and went to their room. Joann and Sheila lay on their beds, hungry and motionless. They waited to be told to clean the kitchen, and hoped there was something left for them to eat.

Sheila heard someone coming down the hall and sat upright in her bed. Before she could warn Joann, the door flew open. Bobby stood there, and he looked from one girl to the next. Then he told Joann to get out, and instructed her to start cleaning the dishes. As Joann stepped through the doorway, Bobby closed the door. He turned to look at Sheila, and gave her the smile that made her feel sick to her stomach.

"Sheila, I had a really bad day today, and you are going to make me feel better. Be a good girl and take care of your daddy," Bobby demanded as he climbed on top of his daughter. Sheila closed her eyes, and at that moment, she wished she were dead, or at the very least, invisible. She cried until it was over, and when he finally finished and climbed off of her, he asked her a question for the first time.

"Do you enjoy taking care of your daddy, Sheila?"

Sheila did not know how to respond to his question, and she prayed for something to come to mind. Sheila looked up at him, trying to figure out how to respond, all the while pulling up the covers so he could not see her. It was to no avail. Upon seeing her try to hide, he pulled the cover off her, to show who was boss. It was also pointless because he had seen every inch of her many times.

"I asked you a question. Didn't you hear me, stupid?" Bobby bellowed. He jumped back on top of her, and this time, instead of molesting her, he laid a terrible beating on her. Bobby just continued to slap and punch her, and tell her what a worthless piece of crap she was. Sheila thought he was going to finally kill her. She was so scared that she peed herself right there in her bed. She thought how she wanted to die. She had never wet the bed in her life, and she was just horrified that he had actually scared the piss out of her. Suddenly, he stopped and looked down at her.

"It's all your fault, you stupid slut. You deserve everything you get," Bobby told Sheila. He climbed off her and left the room. When Sheila realized it was over, and Bobby was gone and not returning, she climbed out of her bed, turned, and stood staring at the wet mattress.

She cried. It wasn't long before Sheila had no tears left, and she went to the bathroom to clean herself off.

Sheila returned to her bedroom with a bucket of soapy hot water and a cloth. She pulled and pulled, until she was able to pull the mattress off the spring and lean it up against the wall. Sheila scrubbed that mattress until she was sure it was clean; she hated Bobby more than she wanted to, and at that moment, she thought he had now humiliated her in every way possible. Sheila could not wait until the day she got to leave, and she knew one day Bobby would pay for everything he had done to her.

When Sheila was finished with the mattress, she left it up to dry, and put on her pajamas and housecoat. She went to the kitchen to see if Joann needed any help, and to see if she could find any food. Joann was just washing the last of the dishes. Sheila grabbed the towel and started to dry the dishes without a word. She didn't dare draw attention to herself.

Joann looked up at Sheila and smiled; she dried her hands and, quietly, she opened the stove and pulled out a small plate of food. She handed it to Sheila and gave her a fork as she took the towel from Sheila, and finished drying the dishes for her. Joann noticed her sister's swollen, red skin and bruising. She thought to herself it would look awful in the morning. Joann was sure she would have at least one black eye, and her lips were already cut and swollen in two places, although she would never point this out to Sheila. There were things in the Parks house that just didn't need to be said.

The moment Sheila and Joann were finished cleaning up in the kitchen, Sheila went to her room. Joann followed her, but when they reached the bedroom, Sheila remembered she had to go into the basement and wash her sheets. They lived in an apartment now, and they didn't have a washer and drier any longer. Sheila took off her sock and prayed she had enough change for the machine. Luckily, she had just enough.

Sheila put the sheets in a bag and prayed she wouldn't have any trouble leaving the apartment. She knew if she was quiet, they wouldn't even notice she was gone. Sheila opened the bedroom door slowly. As she was about to close the door behind her, she felt Joann's hand on her arm. Joann motioned for her to be quiet, and they both snuck out of the apartment. Neither of them said a word until they were safe in the elevator.

The moment the doors closed, Joann looked at her sister and started to cry. Sheila hugged her and told her it was okay, only a few more years and it would be over. That's how Sheila survived. She counted time, and she knew she was almost there. They rode the rest of the ride into the basement silently. The doors opened, and they walked down the hall to the laundry room. Sheila put her sheets in the washer and sat on the bench beside her sister. They sat there for a while before either of them said another word, both lost in their own thoughts.

"I didn't think I was going to survive tonight. I was sure he was going to kill me this time," Sheila confessed to her sister. "I wonder what happened to push him over the edge tonight," Sheila thought out loud. Joann just shrugged and closed her eyes, sitting back on the bench. The girls fell silent again and listened to the sound of the washing machine. It was, in some way, very calming to them.

"I hope it has nothing to do with his job," Joann said. "He was home from work early today. Did you notice? He is definitely out of control. I hope he didn't get fired again." The girls looked at each other with dread. They both prayed Joann was wrong. They grew silent again as they remembered the last time he was out of work. It had been horrible. Bobby had been home for a little over two weeks, and it had felt like a few months; he had beaten Sheila and Hugette so badly, they both had to stay in the house for days until their injuries healed.

Joann helped Sheila fold her sheets when they were dry. Joann gave Sheila a worried look, and Sheila looked back at her with the same expression. Now they knew they had to sneak back into the apartment, and they hoped not to be caught. Sheila grabbed Joann by the hand, and they started down the hall. They got into the elevator. When the doors opened on their floor, the girls got out very slowly. They stood there for a moment without moving.

They started down the hall and stopped in front of the apartment door. Sheila put her ear up to the door to see if she could hear anything. She looked at Joann and winked. Not a sound came from inside the apartment, except for the television. Sheila opened the door slowly. They stepped inside, and Sheila closed and locked the door just as carefully.

*Behind the Drapes*

They made it to their bedroom without Bobby or Hugette seeing them. Thank God, it was over for the day.

Sheila felt her mattress. It was still damp, so she put the sheets on the spring and climbed into Joann's bed. Sheila never asked her sister. She feared having to explain, and she knew Joann wouldn't object. Sheila tossed and turned all night. She couldn't get the images of her father on top of her out of her mind, and she was in a lot of pain. She knew she was going to be stiff in the morning. It was one of the worst beatings she'd ever had.

The next morning, Joann rolled over and looked at her sister sleeping. A tear slid down her face as she saw Sheila's injuries in the daylight. She knew Sheila would be embarrassed when she went to school. However, she knew it would be far worse for Sheila if one of her parents decided she had to stay home because she looked too bad. Joann quietly climbed out of bed, got dressed, and went to wash up.

The alarm went off, and Sheila went to jump out of bed as usual, but she stopped when she felt the pain in her head. She had a terrible headache. Sheila thought it was either the beating or when Bobby hit her in the head with her textbook. Sheila lay back on the pillow for a moment, until she heard the door open. She sat up straight immediately. She was very relieved when she saw Joann walk in.

"Don't rush, Sheila. I'll go put on the coffee and start the bacon," Joann whispered. "Sheila, put some powder on your face so it doesn't look so bad. You don't want to be kept home from school," she warned. Sheila smiled at her sister and got up slowly off the bed. Joann helped Sheila put her mattress back on the spring and make it up. Then she left for the kitchen.

Sheila got dressed and found the powdered makeup hidden just were she had left it. She had bought it just for this purpose, and sometimes it really helped. She hoped it would do the trick this morning. Sheila walked into the bathroom, and was a little startled when she saw herself. She should have known what to expect, but she had been hopeful her face wouldn't be too bad. Sheila did the best she could to cover it up and went to the kitchen.

Hugette and Joann were sitting at the table. Joann looked up and gave her a smile. Her mother, however, never looked up from the spot she was staring at on the table. Sheila poured herself a coffee and sat down at the table across from her mother. Sheila looked at her mother's face and was disappointed when she realized she looked worse than Hugette. Joann got up and made Sheila some toast, then brought it to her with smile.

"Where is he?" Sheila whispered to Joann.

"He left an hour ago. He's out looking for a job," Hugette answered. Sheila was shocked her mother had heard her. It was their worst fears come true. It would be anguish until Bobby found work. Hugette looked up, and, seeing her daughter's face, she told Sheila to stay home from school until it cleared up. Sheila wanted some drugs bad. She was going to school; she needed to get out of the apartment. Sheila had no idea where the anger surfaced from, but all of a sudden, she stood up and banged her fist on the table.

"What is it, Mother? Do you want me here so he will beat me and maybe leave you alone? You are the worst mother on the planet! I am going to school, and I'd like to see you try and stop me," Sheila growled as she leaned over close and stared into her mother's face. Hugette looked up at her, and she saw Bobby in Sheila for the first time. It terrified her. Hugette stood up and quietly left the room without saying a word. Sheila sat back down and realized her hands were shaking. She took a couple of deep breaths as Joann looked at her sister, speechless.

The girls did the dishes and made their lunches for school. They silently walked out the door, down the hall, and on to the elevator. "Sheila, I can't believe what you just said to her. She was terrified of you. Actually, you even scared me! That's some crazy look you had on your face," Joann said, laughing, although she was still a little shaken to have seen her sister become that hostile. Sheila didn't respond. The truth was, it frightened Sheila as well to have anger spill out of her with no control over it.

When they reached the road, they walked to the bus stop without saying a word to each other, and sat on the bench. Sheila opened her eyes to see Steve's car pulling up to the bus stop. Steve beeped the horn and waved for Sheila to come over to the car. Sheila immediately smiled, jumped up, and ran to the car. Steve rolled down the window on the passenger's side, and Sheila leaned in.

"What the hell happened to your face, Sheila? Tell me who did that to you," Steve demanded. He was shocked when he looked at her face.

*Behind the Drapes*

He could tell Sheila had tried to cover it, but it was so obvious someone had kicked the shit out of her, and he was furious. "Get in. We'll go get Kim, and I'll drive you to school," Steve instructed. Sheila saw the look of horror on his face and immediately pulled away from the car. She hated for people to feel sorry for her.

"No thanks, Steve. This is my sister, and we are going to take the bus to school. I'll see you around, and tell Kim I'll see her at school," Sheila said coldly. She didn't want to be rude to Steve, but she felt the wall around her closing. There was no way Sheila would have gotten into that car, alone or with her sister. She couldn't and wouldn't answer his questions, and she hated to lie to the few friends she had. Steve tried to protest and invited Joann to come along, but they both refused. Finally, he gave up and drove away.

When Sheila and Joann got off the bus at school, Kim was waiting at the bus stop. Sheila could see Steve's car parked just down the road. Joann said bye to Sheila and Kim, and ran off to see her friends. Sheila watched Joann with her friends, and she was envious for just a moment. Joann never had to explain black eyes or fat lips. Sheila wished she had been the youngest.

Sheila was pulled from her thoughts as she realized Kim had been speaking to her. Kim stopped talking when she realized Sheila wasn't listening, and started to pull her toward Steve's car. Sheila was about to protest when Kim showed her a joint. Sheila smiled and followed Kim to the car. Steve got out and came to open the door for them. The three of them climbed in, and Steve drove to the empty lot at the end of the street.

They sat there and smoked the joint, and finally, Kim spoke up. "Sheila, what happened to your face? Tell me the truth. You know you can trust me, and please believe you can trust Steve."

Sheila looked at her, then at Steve. He was looking at her with a tender, caring expression. The tears just flew then, and she told them about the night before, although she left out the part about her wetting the bed, and the wounds they couldn't see. Kim listened and suspected there was probably more Sheila didn't want to say in front of Steve.

They sat there quietly and let Sheila get everything off her chest. When Sheila grew quiet and appeared to be finished, Steve demanded she tell someone about her father, like her guidance counselor or the police. Sheila absolutely refused. She tried to explain to Steve and Kim that she only had two more years left, and she didn't want to live in foster care and be a ward of the state.

"If I told on my father, he would kill me. I know it, so I am going to put in my time, and when I turn sixteen, I will move out," Sheila said.

Steve shook his head. "There has to be a better plan," he said. "I'm going to think about it. I will see you after school." Sheila looked at the clock on the dash board and panicked when she saw the time. She was late for school. If her father found out, he was sure to give her another beating.

When Sheila went white, Kim and Steve were alarmed. "What's wrong?" Kim asked.

"I'm late for school," Sheila screeched. "If the school calls my house my father will kill me," Sheila continued as she reached for the door handle. She was terrified.

"Sheila! Calm down, I have a plan," Steve assured her. He would call in sick to work. Then he would phone the school and tell them he was Sheila's father. He'd say she was sick and wouldn't be in school. Then, a few minutes later, he would phone back and say he was Kim's father, and she was sick. He would disguise his voice the second time, of course. Then they could go to his house and hang out for the day.

Kim was ecstatic about spending the entire day with Steve, and she agreed right away. Sheila thought it was worth a try for Steve to call. Maybe the school hadn't already called her house, and she wouldn't get into any trouble with her father. Sheila did not want to go into the school and have everyone looking at her, and have people, especially teachers, asking too many questions. It didn't take Sheila long to agree as well, so Steve started the car, and they drove to his apartment.

Steve lived right downtown. Sheila had never been to this part of the city she had grown up in, and she was surprised how busy it was. She looked at all the people and tall buildings. Sheila was very impressed. Steve turned onto a little dead end of a street. It was more like an alley. There were two small buildings on each side—ugly, old, and falling apart. However, to Sheila and Kim it was paradise; they didn't care. It was Steve's home.

They climbed the stairs to the second floor. When they reached the door, Steve unlocked and opened it. Steve held the door open for the girls. Kim walked in comfortably, while Sheila entered very slowly, looking around. It was dark. They walked into the living room.

There were two sofas, and pillows all over the dark carpeting. In the corner, Sheila saw a record player on a little table, and two very large speakers. Steve turned on a lamp. The windows were covered with dark flags, and the walls were covered floor-to-ceiling with posters of rock groups. Kim poked Sheila and pointed up. The ceiling was covered with posters as well. Both the girls thought it was really cool.

Kim showed Sheila around. The kitchen was tiny, with just a small fridge, an old gas oven, and one small counter with a little sink. The bathroom was even smaller, and it was the dirtiest bathroom Sheila had ever seen. The toilet was filthy, and the tub was no better. There were two bedrooms. One was Steve's, and the other belonged to his roommate, Bill. He was at work, but Kim had told Sheila what a great guy he was. "Kind and sweet," she'd said.

Steve made his calls, and he was sure that the school bought it. The secretary was very pleasant and thanked him for his call, both times. He was sure it was a different secretary the second time. His boss was another story, and he thought he was in a little trouble, but nothing he couldn't handle, he said. Steve rolled another joint. They smoked it and sat back on the couch with their eyes closed, listening to the blaring music coming from the large speakers.

The day was a happy, calm one for Sheila, and when Steve dropped her off around the corner, she was more relaxed than she had been in a long time. Sheila waited at the bus stop for Joann, and when she arrived, she wasn't even aware that Sheila hadn't gone to school. Sheila told Joann that Steve had driven her home from school.

They walked home together and chatted. Joann was so happy to see Sheila in such a good mood. She had been worried that she would have had to answer many difficult questions about her injuries at school. Any questions asked of Sheila usually put her in a terrible mood, and she would be quiet and moody for the rest of the day, almost like she was answering them to herself over and over again in her head.

The elevator doors opened, and the girls walked down the hall. Sheila listened at the door out of habit and winked at her sister—it was quiet. Sheila opened the door, and her father grabbed her and pulled her in. He put her up against the wall by her neck; her feet were dangling off the floor. He banged her again and again against the wall with all his might, and then let her fall.

Bobby bent down and picked her up, and started to punch her in the face with his fist, all the while screaming at her. "Where did you go today, Sheila? I know you didn't go to school, you little slut. Who was the man who called the school today, you tramp?" Bobby just kept screaming the same questions over and over again. He never stopped punching her long enough for Sheila to answer him. Eventually, Sheila lost consciousness, and when Bobby realized it, he just threw her on the floor, spit on her, and walked into the living room.

Sheila wasn't sure how long she had been out, but Joann told her later it had been quite a while. Actually, Hugette and Joann were sure Sheila had died, and they had checked for a pulse several times. Sheila was in her bed when she woke up, and Joann was sitting across from her on the side of her bed, crying. Sheila moaned, and Joann jumped up and came over to her. There was a bowl with water on the side of her bed, and Joann began to clean the blood off Sheila's face.

The door opened. Sheila and Joann froze, too scared to look and see who it was. After a moment, Sheila heard soft footsteps, and she looked up to see her mother putting two plates of food on the dresser. Without a word, Hugette left the room. Joann helped Sheila sit up and put a pillow on her lap. She placed one of the plates on the pillow. Sheila tried to eat, but it was so painful to chew. She tried to put the plate down, but Joann insisted she finish all her supper. Sheila needed her strength, Joann explained. So, to keep her sister happy, Sheila ate all her dinner.

When Sheila and Joann were done eating, Joann took the plates to the kitchen and started the dishes. When she finished, she made her sister a cup of tea. Joann entered the bedroom, and was surprised to see Sheila was gone; she was very relieved to see Sheila come in a moment later. Sheila sat on her bed with a mirror and looked at her face. It was truly grotesque, and she knew there would be no going to school the next day.

# Chapter 9

After Joann had left for school the next morning, Sheila cleared the table, and then started the dishes. Sheila had been right. The moment Bobby had seen her this morning he'd told her to stay home from school, and before he'd left that morning to look for work, he had reminded her. Sheila knew better than try and stand up to him, and she really didn't want to go. This beating was too horrific to try and explain.

At about ten in the morning, Sheila's mother came into the living room, where Sheila had been watching television. She told her she was going to look for work, and she would be back in a few hours, if Bobby came home and asked. Sheila nodded yes without looking up at her mother. Sheila was happy to be alone for once. She didn't have the opportunity very often.

Shortly after her mother left, there was someone banging on the front door. Sheila assumed her mother had forgotten something, like her keys, and she went to open the door. When she opened it, she was shocked to see Kim standing there. Kim bust into tears when she saw Sheila's face; Sheila looked down the hall to make sure nobody was there, and pulled her friend inside. She closed the door behind her.

"What are you doing here, Kim? Are you trying to get me killed? If my father sees you, I'll be in so much trouble."

Kim shook her head no and explained to Sheila that she and Steve had waited downstairs since early that morning, until they saw Bobby and Hugette leave. Steve was at the pay phone across the street, and if one of them came home, he would call up and warn them. When Kim had gotten home and realized the school had figured out the scam and phoned their parents, she had been worried sick.

Kim told Sheila her mother had grounded her for two months, and she was never allowed to see Steve again. Her mother had also told her that she was not to see Sheila anymore. She thought Sheila was a bad influence on Kim. They both laughed at that. It was Kim who was the adventurous one. Sheila had only skipped school because she was going to get a beating for being late anyway, and she had hoped Steve's call might save her.

Sheila told Kim she was fine. She was about to ask her to leave when Kim told her she was running away from home, and she wanted Sheila to come with her. "Don't wait two years and give him the chance to kill you, Sheila. Leave now, with me," Kim pleaded. Kim said that there was no way she would stop seeing Steve. She loved him, he wanted her to move in with him, and he'd said Sheila could come, too. Sheila was terrified at the thought, and when the phone began to ring, she thought she was going to faint from fear.

The girls looked at each other, and Sheila picked it up; it was Bobby. He asked to talk to Hugette, and when Sheila told him she was out looking for a job, he blew up and started screaming at Sheila. Sheila heard something about her mother not thinking he was man enough to take care of his own family. Bobby was yelling so loud that Kim could hear him. Finally, Bobby hung up, but not before he informed Sheila and she and Hugette were stupid bitches. Sheila hung up the phone. She knew at that moment she'd had enough. She told Kim she would pack immediately.

Sheila was back in four minutes. She had the clothing that she wanted and her toothbrush in a paper bag. Sheila put on her shoes and grabbed her jacket, and the two girls left. Sheila turned and locked the door, and they walked to the elevator. The elevator doors opened, and they stepped in. Sheila was trembling. She was terrified and excited

*Behind the Drapes*

about leaving. Then she thought of Joann, and she knew she had to go back. Sheila tried to stop the elevator, but it was already on the way down.

The elevator doors opened, and Sheila saw Bobby coming through the front doors of the building. It was too late to go back. She had to run. Sheila grabbed Kim and pulled her to the stairwell before Bobby could see them. Sheila started to run down, and Kim followed her. They went down one flight of stairs and out a side door that led to the parking lot. They came around to the front of the building and saw Steve in the phone booth. He didn't see them, but he was on the phone, and he was wearing a look of panic, his head cradled with his hand.

The girls ran across the street, and Kim tapped on the side of the phone booth. When Steve looked up and saw them, a huge grin came across his face and he hung up the phone. The three of them ran to the car and climbed in. Steve drove away. Sheila sat there, not sure what to do or how to react. Then suddenly, she started to laugh, and she couldn't stop. It was contagious, and Kim and Steve joined in. Sheila didn't stop until they reached Steve's apartment.

They went inside. Sheila and Kim sat on the sofa, and Steve rolled a joint. He smoked it with Sheila and Kim, and then he left for work. Steve worked in a restaurant. He worked in the kitchen as a cook, and he was very good at his craft. The restaurant he worked in was very expensive and beautiful. It was in an old stone home, someplace Sheila would never eat, she thought, when Kim had pointed it out to her on the drive. Kim had been there many times with her mother and whomever she was married to at the time.

After Steve left, Sheila started thinking of Joann. She had to warn her, and she asked Kim to come with her to the school. Kim agreed, and they jumped on the bus and headed for the school. The whole ride, people were staring at Sheila. She looked awful. Sheila was embarrassed and hated the attention, but she especially hated the pity. One little old lady tried to give Sheila some money, but she refused. People were listening, and Sheila wanted to die.

Kim tried to distract Sheila. She chatted about her new life with Steve. She had so many plans for them. They were going to get married and have kids. Kim wanted at least three children. She asked Sheila to be her maid of honor when they got married. Sheila agreed, not really sure what she was agreeing to. She had never been to a wedding before, but Kim seemed excited about it, so she would do it for her.

When they got to the school, Sheila suggested that they wait for Joann where she usually caught her bus. They still had half an hour, so they decided to go for a walk and smoke a joint while they waited. Sheila was worried about telling Joann she had run away, but she had to warn her. All Sheila could think of was, *What if he tries something on Joann*. Sheila would never be able to forgive herself if that ever happened. She just hoped that if he was going to, he would have already. He had never touched Joann that way, and Sheila hoped he never would.

"Sheila, Sheila! It's time to go," Kim said loudly as she shook Sheila's arm. Sheila had been lost in her thoughts and had not heard Kim talking to her. Kim pointed to her watch, and Sheila realized Joann would just be getting out of her last class. They started back to the bus stop. They didn't have to wait long before Joann came out of the school, talking to a few girls. When she got closer and saw Sheila, she came running over.

"Sheila, what the hell is going on? They pulled me into the principal's office today, and the cops were there looking for you and Kim," Joann told them frantically. "Kim's mother phoned the police when the school called. She called our house looking for Kim and spoke with Mom. When they realized you were both gone the cops are assuming you ran away together."

"Kim your mom is freaking out and she wants the police to find you and bring you home," Joann added. Sheila and Joann looked at each other. They could only imagine what was going on in their house.

The police had come to ask Joann if she knew anything about Sheila and Kim running away. They had also asked if Joann knew where Steve lived. Joann had told them she was shocked with the news, and never heard the girls talking about it; they had certainly never said anything to her about it and she didn't know where Steve lived.

Joann wasn't lying, and the police believed her. However, they told her if Sheila called her, she was to let them know. She had told the cops that she would contact them right away, but Joann assured them both she would never say a word to anyone. Sheila knew she could trust Joann, and the best part was that Joann wasn't mad at Sheila. She was terrified to go home, but she understood why Sheila had to leave. Joann

*Behind the Drapes*

wasn't scared of Bobby the way Sheila was, and they both prayed it would stay that way.

Joann's bus was coming, and she couldn't be late. They all knew that. Sheila gave Joann Steve's phone number and told her to phone if she needed anything, but never to give the number to anyone. Sheila told her she would meet her in a few days, and if their parents were out of the house and she needed to just talk, to phone her at Steve's. Sheila and Joann hugged tightly, and Sheila wished her luck. Then Joann got on the bus, and Sheila watched as it pulled away.

When Sheila and Kim got back to the apartment, Steve and his roommate, Bill, were both home. Steve introduced Bill to Sheila, and they shook hands. Sheila thought he was the complete opposite of Steve. Bill was short and fat with terrible acne on his face. He had greasy, curly black hair and thick glasses. Bill had a great job working for the government and Sheila was pleased to discover that he was one of the nicest guys she had ever met; he was shy and sweet. Sheila didn't trust Bill, because he was a man, but so far he seemed like a complete gentleman.

The four of them chatted and shared a joint. Then Steve had to go back to work. He worked Tuesday through Saturday, split shifts. He had to work from 11:00 AM to 3:00 PM, and then go back from 5:00 PM to10:00 PM. Sheila thought she would hate to work split shifts, but Steve loved his job, and he didn't seem to mind. After Steve left to go back to work, the three of them sat on the sofas and listened to music.

They all seemed to love a rock group called Led Zeppelin. Sheila had never heard of them. She didn't even own a record, but she liked them. Her parents never really listened to music very often. Her father was addicted to his television, and her mother didn't seem to like it all that much. Then Sheila remembered when Hugette, Sheila, and Joann lived alone. Back then, Hugette seemed to listened to music quite often. She even sang along and danced. It was too bad Hugette went back to Bobby, Sheila thought. They could have been so happy without him.

Sheila's thoughts drifted to Joann, and she was worried about what might be happening to her. Sheila tried to push the images from her mind. Bill started to say something, and she was happy to have a distraction. Sheila sat up and heard Bill asking if they were hungry. Sheila hadn't really thought about it; she was used to being hungry, but as he asked, she felt her stomach rumbling. Kim said she was hungry. Sheila didn't say a word. Bill got up and told them he would be back soon. He gave them a joint to smoke while he was gone.

When Bill returned, he had a case of beer and a large pizza for them. Sheila had twenty-two dollars in her sock and tried to give some to Bill for her share, but he wouldn't hear of it. Sheila thanked him. She saw that Kim was devouring a piece, and Sheila hadn't even heard her say thank you. Apparently, Kim was just used to people doing everything for her, and she assumed no thanks were necessary.

Bill handed them each a beer, and for just a moment, Sheila thought of Paula and Marty. She pushed the image from her mind and reminded herself that she had known Kim forever, and she was nothing like Paula. Sheila hoped Bill would be nothing like Marty, and when he handed her a piece of pizza, Sheila accepted it. It smelled so good. It was then Sheila realized she was starving, and she gobbled down two pieces quickly. Bill offered her another piece, and she refused. She was still hungry, but didn't want to be greedy, so she said she couldn't eat another bite.

Kim wasn't shy, and she ate until there was nothing left, then helped herself to another beer. Bill picked up the empty pizza box and put it in the kitchen. When he returned, he brought Sheila and himself another beer. Kim rolled a joint, and after they smoked it, Kim and Bill played a game of cribbage. They tried to teach Sheila how to play. Sheila thought it was difficult, but Bill was patient, and by the end of the evening, she had it mastered. She even beat Kim at a game, which Bill seemed to really enjoy.

When Steve got home from work that night, he brought another case of beer and a box full of food. Sheila offered to give Steve some money and was very disappointed when she found out Steve had stolen the beer and food from his work. Nobody else seemed to think it was a problem, so Sheila kept her thoughts to herself. They all stayed up late that night and drank and smoked a lot of pot.

Bill was the first one to go to bed. At 2:00 AM, he said goodnight and went to his bedroom. He had to be at work by 7:00 AM. Sheila fell asleep on the sofa at about 3:00 AM, and when she got up at around 5:00 AM to use the bathroom, she could hear Steve and Kim giggling from inside his room. She quietly went back to the sofa and fell back to sleep.

It was a small apartment, and at 6:30 the next morning, Sheila heard Bill's alarm clock go off. She heard him get up and go into the bathroom. Sheila lay there, pretending she was asleep. She heard Bill curse as he stubbed his toe coming out of the bathroom. He came back out of his room, and Sheila felt him standing in front of her, staring. It made her feel very uneasy. Suddenly, Bill went back into his bedroom and came back out with a blanket. He placed it softly over Sheila, and left for work.

Sheila lay there, thinking how Bill putting the blanket over her was really the only caring thing anyone had done for her since her uncle Pierre had died. Sheila liked Bill, and she felt like he was going to be a good friend to have around. She fell back to sleep and awoke to Steve screaming. She was startled at first, not sure where she was, but it only took a moment and then she remembered. Sheila looked at the clock and realized it was 10:50 AM. Steve was going to be late for work.

Steve came running out of his room and into the bathroom. Moments later, he ran back into his room, and Sheila could hear him and Kim arguing, something about who was supposed to set the alarm clock. Again, she pretended to be asleep. Steve came running through the room and out the door as Kim yelled something at him about not being a baby. Sheila lay there for about ten minutes. She couldn't fall back to sleep. She was tired, but she knew she wouldn't be able to sleep this late in the morning.

Sheila sat up and reached for a cigarette. She lit it and lay back on the sofa, thinking about Joann and hoping she was fine. She looked around the apartment. What was she supposed to do now? She couldn't go to school, and she didn't know how to get a job. Her father had always told her she was a stupid girl and girls only had to know how to diaper a baby. She needed to speak to Kim; Sheila had always seen Kim as more worldly than she was.

She quietly walked to Steve's bedroom door and opened it slowly. There was Kim, sound asleep, curled up in bed. Sheila closed the door softly and went to open the fridge to see what was there. It was so dirty, she closed the door immediately and decided to clean up the apartment. Sheila looked everywhere, but she couldn't find any soap, sponges, or cleaning supplies of any kind.

She decided to freshen up and go to the store, but when she saw the bathroom up close, she was too disgusted to do anything but change her clothes, splash water on her face, and brush her teeth. There was no toothpaste, so Sheila rinsed her mouth the best she could and left to find a store.

She walked into the bright sunshine and took a deep breath. It was a beautiful day. She asked a lady in the street where she could find a store. The woman stared at Sheila's face and got that look of pity that Sheila hated. Sheila was about to walk away when the woman told her to go five blocks and then turn left. Sheila thanked her and walked to the store.

She counted her money. She only had twenty-two dollars. She was going to have to find a babysitting job soon. Sheila went into the store, trying to ignore the stares, and purchased rubber gloves, bleach, sponges, tea, detergent, soap, toothpaste, and cigarettes. She only had eleven dollars left. Sheila thought she should have planned this better. Eleven dollars was not going to go far. She should have told Kim she would meet her in a few weeks, and then saved her babysitting money.

Sheila turned the key in the apartment door, and as she closed it, she heard some deep voices in the stairwell. She locked the door quietly, and stood there without making a sound. All of a sudden, the voices were on the other side of the door. Sheila almost jumped out of her skin as someone started to pound on the door, and a deep voice said, "Police!"

Sheila just stood there, silently trembling as the banging continued. She didn't know what to do. Finally, it stopped, and she could hear two male voices talking quietly on the other side of the door; then, a business card was slipped under. Sheila picked it up and looked at it. It was the police all right. She put the card in her pocket. She didn't know why. She went over and opened the door to Steve's bedroom. There was Kim, still fast asleep.

Sheila put a pot on the stove and filled it with water to boil. While she waited, she went and brushed her teeth and washed her face. She rolled a fat joint and smoked it. Just as she finished, she noticed the water was boiling. She made herself a cup of tea and poured the rest of the water into the sink, which she then filled with bleach and detergent. By

*Behind the Drapes*

the time Sheila had finished her tea and had a smoke, the temperature of the water was perfect.

Sheila started by tidying up the entire apartment. She cleaned the tables and chairs. She scrubbed the fridge and stove inside and out. Then she cleaned out the sink, put in clean water and detergent, and washed all the dishes. Then, she put them away. Sheila stood looking at the bathroom for a few minutes, then grabbed the rubber gloves and scrubbed it from top to bottom. By the time she'd finished, every inch, including the floor was sparkling. In a few hours, the entire apartment, except for the bedrooms, was spotless.

Sheila jumped in the clean tub and had a hot shower. When she climbed out, she was happy to stand on the clean floor. Sheila hadn't been able to find a clean towel, so she had washed one and let it dry while she had cleaned the bathroom. It was still damp, but it was better than nothing. Sheila got dressed and brushed her hair. She looked at the time and realized she would never make it by bus to see Joann. She was very angry with herself. She promised herself she would go the next day.

Sheila sat on the sofa and rolled a joint for when Kim woke up, but before that happened, Steve got home from work. When he walked in and saw the apartment, he was shocked. He looked at Sheila and asked her what had happened. Sheila just smiled and told him she had been bored. He walked to the bedroom and was surprised to find Kim still asleep. Steve tried to wake her, but she put up a fuss, so he gave up and came back into the living room.

"Now I understand why you were so bored. Has she been sleeping all day?" Steve questioned. Sheila just nodded in response. "You did this all by yourself, Sheila?" Steve said, and again, she only nodded in response. Sheila handed him the joint that she had rolled. He smiled and lit it. Steve handed it to Sheila and asked her, "Did you lose your tongue cleaning today, Sheila? You haven't said a word to me since I got home. You don't have to be shy with me. I won't let you down, Sheila."

Sheila smiled and finally spoke. "Sorry Steve. I have something to tell you, and I'm worried that you will be mad. The police came by the apartment earlier. I don't want you to get into any trouble." Sheila told him everything but she did leave out the part about the cop's card in her pocket.

"Sheila, it's okay, don't worry. It's probably Kim's mother who had them check here. It has nothing to do with you. Kim's mom hates me and I'm sure she blames me for Kim running away," Steve assured her. "If they come back all you have to do is hide and everything will be fine."

Steve tried to wake Kim again, and when she wouldn't get up, he told Sheila he was going to take her out for a burger to thank her for all the cleaning she had done. Sheila tried to protest and said it was the least she could do for him and Bill, for letting her stay there. Steve grabbed Sheila buy the arm, gently. He smiled and offered her a proposition.

"How about I take you to the school to check on your sister, and then you could join me for a burger. Is it a deal?" Sheila couldn't resist. Kim had told Steve enough about Sheila's parents for Steve to know Sheila must be terrified for her sister. If the truth were known, Steve was a little concerned about the police coming by, and he wanted to see what information Joann might have for him.

They got to school just as it was letting out. Sheila and Steve walked over to the bus stop, and Joann was there a minute later. Sheila was so happy when she saw Joann—there was not a mark on her. Joann looked relieved when she saw her sister. She came running over and told Sheila that Bobby had been in an awful mood and asked a lot of questions. Although he had not laid a finger on Joann; Hugette had not been so lucky. They prayed he would find a job soon.

Joann assured Sheila and Steve she had not told anyone anything. Kim's mother had been driving everyone crazy; she phoned the police station and Sheila's parents every hour to find out if there was any news. Bobby had stopped answering the phone, and when the police had dropped by, he had told them he didn't care if they ever brought Sheila home, she was nothing but trouble. Joann told them one of the police officers had given Bobby a dirty look when he said it. The police officer had told Bobby they were minors and should be living with family. When Bobby noticed the look, he told them to get out of the house, and they left.

The cops were definitely looking for Kim. They knew her mother would not stop calling until they found her. When Steve heard this, he became nervous. He cared about Kim and wanted to help Sheila, but not enough to get into trouble with the police. Steve thought to himself that they had better come up with a plan, just in case something went down. Joann's bus was coming. Sheila told her to call if she needed anything, and she would come back to see her the next week. Sheila had to start looking for a job.

Steve and Sheila got back in the car, and, as promised, Steve took Sheila for a burger and fries. Sheila tried to give him some money and he refused, reminding her that he wanted to thank her for cleaning the apartment. They sat in the car and ate. Steve knew Sheila was self-conscious about her face, and he didn't want her to be embarrassed. Discreetly, Steve looked over at Sheila. She was so different than Kim. Kim never would have offered him money when they went out, and she certainly would never have cleaned the apartment.

Steve and Sheila had a nice time, and he actually had her laughing when they got back to the apartment. Steve dropped her off and went back to work. Sheila was surprised that he didn't even come upstairs to see Kim. When Sheila got to the apartment, she was shocked to find Kim still sleeping. It was four thirty in the afternoon. Sheila had never slept that late in her life. Her father would have killed her, and she would never want to miss the whole day sleeping.

Sheila put some water on the stove to boil and made herself a cup of tea. She was sitting at the table playing solitaire when Bill got home from work. Bill walked in the door and looked around, and then he turned and left. Unsure what he was doing, Sheila got up, walked to the door, and opened it. Bill was standing there, looking at the number on the door. Sheila looked at him, puzzled.

"I thought I'd walked into the wrong apartment," Bill said, scratching his head. Sheila laughed and Bill joined in. He walked back into the apartment and looked at the kitchen, and when he went into the bathroom, he shouted with delight. Bill asked Sheila who had cleaned, and when she told Bill she had done it, he thanked her a thousand times. He told Sheila he hated living in such filth, but he had grown tired of doing everything, and had given up months ago.

Bill and Sheila shared a joint, and they were drinking beer and playing cribbage when Kim finally got out of bed. She walked by Sheila and Bill without saying a word. Sheila looked at her friend and couldn't believe how rough she looked without all her makeup. Kim went into the bathroom and took a shower. When she came out, she had the same expression as everyone else. Bill happily told Kim that Sheila had cleaned up the apartment, and Kim responded by shrugging her shoulders and going back into the bedroom.

"Not a morning person, I guess," Bill said, laughing, and Sheila and Bill continued with their game. An hour later, Kim came out of the bedroom looking more like herself, with her makeup on and her hair styled. She looked for coffee and whined when there was none. Sheila offered to make her a cup of tea, but she refused and grabbed a beer. Bill rolled a joint for her to get her out of her crappy mood, and it worked. Within a few minutes, they were laughing and having a great time.

Soon, though, Kim started whining again. "I'm hungry. What's for dinner?" Kim asked no one in particular. Bill and Sheila looked at each other, and although they didn't know it, they both thought the same thing: *what a selfish person*. Kim had spent the entire day in bed while Steve and Bill were at work, and while Sheila cleaned the apartment. Now she expected someone to make her dinner. Sheila thought this was a side of Kim she had never seen, and she didn't like it very much. They had only known each other at school, and the circumstances didn't allow for this side of her to show.

Sheila had suspected Kim's mother spoiled her, but she didn't realize the effect it had on her personality. Kim just assumed somebody would always take care of her. If not her mother, then someone else would always be there to do it. Kim assumed she was special, and people would want to do things for her. Sheila thought how in her life, it was every man for himself. There were very few good people in this world, and if someone did help you, you did everything you could to repay them.

When nobody answered Kim, she got up and looked in the fridge. She closed it and sat back down. "Sheila, you always cooked at your house. Couldn't you make us something for dinner?" Kim pleaded. Bill looked at Sheila and shook his head no, but Sheila got up and pulled some steak, onion, and carrots out of the fridge. Steve had brought home lots of groceries from work. Sheila was really concerned for him, especially with him going in late that morning.

Sheila made a very simple beef stir-fry over some egg noodles, and it turned out to be fabulous. She sliced the carrots and onions finely

*Behind the Drapes*

and sautéed them with butter, garlic, salt, and pepper. She sliced the beef thinly, and added it to carrots and onions with a few tablespoons of beer. She let it simmer on low for an hour, and then served it over the noodles. Just as Sheila was about to serve the plates, Steve came in from work.

"Wow, what smells so good? Who made dinner? Was it you, sleepy head?" Steve questioned, looking at Kim.

"No, it was Sheila. She cleaned the place, and then she cooked dinner. We should keep her around, don't you think, Steve?" Bill remarked, looking at Kim, and it infuriated her. She gave Sheila a disapproving glance.

"Who cares who cooked it. Let's just sit down and have some dinner," Sheila suggested, and they all agreed. However, as they tasted their food, both Bill and Steve started to praise Sheila, and Kim grew visibly upset with all the attention Sheila was getting. Sheila was surprised at all the compliments. She had always been a slave at home, and she had never been thanked for it, let alone praised for it. Sheila was enjoying been good at something, even if it was just cooking and cleaning.

When they were finished dinner, Bill announced that he would do the dishes, and Sheila insisted on helping him. Bill had just put the last dish away when there was pounding at the door. "Police, open up," a deep voice said. Sheila and Kim panicked, but Steve stayed calm. He grabbed Kim and motioned for Sheila to follow. He brought them into the bathroom. He opened the shower curtain and left the curtain pulled to the right. He motioned for the girls to get in.

"Leave the curtain open, and don't move," Steve whispered. Kim looked as if she was going to disagree. "Kim, if it's open, it looks like there's nothing to hide," Steve pleaded with her. She nodded, and Sheila and Kim hugged, trying to squish themselves as close to the wall as possible. They stayed quiet, but they were both terrified. Sheila knew what would happen if they took her home to her father. She stayed as still as possible and pressed herself into the wall.

Steve left the bathroom door open. Sheila could hear banging on the door, and then there were deep voices inside the apartment. She couldn't hear everything, but she made out enough to know they were there for her and Kim. They could hear one voice getting closer. Sheila and Kim held each other and didn't move. The voice came into the bathroom.

The girls were frozen with fear, but a moment later, it was gone. Sheila and Kim didn't dare breathe a sigh of relief while the voices were still in the apartment.

It felt like an hour, although it was twenty-five minutes later when Steve came into the bathroom and told them they could come out. Sheila and Kim were so frightened; it took Steve and Bill another twenty minutes to convince them they could talk. Steve opened the apartment door and showed them that there was nobody listening on the other side. Finally, they started to relax.

Steve rolled a joint, and they spent the next hour laughing and talking about how stupid the police were. It had been so easy to fool them; Sheila was amazed. Steve and Bill had told the police that they had not seen Sheila or Kim since the day before they ran away. Steve had told them he had broken up with Kim the last time he had seen her. The police told them if they saw or heard from Kim or Sheila, they were to contact the police immediately. Steve didn't think the police would be back.

With all the commotion, Kim had lost her angry feelings towards Sheila, and they giggled for hours. They felt they had a special bond, running away together. Having the police looking for them was exciting for them. They were still children, and they observed the experience with immature eyes. Again, Bill was the first to go to bed. He went to his room at 3:00 AM. Sheila, Kim, and Steve stayed up and drank until the sun came up. After one last joint, Sheila fell asleep on the couch. Kim and Steve went into their room.

Sheila awoke the next morning feeling a little woozy. They had drunk a lot of beer the night before. She looked at the time and was surprised to realize it was eleven thirty. She hoped Bill and Steve had made it to work. Sheila quietly opened the door to Bill's bedroom. He was gone, and Sheila was relieved. She was also pleasantly surprised to see how clean his room was. She'd expected it to look like Steve's—dirty and messy.

Sheila opened the door to Steve's bedroom, and she felt so bad for him when she saw Steve in bed next to Kim. Sheila quickly went over to the bed and shook Steve; he jumped up and looked at the clock beside his bed. Steve let out a screech and bolted from the bed. Kim moaned, rolled over, and went back to sleep. Sheila went back into the kitchen

*Behind the Drapes*

and watched as Steve ran from the bathroom, back into his room, and then out the door without a word.

Sheila sat by herself and looked around. She really didn't know what to do with herself. She had a cup of tea and had a smoke; she tried to focus on what she needed most, and that was money. She decided for now to do the only thing she knew. She went to the store, picked up some paper, and made herself some babysitting ads. She hung them up in the building, on the bulletin board by the mailbox.

When Sheila got back to the apartment, Kim was still sleeping. Sheila was hungry, but she didn't want to eat the food without permission. She rolled a joint and realized she was almost out of marijuana. She really needed to find a job. The door flew open, and Sheila jumped. She looked up to see Steve standing in front of her.

It was only one o'clock, too early for Steve to be home from work. Steve was very upset, and Sheila saw he had her babysitting ad is his hand, all crumpled up. Steve turned to Sheila, shook his head, and threw the ad on the table. Sheila sat there and tried hard not to cry. She didn't know what to say to him. She wasn't sure what he was upset about.

"Sheila, what were you thinking? You cannot put up an ad with your name and my phone number in the lobby of the building! What if the cops came back? I could get into trouble," Steve said. He looked at her, not with anger in his eyes, but disappointment. Sheila was so crushed, she burst into tears. She tried to hide it, but Steve saw, and he instantly felt like an ass. He came over to her and hugged her. He told her he was sorry.

"Sheila, I got fired today, and I'm very upset. I have been taking it out on you. I know you want to make your own money, and I think that's great, but you have to be careful from now on, okay?" Steve said softly. Sheila composed herself while Steve continued to hold her. Sheila felt so safe with his hands wrapped around her. Then she felt uncomfortable and guilty for having feelings for Kim's boyfriend. Sheila pulled away from Steve and handed him the joint she had rolled just before he'd come home.

"I'm really sorry about your job, Steve, and I promise to ask you before I do anything stupid again," Sheila said. Tears started to form in her eyes again. Sheila explained that she had put up a couple of other ads around, and she would go get them after they finished the joint. Steve thanked her, and when they were finished, Sheila went to retrieve the other ads, true to her word.

As Sheila came back up the stairs, she could hear an awful argument coming from the apartment. When she reached the door, she could clearly hear Kim and Steve fighting. She was just about to turn and go for a walk when the door flew open, and Steve brushed by her quickly.

Sheila turned just in time to see Steve running down the stairs, and then he was gone. Sheila walked in and saw Kim standing there, crying. Sheila walked up to her friend and held her and let her cry. Sheila didn't understand what could have happened. She had only been gone twenty minutes. Kim finally stopped crying and told Sheila what had happened.

Steve had climbed into bed with Kim and begun to shake her, trying to wake her up. She had complained and told him she wanted to go back to sleep. Steve had become furious and started to scream at her. He called her lazy, immature, and selfish. Kim hadn't understood what the problem was. She wasn't ready to get up yet, and she was mad at Steve for not letting her sleep.

Sheila told Kim about Steve losing his job, and it didn't even seem to worry her. Kim dismissed his feelings and continued to rant about how he was rude and obnoxious. Sheila listened and wondered how two such different people had ever ended up together. The truth was, Steve was just discovering Kim's personality traits. He had never spent more than a couple of hours at a time with her before she moved in. Steve was just as surprised as Sheila to discover what she was really like. Sheila seemed to have much more patience for Kim than Steve did.

Bill came home from work and was not impressed with all of Kim's drama. He'd had a long day at work, and no one except Kim had slept much in the last few days. Bill went to have a nap, and Sheila started to get something going for dinner. Sheila decided to make shepherd's pie for dinner. They had ground beef, potatoes, and onions. Sheila would just have to go pick up some corn. Sheila counted her money. She was getting very low, but they had to eat dinner, so off to the store she went.

# Chapter 10

Sheila reached the front doors of the building. She opened them and took in a deep breath of fresh air. She ran down the stairs and up the alley, as she turned on the next street she saw Steve sitting in his car. Sheila and Kim had been living at Steve's for almost three weeks, and it was going well for Sheila, but Steve and Kim were fighting constantly.

Sheila walked over to Steve's car and tapped on the window. Steve looked up at her and gave her a big smile. He rolled the window down and asked, "What's up?"

"I'm bored so I'm going for a walk. Do you want to come along?" she asked. To Sheila's delight he accepted. They walked silently at first, and then Steve stared to open up to Sheila.

Steve told Sheila he was upset with Kim's behavior. She had always talked about getting married and having kids, but she couldn't even get herself out of bed in the morning, let alone feed herself. She didn't seem to be the person Steve thought she was. Kim didn't even seem to understand the significance of him losing his job. She just assumed he would go get another one, and the bills would be magically paid. Steve was finding all this time with her very frustrating.

Then he said something that scared Sheila: he was thinking of asking Kim to leave. Steve wasn't sure what to do, but he told Sheila that if he did ask Kim to leave, she could still stay for as long as she needed. Sheila didn't know how to respond, so she stayed silent and listened. He told her he was going to see how the next few days went and then decide. For now, he asked Sheila not to say anything. Sheila agreed there was no need to upset Kim for no reason.

They arrived at the apartment, and Steve went back to sit in his car. He needed a little more time to think. Sheila went upstairs and started making dinner. Bill came into the kitchen and told Sheila that dinner smelled good. Bill needed the bathroom, and he was pissed off because Kim was taking forever with her shower. Bill banged on the door and told her to hurry.

Finally, Kim came out, and she and Bill exchanged a few nasty words. It was apparent that they didn't like each other very much. It put a strain on Sheila. She liked them both and didn't want to be stuck in the middle. Bill came out of the bathroom and offered to help Sheila. She thanked him and told him everything was taken care of. With dinner in the oven, Sheila set the table while Bill rolled a joint for him and Sheila.

Steve came into the apartment just as Bill lit the joint. Bill looked up at him with a stern look on his face. "Steve, do you have your rent money?" Bill asked. When Steve shook his head no, Bill was obviously very angry. "Steve, this is the last time. If you don't have your rent, you are out." Bill really liked Steve, but he couldn't keep covering the bills for him every time he lost his job, especially now that he had his girlfriend living there. Bill had been paying for the groceries for everyone for weeks now.

Steve had had enough fighting for one day, so he left. Kim came out of the bedroom just in time to see Steve storming out of the apartment. She ran after him. Bill and Sheila looked at each other. She started first, laughing loudly at the drama of Kim and Steve. Bill joined in, enjoying the moment of calm. Sheila was happy to have a little break from all the fighting. The screaming was making her think about home, and she had begun to worry about Joann.

Bill went to bed after a few beers. He really needed a good night's sleep. Sheila sat on the sofa and looked at the clock. It was just after

8:00 PM. She thought maybe she should call some of the people she had been babysitting for before she left home. Sheila sat there for a while, contemplating the calls. She took a deep breath and dialed Mrs. Quesnel's phone number.

Sheila heard the phone ringing, and she was about to hang up when little Annette answered the phone. She was so excited when she heard Sheila's voice—Sheila was excellent with the children she babysat; they always loved her. Sheila spoke with the child for a moment, and then told Annette to get her mother. A moment later, Mrs. Quesnel was on the phone.

Sheila was very disappointed when Mrs. Quesnel told her the police had been by, asking her and Annette questions about Sheila and some girl named Kim. Mrs. Quesnel didn't want to be involved, and she was very disappointed in Sheila's behavior. She asked her to never call back, and said that if she did, Mrs. Quesnel would call the police. Sheila hung up the phone and was about to cry, but then she realized she had to try again. She couldn't keep living off of Bill, and she was down to $1.27 of her money. Mrs. Quesnel was not the only person she babysat for, and she would just have to keep trying.

Next, Sheila phoned Miss Harris and then Mrs. Baker, and they both said almost the same thing as Mrs. Quesnel. However, Mrs. Baker told Sheila that if and when she came home, she would love to have her back as a babysitter. The children missed Sheila. Sheila thanked them all for their time, and when she hung up from the last call with Mrs. Baker, she couldn't hold the tears back any longer.

Sheila sat there holding the phone with the world closing in around her. She didn't know what to do. She needed money. Sheila sat there, and for just a second, she wished she had never run away. Bobby entered Sheila's thoughts then, and suddenly she realized how safe she felt. Sheila was still crying and feeling completely desperate. Eventually, she cried herself to sleep.

Sheila heard Bill's alarm clock go off. She lay quietly on the sofa, and when she heard Bill in the bathroom showering, she sat up and stretched. A good night's sleep was just what Sheila had needed. She felt refreshed and rested. Sheila hadn't awoken feeling this good in a long time. She felt that everything was going to work out somehow. She didn't know how, but she couldn't shake this positive feeling.

Sheila put on some water to boil for a cup of tea, lit a smoke, and sat at the table. When Bill came out of the bathroom, Sheila asked him if he wanted some tea or something to eat. Bill accepted the tea, but he refused breakfast, thanking her for the offer. Bill commented about Steve and Kim being so loud when they came home fighting at four in the morning. Sheila hadn't even heard them come home; she was disappointed to learn they were still fighting. Sheila remembered Steve's words from the day before. She hoped he wasn't going to tell Kim to leave. The positive feeling left Sheila quickly.

At two o'clock that afternoon, Steve came out from the bedroom, looking like he had been run over by a truck. He grumbled something as he went into the bathroom. Sheila wasn't sure what he said, so she put on some water to boil for his tea. Steve came out of the bathroom and sat at the table with Sheila. He lit a smoke.

"It was awful last night, Sheila. I listened to Kim bitch and complain the whole night. All we did was fight, and I just don't want to put up with her anymore," Steve blurted out. "Sheila, what I said yesterday still stands. If you want, you can stay." Sheila saw that the water was boiling and got up to make them both a cup of tea. She placed Steve's tea in front of him. As Sheila released the cup, he grabbed her hand and looked deep into her eyes.

Sheila pulled her hand away immediately and felt every hair on her back stand up. *They are all the same*, Sheila thought. *Fucking pigs.* "Thanks anyway, but if Kim leaves, I leave," Sheila informed him curtly. Sheila picked up her tea and walked into the kitchen. She poured her tea down the sink. She walked to the door, put her shoes on, and looked at Steve. *What a disappointment he's turned out to be*, she thought.

"Steve, I'm not going to say anything about your offer to Kim. There is no need to upset her more. If she gets up before I get back, could you please tell her I went for a walk and I'll be back soon?" Sheila said. Steve nodded yes and looked down at his tea. He didn't say a word. Sheila left and took a walk around the block. She needed to gather her thoughts and figure out what they were going to do next.

Sheila felt her stomach growl. She was hungry, not having eaten since the night before. She didn't want to spend any more money until she knew what was happening. For now, eating was not a priority. She kept walking in circles for hours. She was really surprised that Steve

*Behind the Drapes*

would throw Kim out, and even worse was making a pass at Sheila. Sheila had always believed that Steve and Kim were in love, but now she knew she was wrong. Where were she and Kim going to go?

Sheila returned to the apartment at 3:00 PM, and as she climbed the stairs, she prayed that Kim was out of bed. Sheila didn't want to be alone with Steve, and she and Kim had to figure out their next move before it got dark out. When she reached the apartment, Steve wasn't there, and she could hear the shower going. She peeked in the bedroom and found the bed was empty. Sheila sat down and rolled a joint for her and Kim. They needed it. She knew Kim was going to be upset. Kim had really believed she and Steve would be married and live happily ever after.

The water stopped. Sheila walked up to the bathroom door and knocked. "Kim, is that you?" she inquired. The door flung open, and Kim stood there crying. She ran into Sheila's arms and let it all out. Kim was so hurt. She'd had this wonderful fantasy of what her life would be like living with Steve, and it had been an awful experience. The worst part was that Steve didn't want to see Kim at all anymore. She was heartbroken. Steve had been Kim's first love.

Kim explained that Steve had woken her up and told her she had to leave. They'd had a terrible fight, and Steve had told her he wanted her out by tomorrow morning. Almost everything Kim said Sheila had heard from Steve the day before, but she never let on. She acted like it was all news to her. Kim told Sheila not to worry about having to move out. She would change Steve's mind—she knew how—and by tomorrow morning, he would be begging her to stay. Sheila wasn't so sure.

Bill came in from work, and Kim informed him of the whole situation before he could even get his shoes off. Bill looked at Sheila and rolled his eyes. She smiled at him in response. Bill sat down and rolled his after-work joint. As he smoked it, everything Kim had just told him started to sink in. If Kim moved out, did that mean Sheila was leaving as well? Bill handed Sheila the joint, too afraid of the answer to ask the question. Bill had become very fond of Sheila over the last few weeks.

The three of them had some beers, and Sheila offered to make some dinner. She still hadn't eaten since the night before, and, with the beer and drugs, she was starting to feel a little queasy. Bill told her not to worry about dinner. He said he would go out and pick up beer and something for dinner, and then he left. Sheila watched Kim pace the floor as she waited for Steve to come home. Sheila didn't want to upset Kim further, but she felt a wave of panic come over as she wondered where they would be sleeping the next evening.

Bill was back within an hour with beer and Chinese food. There was still no word from Steve. They ate their dinner in silence, all lost in their own thoughts. Finally, Sheila broke the silence. "Thanks, Bill, for the great dinner. I've never had Chinese food before. I really like it."

"It's my pleasure," Bill said, and they both looked at Kim, waiting for her to thank Bill, but she said nothing.

Sheila had started to clear the table when she heard the door open. Everyone looked and saw Steve walking in. "Are you hungry, Steve?" Sheila inquired. Steve looked at her with a smile and shook his head no. Steve walked directly to his room and closed the door. Kim grabbed two beers and followed him into the bedroom. The screaming started immediately, and Bill put on an album, turning the volume up.

"I'm not going to miss all the fighting around here," Bill said.

"Me either," Sheila agreed. She finished clearing the table and started to wash the dishes. Bill walked over to the stove and picked up the towel hanging on the handle. Then he turned, leaned back on the stove, and looked at Sheila. Feeling his stare, Sheila returned his gaze. "Bill, I just want to thank you for everything. You are a very nice man, and it was good to get to know you. Very few people would have let a complete stranger into their home, and I appreciate it," Sheila told Bill sincerely.

"Sheila, it was my pleasure to have met you. I just want you to know that you don't have to leave," Bill said in a pleading voice. Sheila looked at him and shook her head no. Sheila turned her attention to the dishes and filled the sink. "I have enjoyed your company. It's been fun having you around, Sheila. I wish you weren't going ... I really like you," Bill whispered. Sheila heard him, but pretended she didn't. She just continued washing the dishes, and Bill started to dry them.

When Sheila finished the dishes, Bill turned down the music. It seemed quiet for a moment, but within a few minutes, Kim started to yell again. Bill turned the music back up, and Sheila went to have a long, hot shower. Sheila stood in the shower and tried to figure out what to

*Behind the Drapes*

do next. She was getting scared. She barely had any money left. What would they eat, and where would they sleep?

There was banging on the bathroom door, and Sheila turned off the water. She climbed out of the shower. "I'll be out in a minute!" Sheila yelled, and hurried to dry off and dress. Sheila opened the door to see Kim standing there, crying. Sheila walked out of the bathroom and held Kim, letting her cry. Sheila looked around the room, noticed Steve's coat gone and Bill's bedroom door closed. Sheila knew then, it was over.

"I couldn't change his mind, Sheila. He wants me gone by the morning," Kim told Sheila through her sobs. "He left and said I had to be gone by nine AM." Sheila had known it was coming. Now she just had to calm Kim down so they could figure out a plan. Bill came out of his room and brought with him a very large joint that he handed to Sheila, telling her to light it. Then he went to the fridge and got three beers.

Bill handed one to Sheila and one to Kim, and sat on the sofa. Sheila lit the joint and handed it back to Bill. When they were finished, Sheila started to pack up her stuff. When Kim saw what she was doing, she started to cry all over again. She ran into the bedroom. Sheila just left her alone and finished packing. It didn't take long; she still didn't have much. When she was finished, she sat on the sofa and let out a big sigh. *What is going to happen next?* Sheila wondered.

Bill reached out and touched Sheila's leg. It startled her, and she jumped away. "I'm sorry, Sheila. I didn't mean to scare you. I just wanted you to know that if you ever need anything, just let me know. I will always be there for you," Bill said in a gentle voice. Sheila believed him. He reached into his pocket and pulled out an envelope. He handed it to Sheila. Before she even knew what it was, she was trying to give it back. Bill gave her a stern look and told her he insisted she take it, and with that he went into his bedroom and closed the door.

Sheila looked into the envelope. There was forty dollars and about ten grams of marijuana. Sheila thought how she shouldn't accept it, but then she counted her money and knew she had no choice. She and Kim needed it desperately. She promised herself she would pay him back one day. Sheila put the money in her sock and hid the drugs in her bag. She picked up a piece of paper and wrote Bill a little note:

> *Bill,*
>
> *Thanks for everything. You are a good man, and I promise one day I will pay you back. You have been a real friend to me, and I will never forget you.*
>
> *Sheila*

Sheila slipped it under his door. Then she went into the bedroom to talk to Kim, but she was asleep. Sheila started to pick up her clothes, which were thrown all over the floor. She placed them in a little pile so it would be easier for her in the morning. Sheila lay on the couch and tried to get some sleep. It took her hours to fall asleep. So much uncertainty lay ahead, and she felt responsible for Kim. She still didn't know what to do. Finally, Sheila drifted off to sleep.

When Sheila woke the next morning, Bill was already gone. She reached for her cigarettes and saw the words "I'll miss you" written on the package. Sheila smiled and looked at the time. It was 7:30, and they had to be out in an hour and a half. Sheila had a quick shower and dressed. She looked into the mirror and saw that her face was almost completely healed. At least there was something to be happy about.

She was already packed and ready to leave at a moment's notice. Now she just had to get Kim up and ready to go. Sheila made them both a cup of tea and rolled a joint. She lightly knocked on the door and opened it. She was shocked to find Kim up and packing her belongings. Sheila handed her a cup of tea, and they shared a joint. Kim went to have a shower, and when she came back, Sheila had breakfast ready: scrambled eggs and toast.

The girls ate breakfast, and then realized it was time to go. Sheila cleaned up from breakfast while Kim put on her makeup and gathered the rest of her things. They left the key Steve had given them beside the long note Kim had written Steve the night before. They took one last look around, and then Sheila closed the door. They threw their bags over their shoulders and started down the stairs to whatever might come next.

Sheila and Kim walked out into the street. It was a beautiful, sunny day. They really didn't know where they were going, so they just walked. After a few hours, Sheila needed to use a bathroom, so they went into a shopping mall. As they were walking around the mall, Sheila noticed a sign in the window of a clothing store that read: "Help Wanted." Sheila pointed it out to Kim and suggested they go in and apply. They needed to make some money to find a place.

The girls went into the store and walked up to a lady behind the counter. They told her they wanted to apply for the job. The woman took a look at them and asked how old they were. Sheila spoke up first. She lied and told her they were both sixteen. The woman didn't believe them for a minute, and then asked why they weren't in school. Sheila told her another lie, saying that they were looking for jobs and planning on taking night classes; their families needed the money.

She gave them each an application, and told them to fill it out and bring it back to her, pointing to two chairs. Sheila asked for a pen. The woman looked annoyed, but gave her one. Sheila sat down on one of the chairs, and Kim followed. Sheila watched the lady, who just stared at them, like she didn't trust them or something. Sheila tried to ignore her, but she hated it when people looked down on her.

Sheila looked down at the application. She filled in her name. Next, she looked at the other questions. She had nothing to write down. She didn't have an address or a phone number. She couldn't even write down her babysitting jobs as references, because they might say something about the police looking for Sheila and Kim. Sheila also didn't know about this one question about a social insurance number. Sheila asked Kim about it, and she didn't know either.

Sheila looked at Kim. She stood up, ripped up the application, and started to walk out of the store. She placed the pen on the counter as she was leaving. Sheila avoided eye contact with the woman, and left the store feeling defeated. When Sheila reached the mall, she walked up to the first garbage can she saw and threw her ripped application inside. Kim walked up behind her and threw hers in as well. They walked out of the mall, both feeling hopeless.

# Chapter 11

Sheila and Kim awoke under the tree. The ground was damp and cold. Sheila and Kim had both developed terrible coughs over the last few weeks, living on the street. Kim's cough sounded much worse than Sheila's, and it had Sheila worried. They only had $2.17, half a pack of smokes, and a couple of joints left. Sheila knew that breakfast would be their last meal for a while.

Sheila lit a cigarette, and they shared it. Kim was coughing so much, and Sheila wanted to get her up off the damp ground. They had to leave before the school opened and there were kids everywhere. Sheila suggested they go get a hot cup of tea and some apples, and Kim agreed. They walked for a few hours and warmed up nicely in morning sun. When they reached the mall, they went directly to the washrooms.

They washed themselves and brushed their teeth and hair. When they left the bathroom, Sheila sat Kim down on a bench, went into the grocery store, and bought four apples and some cough drops. Then she went to the coffee shop and bought two hot teas. Sheila looked down at her hand and realized they only had thirty-two cents left. Sheila walked back to the bench and gave Kim an apple and her tea. She told her to drink it all while it was hot.

Sheila saw the security guard staring at them, and she knew it was time to leave. She pulled Kim by the arm, and they walked out of the mall, back into the street. Kim was getting tired easily, and they had to stop often for her to rest. Sheila wasn't sure what to do now. They didn't even have enough money for another hot tea. Sheila needed to be numb, and she suggested going to the park and smoking a joint, so that's what they did.

The day passed quickly, and before they knew it, they were back under the willow tree, freezing. Sheila and Kim ate the last two apples and worried silently when they would eat again. Kim started to cough, and Sheila surprised her with the cough drops. Kim actually looked grateful and thanked Sheila. Sheila realized how much they both had matured during the last six weeks, especially Kim in the last three. Sheila wondered if Steve would approve of this new Kim—not that he would ever get to see her. Kim's feelings for Steve had turned from love to anger, hatred, and resentment. She blamed him for what she was going through now, and she never wanted to see him again.

What bothered Kim the most was the fact that her mother had been right. Steve had never loved her. He had just said what he needed to, to get her into bed. Kim felt humiliated, and she wouldn't forgive Steve, or ever forget the lesson she had learned about men. When Sheila and Kim talked about it, Sheila always said men were nothing but fucking pigs. Kim wasn't sure they were all bad, but she knew they all lied to get what they wanted.

The next morning, Kim woke with a fever. She looked pale, and Sheila was getting very worried. The night had been especially cold. They were both freezing. They shared a smoke and tried to warm up. Sheila knew they needed to get up off the cold ground. She reminded Kim they had to get going, the school would be open soon. Reluctantly, Kim got up, and they started walking.

It took them a long time to get to the mall that day. Sheila had to let Kim rest every few yards. When they got to the mall, Sheila used the rest of their money to get Kim an apple. With twelve cents left, it was to be the end of food. Kim tried to share the apple with Sheila, but Sheila refused, knowing Kim needed it more than she did. When they finished washing up in the bathroom, the security guard was waiting for them outside in the hallway.

"I don't want to see you two in here again, or I'm going to call the police. You two have been in here every day for weeks. This is not your private bathroom!" he shouted. "Now get out, and don't let me catch you in here again." Sheila grabbed Kim by the arm and walked past him without a word. They left the mall. They walked through the parking lot, and when they reached the other side by the bus stop, Kim had to rest, so they sat on the bench for a while.

By the next morning, Kim's fever had gotten worse, and her cough sounded awful. Sheila and Kim smoked their last joint. Sheila looked over at her friend and noticed Kim was trembling. She was so cold. Sheila took off her coat and felt a panic come over her. She needed to get Kim a hot tea and some food, but how? Sheila had never felt so desperate in her whole life. What was she going to do? Sheila got Kim up, and they started to walk, but Kim couldn't get far before she needed to sit down. She just couldn't stop coughing.

Sheila brought Kim to another shopping mall, a much busier one. Sheila sat Kim on a toilet in the public washroom stall; she locked the door and crawled under it. Sheila told her to get some rest, and she would be back soon with hot tea. Then she ran out of the mall. Sheila was starving, and she knew Kim needed some food to help her fight her cough; she walked for an hour feeling helpless, hungry, and cold.

As Sheila turned the corner, she saw a little old lady carrying a purse, walking alone. Sheila looked around, and she didn't see anybody. The thought just raced through Sheila's head, and she didn't give herself any time to think about it. Sheila walked down the sidewalk, with the old woman walking toward her from the opposite direction. When Sheila was two feet from her, she pounced.

Sheila ran at her and grabbed for her purse. Much to Sheila's surprise, the old woman didn't let go, and suddenly, Sheila found herself struggling with this woman for her purse. Sheila pulled roughly, and the woman started to fall forward. Sheila looked into her eyes and saw her own looking back at her; they were sad and scared. Sheila felt so guilty and ashamed.

Sheila caught the woman before she fell. Sheila helped her steady herself and looked into her eyes. "I'm sorry, I just ..." Sheila blurted out through her tears, but she couldn't explain. Sheila ran and ran, crying. She didn't stop until she was completely out of breath. When

Sheila finally stopped running, she collapsed on the ground for a few moments.

Kim popped in to her mind, and she wondered what time it was. She had to get back, and Sheila was at least an hour-and-a-half walk from the shopping mall. She pulled out her cigarettes, and realized she was almost out of smokes as well. Things were looking bleak. Sheila was really at the end of the line, and she knew it.

An hour and a half later, Sheila crawled under the stall door and looked up at Kim. At that moment, Sheila knew it was all over. She had to prepare for the misery of returning home. Kim was as white as a ghost, and when Sheila touched her hand, she was on fire. Her fever was getting worse. Sheila wet paper towels from the bathroom with cool water and placed them on Kim's head for a moment. Then she put the towels in her pocket and picked Kim up.

"Hey, Sheila. Where is the hot tea?" Kim asked.

"We are going to get some right now," Sheila told her, pulling her up onto her feet. Sheila walked Kim to the front of mall and sat her on a bench. She reached in her pocket and pulled out the card. She looked down at his name. She walked to the pay phone, picked up the receiver, put in her last dime, and dialed the number.

"I'd like to speak with Constable Alain Perron, please," Sheila told the operator. Sheila waited for about five minutes before she heard a very deep voice on the line.

"Constable Perron here," the voice said. Sheila told him who she was and that she was with Kim. She informed him Kim was sick and probably needed to see a doctor—they were ready to go home. As Sheila told the officer this, she felt every hair on her neck stand up. He asked where they were, and Sheila told him. Constable Perron asked her to stay put, and said he would be there in thirty minutes.

Sheila sat on the bench with Kim. As she held her, she thought how nice the police officer had been to her. He hadn't judged her, only offered his service, and she was thankful. She only hoped he wouldn't be different when she met him. Sheila felt Kim shivering from the fever and knew she had done the right thing. She only hoped Kim would see it that way when she was better.

Sheila must have dozed off. When she felt someone shaking her, Sheila opened her eyes and saw the most beautiful deep blue eyes she had ever seen. When Constable Perron saw Sheila open her eyes, he stood up. He was huge. He stood 6 feet 3 inches and weighed in at 243 pounds. He had soft curly black hair, a masculine square jaw, and broad shoulders. He was so large, Sheila was instantly intimidated, until he smiled at her and melted her heart. Constable Perron was a very handsome young man. At twenty-two, he had been a police officer for three years now.

Constable Perron reached out his hand to Sheila. It was enormous, but when she grabbed it, his palm was soft and gentle. Sheila stood up and told him she needed some help with Kim. He picked her up like she was a feather and placed her in the back of the police cruiser. Kim never even woke up.

Constable Perron asked what was wrong with Kim, and Sheila told him she had a bad cough and a bad fever. Within a few minutes, they were in the emergency room at the closest hospital. They took Kim in right away. Constable Perron told Sheila he wanted her to be checked over as well, and they sat down together, waiting for her turn.

"Sheila, is there anything you would like to tell me?" Constable Perron inquired. Sheila looked at him and shook her head no. "We know why Kim ran away, to be with Steve, but your parents say they don't know why you ran away," the officer continued. Sheila just sat there and didn't say a word. She felt she could trust him, but she just couldn't take the chance he would say something to Bobby.

"When I was looking for you, I talked to a couple of ladies you babysat for, Sheila. One of them, Mrs. Baker, told me that you had fresh bruises regularly since she has known you, and sometimes you looked like you had received a vicious beating," Constable Perron said. Sheila still sat there without saying a word, looking down at her hands, shaking her head no. Constable Perron's heart went out to the beautiful, troubled young girl.

Constable Perron told Sheila he couldn't help her if she didn't tell him why she ran away. Constable Perron had seen enough domestic abuse in his short career to know there was something going on in that house, but Sheila was not going to tell him anything. His hands were tied. He told Sheila to keep his business card, and if she ever needed anything to call him. Then it happened. Sheila turned white as she heard Bobby screaming.

*Behind the Drapes*

"Where is the stupid little slut?" Bobby hollered. Constable Perron jumped to his feet and walked up to Bobby, reminding him he was in a hospital. Just then, a nurse called Sheila's name. She got up and followed her down the hall, thankful to get away from her father. They put Sheila in a room and told her to put a gown on. After she did, she lay down on a gurney. The nurse gave her a blanket, and she drifted off to sleep.

Sheila woke to the doctor shaking her; he informed her that Kim had pneumonia, and they suspected Sheila probably did, too. They took her for X-rays, took some blood samples, and brought her back to the room. The doctor listened to her chest and told her to get some rest while they waited for the test results. Sheila asked to see Kim, but the nurse explained that Kim's mother insisted Sheila was not to see her daughter. Sheila would never see Kim again.

Sheila cried herself to sleep and awoke to see the doctor and her mother standing by her bed. The doctor told Hugette that Sheila had to stay in the hospital until the next day. She was lucky not to have pneumonia like Kim. However, she had a terrible lung infection, and they wanted to keep her overnight for observation. Sheila was very pleased to hear the news—she wasn't going to get a beating today.

Sheila hadn't slept in a bed for so long. She felt so warm and comfortable that she drifted off to sleep again, and she didn't move until the next morning. When Sheila opened her eyes, she was surprised to see Constable Perron sitting by her bed. He smiled when he saw Sheila was awake, and he got out of his chair to come stand by her bed. He brushed a piece of hair out of Sheila's eyes, and she felt electricity run through her body from his touch.

Constable Perron told her he had just stopped by to ask her a few questions. Sheila told as much of the truth as she felt she could. She denied ever spending any time at Steve and Bill's apartment, and said they had been living on the street the whole time. Sheila never wanted to get them into trouble, especially Bill. He had been so good to her.

Sheila started to tremble and looked down at her hands when Bobby and Hugette walked into the room. Constable Perron turned to see what had upset Sheila, and he was not surprised to see her parents standing there. He turned and told Bobby he needed to talk to him in the hall. Bobby looked irritated, but followed him out the door.

"Mr. Parks, Sheila refuses to tell me anything, but I suspect from what other people have told me that someone has been mistreating Sheila. Maybe it was abuse that made her run away. What do you think, Mr. Parks?" Constable Perron inquired. Bobby denied having any knowledge of abuse and turned to walk away.

Constable Perron grabbed Bobby roughly by the arm. "I'll be watching you, and if I ever see anything to indicate someone has been beating Sheila, I'll be coming back for you, Mr. Parks." The officer whispered the warning to Bobby. He let go of Bobby's arm with a shove and walked out of the hospital. Bobby watched him leave. For once, he was the one trembling.

The doctor came into Sheila's room and gave her some pills to take. He told her and her mother she was to stay in bed for a least a week. She had to let her body heal, and rest was the best medicine right now. The doctor left the room. Bobby came in and told them he would be waiting in the car, they should hurry. Then he left. Sheila jumped out of bed and felt a little dizzy, but she had heard her father, and she was dressed with her bags ready in a few moments.

Sheila and Hugette left the hospital without saying a word to each other. The ride home was eerily silent, and it made Sheila very worried about what would happen to her once they arrived at the apartment. The drive was too short, and just as Sheila felt the panic wash over her, she noticed Bobby was not pulling into the parking lot. To Sheila's delight, Bobby dropped them off in front of the building and told Hugette he would be home from work two hours late, because he had to make up the time he'd wasted on picking up the slut.

Bobby drove off, and Sheila and Hugette went into the building. The elevator doors opened, and Sheila and her mother climbed in; neither of them had said one word to each other. When the doors opened on their floor, Sheila walked out and started down the hall with Hugette following her. Sheila stopped in front of her door and stared. Her mother opened the door, and Sheila reluctantly entered the apartment. Hugette closed the door behind her. Sheila looked at the closed door and was overcome by a feeling of dread.

Sheila went straight to the bathroom and had a hot shower. Then she climbed into bed. Hugette came in and handed Sheila one of the pills the doctor had given her, with some water. Sheila took the pill, and

*Behind the Drapes*

her mother left the room. Sheila lay on the bed and looked around at her old room. She counted the months until she turned sixteen. Before long, Sheila fell back to sleep.

When she woke up, Joann was sitting on the side of her bed with a huge grin on her face. She was so happy to see Sheila; she had been very worried about her. Joann explained to Sheila that a couple of weeks earlier, Steve had shown up at the school and asked Joann if she had seen Sheila or Kim. When Joann told him she hadn't, he had become upset. He said Sheila and Kim had left a week earlier, and he hadn't been able to find them.

Sheila told Joann she was home and safe, and that was all she needed to focus on. Sheila had no intention of telling her sister about what she had been through; Sheila would take the memories of her experiences living on the street to her grave. It was nothing she cared to see through Joann's eyes. Joann dropped the subject and informed Sheila of what had been going on at home.

Bobby had found a job, and he seemed to like it okay. Well, he didn't bitch about it so much, so Joann just assumed he enjoyed it. Their parents had been fighting constantly since Sheila had been gone. Hugette had received a couple of good beatings. Bobby and Hugette had both stayed away from Joann. Bobby had never touched her, and nobody really spoke to her. Joann had been thankful for the peace and quiet, and had spent most of her time in their room thinking about Sheila.

Sheila was so relieved; at least she didn't have to feel guilty about what Joann had been through. Sheila thought about Kim and wondered how she was feeling, and if she was still in the hospital. She would figure a way to find out what was going on with Kim. Sheila was pulled from her thoughts by the sound of the apartment door slamming. He was home. Joann jumped up and told Sheila to stay in bed. She had to go and get dinner on the plates for Hugette to serve.

Sheila lay in her bed and waited for it to come. She almost welcomed the beating. The waiting was driving her nuts. But Bobby never came near her that night, to the shock of Sheila, Joann, and their mother. However, the longer he waited, the more terrified Sheila became. That night she had nightmares about it.

Finally, the next evening after dinner, the door to her room flung open, and there Bobby stood. Sheila was relieved, just wanting to get it over with. Bobby closed the door and came at Sheila with his fists swinging, calling her every dirty name in the book. He had only hit her a few times when he stopped and stared at her. He seemed to be remembering something, and it made him stop.

Bobby heard Constable Perron's words ring in his head: "I'll come back for you." Bobby looked down at Sheila angrily; he hit her two more times in the stomach and spit on her. Then he smiled and informed Sheila that Hugette was going to the bingo. Bobby told her he would be back in a little while, and she had better be prepared to be a good girl and take care of her father. Sheila lay there crying. The beating had been relatively light, but she knew what was coming next.

# Chapter 12

Sheila awoke with a huge smile on her face. Tomorrow, she would turn sixteen. The time had finally arrived. Her bag was packed and ready to go at a moments notice. Only one more day and she would be leaving her home for good. She reached down and felt her sock. She had saved over four hundred dollars, and this time, Sheila had a plan. It wouldn't be anything like when she and Kim had run away. This time, she would never be coming back.

Sheila sat up in bed and noticed Joann. She was sitting in her bed, hugging her legs and crying softly. "It's almost here, Sheila. You get to leave soon, but I'll still be here for two more years. What if he starts with me once you're gone? What will I do?" Joann asked through her tears. Sheila ran to her sister and hugged her. *It will be the same as when I ran away*, Sheila prayed silently. Sheila just assumed her father hated her more than Joann and Pauline, and that was why he hurt her most. Or maybe she had done something she wasn't aware of.... In any case, it didn't matter. It was over.

"I'm sorry, honey, but I have to leave. You know that. We have talked about this many times. As soon as I get settled, I'll let you know where I'll be living, and if he comes near you, Joann, you run away and live with me. Remember, Joann, he never touched you when I ran away, and he probably won't touch you now."

Sheila looked at the clock. "I have to go start breakfast. Get cleaned up, and come down and eat. We have to leave for school soon," Sheila said as she changed her clothes and ran out the door. Sheila put the coffee on and started bacon and eggs for Bobby and Hugette. Then she started the oatmeal for her and Joann. They were not allowed to ever have bacon and eggs. These were only for her parents.

Bobby came into the kitchen, grabbed a coffee, and sat down. "How long until breakfast?" he snapped at Sheila. *One more day*, Sheila thought as she handed his bacon and eggs to Hugette to serve to him. Hugette still made a big deal about handing Bobby his meals. Bobby ate his breakfast and grabbed his lunch box, and without a word to anyone, he left.

"What are your plans tomorrow, Sheila?" Hugette inquired without looking at her daughter.

"I think you know the answer to that," Sheila responded. "Mom, I'll be gone soon, and you will probably never see me again, so if I add correctly, you have lost four of your five children so far. If you're smart, you will be a mother to Joann and protect her from that animal, before you lose her too. Remember, Mother, when Joann is gone, you will be left here alone with him for the rest of your life." Hugette ran from the room in tears, realizing her daughter was right.

Sheila and Joann finished their breakfast, and Sheila did the dishes. Then they left for school. Joann was going to miss not having Sheila around. She could remember easily when Sheila had run away. It had felt like years, and it had only been forty-six days. Sheila had no plans to continue with school, so Joann wouldn't even see her there. Joann couldn't wait until it was her turn to go.

Sheila had to find a job to survive, and that left no room for school. However, before she left, she checked with student services. They connected her with a guidance counselor. He was a very nice man. He explained to Sheila what a SIN number was, and helped Sheila obtain one. Now she could get a job. What pleased Sheila most was learning how to properly fill out a job application. This time, no one would be looking down on her.

Sheila had already informed the school and the guidance counselor she was leaving school. The counselor had spoken to Sheila and tried to change her mind, but she was stubborn. Sheila didn't listen to a word he said. He was a man, and what did he know about her? She sat there, and when he was finished talking, she smiled and told him she would try and come back next year. Then she left the room.

That evening at dinner, Bobby told Sheila that even though she was turning sixteen the next day, he would allow her to continue living with them until she finished high school. Sheila almost laughed out loud, but she stopped herself. She didn't want to look for a new job the next day with a black eye. Sheila looked at her father and thanked him for the offer. Bobby threw fifteen dollars to Hugette, and told her she could go to bingo. With a big smile on her face, Hugette picked up the money and left the table to go get ready, without even finishing her meal.

Sheila was in disbelief. Even on her last night at home, her mother would leave her alone with that monster. Hugette had clearly not listened to anything that Sheila had told her that morning at breakfast. Bobby got up and left the room. *Not tonight*, Sheila thought. She didn't want to do it. All of a sudden, Sheila heard the apartment door close and Hugette yelling good-bye. Anger started to build in Sheila that she had never allowed to surface before. *Not tonight!* Sheila thought.

Sheila told Joann that if anything happened tonight, Joann should go to the corner store and wait there until Sheila came. No sooner had Sheila got the words out than Bobby came into the kitchen. He told Sheila to make him a cup of tea and went back to the sofa. "Go now, Joann," Sheila whispered, and she put the kettle on. Sheila grabbed the large cup and a teabag. When the tea was ready, Sheila walked into the living room with a determined mind. He was not going to hurt her anymore.

When Sheila entered the living room, she told her father that Joann had gone out to play. Bobby told her to put the tea down, and to be a good girl and take care of her daddy. An enormous smile came across her face. Sheila walked closer to him, and closer. Bobby was excited to see her smile. When Sheila saw the enormous bulge in his pants, she took the hot tea and threw it at his crotch. Bobby jumped up screaming, and Sheila kicked him with all her might, right between the legs. Bobby fell to the floor moaning. "Not tonight or ever again!" Sheila screamed at her father, and she ran from the apartment.

When Sheila arrived at the store to meet her sister, she was still laughing hysterically, but her laughter soon turned to tears. It was finally over. She had waited her whole life for this moment, and now that it was here, she was terrified. She told Joann what happened, and at first Joann laughed as well, but then she realized she still had to go home. They sat together in silence for a long time, and then Joann looked at the clock in the store. They both knew she had to go home.

"I'll be waiting for you outside of school tomorrow afternoon," Sheila assured her sister. She sat there watching Joann until she was out of sight. Not knowing what to do and where to go, Sheila sat there for hours. She noticed a man watching her from a parked car, so she got up and went into the store. Sheila bought some cigarettes and a small milk. She asked the clerk for a plastic bag. Sheila remembered how the cold ground was not good for you. Sheila paid the clerk and left the store.

When Sheila got outside, the man and the car were gone. She was relieved. She started to walk in no particular direction, and, as night fell, she was faced with the question of where to sleep. Sheila had enough money to get a hotel room, but she didn't want to waste any money on luxuries. She knew that with the plastic bag to keep the damp ground away from her, she would be okay for a few nights. She was still a little scared, because this time she didn't have Kim with her. This time, she was alone.

Sheila had never seen Kim again. However, a few months after Sheila had gotten out of the hospital; Bobby had beaten her and told her to stay home from school. She really couldn't understand it, since she only had a few little marks on her face. Bobby seemed to be so nervous and cautious about anyone seeing marks. On this day, Joann had come home from school with a letter. Kim had come to the school looking for Sheila, and she had asked Joann to deliver it. Sheila had read it a thousand times, and she pulled it out now.

*Dear Sheila,*

*I just want to say thank you for being such a good friend. I wanted to make sure you know I'm not upset with you for calling the police. The doctor told my mother you probably saved my life. I didn't get out of the hospital for three weeks, and then I had to stay in bed for another two.*

*Sheila, we had a great adventure and I will never forget it. I'm sorry you had to go home to your father, and I'm sorry I'm not there to help you through it. My mother is sending me away to boarding school. It's in the United States, over eleven hours away. Sheila, I'm going to miss you and I will always be your friend and I hope to see you again someday.*

*Love Kim*

Sheila folded the letter and put it away in her pocket. She wondered where Kim was and what she was doing. It was spring, but the nights were still cold. All Sheila had on was a light sweater and jeans with no coat, and she was quite chilly, but she didn't mind. She was free, and tomorrow she would find a job. Sheila noticed she was close to Golden Street. She knew exactly where she would sleep that night.

Twenty minutes later, Sheila placed the plastic bag on the grass. It was still a little damp. She sat on it and placed her back tightly on the trunk of her willow tree. She looked around. Not much had changed. Sheila drank her milk and had a cigarette to try and warm up. Then she smoked a joint to relax, and soon, she drifted to sleep.

When Sheila awoke the next morning, it was to the sound of children's laughter. The sun was shining brightly, and she knew it was going to be a good day. Sheila walked over to her old school. As she watched the children play, she wondered how many of these little children lived in a hellish home, and Sheila said a little prayer for them and Joann. She hoped her sister was okay. She went into the school, used the bathroom, and washed her face. Sheila emerged back into the sunshine with a hop in her step as she thought, *This is the first day of the rest of my life.*

Sheila walked through the gate, and in the daylight, she was disgusted by the project. It was so dirty and run-down. It was worse than Sheila remembered. She walked over to her old house and thought of her life and the horrors of unit 8. As she stood there staring, Sheila promised herself she would never allow herself to ever think about the things that had happened to her. Bobby, Hugette, Marty, and Paula were wiped from her mind for good.

Sheila jumped on a bus, and when the bus drove by a mall, she got off. She walked back to the mall and went to the drugstore. Sheila bought a hairbrush, toothbrush, and toothpaste, plus a few other things she would need. She stopped at a sporting goods store and bought a waterproof backpack to keep her only belongings dry. Then she went into a clothing store and bought two new sweaters, a pair of pants, and a warm jacket.

Sheila went into a bathroom in the mall and washed up. She brushed her teeth and hair and changed her clothes, just like old times. She was just about to place her old clothes in the backpack when she realized she didn't want anything from her past to remind her. She threw her old clothes into the garbage can. Looking in the mirror, she thought she looked good in her new clothes, but she needed to eat. She was getting hungry.

It was 12:30, and she hadn't eaten all day. She went into a restaurant and ordered a sandwich and fries with a big glass of milk. She counted her money. She was down to $273. Sheila knew she had to get a newspaper and look for a job.

Just as Sheila was leaving the restaurant, she bumped into a man. "Oh, I'm so sorry," Sheila told him. He looked down at the body and was enjoying it, until he reached her face. Then he blushed.

"Sheila, I'm so sorry. I didn't recognize you. I haven't seen you since you were around eleven. You sure have grown up. How's Rick doing?" the man said.

When Sheila heard Rick's name, she remembered him. It was Scott Stewart, Rick's friend from the project. Scott was a short man with a warm smile. He had dirty blond hair and green eyes, and he was always smiling—a very friendly person. He had always liked Sheila and her brother. He had heard the rumors around the project about the beatings from Bobby. He had seen the bruises on Rick, and he felt sorry for them all.

He invited her to come back into the restaurant for coffee, and she did. Where did Sheila have to be? And she had always liked Scott. Scott had gone to school with Rick, although, as Sheila discovered, they didn't see each other too often anymore. Scott hadn't lived in the project for three years. He loved to chat. That was obvious, and it gave her a chance to get a little information on her brother. She hadn't seen Rick in a very long time.

Scott informed Sheila that he lived with a girl named Brenda and they were engaged. It was apparent he loved her. Scott had come to the restaurant to meet Brenda. She was just finishing work, and they had some errands to do. Scott asked Sheila what she had been up to, and Sheila explained she was out looking for a job, any job that paid.

Sheila looked up and saw a girl walking over to the table. She looked nice, and she had a big smile on her face as she approached them. She bent down and kissed Scott as she reached the table. "Oh, sure, I leave you alone for a little while, and here I find you sitting with a beautiful woman," Brenda said in a teasing voice. *What beautiful woman?* Sheila thought. *It is only me and Scott.* She still had no idea what a beauty she had grown up to be.

Scott stood up and reached over to the next table. He brought over a chair so Brenda could join them. Brenda was a tall, thin girl with dark eyes and hair, and she had a lovely smile. "This is Sheila Parks," Scott said. "I went to school with her older brother, Rick. I almost knocked her over when I was coming into the restaurant to meet you, so I asked Sheila to join me for coffee while I waited for you," Scott explained.

"It's very nice to meet you, Sheila," Brenda told her as she reached over and shook Sheila's hand. Sheila liked her right away. She smiled back and shook Brenda's hand. Scott ordered a coffee for Brenda; she reached over and touched his arm softly in thanks. Sheila thought how sweet it was. Maybe there were good men out there, but not for Sheila. She never wanted one. Scott told Brenda that Sheila had just been telling him she was here looking for work. "What kind of work are you looking for, Sheila?" Brenda inquired.

"Well, all I've ever done is babysitting, but I'm willing to try anything. I need a job," Sheila explained. Sheila didn't want to go into any details with Scott and Brenda, and she thought it was time to go, before they asked too much. "Well, I should get going. It was very nice to see you, Scott, and to meet you, Brenda," Sheila said sincerely as she got up to leave. Brenda looked at Scott and then at Sheila. She smiled and pulled Sheila back into her chair softly.

"Not so fast, Sheila. I might be able to help you with a job. I'm the assistant manager at Snack Stop, the fast-food restaurant downstairs, and we are looking for someone right now. Cheryl, the manager, is putting an ad in the newspaper today. Do you want to go meet her?" Brenda inquired. Sheila beamed and nodded yes. Could this happen? she wondered. Could she find a job on the first day?

Brenda suggested that they finish their coffee, and she gave Scott a list of things to get at the grocery store. They would meet him there when they were finished speaking with Cheryl. Scott smiled and gulped the last of his coffee. He wished Sheila good luck, and he was gone.

The girls finished their coffee as Brenda told Sheila about the job. Basically, Sheila would take orders and do the cash, thirty-eight to forty-two hours a week. The pay was $5.95 an hour and she could eat free. It was more than Sheila had hoped for. She would have shoveled shit and been happy to be making money. When they finished their coffee, they left and went to meet Cheryl.

When they arrived, Sheila looked around. It reminded her of a cafeteria, and when she saw the uniforms the girls were wearing, she giggled to herself. They were bright orange with brown trim, and Sheila loved it all. Brenda told her to have a seat at one of the small tables, and she left. Five minutes later, Brenda arrived with a very large and very loud woman, and introduced them. She was about 250 pounds with long straight black hair and a warm smile. The uniform made her look enormous.

"So, Brenda tells me you are the person for the job, but I have a few questions," Cheryl said. She really intimidated Sheila, who sat there and trembled while trying to hide it. "Do you have any experience?" Cheryl asked. She was so nervous, and she tried to find the words. Then she thought of what the guidance counselor had told her, and the words came to her quickly.

"Not with this line of work, but I have years of working experience. I'm never late and always follow instructions carefully. I am a hard worker, and I would not let you or Brenda down if you give me a chance. You will not regret it for a moment," Sheila assured her. Cheryl sat there and listened. She didn't say a word for what seemed like an eternity. Finally, she looked at Brenda and smiled, and Brenda looked at Sheila and smiled.

"Sheila, you can start tomorrow morning at six AM. Brenda will train you. I have a good feeling about you, Sheila. Brenda, you can get her a uniform, and I'll see you tomorrow afternoon, when I come in to work." With that, Cheryl went back to her office. Sheila almost jumped out of her chair and kissed Brenda, but she thought better of it and just thanked her instead. Brenda went to get her a uniform and told her she needed to wear plain white shoes to work.

Sheila walked to the grocery store with Brenda; it was in the mall, not far from Snack Stop. Sheila thanked Brenda a hundred times by the time they arrived at the grocery store. "You got the job yourself, Sheila. I only introduced you to Cheryl," Brenda assured her. Just then, Scott yelled to them. He was in one of the checkout lines. They walked over to meet him.

"How did it go?" Scott asked. He looked at the smiles on their faces, and he knew. "That's great. I knew you'd get it," Scott said. Sheila thanked him for introducing her to Brenda. "My pleasure," he said. Brenda invited Sheila to come to their house for dinner, but she had to get shoes, and she couldn't wait to tell Joann about her new job, so she refused this time. They both tried to persuade her to change her mind, but they couldn't. Sheila told Brenda she would see her at 6:00 AM sharp, and with a wave, she left feeling very proud of herself.

Sheila looked at the time. It was two o'clock, and she had to meet Joann at her school by three, so she had to hurry. She ran to a pay phone and called to see which bus to take. Then she ran to the bus stop. Sheila arrived at the school with ten minutes to spare. She jumped off the bus and ran to their spot. She sat down on the bench and had a cigarette while she waited for Joann. For the first time that day, Sheila noticed how stiff her back and neck were from sleeping sitting up against her tree. *Not too much longer*, Sheila thought.

Joann arrived, and she was so happy to see her sister. Joann had barely slept because she was so worried about Sheila. They hugged and started to walk. Joann told Sheila how Bobby had acted when she got home the night before. Thinking it was Sheila, he came to the door screaming. When re realized it was Joann, he told her to get out of his sight. She had gone right to her room and stayed there all night. When their mother got home, Hugette and Bobby had a terrible fight.

That morning, when Joann went down to start breakfast, Hugette was sitting there with a black eye and bruised lip. She asked Joann if she knew where Sheila was, but Joann lied and said no. When Bobby came into the kitchen, he told Joann that Sheila was no longer part of the family, and her name was never to be spoken in his home again. Then he reminded Joann that she would be sixteen in less than two years, and she had better start thinking about where she would live. Then he left for work. Without saying a word to her mother, Joann had breakfast, cleaned the dishes, and left for school.

Joann looked at Sheila and realized that her sister looked better than okay. She had a sparkle in her eye that Joann had not seen in a long time. Sheila was wearing new clothes, and Joann thought she looked very pretty. "Where did you sleep last night, Sheila?" Joann asked.

"Under my willow tree," Sheila replied. She told her sister everything that had happened to her in the last twenty hours: walking and finding herself near Golden Street and going to her tree, somewhere she felt safe. Sheila told her about Scott and Brenda, and the best news of all, her new job. Joann was so happy for her sister. Sheila explained to Joann that she wasn't sure when she would be back to see her, because she wasn't sure what her hours would be at her new job.

They stopped at a pay phone so Sheila could look up the phone number for the Snack Stop and give it to Joann. Sheila told her only to use it in case of emergency. She said if she was not there, she could leave a message. Sheila would come to her when she got it. They were close to the building, and Joann had to go home and start dinner. The two sisters hugged, not knowing when they would see each other again. Sheila stood there watching her little sister walk away, and when she couldn't see her anymore, she walked to the bus stop.

Sheila went back to the mall to buy some white shoes for work, and a little battery-powered alarm clock. She went to the grocery store, where she bought a few apples and some milk for dinner and breakfast, and a newspaper. Now Sheila had to find a place to live. Sheila knew there would be no buses running at five in the morning, so she timed how long it would take her to walk. When Sheila got to her tree, it had taken her one hour and fifteen minutes. Sheila realized she was hungry, so she had her milk and two apples.

She had got some paper and a pen from her sister, so she sat down under her tree and figured out her finances. At forty hours a week and $5.95 an hour, she would make $238 a week. That would be $952 a month, approximately. Sheila figured she could afford between $350 and $400 a month for rent. She got out the newspaper and looked up some rooms for rent. They were all around $250 a month, so she felt relieved.

Sheila smoked a joint to calm her nerves. It was starting to get dark, so she set her alarm clock for 3:30 AM and tried to get some sleep. She pushed her back into the trunk of her tree and hugged her legs. It was still scary outside alone at night, but things were looking a lot better than the night before. Sheila had a job now, and it was only a matter of time before she would have a bed to sleep in. Soon, she drifted off to sleep.

When she awoke the next morning, it was still dark. The sound of the alarm clock echoed in the silence. Sheila quickly turned it off and sat there quietly, in case anyone was out there and heard it. Once she was sure nobody was around, she packed up her things and, throwing her backpack over her shoulder, she started on her walk. A few blocks from the mall there was a twenty-four-hour gas station. She used the bathroom to wash her hair and get ready for work.

Sheila came out of the bathroom with wet hair, wearing her uniform. The sun was rising, and the air was starting to warm up. She hoped her hair would be dry by the time she got to work. When she handed the clerk back the key to the bathroom, he gave her a strange look. Sheila bought a coffee and some smokes, and gave him a big smile. He smiled back, and she knew he wouldn't say a word. Sheila looked at the clock. It was 5:15 AM, so she started to walk the short distance to work, eating an apple as she went.

When Brenda arrived at the Snack Stop, Sheila was standing there waiting. Brenda looked at her watch—it was only 5:35 AM—and she smiled at Sheila. Brenda unlocked the door, and they went in. Brenda turned on the grill and the fryers and went to put her uniform on. When she came out, she handed Sheila a form and told her to fill it out.

Sheila looked at it with terrified expression that Brenda noticed. She assured Sheila that it was just a standard employee form: name, address, phone number, social insurance number, and emergency notification.

Sheila filled in her name and social insurance number and stared at the rest of the questions. *I can't put in willow tree in park for my address*, Sheila thought. Brenda came over and looked at the form. It was almost blank. Brenda told Sheila she would help her with it after their shift, and they started to work.

When Cheryl arrived at 1:00 PM, Sheila looked as if she had been working there for years. She had the cash register mastered, and she was always doing something, wiping down a counter or cleaning the tables. She handled the customers with a cheerful manner. Cheryl was impressed, and when she spoke to Brenda, she was sure she had made the right decision.

Brenda had been shocked by how easy it was to train Sheila. She only had to say something once and Sheila had it down pat. Sheila had been raised in a home where, if you missed any instructions, you would get a beating, so she had learned to pay attention instinctively. She had also developed an excellent memory. Most importantly, Sheila always kept working. She was always terrified to disappoint anyone who was in a position of authority over her, another character trait she'd developed in her childhood.

Brenda was very surprised how mature Sheila was for her age, and the best part, Brenda thought, was she was fun to work with. She liked to be around Sheila. For Sheila's part, in the last two days she had been more relaxed than she could remember. She wasn't always looking over her shoulder to see if her father was coming. She had never felt so free, and she loved it. Brenda invited Sheila to come for dinner, and this time, Sheila accepted. She was in no hurry to go to the willow tree where it was cold and lonely.

When they arrived at Brenda's place, Sheila was uneasy, realizing the house was a few blocks from her parents' apartment building. But she pushed the thought from her mind and went in. It was a four-bedroom house. Brenda and Scott rented a big basement bedroom, and a friend of theirs named Tony owned the house. Tony's bedroom was downstairs in the basement as well, and there were two bedrooms upstairs. A guy named Jack lived in one, but he was away visiting his parents in another province. Sheila wasn't sure about the last one, because Brenda didn't mention it.

The house was nicely furnished, and it had a warm feeling to it. Brenda and Sheila chatted while they cooked dinner, and they laughed a lot. Then, Brenda asked Sheila a question that made her feel uncomfortable. "So Sheila, do you live with your parents?" Brenda said innocently. Sheila felt torn. She hated the direction of the conversation, but she wasn't ready to leave. She was having fun.

"No," she said. "I just moved out a couple of days ago. That's why I was looking for a job. I'm staying with a friend right now, until I find a place," Sheila lied. She would never admit to anyone she was sleeping under a tree. "I don't speak to my parents, Brenda. Can we just leave it at that?" Sheila pleaded as her eyes filled with tears. She quickly composed herself and hoped Brenda hadn't noticed. Brenda had, but she never let on.

"Sure," Brenda answered with a smile. She had an idea, but she would wait to speak to Scott before she told Sheila. Dinner was just about ready, so Brenda suggested they sit in the living room and relax while they waited for Scott. As Brenda sat on the sofa, she reached under the side table and pulled out a cigar box. She opened it. It was full of pot. When Sheila saw it, she smiled and pulled a joint out of her sock. They both started to laugh.

Just then, Scott arrived. "What's so funny, ladies?" he asked. Sheila felt so grown-up being called a lady. She listened as Brenda explained. Scott playfully took Sheila's joint and lit it. When they were finished, they went into the kitchen and ate their dinner. Sheila thought it was the most enjoyable dinner she had ever experienced. As soon as they were finished, Sheila jumped up and started to clear the table.

"What are you doing, Sheila? We did the cooking, so Scott will do the cleaning. It's only fair. Put that down and let's get a beer. I'll roll a joint for us for when Scott is done with the dishes," Brenda instructed. Sheila did what she was told, but she was in shock at the thought of a man doing dishes. She had never heard of such a thing. She couldn't ever picture her father or brothers doing women's work, but she definitely enjoyed the thought. Scott didn't even seem to mind; he just got up and got started cleaning while he whistled a happy tune.

Brenda put on the television and retrieved her box from under the table. She plopped on the floor with her legs crossed. Scott came in, and they sat on the floor smoking the joint as they watched television.

Brenda suggested that they play cards, and they all agreed. As they were going into kitchen, Brenda told Sheila to get another beer for everyone, and she and Scott would be right back. They had to talk for a minute. Brenda grabbed Scott by the arm, and they went to their room in the basement.

Sheila did as she was asked and got three beers from the fridge. She placed them on the table. Sheila heard the front door close, and a moment later a very short, balding chubby man came into the kitchen. It was Tony. He owned the house; he was a divorced man in his late thirties who was always trying to pick up young girls. Tony was sleazy but harmless. He wouldn't hurt a fly, and he knew what no meant. He stopped in his tracks when he saw Sheila. He looked her up and down, and he had an instant crush on her.

Just then, Brenda and Scott came back into the kitchen and introduced everyone. Tony flashed Sheila a big smile and shook her hand. Sheila smiled back and returned the shake. "We were just about to start playing cards. Do you want to join us?" Brenda asked him. He accepted, grabbing a seat next to Sheila. They taught her how to play euchre, and they all had a great time.

Sheila got up to use the bathroom, feeling a little woozy. Enough beer, she thought. When she returned, Sheila looked out the window and saw it was dark out. She had to get going. She thanked Brenda and Scott, and told Tony it was nice to meet him, and she was just about to leave when Tony asked her to wait for a minute.

"Brenda and Scott were just telling me that you are looking for a place to live. There is a free bedroom upstairs if you want, Sheila. If you paid me $100 a month and supplied your own food, I would be happy with that. What do you think?" Tony asked. Sheila couldn't believe it—$100. All the ads she'd seen were for over $200 a month. Sheila thought she would feel safe here with Brenda and Scott, and she needed a roof over her head.

"When could I move in?" Sheila inquired. Tony told her tonight, and Sheila bent down and pulled the money out of her sock. Sheila paid him two months' rent in advance. Tony was even happier when he had two hundred dollars in his hand. Everyone thought it was a perfect plan. Sheila was ecstatic, and Brenda brought her up to see her knew room.

*Behind the Drapes*

It turned out to be furnished, and Sheila almost cried. There was a bed, a desk with a chair, a lamp, two dressers, and an armchair. Sheila thought it was the most beautiful room she had ever seen. It was dirty, but Brenda promised to help her clean everything the next day after work. They went back to the kitchen and played two more games of cards, then decided it was time for bed. Then, Sheila went to her room. She couldn't wait to tell Joann about her new room and how close to her she would be living. Sheila slept in a bed that night and cried herself to sleep. For the first time in her life, Sheila cried happy tears.

# Chapter 13

Brenda and Sheila were in a hurry to get out of work. Brenda was balancing the cash, while Sheila was running around making sure everything was done for Cheryl before they left. They were having a party that night, and they couldn't wait to get home. They had been living and working together six months now, and they had become very good friends. They were having a Halloween party. Sheila had never been to one, and she was very excited.

Sheila loved her home and her job. She worked Monday to Friday, 6:00 AM to 2:00 PM. She had got a raise a few months back and now she was receiving medical and dental insurance. She saw Joann every Saturday. Joann would come over after she finished her housecleaning and visit for the rest of the afternoon. They always had such nice visits.

Bobby had never come after Joann the way he had with Sheila. Sheila was happy about that, but it made her angry with herself. Had she done something to deserve it? Something to make him do it, or maybe she encouraged him in some way she wasn't aware of? As always, Sheila pushed the thoughts from her mind with the help of drugs and alcohol. Even though Sheila was only sixteen, all her friends were in their twenties, and no one really thought of Sheila as a child. She always just partied along with them.

"Okay, you two, get out of here, and I'll see you at about ten thirty tonight; as soon as I can get out of here, I'll be right over," Cheryl told Sheila and Brenda. They thanked Cheryl, grabbed their stuff, and went to the front of the mall to hail a cab. They had groceries Sheila and Brenda had bought on their lunch breaks, and they were not about to carry them on the bus. Brenda told Sheila to go to the curb and wave down a cab. Within ten seconds, there were two, arguing who had got there first. Sheila still had no idea how beautiful she was, but Brenda could see it fine, and she smiled as she placed her bags into the backseat of one of the cabs. Sheila followed her.

Once Sheila and Brenda had all the food cooked and the decorations up, they shared a joint and had a beer. After they'd relaxed for an hour, they went to put on their costumes. Brenda dressed as a witch and Sheila dressed as a cat. They both looked great. Scott arrived then, and he raced downstairs to get dressed. He returned as Spiderman. He entered the room, picked up Brenda, and started spinning her around, begging her not to cast an evil spell on him. They all laughed.

Sheila had never wanted a man in her life, but after spending the last six months with Brenda and Scott, she was starting to think maybe she was wrong. Maybe all men were not like her father. Maybe there were some more out there like her uncle Pierre and Scott. Sheila was pulled from her thoughts as she heard Scott calling her name.

"Sheila! Hello, Sheila! Are you there?" Scott was calling.

"Sorry Scott. I guess I was lost in my thoughts," Sheila said.

"That's okay. Did you hear what I said? I ran into your brother Rick today. I told him you were living here and invited him to come over tonight for the party. He said he would try and make it, and he told me to tell you he said hi," Scott told her. Sheila realized she hadn't seen her brother since he had moved into Ralph's place. She hoped he would show up.

People started to arrive. The party was in full swing when Sheila felt someone hug her from behind. She turned to see Rick standing there. Sheila jumped into his arms and gave him a big kiss. "It's so good to see you, Rick!" Sheila hollered over the loud music and screaming people.

She ran to the fridge, got him a beer, and offered him something to eat.

"I'm not hungry, but could I get a beer for Ralph? I brought him with me," Rick said. Sheila grabbed another beer, and they went to find Ralph. He gave Sheila a hug when he saw her, and the three of them tried to chat over the noise. "Is there somewhere we could go and talk where it's a little quieter?" Rick asked. Sheila brought the two of them to her room.

Sheila was very proud of her room; she and Brenda had fixed it so nice. It was the nicest room Sheila had ever had, and she was happy to show them. They both told her it was great, and it made Sheila very happy to hear it. Rick sat in the armchair and Ralph sat on the chair by the desk. Sheila pulled a joint out of her nightstand and asked the boys to join her. "You sure have grown up, Sheila," Rick commented.

"You sure look good, too," Ralph added. Rick told Ralph to stay away from his little sister, and they laughed, sharing the joint.

When Sheila went downstairs to get more beer, the party was still going strong. She felt someone staring at her, and she saw a guy sitting in the kitchen with Tony. They were talking, and the guy was smiling at her. It was no one she knew, and men always stared at her, so she didn't pay any attention. She started back up the stairs to her room.

"Are you going to spend the whole night in your room, Sheila?" Tony hollered after her. Sheila came back down and told Tony her brother was here, and she hadn't seen him in years. She needed to talk to him, and it was too loud downstairs. She assured Tony she would be down soon. When Sheila got back to her room, Ralph had some white powder out on her desk.

"Do you want some, Sheila?" Ralph inquired. Sheila didn't even know what it was, but she didn't want to appear like a child, so she nodded yes and handed everyone a beer. Sheila sat back on her bed. She and Rick chatted about Joann, and life. They never spoke about their parents. Sheila watched Ralph chopping the white stuff and neatly putting it into lines on the desk surface.

Ralph asked Rick for a bill, and Rick pulled out of his pocket the largest amount of money Sheila had ever seen. There must have been thousands of dollars. Sheila watched as Rick peeled a crisp hundred off the roll. There was another one right underneath. It appeared they were all hundred-dollar bills, and the roll was thicker than the end of a baseball bat. Rick handed Ralph the bill, and he rolled it up.

Ralph placed the rolled bill on one of the lines of white stuff, bent down, and put the other end of the bill to his nose. He sniffed the powder up into his nose. Sheila was confused, and Rick noticed the look on her face and he explained. Rick told her it was cocaine, and it was wonderful. He explained that he sold it, and that's how he made all the money. He told Sheila she would love it, and he told her how to do it.

Sheila did as Rick instructed and went to the desk, taking the bill from Ralph. She sniffed up a line. It burned at first. Two minutes later, Sheila felt better than she had her whole life. She was happy in a way she had never felt before. They stayed in her room and missed the whole party. They drank and smoked and sniffed cocaine into the wee hours of the morning, and when Sheila went down to walk Rick and Ralph to the door, the party was over. Everyone was gone.

The next day, when Sheila awoke, her head felt as if it might explode. She looked at the clock and was shocked to see it was 12:15 PM. It was the worst hangover she had experienced in the last six months, and Joann would be there in less than two hours. She dragged herself out of bed and opened her door to go to have a shower. She noticed the door across the hall was opened. It had never been open in all the time Sheila had lived there. Sheila peeked in, but there was no one there, so she went and had a shower.

Sheila felt a little better after a shower. She dressed and went down to the kitchen. As she reached the bottom of the stairs, all she could hear was laughter, and it brought joy to her soul. She walked in and saw Brenda, Scott, Tony, and the guy who'd been sitting with Tony last night at the party. The guy was telling a story, and everyone was laughing hysterically.

Sheila walked to the coffee pot and poured herself a cup of coffee. She said good morning to everyone as she sat at the table. "Well, how you feeling, missy? Everyone missed you last night. Cheryl was sorry she missed you. It was a really good party," Brenda said. Before Sheila could respond, the new guy got up and walked around the table. He stood beside Sheila with an outreached hand.

"Jack Currin is my name. It's nice to finally meet my new roommate," the guy told Sheila. She stood up, shook his hand, and smiled. At that moment, Jack fell in love with Sheila, and vowed to himself that she would be his. Jack appeared to be a gentleman. He kept his eyes on hers. Sheila was impressed because he was one of the first men who had not stared at her chest. Jack had checked out Sheila's luscious figure, but he was smart enough to be discreet.

"It's nice to meet you as well," Sheila replied. Jack was twenty-five years old, and he was a carpenter. He was tall and thin, with dark hair and hazel eyes that he kept covered with dark glasses. One quality that Sheila noticed right away and loved was Jack's sense of humor. He was always making everyone laugh, and he seemed really laid back. After the stress that had been Sheila's existence, she appreciated laughter. Sheila thought she enjoyed the atmosphere in the house much better with him there. She was glad he was back.

Brenda rolled a joint, and they had coffee and talked and laughed. Sheila could not remember when she had laughed so much. Jack had the best stories. Scott was sitting next to Jack, and when Scott offered him the joint, Jack didn't take any. He just passed it to Tony. Sheila was surprised. She hadn't met any of Brenda and Scott's friends that didn't smoke dope. Jack didn't seem to mind everyone else smoking, though. Just then, there was a knock at the door. Sheila remembered Joann, and she ran to get it.

Joann was standing there, all bundled up at the door; it was November first, and it was cold. Joann thought her sister looked terrible today. *Another hangover*, she thought. She was getting used to seeing Sheila like that. Sheila invited her in and ran to get her coat. They were going out for lunch and shopping. Joann and Sheila walked to the bus stop. Sheila told her all about seeing Rick, and what he had been up to. As per Rick's instructions, Sheila gave Joann his phone number and told her to call if she needed anything.

They were standing at the bus stop when a blue truck pulled up. It was Jack. "Need a ride, ladies?" he inquired. It was cold, so Sheila said yes, and they climbed in. "Where to?" he asked them, and Sheila told him of their plans. She introduced Jack and Joann. He told them stories and had them laughing all the way to the mall. When they arrived, Jack said he was hungry and asked if he could join them. Sheila looked at Joann, and she smiled. Joann enjoyed Jack's company as much as Sheila did. He parked the truck, and they went into the mall.

They were seated at a nice corner table, and they had a wonderful afternoon. As it turned out, their lunch lasted three and a half hours. Joann looked at her watch, which Sheila had bought for her. Sheila always bought Joann little things whenever she could. "I have to go now, Sheila. I'm going to be late if I don't leave now," Joann said in a panicked voice.

"It's okay, Joann. I'll give you a lift. Don't worry, I'm a fast driver," Jack assured her. He had asked Scott about Sheila, so he knew a little about her background. He didn't want to be the cause of any trouble for Sheila or her sister. Sheila glanced at him with a relieved look in her eyes. She thanked him and asked the waitress for the bill.

When the waitress came back and put the bill on the table, Jack grabbed it. Sheila tried to protest, but he wouldn't hear of it. He paid for everyone's lunch, and they thanked him several times on the way to Joann's place. Jack got Joann home with five minutes to spare. She jumped out and told Sheila that she would see her next Saturday. Then she thanked Jack one last time for lunch and the ride, and ran into the building.

Sheila watched Jack silently as they drove home. She had learned a lot about him at lunch. He was the youngest of two children, and his parents lived in British Columbia. That's where Jack had been the last eight months, building his parents' a new home. His family was very close and he loved his parents very much. From what Sheila gathered, he had loving and supportive parents. She wondered how different she would have been if she'd had different parents. Sheila liked Jack very much, she decided. He was very nice to her and her sister.

That night, everyone was pretty tired from the night before, so they decided to watch movies and order pizza. Tony had a date, and he was already gone, so that left Brenda, Scott, Jack, and Sheila. Jack and Scott left to get movies and pizza, and Brenda and Sheila agreed to tackle the dishes from the night before. The girls chatted and started the dishes. Then Brenda got serious and gave Sheila a little friendly advice.

"Sheila, you know I care about you, and sometimes I forget you are only sixteen. I just wanted to warn you that Scott told me some things about your brother Rick this morning. I know he does cocaine and maybe sells it. It's a bad drug, Sheila, and it can ruin your life if you're not careful. I'm not your mother, and I don't want to preach, but you have to promise me you will not get hooked on that stuff."

"I promise, Brenda. I just tried it last night, that's all. I'm not going to do anything foolish. You have helped me out so much, and I won't let you down," Sheila assured her. Brenda smiled. They finished the dishes and relaxed on the sofa with a joint while they waited for the boys to get back.

Jack and Scott arrived, and they had their pizza and watched a movie. Scott was falling asleep on the couch, and Brenda told him to go to bed. He got up and went downstairs. When the movie was over, Brenda said goodnight and went to bed. Jack got up and got another beer, and brought one out for Sheila. He put in another movie and stretched out on the floor. Sheila sat on the sofa and wondered if Jack would make a pass at her now that they were alone, but he never moved. When the movie was over, Jack said goodnight to Sheila and went to bed.

Sheila sat there on the sofa, feeling lonely. She thought about Brenda and Scott and the relationship they had. They always seemed so happy. She thought about Jack and how nice he had been to her, and how he made her laugh. Sheila felt tears rolling down her face, and for the first time in her life, she wanted to go to a man and take care of him. Sheila knew she would never enjoy it, but she wanted to do it for Jack.

Sheila got up, turned off the television and the lights, and headed up the stairs. Sheila Parks did not want to be alone anymore. She wanted a man to take care of her and keep her safe. When she got to the end of the hallway, she looked from her door to Jack's. After a moment, she opened Jack's door and walked in.

Jack was sitting on his bed, setting his alarm clock. He looked startled but happy when he saw Sheila standing there. Sheila stood frozen, not knowing if she should stay or go. Then slowly one by one Sheila undid the buttons of her blouse until it fell from her shoulders and landed on the ground.

Jack stood up. A smile came across his face as he walked over to Sheila. "Sheila, I've wanted to be with you since the moment I met you, but you are only sixteen, and I'm twenty-five. I know it's not right for me to be with you, but I do want you. Sheila, are you sure that this is what you want?" Sheila nodded yes, and he took her by the hand and walked her to the bed.

Jack kissed her and caressed her softly and told her how beautiful she was. Jack never hurt her, and he was as gentle as could be as he made love to her. When he was finished, he rolled off her and lay there for a moment. Then he rolled back and held her. Sheila didn't enjoy it, but she pretended she did, and she didn't regret it for a moment. Lying there with Jack, feeling his arms wrapped around her, and knowing he was happy with her was worth it, Sheila thought. She drifted off to sleep, feeling safe and happy.

The next morning, Sheila awoke to feeling Jack's arms around her, and she was still happy with her decision. Jack started to kiss her and tell her how happy he was. They lay there talking and giggling for hours, until finally they got up and went down for coffee. They walked into the kitchen holding hands, and Brenda, Scott, Tony, and his date were already up and finishing breakfast. Tony introduced his date to Sheila and Jack. Her name was Wendy. She worked for Tony, and she had the most annoying voice any of them had ever heard. However, she was a nice girl.

Sheila was about to go for the coffee pot when Jack told her to sit down. He would get coffee for both of them. Sheila thought she could really get used to being treated like this, and she sat down with a big smile. Brenda looked from Sheila to Jack and waited for one of them to explain, but neither of them offered any explanation. Jack brought Sheila her coffee and asked her if she wanted to go out for breakfast. She said yes, and picking up her coffee, she went to have a shower.

"Yes, Sheila and I are together, and I don't want anyone to say a word about it. I would never do anything to hurt her, and I will always take care of her," Jack announced after Sheila had left the room. They all looked up at him with disappointed looks on their faces. Only Brenda had the nerve to say what they were all thinking.

"Jack, she is too young. She is only sixteen years old. She is too young to know what she wants. You are making a big mistake," Brenda said. Jack told her she was wrong and climbed the stairs to his room. He sat on his bed fuming and thought how he would prove them all wrong. Sheila would be happy. She came into the room then, wrapped in a towel, looking so beautiful and so young. He realized, only for a second, that Brenda could be right.

# Chapter 14

Sheila woke with Jack's arms around her. The sun was shining in through the opened drapes, and she knew it would be a good day. She turned to kiss Jack good morning and saw him smiling at her. He gave her that look, and she shook her head no. She hated doing it, especially in the morning when she had not consumed any drugs or alcohol. He pleaded, and Sheila gave in, hoping he would be finished soon.

Sheila climbed into the shower, scrubbed herself down, and cried. She didn't know why she was crying. Jack was so good to her, but she knew she didn't love him the way he loved her, and she didn't know what to do. Sheila wondered if she was being selfish and unfair to Jack by staying with him. She didn't know if she even wanted to stay. She composed herself and finished her shower. She got changed into her work uniform and went downstairs for breakfast. Brenda was already their whistling and cooking eggs.

"Do you want some scrambled eggs, Sheila? There are more than enough," Brenda asked. She hungrily accepted. The girls had breakfast together and chatted. Jack finally appeared, looking a little hung-over, and poured himself some coffee. Sheila had discovered over the last six months that although Jack didn't do any drugs, he made up for it drinking alcohol. He loved his beer. Jack offered them a ride to work, as usual, and Sheila accepted.

Jack worked for himself, so he had a flexible schedule. Sheila cleaned up the kitchen while Brenda changed into her uniform, and then they left. A couple of blocks from work, Sheila asked Jack to pull over and asked Brenda if she would mind walking the last few blocks with her. It was a beautiful spring day, and Sheila wanted some fresh air. Brenda looked at her watch. They had lots of time, so she agreed. The moment Sheila stepped out of the truck she threw up her breakfast and almost fainted. Brenda caught her just in time.

Jack and Brenda agreed that Sheila was sick, and she should go home to bed. After much protest from Sheila, she agreed. They drove Brenda to work, and then Jack drove Sheila home. She went straight to bed. By noon, she still couldn't keep water down, so Jack convinced her to go to the doctor. She phoned her family doctor, and he told Sheila to come in right away. Jack wrapped her in a blanket, and off they went.

Sheila came out of the examining room white as a ghost and walked right past Jack, out the door. Jack ran after her. He caught up to her at the elevators, and when he turned her around, her face was covered in tears. He pulled her close and hugged her, imagining the worst. The elevator door opened, and they walked. Sheila never said a word until they were sitting in the truck.

"My doctor thinks I'm pregnant, Jack," she blurted out. Sheila started to cry, and he sat there shocked. "You don't need to worry, Jack. I'll take care of everything myself. I would never make you do something you're not ready for. I don't even know what I want to do," Sheila explained through her tears. Finally, he reached over, hugged her, and told her everything was going to be okay. They stayed like that, holding each other for a long time.

Finally, Jack pulled away and told her first and foremost not to worry until they knew for sure. Sheila had told him the doctor would call with the test results within twenty-four hours. However, Jack knew she was pregnant. That morning, when he had made love to her, she had felt different inside, and he just knew. When Jack pulled into the driveway, they both got out of the truck in silence, and Sheila went right back to bed. She didn't even come down for dinner, and when Brenda went up to check on her, she pretended to be asleep.

*Behind the Drapes*

That night when Jack went to bed, he brought Sheila a cup of tea and held her close. Neither of them got a moment of sleep. They just lay there waiting until morning came. The moment the sun came up, Sheila turned on her side and looked at Jack. She knew she didn't love him, not the way she should. Whatever decision she made, she had to assume she would be alone.

The doctor's office called at 3:15 PM, and they confirmed it. Sheila was pregnant. Sheila and Jack had both stayed home from work that day, and they were alone when they got the news. Sheila never shed one tear. She had thought long and hard the night before, and she was going to have the baby, with or without Jack's help. Sheila thanked the nurse for calling, took Jack by the hand, and led him to the sofa. They sat down.

"Jack, I'm pregnant, and please don't say a word. I've given it a lot of thought, and I am having this baby and I'm happy about it. I know it won't be easy, but I want to do it. You don't have to be a part of this if you don't want. I will never come to you for money, even if I have to live on welfare." They both knew how much Sheila hated the thought of being on welfare.

"I want this baby to have a happy childhood, Jack. Not like the one I had." Sheila had never told Jack too much about her childhood, but he was a smart man, and he knew it had been rough. She never spoke to her parents, and he was in the same bed with her when she awoke screaming with her nightmares.

"May I speak now, Sheila?" Jack asked, and she nodded yes. Jack picked up her hand and held it. "Sheila, I love you, and I've told you I would take care of you, and I meant it. I want to be a part of your life and the baby's. Sheila, I want to marry you, and I know you've told me in the past that you never want to get married, and I won't push you, but that is how I feel." Sheila said no to the marriage proposal, which Jack had expected. But she was happy to try and raise the baby together.

Sheila didn't love Jack the way he loved her, but the way she saw it, she could be a single parent now or try to make it work with Jack, and if it didn't work out, she would be a single parent later. She had to try and make it work for the baby, and she didn't want to live on welfare.

Sheila walked up to her room, took her pot out of her nightstand, and put it on the table. Jack looked at her, and she told him not to worry, it was for Brenda. If Sheila was going to have a baby, she was going to have a healthy one. Sheila never touched drugs or alcohol for her whole pregnancy.

That Saturday when Joann came for her visit, Jack took them out to a really nice restaurant for lunch. Joann noticed her sister didn't look hung-over this weekend. Joann thought she looked beautiful. It had been a long time since Joann had seen her sister without a hangover on a Saturday afternoon. As Joann looked more closely, she realized that Sheila was happier than she had seen her in months. Joann was aware of Sheila confused thoughts in regard to her life with Jack. Joann liked Jack, but her sister's feelings were more important to her.

Jack handed Joann a menu and asked her, "What are you having, Aunt Joann?" Joann gave Jack a confused look, and Sheila told her then about the baby. She was so happy for them. Jack was obviously very happy about the baby, or maybe it was because he thought with a baby, he would always have Sheila, Joann wondered. Joann told them how happy she was for them, and Sheila filled her in on the plans they had made.

They didn't want to raise the baby in a party house. They had to move. They were going to look for an apartment for now. Jack assured Joann she was always welcome, no matter where they lived. Sheila was going to continue to work for a while longer, and Jack planned to concentrate more time and effort into his business. No wife of Jack's would ever work, and he made that perfectly clear. For the time, Sheila was happy with the thought of staying home with the baby. The three of them had a wonderful lunch, and then Jack took them shopping and bought them each a new watch.

Brenda was excited with the news, until she realized they were going to move. Brenda and Sheila had become close friends, despite the difference in their ages. Brenda was going to miss her. She was happy to hear Sheila would keep working for now. Though, Brenda was sure they would never be as close again; it would never be the same. Brenda had been quite pleased when Sheila gave her the drugs. Brenda new Sheila would be a good mother. Sheila wasn't so sure, and she worried, but she knew she would never be like her parents.

Scott congratulated them both. He asked if Rick knew, and Sheila told him no. She asked him not to say anything if he ran into him.

*Behind the Drapes*

Sheila wanted to tell him herself. She had only seen Rick once since Halloween, and he had never even met Jack. Sheila thought she would tell him soon.

Tony was sorry to see them go, but he already had more people to move in, and, as it turned out, he would be getting more rent from the new tenants, so he was happy. He told them to drop by anytime, and told them he would help them move. Scott and Brenda offered to help them move as well. Sheila would miss them all, especially Brenda and Scott. She owed them so much. In many ways, Sheila always thought of Brenda as a big sister. She hoped they wouldn't lose their friendship.

The day they moved was a beautiful sunny day, and they had lots of people to help. They had found an apartment within three weeks that was big and cheap, a two bedroom on the ground floor. The back entrance of the building led right to a park with a path that led right to a beach. Sheila loved it, and she was excited about the move. It was further for Joann to get to, but Jack assured Sheila he would go pick her up anytime Sheila wanted, which made her happy.

Jack, Scott, and Tony moved in the big furniture, while Sheila and Brenda unpacked boxes. The girls had come the day before with Joann and cleaned it top to bottom. Brenda and Joann did most of the work. Now that Sheila was pregnant, no one let her do anything. Sheila loved the attention and was truly enjoying her pregnancy, except for the morning sickness, but the doctor had assured her it would pass. He said everything looked good. Sheila was going to see an obstetrician the following week.

By seven o'clock that evening, the entire apartment was unpacked. The bed had been set up and made, the dishes unpacked, and even the pictures were hung on the wall. Sheila loved pictures. When she was young, her home had seemed so empty and bare, like her life. Now, Sheila wanted her walls filled with pictures and colour, and hopefully her life would follow suit.

They ordered pizza for everyone for helping. By nine o'clock that night, Sheila and Jack were finally alone in their new home. Sheila cleaned up the plates from the pizza, and Jack collected the empty beer bottles. Sheila stood in her new kitchen and started to cry. "What's wrong, Sheila?" Jack inquired.

Sheila looked at him with a big smile, and, still crying, she managed to say, "I'm so happy." Jack reached out and pulled her tight against him. Sheila held Jack close and thought maybe she could love him. At least, she would try. They went and curled up on the sofa and watched television together. As Sheila looked around the room, she was so pleased with what she saw. She and Brenda had done a great job with the decorating. Sheila loved her new home.

Joann came into the apartment Saturday afternoon, and she loved it. She was very excited and pleased for her sister. It was not the greatest apartment, but it was certainly the nicest place Joann had ever seen. There were so many pictures on the walls, plus Sheila and Brenda had gone to a few garage sales and bought some lamps and an old table set for the apartment. It felt like a home. Joann never wanted to leave.

Every Saturday, Jack took Sheila and Joann out to lunch. It had become a tradition, but today Sheila wanted to stay in and cook in her new kitchen. She made them a terrific lunch, and they sat at the table for hours talking. Jack had them laughing so hard, Joann choked on her milk. When the time came that Joann had to leave, Jack and Sheila drove her home and told her they would see her the following Saturday. Jack stopped and picked Sheila up some ice cream on the way home.

# Chapter 15

Jack kissed Sheila, and he left for work. Sheila went to the kitchen and started to clean up from breakfast. Sheila had been finished with work for six weeks now, and she was enjoying staying home. Sheila's belly was big. She was due in two weeks, and she was getting very excited for the baby to come. Sheila was washing the dishes and thinking of everything she had to do that day, when she heard banging at the door.

She went to the door and looked through the peephole. All she could see was Joann standing there crying, and there was someone else, but she couldn't make out who it was. Sheila flung open the door and was shocked to see Hugette standing there with Joann. Sheila grabbed her sister, instinctively pulling Joann into the apartment to protect her. "What's wrong?" Sheila asked her sister.

"Can I come in for a minute, Sheila?" Hugette inquired. Sheila reluctantly nodded, and she and Joann stepped aside to let her in. It was obvious Hugette had recently been beaten by Bobby. She was all bruised and swollen, and this time she had a cast on her arm. "I'm leaving your father, and I have a place to stay, but there is no room for Joann. She has nowhere to go. Can she stay with you?" Hugette blurted out.

"Joann can always stay with me," Sheila answered with hatred in her voice. Hearing this, Hugette opened the door and left without even saying bye, or asking about Sheila's obvious pregnancy. Joann was crying, and Sheila couldn't get any information right now, so she brought Joann into the kitchen, made her a cup of tea, and let her cry it out. Finally, Joann looked up at her sister and told her she was sorry.

"For what Joann? Sorry for what!" Sheila demanded. "For having parents who don't care about you? There is nothing for you to be sorry about. You will move in here, Joann. Think about it. It's over. You are out and you didn't have to wait until you were sixteen, although you will have to share a room with the baby," Sheila said. Joann didn't care. She would have slept on the floor, and she realized her sister was right. It was over. Joann started to laugh, and Sheila joined in. Now, Sheila thought, she just had to break the news to Jack.

Joann and Sheila spent the day together. They tidied up the house, and Joann helped Sheila wash the bedding for the crib and set it up. Joann told Sheila everything that had happened the night before. Bobby had come home in an awful mood, and Hugette was whining about going to bingo. He had just flipped out and beat her up. The next morning, after Bobby went to work, Hugette told Joann she had to help her get dressed and take her to the hospital.

Sure enough, Bobby had broken Hugette's arm and given her a slight concussion. When they were leaving the hospital, Hugette had stopped at a pay phone and made a few calls. She walked up to Joann and told her she was not going home. She was going to stay with her cousin, and there was no room for Joann. Hugette asked her if she had anywhere to go, and when Joann said no, Hugette had demanded to know Sheila's address. They had taken the bus to Sheila's in silence, and Sheila knew the rest.

Sheila scolded her sister for saying she had nowhere to go. Sheila reminded her that she always had a place to go as long as Sheila was alive. Just then, the phone started to ring, and Sheila went to pick it up. It was Jack calling to check on her. Sheila told him everything that had transpired, and when she hung up, she walked up to Joann and told her what Jack had said. He was happy to have his adopted little sister moving in. Sheila and Joann started to cry, happy tears.

That night when Jack got home from work, he told Joann she could stay for as long as she wanted. Jack had even stopped and bought her a mattress and box spring on the way home. The three of them had dinner and laughed as Jack told them stories of his day. Sheila and Joann did the dinner dishes, and Jack took them out for ice cream. Even though it was the end of October, Sheila was still craving ice cream.

That evening, Sheila and Joann made up her new bed next to the crib, and they sat and watched television together. Joann thought she had never been more relaxed. Sheila looked over at her sister, and, seeing the smile on her face, she knew she didn't have to worry about Joann anymore. Bobby and Hugette could finally be forgotten about completely. Now that Joann was not living there anymore, Sheila could stop worrying about what he might do.

The next day, Jack had his breakfast and left for work. Joann decided to take the day off school and get adjusted. Sheila phoned and found out what buses she had to take to school, and later that morning, they rode the bus to school to time the trip. They stopped at the mall, and Sheila bought Joann some new clothes. She only had what she was wearing, and there was no way they were going to the house to get anything. When they got home, they had lunch and went for a long walk. Sheila and Joann walked in silence, both the girls lost in their own thoughts. Joann was thinking about her future, and she was hopeful.

Sheila thought about the baby and giving birth. It would be soon. Sheila was very mature for seventeen, but the fact was, she was still a kid, and she was getting a little scared about the delivery, and parenthood. Sheila reminded herself that she had survived her father's beatings. How much more painful could labor be? And as for the parenting, she promised herself she would never treat her children the way Bobby and Hugette had treated theirs. Sheila vowed to herself she would just do the opposite of whatever her parents would have done. She had hoped everything would work out.

Jack was extremely supportive of Sheila, and it helped her immensely. At this time in their lives, Sheila and Jack were truly content. Sheila was enjoying staying home and taking care of the house, and she was anxious for the baby to come. She had had a perfect pregnancy—except the morning sickness, but that had been over for months. For the first time in years, Sheila was completely free from drugs, alcohol, and her parents, and she was blossoming.

Sheila had never looked better. She was healthy and glowing. Jack was proud of Sheila, and he loved her. Their home was a happy one. Joann had commented several times to them that she loved the peace and tranquility of the apartment, and she especially loved Sheila off the drugs and alcohol. Sheila was calm, and she seemed to lose her angry edge. The only thing that bothered Sheila was that she knew she didn't love Jack the way he loved her, but she hoped she would grow to love him more over time.

Sheila broke the silence and suggested that they head back to start dinner. Joann agreed, and they chatted on the way home. Sheila and Joann saw a man fixing a flat tire of a really nice sports car on the side of the road. As they got closer, they realized it was Rick. They stood there frozen and looked at each other, then stared at him, not sure of what to do. Rick turned and looked at them as if he felt the stare. He then smiled and walked over.

He gave Joann a big hug. Then, he looked at Sheila and rubbed her huge belly. "What is this?" Rick inquired. Sheila told him everything about Jack and her new baby. Joann happily informed him that she was living with Sheila and Jack, and pointed to their building. Rick seemed happy with the news, and he was doing well. He still lived with Ralph in the project, something that shocked Sheila. Sheila had terrible memories of that place. She couldn't imagine anyone wanting to live there.

Rick was working in a big hotel downtown as a waiter, and he still had his other business of selling drugs. He flashed a big roll of bills to the girls, and they were very impressed. He was on his way to work and was running late. He took their phone number and told the girls he would call the next day and take them to lunch. Sheila and Joann were so excited. They had always looked up to Rick. They let Rick get back to his tire, and they walked home, talking happily about seeing Rick the next day.

That night at dinner, the girls told Jack about seeing Rick and their lunch plans. Jack was pleased. He knew how much it meant to Sheila and Joann to see their brother. Sheila had made Jack's favorite dinner, tuna casserole, and they had a pleasant meal. Sheila and Joann cleaned up the dishes afterward, and when Jack suggested ice cream, Sheila said no. Jack and Joann were surprised, but Sheila said she was very tired and wanted to go to bed early. They sat down to watch television, and within ten minutes, Sheila was asleep on the sofa. Jack woke her up and sent her to bed.

Sheila awoke at 1:00 AM. She was feeling very uncomfortable, and decided to get up and walk around. She had some lower-back ache, and a restless feeling came over her. She just walked the halls of the apartment for hours. Just after 3:00 AM they started. Sheila's first contraction was strong, but she wasn't sure what it was. By the time her fourth contraction came, she was pretty sure she was in labor and went to wake up Jack.

Jack jumped out of bed with a terrified, nervous look on his face, and he scrambled to get dressed. Sheila changed her clothes. She was excited and scared. She went to wake up Joann and tell her the baby was coming; they were going to the hospital. Joann was so excited. She knew she wouldn't be able to sleep, so she got up and told them to call as soon as there was any news. Jack was running around the apartment panicked, and Sheila had to take charge. She grabbed her suitcase—it had been packed for weeks—got Jack's car keys, and took him by the hand. Then they left.

They arrived at the hospital, and, after a quick exam, they confirmed Sheila was in labor. A nurse brought her into a room and told her she would be back to check on her soon. Sheila's contractions had become stronger, and the pain was intense. She tried to be brave with Jack there, but at times, it was very difficult to hold back the tears. Jack had decided to come into the delivery room. He wanted to be with Sheila for the whole experience.

Finally, the nurse returned and checked Sheila. She informed them it was almost time to go into the delivery room. Sheila asked for something for the pain, and the nurse told her it could delay the delivery, so Sheila decided against it. The doctor arrived a few minutes later and told Sheila it was time. They brought her into the delivery room, and she started to push. The pain was awful, and she wanted it to be over. It had been hours, and Sheila was getting exhausted. The doctor just kept telling her to push, and she did.

Finally, at 9:06 AM, their son was born. He weighed seven pounds eight ounces, and he was beautiful. Ten fingers and ten toes, Sheila counted as soon as they placed the baby in her arms. Sheila and Jack were laughing and crying, and then the baby started to cry as well. The doctor told Sheila the baby was perfectly healthy, and she had done a great job. Jack agreed. The nurses told them they hadn't seen such a cute baby in a long time. *He is perfect*, Sheila thought as she held her son.

By eleven o'clock, Sheila was in her own room and fast asleep. Jack told the nurse he was going home for a shower, and asked her to tell Sheila he would be back soon when she woke up. Jack kissed Sheila good-bye and stopped by the nursery to see the baby again. He was so proud of his new family, and he loved Sheila more at that moment than he ever had. Jack left the nursery and went to the pay phone to make some calls, all the while with a huge smile on his face.

He phoned Joann first, and she was thrilled. He told her he would be home soon, and he would bring her back with him to see Sheila and the baby. Then he phoned work and told them he would not be in for the next few days. Jack picked up the phone again and made a call he knew he should have made a long time ago. He dialed the phone, and his mother answered. "Hi, Mom. It's Jack. I have some news," he told his mother cheerily.

Jack's parents were in their late sixties. They hadn't started their family until they were in their late thirties. Jack loved and respected his parents. They had always been excellent parents, and he knew they would be supportive. Jack didn't know how to tell them his seventeen-year-old girlfriend was pregnant, and now they had a new baby and weren't married. So he started with a lie and told them Sheila was twenty, and they were planning on getting married in the summer.

Martha and Edward Currin were ecstatic with the news. This was their first grandchild. Martha told Jack they would plan a trip down in the spring. She couldn't wait to meet Sheila and see the baby. Jack promised to send pictures right away. Martha told Jack that she would call his sister Julie and give her the good news, and then she scolded him for not telling them sooner. Martha and Edward told Jack to call if he needed anything, and they loved him, and to give their best to Sheila. Jack hung up the phone wishing he had told them earlier, and knowing he would have to convince Sheila to marry him before his parents arrived.

*Behind the Drapes*

When Sheila woke up, her room was quiet. She got out of bed, went down the hall to the nursery, and got the baby. Sheila went back to her room, stopping at the nursing station to get a bottle for the baby. The nurse told Sheila that Jack had gone home for a shower and would be back soon. Sheila was happy to have some time alone with the baby, and she realized that she and Jack still had to name their son.

Sheila sat on the bed and looked at the adorable little creature in front of her. He was the most beautiful baby Sheila had ever seen, and she loved him with every ounce of her being. This is the way she knew she should love Jack, but it wasn't there. As she fed the baby his bottle, Sheila watched him and thought Jesse should be his name. Sheila couldn't wait for Jack to get there and discuss it with him.

Jack entered Sheila's hospital room with a big bouquet of flowers and a teddy bear. "How are my lovely girl and son doing?" Jack inquired. Sheila looked up with a big smile in response. The baby was sleeping in the bed with Sheila, and she was just watching him. Jack bent down and gave them both a kiss. "Sheila, I can't believe how beautiful he is," Jack said.

"I know, every time I look at him, I can't believe it. He is happy and safe; we are going to keep it that way. Jack, I want to name him Jesse," Sheila said. Jack liked the name, and they decided on Jesse Currin. "Where is Joann? I thought you would bring her to see the baby?" Sheila questioned.

Jack explained that when he got home, Rick had been there with Joann. He had phoned to take Sheila and Joann to lunch, and Joann had told him the news about the baby. He had shown up at the apartment a few minutes before Jack had arrived. Rick and Joann were going to lunch and then coming to the hospital.

Jack thought so far Rick seemed like a nice fellow, but there was something that bothered him about Rick. Maybe it was the way Sheila and Joann looked up to him. He wasn't sure what it was, but Jack realized Rick was Sheila's brother, and he would make an effort to get to know him better, with an open mind. He hoped his feeling about Rick would change. Jack didn't mention it to Sheila; he wanted her to stay happy and stress free.

Joann and Rick arrived at the hospital a few hours later. They brought Sheila and Jesse presents. Sheila opened the baby's first. It was a cute little sleeper and matching blanket. Sheila opened hers and it was a new bathrobe. It was bright orange, Sheila's favorite colour. Sheila thanked them both, and as she tried the robe on, she put her hand in the pocket and felt something. Sheila pulled out a bag, and it was full of marijuana. She shoved it back into the pocket.

Rick smiled and said, "Sheila, that is for when you get home. You have been a good girl too long. It's time to have some fun again." Sheila heard the words "good girl," and a chill went up her spine. She pushed the image from her mind. Sheila realized Rick had no knowledge about the sexual abuse, but she had hoped not to hear those words again.

Sheila looked over at Jack and promptly hid the pot in her suitcase. Joann quickly changed the subject, and at that moment Jack knew what it was about Rick he didn't like. Who would bring illegal drugs into a hospital for their little sister after she had just given birth to her first child at the age of seventeen?

Joann fell in love with Jesse the moment she saw him. He was so little and cute. Rick thought he was pretty special as well. Sheila changed his clothes and put on the new sleeper that Rick had bought for him. Jesse looked adorable. The four of them chatted for a while, and then Rick invited Jack out for a drink to celebrate the birth of his son. Jack reluctantly accepted. Joann decided to stay at the hospital with Sheila. Jack would pick her up on his way home.

Sheila and Joann had a wonderful visit. Jesse was a very good baby. He never cried. Sheila had only heard him cry in the delivery room right after he was born. Joann told Sheila about her lunch with Rick. He had taken her to a fancy restaurant, and she had been very impressed. Rick had smoked a joint in the car and had offered some to Joann. Joann told Sheila she had refused because she was scared. Yet, she had really wanted to take some. Joann didn't want Rick to think she was a child, although she was only fifteen. She told Sheila that next time she would try it.

Sheila knew at that moment she should tell Joann not to use drugs. On the other hand, Sheila was certain that the moment she got home, she would have some of the pot in her suitcase. Seeing that image in her mind had shaken Sheila; she needed to forget. Sheila changed the subject and started to talk about bringing Jesse home.

Jack returned a few hours later and brought Sheila a hamburger and fries. Sheila didn't like the lunch the hospital had served, and she was starting to get homesick. She hadn't even spent the night yet. Jack reminded her it was only two more days, and then she and the baby would be home with him. The thought of being home with Jesse was music to Sheila's ears; she couldn't wait to tuck him into his crib.

"Jack, did you have a good time with Rick?" Sheila inquired. Jack really didn't answer. He just smiled and told Sheila how beautiful she was. He told Sheila he had phoned his parents, and they sent their best to her and the baby. Jack wanted to wait until Sheila was home before he told her about their visit and the little white lies he had told them. He knew Sheila would be fine with the one about her age, but the marriage was something totally different.

It was getting late, and the nurse came to take Jesse to the nursery for the night. Before she left, she told Jack and Joann that Sheila needed her rest. Jack agreed, and he and Joann decided it was time to go. Sheila reminded Joann what buses to take to school, and then she reminded Jack to give Joann some lunch money. They both laughed and told her they could take care of themselves; Sheila only had to take care of Jesse.

Joann gave Sheila a hug and told her she would be back tomorrow to see her. Jack kissed Sheila and told her he loved her and was very proud of her. Sheila smiled up at him. He was such a good man, and she would do everything she could to make him and Jesse happy. Jack told her he would return in the morning, and they left. Sheila lay there, thinking how lucky she was to have such a loving man in her life, and a beautiful, healthy son. There was nothing else in the world she needed.

# Chapter 16

Sheila sat on the floor while Jesse played in front of her. Jesse giggled and smiled up at his mother as she spoke to him. She was telling him that Joann would be home from school any minute. She told him in a singsong way that he loved. Jesse was six months old and a very enjoyable baby. He only cried when he wanted something, and he rarely needed anything—Sheila was a good mother. Sheila heard the door open. She heard more than one voice, and in walked Joann and Rick.

"How was your day?" Sheila inquired. Joann shrugged and looked at Sheila with red, glossy eyes and that look that Sheila recognized. Sheila knew she was high, and so was Rick. "You two didn't wait for me to smoke?" Sheila complained. Rick smiled, pulled a huge bag of pot out of his jacket, and placed it on the table. "Jesse goes down for his nap in twenty minutes. We can smoke it then," Sheila said. Joann came and sat on the floor with Sheila and Jesse.

Joann loved Jesse as if he were her little brother. They shared a bedroom and had a close bond. Jesse saw Joann, and he started to giggle and kick his feet. Sheila and Joann were living in a new world where it was happy and safe. It was the only thing either of them had ever wanted. Rick came over and played with Jesse as well. The three

*Behind the Drapes*

of them just sat on the floor, admiring Jesse and loving him. Sheila looked around and thought how lucky Jesse was to be growing up in this environment. He would have a better life than Sheila, and she was grateful.

After they played with Jesse for an hour, Sheila put Jesse down for his nap, and he went right to sleep. When she walked back into the living room, Rick had already lit the joint. The three of them smoked it and giggled and chatted. Sheila told them how nervous she was to be meeting Jack's parents the next day; they had been unable to come until now. She was also meeting his sister, Julie. Jack's parents were going to be staying at Julie's house, and she was cooking everyone dinner. She lived an hour away from Sheila and Jack.

Rick told Sheila he could fix her problem and gave her some white powder, which she recognized right away. It was the stuff Rick had given her at the Halloween party when she lived with Brenda. Sheila refused and told Rick how sick she had been the next day. Rick explained that it was because she had been drinking alcohol, and Sheila rarely drank anymore. Sheila never had a drink during her pregnancy, and since Jesse had been born, she only drank once in a while. Rick told her if she used the cocaine without drinking, she would be fine the next day, and she would be the hit of the party when she met Jack's parents.

Sheila took it, and then she thanked him. Sheila told Rick about Jack lying about her age, and how he was pressing her to get married. Sheila didn't really mind him lying about her age, but she didn't want to get married. When Rick inquired as to why she didn't want to get married, Sheila explained that she didn't love Jack enough.

Rick became angry and looked at Sheila with a scary expression. "Sheila! Are you crazy? Do you know how lucky you are to have Jack? He loves you and he treats you well. Marry him, Sheila, and if it doesn't work out, then you get a divorce and he will have to take care of you and Jesse. Don't be stupid, Sheila. Jack comes from a rich family and you could get some."

Sheila tried to explain that she didn't want to take advantage of Jack because she cared for him, but Rick would not listen. It took Rick two hours, but he finally convinced Sheila that there was no harm to be done by trying to make it work. It would make Jack happy, his parents would get off their backs, and it would give Sheila and Jesse a little security.

When Sheila finally agreed, Rick gave her a hug and told her she was making the right decision. Joann had agreed with Rick. She was very fond of Jack and knew how well he treated Sheila and Jesse.

When Jack got home from work, he was exhausted. It had been a long week and it was finally over. He sometimes worked on weekends, but not with his parents in town. Jack hadn't seen his parents for well over a year, and he missed them. Sheila greeted Jack at the door with Jesse in her arms and gave him a big kiss. Rick had left, and Joann was taking a nap before dinner.

Jack went to the fridge and got himself a beer. Although Sheila didn't drink anymore, Jack still consumed enough for both of them. Sheila never thought twice about it. That was just the way it was. Jack drank, and Sheila smoked pot. Jack went into the living room with his beer and sat on the sofa. Sheila followed with Jesse in her arms.

"Jack, Rick picked up Joann at school today and drove her home. He came in with her, and we had a chat about you and I getting married. He made me see that I was wrong, and I want to marry you," Sheila told him. Jack jumped up and grabbed Sheila. He kissed her and hugged her. He couldn't believe what he was hearing. He hadn't known what he was going to tell his parents the next day.

Jack could not imagine that it was Rick who had convinced Sheila. He had been trying to convince her to marry him ever since she had gotten pregnant with Jesse, and all it took was one talk with her brother. Jack knew that Rick had influence over Sheila, but he hadn't realized to what extent. Maybe Jack had been wrong about Rick. He was obviously on Jack's side about the marriage. In the end, it didn't matter what had changed Sheila's mind. She was going to marry him, and he could not be happier.

That night, Jack took Sheila, Jesse, and Joann out to dinner to celebrate. They went to Sheila's favorite place. It was an Italian restaurant, and she loved their lasagna. When they were finished eating dinner, Jack ordered dessert for Sheila and Joann. He picked up Jesse and told the girls they would be right back; he just had to run to the mall next door. Sheila told him to wait and they would go together, but Jack insisted, and he left with Jesse.

Sheila and Joann had their dessert and talked about the wedding. Before long, Jack was back with Jesse. He paid the bill, and they went

*Behind the Drapes*

home. When Jesse had had his bath and was in bed for the night, Jack asked Sheila to come into the bedroom with him. Sheila immediately thought, *No, not tonight*; Sheila still hated to make love with Jack, but she gave in from time to time. She knew he was a man, and he had needs.

Jack sat Sheila on the bed. He reached over, picked up her left hand, and told her he loved her. Then, he pulled a small box out of his pocket and opened it. Sheila looked down, and there it was: a diamond ring. Sheila had never seen such a beautiful ring. It was small, but to Sheila, it was huge. Sheila had never owned a ring, diamond or otherwise. Jack took the ring out of the box and placed it on her left ring finger.

"Will you marry me Sheila?" Jack asked her. Sheila started to cry and only nodded yes in response. Then she hugged him. Jack laid her on the bed and started to remove her clothes slowly, as he kissed her neck. *I've made a mistake*, Sheila thought and closed her eyes tight, praying it would be over soon.

The next afternoon, Sheila finished packing Jesse's bag. It always amazed her how much one little baby needed. Sheila was getting so nervous, even her hands were shaking. Jack told her there was nothing to worry about, but Sheila was worried Jack's family wouldn't approve of her. Jack told Sheila he wanted to leave in ten minutes. She went into the bathroom and pulled the bag of cocaine out of her pocket. She stared at it. Sheila decided she didn't want to meet Jack's parents and sister while she was using cocaine, so she put it back into her pocket, and they left.

Jack knocked on the door and Julie opened it. She invited them into the house. Julie was in her early thirties and very tall. She had blonde hair and golden skin. What Sheila liked the most about her was her warm, friendly manner. When Julie saw Jesse, she squealed like a little girl. Julie yelled for her parents to come and see the baby. Jack introduced his sister to his future wife and son.

Martha and Edward entered the hallway, and Sheila was shocked by their appearance. Hugette and Bobby had been very young when they started their family, but Jack's parents had waited until they were ready financially before they had children. To Sheila, they looked like Jack's grandparents. They were both totally gray, with big sweaters and warm slippers. Sheila discovered they were the most wonderful people she had ever met. She actually felt a little jealousy toward Jack. He was so lucky to have had parents who loved and cared for him.

They sat in the living room, with which Sheila was very impressed. She had never seen such a nice house, except on television. The house was big and lavishly furnished, and only one person lived there. This amazed Sheila. They chatted before dinner and Jesse was so charming. Everyone adored him. Jesse entertained everyone with his smiles and giggles; he really was a happy baby. Martha and Julie both commented on it and told Sheila it was obvious that Jesse was well taken care of.

Sheila sat there and thought how nice it would have been to be a part of a loving family. Sheila gave Jesse his bottle, and Martha and Julie got dinner on the table. Jesse played quietly while they ate. The meal was delicious. It was all so fancy that Sheila was intimidated. She wasn't sure which fork to use, but Sheila was enjoying herself as they chatted. But then it happened, and Sheila started to shake.

"Tell me about your family, Sheila. Where do they live?" Edward innocently inquired. Sheila didn't know how or what to answer; she looked to Jack for help. Sheila had never told Jack the whole story, but he knew it had been bad and Sheila did not like talking about it. Jack told his parents that Sheila didn't see her parents, and Martha and Edward looked very confused. Mr. and Mrs. Currin could not imagine any parents not seeing their children.

Sheila excused herself from the table and rushed to the bathroom. Sheila locked the door and stood looking in the mirror. She hated what she saw in her reflection, and she knew everyone else saw it as well. Sheila reached into her pocket and pulled out the little bag. She snorted two lines, and within a minute, she felt much better. Sheila washed her face and dried her eyes, and she returned to the table with a confident smile.

Sheila was feeling much calmer as she sat down and listened to the conversation. She realized everyone was excitedly planning a wedding—Sheila's wedding. Sheila sat there and listened, and she thought how strange it was they were making plans without even asking her opinion, when it was her wedding, after all. Finally, Julie stood up and started to clear the table. Sheila immediately started to help, but Martha demanded Sheila sit down. She helped her daughter clear the table.

*Behind the Drapes*

Edward and Jack went into the living room, and Sheila sat there alone, feeding Jesse his dinner. Sheila looked down at her son. This was his family now, and Sheila vowed to keep the peace. Jesse finished his peas and carrots and let out the loudest burp Sheila had ever heard. Everyone ran into the room and started to laugh. Jesse looked up at his mother, and then, looking around at everyone else, he started to giggle. This got everyone laughing harder.

They all moved into the living room, and Sheila sat on the floor with Jesse. Everyone else sat on the sofas. Julie served Jack and Edward brandy, and Martha and Sheila had tea. Jesse entertained the crowd, and Sheila looked around the room, listening to them talk and laugh, and wondering what her life would had been like if she had been raised in a loving family. It was all okay, though, Sheila thought. Jesse would grow up in this family, and that was all that mattered.

Edward told them that he wanted them to get married right away, and he would give them ten thousand dollars for a down payment on a house. Edward was not offering; he was demanding they take the money and buy a house. Sheila tried to object, but he was insistent. Julie was sweet and tried to help. She told her father it was the first time they were all meeting, and they should be getting to know each other. Maybe this could be a conversation for another visit. Sheila excused herself, went back to the bathroom, locked the door, and did a few more lines of cocaine.

Sheila came back into the living room feeling better. She finished her tea and looked at her watch. "It's getting late, and we should be leaving soon. It's almost time for Jesse to go to bed, and we have an hour's drive ahead of us," Sheila said to no one in particular. Jack agreed and jumped up. She started to gather Jesse's things. Sheila offered to help Julie with the dishes before they left, and Julie giggled.

"The dishes are my job and everyone knows that," Edward explained. "I enjoy doing them. It relaxes me after dinner." Sheila was in shock. The man of the house doing the dishes? She almost laughed out loud when the image of Bobby doing dishes entered her mind. It occurred to Sheila for the first time that maybe the way she grew up was the exception and not the rule. Jack and Sheila arranged to meet Edward, Martha, and Julie for brunch the next day at a restaurant. Then they left.

Nancy Prudhomme

While Jack and Sheila were on their way home, Sheila never stopped talking for a minute. Jack had to tell her several times to slow down; she was talking a mile a minute. This was mostly due to the effect of the cocaine. Jack wasn't aware of her using coke, so he just thought she was upset, and he got the message loud and clear. Sheila didn't want a big wedding, and she didn't want to buy a house. Everything was perfect now, and Sheila didn't want anything to change. She had only agreed to marry Jack the night before, and already it was getting her stressed out. Sheila informed him she would not move, and that was that.

Jack just agreed with whatever he had to. Sheila was very upset, and he wanted her to calm down. He rarely saw her like this, and he didn't like it. Jack did agree that a big wedding was not what they wanted, and he said they would talk about the house another time. Jack wanted to buy the house. He knew it was important for their future. Jack thought he would talk to Rick and see if he could help.

When they arrived home, Sheila went to get Jesse ready for bed, and Jack asked Joann to roll a joint for Sheila because she was a little stressed out. He went into the kitchen, made a pot of tea, and got himself a beer. Jack went into the living room, and Joann told him the joint was ready. Joann asked what had happened, and Jack told her everything. Joann listened, and she had to agree with her sister. Why ruin a good thing? But it was their life, and Joann kept her thoughts to herself. Sheila came into the room and sat on the sofa. Seeing the joint, she smiled and picked it up.

The next morning, Sheila got out of the shower and heard two male voices. She knew one was Jack, but she couldn't make out the other. She prayed it wasn't Edward and rushed to change. Sheila walked into the kitchen and smiled when she saw Rick holding Jesse. Sheila crabbed a coffee and leaned on the kitchen wall, saying good morning to everyone.

Rick and Jack looked up at her. Sheila had become such a beautiful woman. Now that Jesse had been born and she had lost the baby weight, Sheila was different. She seemed to have lost all her own baby features. Rick really hated to admit it, but Sheila looked exactly like her mother. He would never say that, though. He knew it was the last thing Sheila wanted to hear.

*Behind the Drapes*

"What brings you by so early on a Saturday morning? Joann isn't even up yet," Sheila said.

"I was just leaving to go to my friend's cottage when Jack phoned and told me you needed some pot. So here I am," Rick said with a grin. Sheila looked at Jack, smiled, and walked over to give him a kiss on the cheek. Jack always treated her well. Sheila went over and picked up Jesse from Rick. She fed him his breakfast. Jesse was in excellent humor as usual, all smiles and giggles.

Jack got up and grabbed his keys. "Sheila, I have to go to the beer store, and I'll go now before it gets too busy. You can visit with Rick, and I'll be right back." Jack left, and Sheila finished feeding Jesse as she chatted with her brother. Sheila told Rick he had been right about not drinking. She felt fine, but Sheila wanted more cocaine. Rick happily gave Sheila more, and some pot as well. As always, he wouldn't take any money.

After Sheila had cleaned up the baby, they went into the living room so Jesse could play on the floor with his toys where Sheila could watch him. Joann came in, mumbled something about coffee, and went to the kitchen. "Sheila," Rick said, "Jack and I had a chat when I first got here, and I want to talk to you about Jack's father's offer to give you money for a house." Sheila tried to object, but he stopped her and continued.

"Do you know how much Dad wanted to buy a house, Sheila? I think you are too young to remember, but I do. That's all he used to talk about. Then one day he stopped talking about it. I guess he gave up because he knew he could never succeed. If you and Jack bought a house, he would be so jealous. Think about it, Sheila. Despite all the beatings he gave us, we are going to make something of ourselves and have a better life than him."

Sheila sat there silently for a while, and then she looked up at her brother. She knew he was right. If Bobby or Hugette ever found out, it would infuriate them, which was enough for Sheila. Sheila and Jack were going to buy a house. "Oh, how smart you are, brother dear," Sheila told Rick, laughing. Joann came back into the room with coffee, and Sheila told her the good news. With his work done, Rick hugged his sisters and left.

Jack arrived home with a dozen roses for Sheila, and one long-stemmed rose for Joann. The girls thanked him, and Sheila told him her decision about the house. Jack was so happy; he knew he had made the right decision phoning Rick. The house was the real reason he had phoned Rick. The pot was just to keep Sheila calm. Jack had come to discover that a high Sheila was a calm Sheila, and he wanted her to stay that way.

Brunch with Martha and Edward was quick and painless for Sheila. She had her little white bag in her pocket if she needed it. However, it wasn't needed; Jack's parents didn't ask Sheila any personal questions, and they were very pleasant. Martha and Edward were returning home the next morning, and they wouldn't be back until the wedding. Julie asked Sheila and Jack over for dinner the following Sunday, and Jack agreed.

As soon as he had said yes, Jack realized he shouldn't have accepted the invitation without checking with Sheila. He looked over at her with a nervous look, and she smiled at him. Jack was relieved. That smile told him everything would be fine. After everything Jack had done for Joann, Sheila had no problem spending time with his sister. After all, Julie was a very nice person, and Sheila liked her. It would only be her, not Martha and Edward.

Edward asked the waitress for the bill and Martha made Sheila promise to call her as soon as she and Jack had decided on a wedding date. They all got up together and walked outside, after a short argument about who was going to carry Jesse; Martha won. Edward and Martha said good-bye to Jack and gave him a hug. Then they both gave Sheila a hug and welcomed her into the family. Sheila was very touched. Martha, Julie, and Edward kissed Jesse several times. It was obvious they all loved him. Julie told Sheila and Jack she would see them the next weekend, and the three of them drove away.

Jack asked Sheila if it would be okay if they drove around for a while on the way home, to look at some houses for sale. Sheila was actually enjoying herself, writing down the phone numbers and addresses of the for sale signs. After they saw about ten, Jesse started to fuss. He was getting hungry, so they started home.

By the time Sheila had Jesse fed and down for his nap, Jack had phoned every ad. It was apparent that even with Edwards's generous gift of the down payment, the homes in the city were far too expensive for them. Jack made decent money, but they were not in a position to have a large mortgage payment. Where they were living now, all the utilities were included in the rent. Once they moved into their own home, they would have to start paying all the utilities. The bottom line was, they could not afford to buy a house in the city.

Sheila thought that was the end of buying a house, but when she innocently mentioned it in conversation that night at dinner, Jack became very irritated. "Sheila, I thought it was settled and we were going to buy a house!" Jack hollered at her. Sheila and Joann both jumped, partly because it reminded them of Bobby, and partly because they had never seen Jack get angry that way before. The moment Jack saw them jump, he felt bad, and he told them so.

"I don't understand, Jack. If the houses are too expensive, then how do we buy one?" Sheila said. She was truly confused. She didn't know anyone who owned their own home. Jack looked at Sheila with a frustrated expression and explained it to her. If they could not afford a house in the city, they would have to move out to the country until they built up equity. In about five years, they could afford to buy in the city. Sheila and Joann looked at each other and wanted to cry.

Jack assured them both he would look for a three-bedroom house— one room for Sheila and Jack, one for Jesse, and the last for Joann. He told Sheila and Joann that they would look for something close to the city. Sheila and Joann felt a little better, but neither of them wanted to move out of the city. Sheila and Joann had always lived there, unlike Jack, who had lived all over the world. Edwards's first career had been with the military. He had been a pilot, and they had lived all over. Jack was familiar with moving to different cities, but Sheila was not.

The three of them finished their dinner in silence, lost in their own thoughts. Jack grabbed a beer from the fridge and went to sit on the sofa. Sheila and Joann did the dishes and chatted about how it could be a new adventure. In Sheila's heart, she knew it was a bad decision, but she had told Jack they could buy a house. Joann chatted about her own room. She had been sharing her room with Jesse, and she loved him. Nevertheless, it would be nice to have some privacy.

Sheila and Jack spent the next three weekends looking for a house. Because of the price of the homes, each weekend they went further from the city. Jesse stayed home with Joann. Sheila and Jack left early every Saturday and Sunday morning. They didn't return until it was dark.

On the third Sunday, Sheila and Jack stopped for lunch at a truck stop on the highway. Jack looked over the map and told Sheila there was a little town ten minutes away from where they were.

They decided to stop there to look around, and then head for home. Neither of them was hopeful. They had been looking every free moment and hadn't liked anything in their price range. Cedar Falls was a small town. The population was just over six thousand. As they drove there, Sheila calculated that it was a little over an hour from the city. Sheila prayed Jack didn't see anything he liked. It was too far.

Sheila had to admit it was a pretty little town. They drove down the main street, and Sheila spotted a realty office. They stopped and went in; there was a short chubby man with a huge smile sitting at a desk. He was dressed in jean overalls and a denim shirt. He made Sheila feel comfortable and relaxed, and they liked him right away. His name was Walter. He offered Sheila and Jack coffee, but they declined.

Jack told Walter what they were looking for and their price range. Walter told them he knew the perfect house. The people were asking what Jack wanted to spend, although Walter felt they could get it for about five thousand less. The house had just gone on the market that morning. Walter had been on his way over to measure the house for the ad. He asked if they wanted to come with him and look at it; Jack said yes and grabbed Sheila by the hand.

It was a nice house on a quiet street. It was an ugly brown, but Jack assured Sheila he would paint it a new color. It was on a half acre of land; it had three bedrooms, two bathrooms, a huge kitchen, and a large living room. There was a long porch and a double garage. Sheila could see Jack loved it. She liked it, but she still felt it was too far from the city. Jack helped Walter measure the house, and Sheila walked around. She knew this would be their new home, whether she liked it or not.

When Jack and Walter finished measuring the house, Jack asked Walter if he and Sheila could have a few minutes alone. Walter was happy to oblige and went out into the yard. Jack told Sheila that he wanted to make an offer on the house, and Sheila reluctantly agreed. Jack was so happy. He explained to Sheila all the renovations he would do. Jack promised Sheila it wouldn't be forever, just until they built up enough equity to move back to the city.

*Behind the Drapes*

Sheila was enjoying seeing Jack so excited, and she thought about Jesse and the backyard he would have to play in. Sheila went to the door and called Walter. He entered the kitchen, and Sheila told him they wanted to place an offer on the house. They went back to Walters's office, and he started on the paperwork. Once everything was signed, Walter left to go see the owners and present the offer. He told them he would have an answer in about an hour.

Jack took Sheila to dinner while they waited. They went to a place along the river Walter had told them about it. Sheila liked the restaurant. She enjoyed the atmosphere, and the food was good. Sheila went to the pay phone and phoned Joann to tell her they would be late. Joann said everything was fine. Jesse had just finished dinner, and she would give him his bath and put him to bed. Sheila appreciated how wonderful Joann was, helping with the baby, and she told Joann so once again. Joann told Sheila the same thing she always did: Jesse was her baby too, and she loved him.

Sheila and Jack arrived back at Walter's office, and he was there waiting. The sellers did not accept the offer. They had come back with an offer of two thousand more than Jack had offered. It was still four thousand lower than what Jack had wanted to spend. He looked at Sheila and told her they were going to accept. Walter was thrilled. He told them he had never sold a house that had not even been listed or advertised before. He said it must be fate. Sheila and Jack signed all the papers. They owned a house, and the deal would close in six weeks.

The drive home seemed so long as they sat in silence. Sheila she was stressed out. All she could think about was all the money they owed now. Plus, they were moving, and it was so far from the city. Would Joann hate the idea? Sheila was already regretting the decision, but Jack was smiling from ear to ear.

Jack was so happy with their purchase, and he didn't think he would mind the commute into the city for work. He thought the hour drive would be a peaceful way to start and end the day. Jack had always wanted to buy a home. His parents had always owned their own homes and had taught their children the importance of buying real estate as an investment. Jack couldn't wait to get home and phone his parents. Sheila was dreading telling her sister.

When Sheila and Jack entered the apartment, Joann walked up to them and handed Jack a beer. He thanked her. She looked at Sheila and told her Jesse was fast asleep, and she had a joint ready for them. They went into the living room, and Jack told Joann all about the house they had just bought. She was very excited, until she found out how far it was. Jack reminded them they would have a new house, but it would still be a happy home. Sheila and Joann knew he was right, and they both tried to be more enthusiastic.

Jack phoned his parents, and they were very pleased. Edward told Jack he would wire the money into his bank account the next day. Martha got on the phone and asked about the new house. She wanted to know if there was any new information on a wedding date. Jack told Martha they had been very busy looking for a house, and now that they had found one, they would focus on wedding plans. Jack thanked his parents again for their generous gift and said goodnight.

The next morning, Sheila woke up, ran into the bathroom, and vomited. Jack knocked on the door and asked if Sheila was okay. Sheila opened the door and looked up at Jack. She was crying. Jack held her until she stopped crying, and then he asked her what was wrong. She told him her suspicion. Sheila thought she might be pregnant. Her period was late, but she had been so stressed out since Jack's parents' visit, and then looking for a house, Sheila had thought she was late due to stress. Now she knew better—she recognized the feeling of morning sickness.

Jack was ecstatic. He wanted two kids. Sheila hadn't really thought of it. She only focused on trying to be a good mother to Jesse. More children had never really occurred to her, and she and Jack had never really discussed it. Sheila thought it was a bit soon. Jesse was only seven months old. He would be a little over a year when the new baby came, probably still in diapers. Sheila decided to make a doctor's appointment and not panic until she knew for sure.

A week later, the doctor's office called with the test results: Sheila was pregnant again. When she told Jack, the first thing he said was they had to get married before the second baby came. *Great, more stress. That's what I need right now,* Sheila thought. Sheila had known she couldn't put it off forever. Jack's parents had been phoning every night to see if there was any news. Sheila knew as soon as they found out about the new baby, the pressure would intensify.

That night, after dinner, Jack was sitting on the sofa having a beer, and Sheila came into the room with a calendar. "Would you like to pick a date, Jack?" Sheila inquired. He looked up at her with a big smile and pulled her down onto the sofa. Sheila giggled, and Jesse smiled up at the two of them from his blanket on the floor. "I thought it would be easier to tell your parents about the new baby if we have a wedding date picked out," Sheila told him, and Jack thanked her with a kiss.

Sheila would marry Jack in eight weeks, before she started to show. They agreed on a very small wedding. Jack's sister, Julie, had been dating a judge, Joseph Monteizo, and he offered to marry them. Sheila and Jack just had to go down to city hall and pick up the license. Joseph was quite a bit older than Julie. They had been dating for eight months and seemed very happy. He was a tall stocky man with soft brown eyes and a warm smile. Joseph had been at Julie's for dinner the last time Sheila and Jack had gone. They both thought he was a nice man, and Sheila was happy to have him marry them.

Julie wanted to have the wedding at her house. Joseph could perform the ceremony in her yard, and she would cook a huge meal for everyone. Sheila and Jack took her up on the offer. Sheila was happy to have someone help her with the arrangements. Sheila told Julie she would help her with all the cooking and anything else she needed. Julie told Sheila she was happy to do the work. Julie enjoyed cooking, and it made her happy to help her brother and Sheila. And with that, the wedding was planned.

# Chapter 17

Sheila stood on the porch of her new house and watched as the moving truck came down the long driveway. She had arrived a few minutes earlier. Brenda had driven Sheila and Joann up in her car. Brenda and Scott had come to help them with the move. Tony had also shown up to lend a hand. Rick had arrived at the apartment just as the truck door was being closed. He apologized for being late and promised to make up for it when they were unloading the truck.

Jack and Tony jumped down out of the big truck, both with a beer in their hand. A few moments later, Rick's sports car pulled up. Rick and Scott got out, and a big puff of smoke followed them out of the car. Apparently, they'd had a few joints on the way up. Rick and Scott walked up to the porch, and Jack gave them both a beer. Brenda watched as they all started to get a little too comfortable, chatting and drinking beer.

"There will be no more beer until that truck is unloaded!" Brenda shouted at the four men. She picked up the cooler that was beside Tony, put it in the trunk of her car, and locked it. Sheila admired Brenda's assertive personality. The guys bitched a little, but got right to work. Within three hours, the truck was unloaded and the larger furniture was in place. Sheila wanted to get as much done as possible today. Julie had picked up Jesse that morning and would be home with him the next afternoon.

Scott got the cooler of beer from Brenda's trunk and brought it into the kitchen, and the four guys drank beer and talked. The girls unpacked the bedrooms and made up all the beds, including Jesse's crib. Sheila knew she had to get Jesse out of his crib and into his new bed soon, because the new baby would need the crib. But she would worry about that after the wedding. It was coming up soon—only two more weeks. Sheila was a bag of nerves, and she was pregnant, so she didn't have the luxury of doing drugs to help her through it.

When the girls finished setting up the bedrooms, Joann offered to tackle the bathroom, while Sheila and Brenda unpacked the kitchen. They walked into the kitchen and noticed the boys were getting very loud. Sheila knew she had to get some food into them soon. She phoned and ordered a few pizzas, which arrived just as she and Brenda had finished the kitchen. Sheila went to get Joann, and found she was already on her way down the stairs.

They all ate pizza and chatted. Everyone was tired. It had been a long day, and everyone had worked hard. Even Rick had kept his promise and worked really hard. He was the first to leave; he gave Joann some pot and told both his sisters to call if they needed anything. Jack and Sheila both thanked him for all his help. Rick told Sheila he would be back in a couple of weeks to visit, and he left. Sheila watched as his car peeled out of the driveway. *What a great brother*, Sheila thought.

Tony left a few minutes later with Brenda and Scott. Brenda had told Tony she would drive him back to his vehicle. Sheila reminded them about the wedding and ensured they had the correct address for Julie's house. Once the house was quiet, Sheila realized how tired she was. She quickly tidied up the kitchen and went to change into her pajamas. As Sheila walked through the house on her way to her bedroom, she saw that they really had got a lot accomplished that day. She was very pleased. Sheila thought there would be no problem having the house completely finished by the time Jesse arrived tomorrow afternoon.

The next morning, Sheila woke first and quietly climbed out of bed. She went downstairs to the kitchen and made a pot of coffee. She had started the dishes when Joann came into the kitchen. Sheila told her to sit down, and she got herself and Joann a coffee, and sat down with her. Joann told Sheila she couldn't remember when she had had such a peaceful sleep. Sheila agreed. She had also slept well; it was so quiet at night in the country. They were used to the sounds of the city: police, fire truck sirens, and people yelling at all hours of the night. They had to agree that it was, at least, a calm and peaceful place to sleep.

Jack came into the kitchen an hour later, and Sheila got him some coffee. Sheila reminded Jack they had to get some groceries before Julie got there with Jesse. Jack told Sheila and Joann to get dressed, and he would take them out to breakfast. They would get the grocery shopping done afterward. They all agreed. They were all hungry and they had another full day ahead of them.

After they finished the shopping, Jack drove by the high school to show Sheila and Joann where it was. Sheila was going to register Joann for school on Monday, and she had to know where to take her. It was a very attractive school. Sheila thought it looked like a university in the States she had seen on the news, although it was much smaller. Joann really liked it, and she couldn't wait to go. She was getting excited about maybe starting a new life where no one knew her.

Sheila was completely finished unpacking by the time Julie got there. Julie was very impressed. She had assumed the house would be full of boxes and disorganized, but it was spotless. When she mentioned it to Sheila, Sheila told her she'd had lots of help from Joann and Brenda, and it was Julie taking Jesse for the night that had been the biggest help of all.

Jesse almost dove from his aunt's arms to get to Sheila. Sheila scooped him up quickly. She had missed Jesse. It was the first time they had been away from each other for more than a couple of hours. Julie told Sheila that Jesse had been an angel, and she would be happy to babysit anytime. Sheila thanked her again, and as she cuddled her son, Sheila took him and Julie on a tour of the house.

When they arrived upstairs, Joann's door was closed, and Sheila knocked. Joann answered the door and greeted them with a smile. Sheila introduced Joann to Julie, and Julie reached out and shook her hand, returning the smile. When Jesse saw Joann, he started to kick and squeal, and Joann took him from his mother's arms. Julie was shocked to see how young Joann was. When she heard that Sheila's sister was

*Behind the Drapes*

living with them, she'd just assumed she would be older. Then Julie looked at Sheila more closely, and realized there was no way they were telling the truth about her age. She was a lot younger than Jack was letting on.

Julie liked the house, and Sheila wasn't sure what Jesse thought, but he was smiling and cooing, and she thought that must be good. Sheila offered Julie a cup of tea, and they went into the kitchen. Sheila loved the kitchen; it was so big and bright. It was her favorite room of the house. Sheila put the kettle on while Joann, with Jesse in her arms, sat at the table. Julie and Sheila joined her. They had their tea and chatted. Jesse let out a big yawn, and Sheila knew it was time for his nap.

When Sheila returned to the kitchen, Jack was back from the hardware store. He told Julie about his plans for renovating the house. Jack was ready to get started immediately, and he had been out shopping for supplies. Julie was enjoying seeing her brother so enthusiastic about a project. Julie looked at her watch and told them she had to leave; she was meeting Joseph for dinner. Sheila again offered to help with the meal for the wedding, and Julie assured her everything was under control.

Once Julie had left, Jack got right to work and ripped the dark, dingy paneling off the walls. The entire living room was covered in paneling. It made the room look dark and gloomy, and Sheila and Jack both agreed it had to go first. Once the first piece of paneling was off, they realized there were three layers of wallpaper underneath. It would be a much larger job than they'd originally thought. Joann and Sheila helped Jack, but it was slow going, and it wasn't long before Jesse woke up crying, being in a strange room.

Sheila ran up to his room, and as soon as he saw his mother, Jesse's tears turned to smiles. Sheila brought him downstairs and fed him his dinner. She asked Joann to peel potatoes for dinner, and Joann was happy to oblige. When Sheila was finished feeding Jesse, she got dinner on the table and called for Jack to come eat. When he didn't come right away, Sheila went into the living room to get him.

When Sheila walked into the room, she stopped in her tracks and stared. It was a disaster zone. There were pieces of wallpaper thrown about, and the carpet was soaked from the water Jack had been using to soften the paper. Sheila looked at Jack and shouted at him, "Jack I was only out of the room for an hour! How did you make such a mess?"

Sheila bent down and started to pick up the paper. The tears came, and she couldn't stop them.

Jack came to her and told her he would get to it later, but Sheila knew that could be days from now. Jack was smart and a hard worker, but he was also a procrastinator. Sheila kept on picking it up, and Jack went to have his dinner. Joann came and helped Sheila clean up. Then they went to eat a cold dinner. Jack went right back into the living room and continued to peel the paper, making another mess.

Sheila and Joann finished their dinner, and Sheila went to give Jesse his bath and get him ready for bed. When she came back downstairs, Jack was still peeling, and Sheila went into the kitchen, where Joann was just finishing the dishes. Sheila thanked her sister and put the kettle on for tea. Joann excused herself and went into the garage to smoke a joint. Sheila couldn't wait for the baby to come so she could smoke one as well.

Time flew, and before Sheila knew it, the day of the wedding had arrived. It was a warm, sunny day. She was so nervous, and she tried to convince herself she was doing the right thing for her children. Rick was going to give her away, and Joann was going to be her maid of honor. Jack had asked Tony to be the best man.

Sheila was on her way to Julie's house with Jesse, Joann, and Brenda. Sheila thought she just had to get through the day. Tomorrow, it would be over, and life could be calm again. They had moved into the new house, and tomorrow, the wedding would be a thing of the past. Sheila arrived at Julie's house and put on her wedding dress. She had purchased it from a catalogue of a department store. It was a perfect fit, and Sheila looked beautiful in her simple white gown.

The wedding was small, only twelve people in total. Julie had outdone herself. The decorations were unbelievable. There were flowers and bells everywhere. It was beautiful. The ceremony was quick and simple. Joseph presided, while Joann and Tony stood next to the couple. Julie held Jesse during the ceremony, while Martha and Edward sat close. On the other side sat Tony's date, Rick and his date, and also Brenda and Scott.

The meal was elaborate and delicious. Everything was perfect. Julie had cooked a seven-course meal, and everyone enjoyed it. Edward made a speech and officially welcomed Sheila into the family. Rick made a

*Behind the Drapes*

toast to the couple and welcomed Jack into the family. Brenda said a little something about when Sheila and Jack had first met; she had disapproved in the beginning, but as time passed, she realized she had been wrong. Sheila hoped Brenda was right.

At eight o'clock, Sheila and Jack left. Rick had rented a hotel room for them at the downtown hotel where he worked. Julie would keep Jesse overnight, and Sheila and Jack would pick him up in the morning. Rick and his date would take Joann home and stay overnight with her, so Sheila didn't have to worry. Everyone left after Sheila and Jack had gone, thanking Julie for a wonderful day.

When Sheila and Jack arrived at the hotel, there was a fruit basket from Tony, a cheese tray from Brenda and Scott, and a bottle of champagne from Rick. Sheila had a few sips of champagne, and she and Jack made a toast to each other. Jack promised Sheila he would always be kind and gentle with her. He would always take care of her and the kids. Sheila promised Jack that she would always try her best to be a good wife to him and a good mother to their children. Sheila and Jack clanked their glasses together and sealed their toast with a kiss.

# Chapter 18

Sheila walked out into the sunshine and sat down on a lawn chair next to Joann to watch her children play. Jesse was almost two and a half now, and he was running around, talking a mile a minute to his brother, Keegan. Sheila had given birth to another son and she had been thrilled; they called him Keegan Currin.

Joann and Jack had wanted a girl, but Sheila never wanted to have a daughter and the moment Keegan was born, Sheila had her tubes tied. Two children were more than enough, Jack and Sheila had agreed. Sheila thought if she had a daughter, she would always be suspicious of the men around her baby, including Jack. Sheila appeared to not only look like her mother, but to be as fertile as Hugette. Sheila did not want to have five children by the time she was twenty-five.

Keegan had just started to walk. He was fifteen months old. He was slower to talk than his brother. Keegan was a happy baby, just like Jesse had been. Jack had installed a large fence off the porch, and it had made things much easier for Sheila. She was able to let the kids stay outside by themselves for short periods of time when she was alone, just enough time to grab a drink for the boys or grab the phone.

*Behind the Drapes*

Jack was at work, and Sheila and Joann were waiting for Rick. He was coming up for a visit. Jesse saw his car first and started to scream his name. The boys loved their uncle Rick. Rick pulled up the driveway, and the boys ran over to the fence, calling him. Keegan's words were still not understandable, but it was obvious he was happy to see his uncle. Sheila walked over and picked up Keegan. She grabbed Jesse by the hand and walked over to open the gate.

Rick got out of the car, came over, and picked up Jesse. Jesse begged Rick to go for a ride in his car, and Rick promised to take both the boys for a ride before he left. Sheila asked Rick if he had brought her a treat, and he nodded. Rick handed Sheila a bag of marijuana, and she gave it to Joann, asking her to go into the house and roll a joint. Joann happily took the bag and went into the house.

Sheila and Rick sat down, and the boys pulled at Rick's pant legs, begging him to come play with them. Sheila told the boys to give her and Rick a moment to talk, and then their uncle would play with them. Jesse and Keegan quietly went to play. Sheila told Rick she had something serious to talk to him about. She was very worried about Joann.

Sheila explained that when Joann had first started at her new high school, she had been very optimistic. Joann was shy, and she had not made many friends. They were from the big city and used to the fact that people came and went. In this small town, it was very hard to fit in. Joann had tried, but everyone had grown up together and had formed little cliques. There was no room for any outsiders. And that was what Joann was to them, an outsider. She felt like one, too. These people were different. Everyone seemed to have money. It wasn't like the project. Worst of all, they were rude to Joann.

Joann had gone to school, come home, put her pajamas on, and sat on the sofa until bed, then done it all again the next day. On the weekends, Joann had never even got out of her pajamas. When the next school year came, Joann had dropped out. She had been sixteen, and there was nothing she or Jack could do. Ever since she'd stopped going to school, all she did was sit around, smoke dope, and watch TV. Sheila was really worried about her. Joann was seventeen now, and she should be out with people, meeting boys, not stuck in a little town with her sister and living a miserable life.

Rick agreed it was cause for alarm and said to let him think about it for a little while. He went to play with the boys. Sheila yelled to Rick that she was going into the house for a few minutes, and walked onto the porch. Joann was just coming out, and she told Sheila the joint was ready. They decided to smoke it alone while Rick played with the kids. They went into the garage.

Jesse and Keegan finished their lunch, and Sheila put them down for their nap. She told them that when they woke up, Rick would take them for a ride in his car. Both the boys went right to sleep. Sheila made some sandwiches and a veggie platter; she brought it outside and placed it on the picnic table with a big pitcher of ice tea. Sheila, Joann, and Rick ate their lunch outside and enjoyed the sunshine.

"Joann, I have something to ask you," Rick said. "I know of a job opening up in the gift shop at the hotel where I work. Are you interested in taking it?" Sheila and Joann were stunned. Sheila didn't want Joann to leave. She just wanted some advice to help her get Joann out of her slump. Joann looked at her sister, and Sheila saw the excitement in Joann's face. Sheila knew this was the right thing for her sister to do.

Rick explained that he had a very large enclosed storage space in the loft of the house he was renting, and he could renovate it into a bedroom. Rick lived in the upper two floors of a beautiful old home right in the heart of the downtown core. Rick suggested maybe Joann was ready for a change, and Rick said he could use someone to help him with the cleaning. Rick agreed to allow Joann to live there for free if she did some housecleaning.

"I have never had a job. I'd like to try, but I'm scared. What should I do, Sheila?" Joann asked her sister nervously. Sheila told her sister she should try and get the job, and if it were meant to be, she would be hired. Sheila also reminded her sister she could not continue to live the way she had been. Joann needed to start acting like a seventeen-year-old and have some fun. Maybe Rick was right, she said. Maybe Joann was in need of a change.

Joann agreed and told Rick she wanted the job. They discussed it and decided that Rick would go to work that evening and set up the interview. Sheila mentioned that Jack could drive Joann in the morning if Rick could set something up for the next day. Rick told Joann that he would start the renovations to the loft that night after work. Rick

*Behind the Drapes*

thought Joann should move, and if this job didn't work out, he would find her something else. She needed to get back to the city.

Jesse and Keegan woke up from their nap, and Rick took them for a spin in his car. Sheila and Joann chatted about her possible move back to the city. Sheila desperately wanted to go back to the city, and she had felt that way since the day she left. The more Joann thought about it, the more she liked the idea. For the first time in her life, she would have her own money. Joann had never babysat the way Sheila had, and she certainly had never worked. Sheila and Jack got her what she needed.

Rick returned with the boys twenty minutes later. Jesse and Keegan were smiling ear to ear, and Jesse told his mother about their adventure. They had seen a cow and named him Jean-guy, and he had a big bell. Keegan added his few words, which nobody could understand but Jesse, who translated for everyone. "He said the cow was blue," Jesse informed them, and they all laughed.

Sheila got the boys a drink, and they went to play. Rick told his sisters he had to get going or he would be late for work. He told them he would call them in the morning and let them know about the job. He went over to the boys and wrestled with them for a few minutes, and then, despite their protests, he left. They watched as his sports car pulled out of the driveway.

That evening, the phone rang as they were sitting down to dinner, and Sheila picked it up. Rick was phoning to tell them he'd talked to the manager of the gift shop, and Joann had the job without an interview. Rick made some comment about the manager having a crush on him. Joann would start in two weeks. Rick said he had to go, and he would call the next day. Sheila hung up the phone; she felt like she had lost her best friend, and in many ways, she had.

Jack and Joann looked at Sheila nervously, wondering what the bad news was. Sheila hadn't even had time to tell Jack about Rick's visit or Joann's possible job, and now it was all over. Joann was leaving. Sheila came back to the table and sat down. She really tried to fake a smile, but it was so obviously not real. Sheila told Joann what Rick had said. She squealed with delight and ran from the table.

"What is this about?" Jack questioned. Sheila told him all about Rick's visit and their conversation. Jack was surprised, but he was ecstatic about the news, which upset Sheila, who was crushed. Jack had known that Sheila was worried about her sister, but he'd never imagined that Joann moving would be a solution. Jack reached over and grabbed Sheila's hand. He winked at her with a smile.

"Now we can have some privacy," Jack purred. Sheila looked at him and thought that was exactly what she was afraid of. Jack started to eat his dinner, and Sheila called Joann back to the table to finish her dinner. Joann barely ate any of her dinner. She just chatted excitedly about her move back to the city. Sheila was very happy to see Joann in such a good mood, but she knew she was really going to miss her sister.

The next two weeks flew by too quickly for Sheila. Joann was working at one of the biggest hotels in the city as a cashier in the gift shop. She would be working Monday to Friday, 7:00 AM–3:00 PM. It was the Saturday before Joann was starting work, and Rick would be there soon to pick her up. Rick had called the night before and told them he was completely finished with Joann's new room, and it looked great. Joann couldn't wait to see it.

Sheila was looking out the window, and she saw Rick in a big truck pulling into the driveway. Sheila couldn't believe it. Rick was early. Rick was always late, and he picked today to be on time. Sheila yelled to Joann that Rick was here, and she came running into the room, past Sheila, and out the door to meet him.

They came back into the house, and the boys jumped on him. Jack came up from the basement and got himself and Rick a beer. They sat down and chatted for a few minutes, and then Jack stood up and suggested they get started. Sheila was so angry all of a sudden. *What's the big rush?* she thought. However, everyone else thought it was a great idea, and they started to load the truck. They were completely loaded forty minutes later. Sheila suggested they have a beer, but Rick declined.

Sheila felt a panic come over her. She asked Rick in a whisper if he had any cocaine. Sheila hadn't done it in years, but all of a sudden pot wasn't enough. Rick smiled and handed her a baggy discreetly. Neither of them wanted Jack to see. Sheila hugged her sister tightly. It was hard to let go, but she knew she had to. Joann let go, and she was crying. She would miss Sheila just as much as Sheila would miss her. Sheila started to cry, too.

*Behind the Drapes*

Jack and Rick calmed them down, and Rick and Joann left. Sheila watched the truck drive down the driveway and turn down the street, and when she couldn't see it any longer; she went to the bathroom and locked the door. Sheila pulled the little baggy out of her pocket and looked at it. "Welcome back, old friend," Sheila whispered to the baggy, and she did two large lines of coke.

Sheila walked back into the living room. Jack sat on the sofa and drank a beer while Jesse and Keegan watched a cartoon on television. Sheila walked into the kitchen, opened a beer, and took a big gulp. She rolled a big joint and yelled for Joann to join her. She started to bawl like a baby when she heard no response and realized she was alone. Sheila went into the garage and sat there alone, smoking her joint while she cried.

Sheila came back into the house, helped herself to another beer, and started dinner. Sheila called Jack and the boys for dinner. Jesse and Jack came into the kitchen with Keegan waddling behind them. Sheila washed the boys' hands, and they sat down to eat. Sheila was so quiet at dinner. Jesse asked his father what was wrong with Mommy, and Jack told him she was sad, but she would feel better soon. She excused herself, went to the bathroom, and locked the door. Sheila thought, *Yes, Jack. I will feel better soon.*

That night, when Sheila and Jack went to bed, he pounced on her before she was even under the covers. Sheila pleaded with him that she was too tired, but he was persistent. He told Sheila he had waited for years for them to be alone, and he wanted to enjoy his newfound privacy. Sheila told him she would be right back and went to do some more coke; Sheila came back to bed and lay down. She prayed it would be over soon, and closed her eyes tight.

# Chapter 19

Sheila sat on the floor with her sons, and they played with building blocks. Joann had been living in the city for four months now, and to Sheila it had felt like four years. Sheila had never been so lonely in her life. Joann had never been happier since the move back to the city. She had become something of a social butterfly. Sheila was pleased for her sister, but she missed her so much.

"Mum! Mum!" Keegan hollered excitedly. Keegan wanted his mother to see the tower he had made with his blocks. He was very proud of himself. Sheila looked over and smiled at her baby, and told Keegan it was beautiful. There was no doubt that Sheila loved her children. She had been blessed with two beautiful and happy boys. Still, they were not enough.

Sheila didn't know anyone in this town, and she was alone with the Jesse and Keegan at least 85 percent of the time. It was depressing her, and this made her feel guilty. She reminded herself how lucky she was to have a nice house to live in. She and the children had food on the table, and Jack treated them well. Sheila hated herself for her thoughts. She tried so hard to be happy, but at nineteen, she needed something

*Behind the Drapes*

more. Even the pot wasn't having the same effect, and she rarely saw Rick to get the good stuff.

Sheila looked up at the clock and told the boys it was time for their nap. They helped Sheila pick up the toys. Jesse told Sheila they needed a drink before bed. Jesse and Keegan were good little boys, and when they had finished their apple juice, they marched up the stairs to their rooms as Sheila followed. She tucked them both in their beds and sat at the top of the stairs, waiting. They were both asleep within five minutes, and Sheila went directly into the garage to smoke a joint.

Sheila came back into the house and made a cup of tea. She went into the living room and switched on the television. Sheila stared blankly at the screen, and her mind drifted. She fantasized about running away. She thought about having a job and lots of friends. She knew Jack would always take care of the boys; he had a loving family to help him. Then Sheila thought about having to tell Jesse and Keegan she was leaving, and the guilt and tears returned. She hated herself at that moment.

The phone rang, pulling Sheila from her thoughts. She ran to pick it up. It was Joann. She had gotten off early at work because of a union meeting, and she had skipped the meeting. She chatted excitedly about the past weekend and all the fun she had been having. Joann had met a boy she liked. Sheila was happy for her sister, but so envious. Sheila cried as she listened and did her best to hide it.

"Sheila, is everything alright? You sound upset," Joann asked. Sheila told her she was fine; she just missed her. It had been five weeks since Sheila had seen her. Actually, they had only seen each other three times since the move. Every few weeks, Rick would bring her up for a visit, but it was only for a few hours, and the visits seem to be further apart every time. Jack had been getting upset about the phone bills. It was long distance, so even the calls were limited now.

Joann told Sheila it was time for a break, and she needed to get away. Joann invited her down for the weekend. Just the thought of getting away lifted Sheila's spirits. Joann explained that Rick was having a big party Saturday night, and Sheila could bunk in with Joann. They could go to the clubs to dance, and Rick would pick them up after he got off work at around 11:00 PM. Joann suggested Sheila talk to Jack, and said she would call back later that night.

Sheila hung up the phone with a skip to her step. She decided to make a special dinner for Jack. She ran to the bookcase and started to look through her cookbooks to get some ideas for what to make. Sheila put the radio on and was singing away when Jesse came walking into the room. He smiled up at his mother, and Sheila picked him up and started to dance with him around the room. Jesse giggled.

Sheila heard Keegan calling for her, and she and Jesse went to get him. Sheila made the boys a small snack and told them to go play in the living room; she had to start to make dinner. Sheila had decided to make lasagna. She wanted to get it ready now, so she could just put it in the oven when Jack arrived. Sheila was never sure when he would be home. With the long drive and the overtime he had been working, she just played it by ear.

Sheila finished all the prep for dinner, and she and the boys went out to play while they waited for Jack to get home. By six o'clock, he still wasn't home. The boys had to eat soon, so Sheila brought them into the house and put dinner in the oven. She put a cartoon on for the boys, cleaned the dishes, and set the table. Just as Sheila was about to call the boys for dinner, she saw headlights in the driveway. Jack was home.

Lately, Jack's arrival was everything to Sheila. He was her only adult company. Jack walked into the house, and Sheila greeted him by jumping up into his arms and wrapping her legs around him. Sheila gave him a passionate kiss and told him dinner would be on the table in five minutes. She went to get Jack a beer, and he went into the living room to see his sons. Sheila heard the kids squeal with delight. Daddy was home.

Jack was thrilled with the lasagna, and the boys like it, too. Sheila got Jack another beer, and she thought, *Now is as good a time as any.* She sat down and looked at Jack with pleading eyes. Jack saw the look, and he recognized it. "What's up, Sheila? What do you want?" he asked. Sheila smiled and told him about Joann's phone call and invitation. Sheila had no idea how Jack would react. She had never asked for anything like this before.

Jack reached over and took Sheila's hand. She was not expecting what came next. "Sheila, you are cooped up here all the time with the kids. I know how young you are. You need to have a little fun and excitement. I think it's a great idea, and the boys and I can have a men's

*Behind the Drapes*

weekend. Nothing but beer and hammers," Jack joked. Sheila started to cry happy tears. She jumped out of her chair, hugged him, and gave him about twenty kisses. The boys giggled.

The phone rang, and it was Joann. Sheila told her what Jack had said, and she was very happy with the news. Sheila and Joann giggled and talked about everything they would do. They were both very excited for the coming weekend. Joann mentioned that she had told Rick Sheila might be coming down for the weekend. He had said it was a perfect weekend for a visit, with the party and everything. Sheila hung up the phone with a happy feeling she had not felt in a long time.

That night, as Sheila and Jack climbed into bed, he reminded Sheila how he had been so understanding about her weekend away, as he put his hand up her pajama top. Sheila thought to herself that she would probably want to go away again, so she might as well give in and make Jack happy. For the first time in Sheila's life, she became the aggressor. She climbed on top of Jack and pulled her top off. Sheila knew what men wanted. Her father had taught her well. She kept her eyes open, and she stayed in control.

The reaction Sheila received from Jack was unbelievable. He seemed to really enjoy her in an aggressive role. Sheila was able to almost enjoy herself. With her eyes open, she knew where she was and who she was with, and that made her feel safe. With Sheila being in control, she didn't feel like a victim, and she thought if she had to do this awful thing, she would have it her way from now on. Sheila was now in control, and Jack didn't seem to mind.

The next morning, Jack brought Sheila a cup of coffee in bed and told her he had taken the day off work. He had already started breakfast, and he would send up Jesse to get her when it was ready. Jack told her to stay in bed and relax, and handed her the newspaper. All this pampering shocked Sheila. She sat there drinking her coffee and staring blindly at the newspaper. Then it hit her.

Jack's pampering was due to their sexual experience the night before. Sheila was dumbfounded. Could this be the secret to men? Just give them sex, and you could have anything you wanted? Sheila allowed herself to remember the past for a brief moment. She remembered how Bobby had treated her differently after it had started. Sheila would try an experiment and test her theory soon.

Jesse came running into the bedroom with Keegan following. They jumped on Sheila's bed and told her breakfast was ready. Sheila gave her children a big kiss and began to tickle them as they giggled. She got out of bed and put on her bathrobe. Taking her boys by the hand, they went down for breakfast.

As Sheila reached the bottom of the stairs, she could smell the bacon cooking, and she realized how hungry she was. Jack had made apple pancakes and bacon, "apple cakes," as Jesse called them. They had a wonderful breakfast together and chatted and laughed; Jesse had definitely inherited his father's sense of humor. He had them laughing so hard. Sheila and Keegan thought they were both hysterical.

When they were finished with breakfast, Sheila got up to start the dishes, but Jack insisted on doing them. He told Sheila to go have a shower; they had a surprise for her. Jesse and Keegan giggled and tried to hide their smiles. They were obviously in on the secret. Sheila was happy to oblige, and she went to shower and dress as Jack started to clean the kitchen with the boys help.

Sheila took a long, hot shower and felt great as she stepped onto the mat. She dressed and went downstairs, excited to find out what her surprise was. The boys were watching cartoons, and Jack was just finishing cleaning the kitchen. Sheila walked in, and he looked at her and smiled. "You are sure a beauty, my love," Jack commented, and Sheila blushed.

Sheila was never able to see herself the way other people saw her. Even now, she had no idea how beautiful she was. "So where is my surprise?" Sheila asked.

Jack told her to be patient, and he yelled for the boys. "Turn off the television," he said. "It's time to go!" They came into the room, and Jack handed them their coats. They piled into the car, and Jack drove to the local mall. It was very small compared to the city malls, but there were a few little stores Sheila loved.

Jack pulled up to the front doors and put the car in park. Sheila looked at him strangely and wondered why he was not parking the car in the lot. Jack handed her a credit card and told her to go and buy herself something nice to wear to the party. Sheila had not spent money on herself for years, and all her clothing was really outdated. Jack wanted her to have something nice to wear.

Sheila squealed with delight. "Oh, thank you, Jack! This is the best surprise," she said. Jack explained that he and the boys had to go to the lumberyard and run a few errands. They would be back to pick her up in an hour or so. Sheila kissed him and the boys, and told them she would see them soon. Sheila thanked Jack again and went into the mall.

Sheila had a lot of fun shopping. She tried on several new outfits. Jack had not given Sheila a limit on what to spend, but she was careful not to take advantage of his generosity. It took Sheila a while to decide on something, and then she saw a manikin with the most beautiful pants and a blouse. Sheila found a sales girl and asked her about it. It was on sale for right around what Sheila wanted to spend. The girl got it for her and she tried it on.

When Sheila came out of the dressing room to look in the mirror, the sales girl gasped. The outfit looked excellent on Sheila. The pants were a soft tan color, and they fit perfectly, showing off her tiny waist. The blouse was deep red, and it looked beautiful with Sheila's hair and skin. It also accentuated her full breasts with the low neckline. It was by no means a sexy outfit, but on Sheila it looked incredibly sexy. She bought it, hoping Jack would like it.

Sheila had been shopping for sixty-five minutes, and when she saw her watch, she ran to the mall doors. She was relieved when Jack and the boys were not there yet. Sheila leaned on the wall, and in just a few minutes, they pulled up. She climbed into the car, and Jack handed her a bouquet of flowers. Sheila thanked him, thinking this was the most enjoyable day she'd had in a long time, and she was grateful.

That evening, Sheila finished cleaning up from dinner and came into the living room. She told the boys it was time for their baths. Jack told Sheila to go into the garage for a smoke, and then open the bottle of wine he had bought; he would take care of everything. That evening, Jack gave the boys their baths and tucked them into bed.

When he arrived back downstairs, Sheila was waiting for him in the living room with the bottle of wine and two glasses. Jack told Sheila the boys wanted to say goodnight. He asked her to try on her new outfit for him while she was upstairs. Sheila went upstairs, kissed Jesse and Keegan, and went into her room to change.

Sheila checked on them again, and Keegan was fast asleep, but Jesse was still awake. When he saw his mother, he smiled. "You look pretty, Mommy," Jesse commented, and it made Sheila very happy. She thanked him and told him she had bought it that day at the mall. "Go to sleep, Jesse," Sheila said then. "I will check on you in a minute."

When Sheila walked into the living room and Jack looked up at her, he threw himself on the floor and pretended to be having a heart attack. "Sheila, you have just stopped my heart. You look so beautiful," Jack said as he clutched at his chest. Sheila laughed at Jack's antics; she was pleased with his reaction.

The truth was, the moment Jack saw Sheila in her new outfit, he became a little nervous about her trip to the city. Jack had complete faith in Sheila. She had never given him a reason not to trust her, but it was the men whom she would meet that worried him. Jack reminded himself that Sheila would be with Rick, and he would make sure no one came too close to his sisters. And Jack knew how much Sheila deserved the time away.

When the weekend finally came, Sheila stood at the kitchen window and stared at the driveway, impatiently tapping her foot on the floor. She was waiting for Jack to get home, and he was running late. Her bus for the city was leaving in an hour, and Sheila did not want to miss it. She had been waiting all week for Friday to arrive, and it was finally here. Sheila was so excited about her trip to visit Joann.

She had not been to the city since her wedding, and she missed it a lot, but not half as much as she missed Joann. Finally, Sheila saw Jack's headlights in the driveway. Jack and the boys were going to drive her to the bus, which left from the gas station in town. On Sunday afternoon, Jack and the boys were going to pick Sheila up at Rick and Joann's. Jesse and Keegan missed Joann as well. They were excited to go visit her.

Jack came in the door, and Sheila started giving him instructions for the weekend. Sheila had prepared two casseroles, which were in the fridge, one for tonight and the other for tomorrow. Jack laughed at Sheila and reminded her they were his children too, and he knew how to take care of them. "The boys and I will be fine," he said. "I just want you to relax and enjoy your weekend."

Jesse and Keegan were watching cartoons. Sheila went up to them and told them she was leaving soon. She reminded them to be good boys for their father. They told their mother they would be good and help him. Jesse told Sheila he would take care of everything. He thought he was so grown-up, next to his little brother. Sheila always thought Jesse and Keegan's relationship reminded her of she and Joann's when they were young, and it made Sheila happy to realize they shared such a deep bond.

# Chapter 20

When the bus pulled up at the station, Sheila thought how big it was compared to the gas station she'd left from. *This is the city*, Sheila thought, and she smiled. She climbed down the stairs and looked around, and there she was. Joann was waving frantically at Sheila. Sheila threw her bag over her shoulder and ran to her sister. Then she put her bag down and stood in front of Joann, staring. Joann looked so different, and happy.

Joann had on a tight pair of black slacks, high heels, and a white blouse under a black leather coat. She was wearing makeup, and her hair was curled and tied up with a clip. Little wisps of hair were flying about in the wind. Sheila thought she looked so grown-up. She was impressed with her sister's new look. Joann was stylish and trendy, and Sheila thought she had never seen her sister look better.

Sheila followed as Joann grabbed her hand and pulled her through the crowded bus station. When they reached the front of the station, Joann walked up to a row of cabs and started to walk down the row, looking inside each one. At the back of the row, one cab started to beep its horn. Joann pulled Sheila, and they ran to the beeping cab.

*Behind the Drapes*

"It's Brother. He's going to drive us," Joann explained. Sheila was confused. Rick was driving a cab now? When they reached the car, Joann opened the door for Sheila to get in. Sheila climbed into the backseat and looked up. There, looking back at her, was a man, but it certainly wasn't her brother. He was a large Greek man with a big smile. He reached over and shook Sheila's hand.

Joann explained that this was a friend of Rick's. They worked together as waiters at the hotel, and Brother also drove a cab. Brother was a nickname that Rick had given him, and now everyone called him by it. Brother told Sheila he was very happy to meet her, and that any sister of Rick's was a friend of his. He had a thick accent, and Sheila found him charming.

Brother drove them home and came in with them. He waited while they changed. Joann explained that they were going to have a late dinner at the hotel with Rick. Sheila changed into her new outfit. She'd been planning on saving it for the party, but Sheila knew the hotel was fancy and she wanted to fit in. Jack had given her one hundred dollars to spend over the weekend, and if she had to, she would buy something new the next day.

Joann only changed her blouse. She went from the white one to a gold sleeveless number that looked very sexy. Joann told Sheila she loved her new clothes and she looked lovely. For once, Sheila felt good about her appearance. Sheila returned the compliment, and told Joann how impressed she was with the changes in her. When the girls went into the living room where Brother was watching television, he whistled loudly and commented on how beautiful Rick's sisters were.

They pulled up in front of the most beautiful building Sheila had ever seen. It had to be over one hundred years old, and it looked more like a castle than a hotel. Sheila thought the building was impressive, but she was not prepared for the interior; it was the most elegant thing she had ever seen. Joann had told her it was nice, but she had never gone into detail.

Brother walked them to the main dining room. When they entered, he took their coats to the coatroom. Brother returned and told them to have an enjoyable dinner, and he would see them later at the club. Sheila looked at the large wooden tables with the high-backed chairs, thinking the entire hotel was breathtaking. Rick saw them at the door and walked over to them with a big smile. He gave them both a kiss and said hello, then walked them to their table.

The table was beautifully set for two; it was by a large window with a magnificent view of the downtown core. It was dark, and there were lights shining everywhere. *It is glorious,* Sheila thought. Rick gave them the star treatment. He ordered their food for them and brought them over a bottle of wine. He was working, so he wouldn't be able to eat with them, but he wanted to treat them to a nice evening. When Rick got off work, he would take them to a few clubs.

The first course was a clam chowder, followed by Caesar salad, and next, lemon chicken served with wild rice and the best vegetables Sheila had ever tasted. For dessert, Rick served them coffee, liqueurs, and a chocolate torte. Both the girls were stuffed, and by now, it was almost midnight. They were the last ones in the dining room.

Sheila and Joann chatted. They were having a wonderful evening. When Sheila told Joann what fun she was having, Joann informed her it was only the beginning; there was more to come. It was late, and Sheila let out a yawn just as Rick was bringing them more coffee. He smiled at Joann, handed her something, and told her to take Sheila to the powder room.

Joann smiled at her brother and got up from the table. She told Sheila to follow her. They walked down a long, beautiful hallway and into the most luxurious bathroom Sheila had ever seen. Joann walked into a stall and pulled Sheila in with her. She locked the door behind them. Joann pulled out a bag of cocaine and started to cut up lines on the back of the toilet. She cut up four, two for each of them, and bent down and snorted two.

Joann handed Sheila the straw, and Sheila couldn't believe her eyes. Her little sister was doing cocaine. Joann, seeing the look on Sheila's' face, reminded her sister she was almost eighteen and an adult. She worked and had her own place. Nobody was going to tell her how to live her life.

Sheila knew she was right. Sheila was doing it, so who was she to tell Joann it was wrong? Sheila took the straw from her sister, bent down, and snorted her lines. Then they went back to having a fun evening. Sheila and Joann returned to the table wide awake. Rick had gotten

*Behind the Drapes*

them more liqueurs, so they sat down and chatted, waiting for Rick to finish work.

Sheila and Joann were laughing about nothing as Rick walked over to the table in jeans and a shirt. He was obviously finished, having changed out of his suit. It was 1:15 in the morning, and they were going out clubbing, as Rick described it. Brother came walking in, and Rick told them their chauffeur had arrived. They all laughed, and Brother went to retrieve Sheila and Joann's coats. He returned a moment later, and they left.

They piled into Brother's cab, and Rick told Sheila that Brother was off work. Still, they left the sign on top of the car to avoid the police, and they always found better parking. Rick cut up more coke for everyone, and Joann lit a joint. They arrived at a plain row of storefronts that where all closed; at the end, there was a door into the building. There were no windows, and Sheila didn't have a clue where this club was. There wasn't even a sign.

Rick went up to the door and knocked. Sheila could see someone looking through a peephole, and then the door flew open. The largest man Sheila had ever seen was standing there with an enormous smile. He grabbed Rick and gave him a hug. Rick pulled free, laughing, and introduced Tiny to Sheila. He already knew Joann and Brother.

He invited them all in, shook Sheila's hand, and told her and Joann to have fun. Once they got by Tiny, Sheila could hear loud music. They walked down a short corridor and a long flight of stairs. At the bottom was a door with another huge man standing there. He greeted everyone, same as the man upstairs, and allowed them to pass, telling them to have a good time.

They walked through the door, and the sound of pounding music filled the air. There were people everywhere. The place was packed. There was an enormous bar to the left and a large dance floor with a DJ booth to the right. The entire remainder of the club was covered with sofas and large armchairs, with small coffee tables here and there.

They made their way to the bar. There were three bartenders working, and they all seemed to know Rick, Joann, and Brother. One really handsome one came over and screamed hello. Rick ordered everyone a beer, and Joann pulled Sheila onto the dance floor. The music was pounding in Sheila's ears. She could feel it in her entire body. She and Joann danced for half an hour before they went to back to the bar.

They were both really thirsty and downed their beers. When Joann waved to the handsome bartender, he literally came running over. Joann smiled at him and asked for another beer for her and Sheila. Joann tried to introduce them, but the music was so loud Sheila couldn't hear a word. Sheila and the bartender just smiled at each other and waved. Joann grabbed her beer and pulled Sheila by the hand to the bathroom.

They arrived in the bathroom and waited for a free stall. When one opened up, they went in and did some more coke; Joann explained that she and the bartender who served them had been dating, and Sheila had to keep it a secret from Rick. His name was Luc. He and Rick played hockey together and were really good friends. Joann and Luc had been dating for five weeks behind Rick's back, and he had no clue anything was going on. Luc was twenty-nine and much too old for Joann, but Sheila promised to keep her sister's secret.

Joann and Sheila went to find Rick. He was talking to a few guys who, when they saw Sheila, all started making passes at her. They were very pushy, and Rick stepped in, telling them she was his little sister, and she was married with kids. This seemed to stop them in their tracks. Sheila and Joann went back to the dance floor and danced the night away. They had a blast. It was more fun than Sheila had ever had, and she loved it.

They arrived home at 4:30 AM. Rick and Joann both lit joints, and Sheila joined them in smoking them. A few minutes later, everyone went to bed. It took Sheila almost two hours to fall asleep from the effects of the coke. It had never bothered her like this before, but Sheila had never done as much as she had tonight. Finally, Sheila drifted to sleep, thinking about the exciting night she'd just had.

Sheila woke the next afternoon with a terrible sinus headache. She looked over, and Joann was already up. Sheila got up, and went to brush her teeth and wash her face. When she came out of the bathroom, she smelled coffee, and she followed the smell right to the kitchen. Rick and Joann were sitting there having coffee. Sheila walked over to the pot and poured herself a large cup. Then she sat down at the table with them.

*Behind the Drapes*

"Good morning, sleepy head," Joann said with a smile. Sheila smiled in response, and Rick threw a bottle of aspirin at her. Sheila took two and washed them down with a gulp of coffee. Rick lit a joint and passed it to Sheila. He told her it would make her feel better. Rick got up and started to cook breakfast. He and Joann had a system. Rick did all the cooking, and Joann did all the cleaning and dishes. Rick thought of himself as quite the chef, and he *was* quite good, having learned a lot working at the hotel.

The three of them ate their breakfast and chatted. Sheila thanked Rick for the lovely dinner. "So that is how the other half lives," Sheila commented. They all laughed and chatted about when they were kids, though they didn't touch on anything too heavy. It felt good, almost therapeutic to laugh about issues that had given all three of them such deep scars.

All of the children of Bobby and Hugette Parks had scars. The five of them had different types of scars, but nonetheless, they all carried their past on their shoulders. "Have either of you ever heard from Pauline or Peter?" Joann asked her siblings. Sheila and Rick both shook their heads no, and they all sat in silence wondering where they were, hoping they were together and happy.

Rick left to go play hockey, and Joann and Sheila went shopping. They took the bus to the mall where Sheila used to work, and it brought back so many memories. They went by the Snack Stop, but Sheila didn't recognize anyone, so they didn't stop in. Brenda hadn't worked there for over a year, and Sheila wasn't sure about Cheryl, but she didn't see her there. Sheila and Joann went off in search of a new top for Sheila to wear at the party.

Sheila and Joann had a great afternoon together. They tried on hundreds of outfits and had a ball. Joann bought a couple of new tops, and Sheila found a beautiful orange top that would match her new pants perfectly. They heard over the loudspeaker that the mall was closing, and Sheila looked down at her watch. It was already 6:00 PM. They walked to the bus stop and waited for the bus.

"Look, Sheila. Isn't that Paula, the girl we used to hang out with in the project?" Joann said. Sheila looked, and sure enough, it was Paula. The awful memories flashed in Sheila's mind. She grabbed Joann's arm and started to run in the opposite direction. Joann didn't know what was going on, but she followed her sister instinctively. Sheila was trembling and tears filled her eyes when she finally stopped running; they had run four blocks.

"What was that about, Sheila?" Joann asked. Sheila just shook her head no and asked Joann to light a joint. They were close to a park, and they walked and smoked the joint in silence. Joann didn't know what had happened with Paula, but it clearly seemed to upset Sheila. She decided not to pry. If Sheila wanted her to know, she would tell her. But Sheila never would tell her or anyone.

They came out of the park and walked back to the mall. Paula was gone, so they waited for the bus. When they got home, Rick was getting ready to leave for work. Sheila asked him for some coke, and he gladly gave her some. Sheila and Joann did a few lines. Joann called for Chinese food, and then Sheila called to check in with Jack and the boys.

Jack told her all was well and asked if she was having fun. Sheila told him about the night before and the great dinner. Sheila asked to talk to the boys, and Jesse got on the line. He said he was taking care of everyone. Keegan got on and told his mother he missed her, and Sheila reminded him only one more sleep and she would be home. Jack got back on the line and told Sheila he would be there the next day at 2:00 PM to pick her up. They said their good-byes, and Sheila hung up.

Sheila and Joann ate their Chinese food and had a nap. Neither one of them had slept much the night before. Sheila had woken up and 12:30 PM, but she hadn't fallen to sleep until after 6:00 AM. Joann woke Sheila up at 9:45 PM and told her she was going for a shower to freshen up. She had a few lines waiting for Sheila.

Sheila looked down at the cocaine and thought she had better not. She couldn't afford to be too sick the next day with the kids. Sheila sat there alone with her thoughts, and she started to think about Paula. Sheila pushed the image from her mind, picked up the straw, and snorted the coke. She rolled a couple of joints and went to see if Joann was finished with the bathroom.

The girls finished getting ready. They smoked a joint and did a few lines while waiting for Brother to pick them up. They were going to a club Joann liked, and Rick would pick them up after work to go home for the party. They heard Brother knocking at the door, and Joann went

*Behind the Drapes*

to let him in. He came into the living room, greeted Sheila, and lit a joint. Brother asked Joann for a few lines, and Sheila gladly cut some lines for everyone.

Sheila and Joann arrived at the club. Sheila thought this one seemed nicer than the one they were at the night before. There were tables and chairs everywhere, and a dance floor. There were windows around three sides of the building. It was busy, but you could walk around easily. Sheila and Joann went to the bar to order drinks. The bartenders both waved at Joann, and the pretty one named Sammy came over.

Sammy was a beautiful girl with a big smile and a thick French accent. Joann introduced Sheila to her, and they ordered a couple of Caesars. Sammy was back in a flash, and the girls grabbed a table. A steady stream of people—men and women—came by the table to chat with Joann. She seemed to know everyone. Joann and Sheila went to the bathroom and did some more lines, then hit the dance floor.

Sheila was dancing with a very attractive man when Joann tapped her on the shoulder and told her it was time to go. They went up to the bar and asked Sammy for their bill and three tequila shots. Sammy came over with the tequila and Joann handed one to Sheila and Sammy. She picked up the last one. They toasted to a good night and downed the tequila. Joann and Sheila split the bill, and they were just about to go out to wait for Rick, but then he appeared at the bar.

Rick ordered three more tequilas and they each did another shot. They left the club and got into Brother's cab. Rick pulled out a couple of joints and lit them one by one. He passed them around the car. By the time they arrived at the house, Sheila and Joann were both feeling pretty drunk. Rick suggested they have some water and some more coke so they could stay up for the party.

Joann agreed and got them both a vodka and water, while Rick prepared the lines of coke. Joann handed Sheila her drink and winked at her. Sheila took a sip and nearly choked, it was so strong. Sheila and Joann looked at each other and started to laugh. Rick put the music on loud, and people started to arrive. Within an hour, there must have been fifty people in the house.

Men anxious to get to know her surrounded Sheila. She was enjoying all the attention. Sheila chatted with some people she hadn't seen since she'd lived in the project. Most of them were Rick's friends, and they all told Sheila the same thing: you have really grown up to be a beauty; I haven't seen you since you were just a kid. The drinks and drugs kept flowing, and people kept arriving.

Finally, at about eight the next morning, people started to leave. By nine, only Sheila, Joann, Rick, Ralph, and Brother were left. Ralph was passed out on the floor, but the rest of them were still wide awake from all the cocaine they had consumed. Brother got up and told them he had to get going or his wife would kill him. Sheila wasn't even aware he was married until then. He left, and only the Parks kids remained.

"I don't want to be married anymore. I think I want a divorce," Sheila blurted out. Shocked, Rick and Joann looked at each other, then at Sheila. It was so out of the blue that Rick and Joann assumed she must be kidding, so they started to laugh. It didn't take long before they knew she wasn't joking. Sheila started to cry, and she just couldn't stop. Joann came close to her and hugged her. Sheila hadn't said anything about this all weekend, and Joann didn't understand what had happened.

"What the hell is going on, Sheila? Where is this coming from?" Rick demanded. Sheila started to explain to them how she had been feeling ever since Joann had moved back to the city. Sheila was miserable. She was living in a new place where she didn't know a soul, and she spent all her time alone with the kids. Sheila made it very clear that she loved her boys, but she had never loved Jack, and ever since the move she hadn't been happy at all.

When Joann lived with her, it was bearable, but now all she did was dream of running away. Jack was barely ever home, and Sheila was so lonely, she was about to break. Jack had even been complaining about the phone bill, and now all her phone calls to Joann had to be approved by him. Sheila hated not having her own money. She had to rely on Jack for everything. She didn't even have her driver's license, so she had to rely on Jack for her transportation as well. Sheila reminded Rick that he had told her to try the marriage, and if it didn't work out she could get a divorce.

"Sheila, has Jack been treating you well?" Rick inquired. Sheila nodded yes as the tears continued to stream down her face. Jack was a good husband. That wasn't the problem. Sheila was miserable, and she couldn't go on living or feeling this way. "I think you need to make some changes in your life, Sheila. You don't need a divorce. You just need to fix the problem," Rick continued.

"Changes; what changes are going to make me feel better? Jack knows I hate living there, but he says we have to stay until we build up equity. It's going to be years before we can afford to move back to the city," Sheila cried. She felt so guilty about her feelings. She knew most people would kill to have a good husband and beautiful children like she did. But Sheila wanted a new life, something more exciting. She was tired of staying at home, being just a mom. This weekend, she had observed the exciting lifestyle her sister and brother lived, and she wanted a piece of it.

"Sheila, why don't you just get a job and meet people?" Joann pleaded. "I have so many friends since I got my job. I bet if you meet people, you won't mind living there so much." Joann loved Jack like a brother, and she didn't want to see them break up. If Sheila only knew how much Joann envied her, she thought. She had a loving family, and Jack treated her so well.

Sheila knew that Jack did not want her to work, but she conceded that maybe Joann was right. If she had some friends, then it would be more enjoyable. But Sheila reminded Joann how tough it had been for her to make friends when she was living there. Rick and Joann made Sheila realize that was kids in school, but this was adults in the real world. Rick also felt that Sheila should get her driver's license so she wouldn't feel so isolated. He said all Sheila needed was a little more in her life—a job, friends, anything to add a little excitement.

After hours of Rick and Joann convincing Sheila, she decided she needed a little independence rather than a divorce. Sheila looked down at her watch and let out a screech when she realized it was 11:20 AM. Jack would be there to pick her up in three hours, and she hadn't even slept yet. Rick told her not to panic and gave her a bag of cocaine to take home with her. "This will keep you awake as long as you need," he said. "But for now, I think we should all try and get a little sleep."

Jesse and Keegan looked so happy when Sheila saw them. They ran and jumped into her arms. When Joann entered the room, they ran to her and told her how much they missed her. Sheila made some coffee and apologized to Jack for having to bang on the door so long. Nobody had heard them knocking, and finally Jesse had tried the knob, which wasn't locked, so they came in. Sheila had awoken to Jack and the boys yelling for her, and she'd jumped out of bed and run down the stairs.

Jack was in fine spirits. He wasn't upset at all. He'd assumed Sheila would be tired after her weekend away. They had their coffee while Jesse and Keegan told them about their weekend. They let it slip to their mother that Jack had built something for Sheila. All Sheila wanted to do was go home with her family and sleep. She went upstairs with the boys following to pack her things.

Sheila came back downstairs and told Jack she was ready to go. Sheila thanked Joann for a great weekend, and they left. Sheila and the boys slept the whole way home, and when they pulled into the driveway, Jack woke them up. "We're home," he said. Sheila felt awful. She was tired and hung-over. However, when she walked into the house, she felt better just being home. Sheila went into the bathroom and locked the door. She knew how to get through the rest of the day.

# Chapter 21

Sheila awoke the next day still not feeling totally recuperated after the weekend. She felt a little down and guilty, and she didn't even know why—she hadn't done anything wrong. She realized it was probably due to the reaction she knew she would get when she mentioned getting a job to Jack. She pulled herself out of bed, and as she went down the stairs, she could hear Jack singing in the shower. Sheila wished she felt that happy.

She walked into the living room and looked at the coffee table Jack had made for her. It really was lovely; Jack was talented. Sheila went into the kitchen, put on a pot of coffee, and sat at the table lost in her thoughts. Sheila jumped when she felt something on her neck. She turned around and saw Jack standing there. He laughed at startling her and poured them both some coffee.

Sheila and Jack enjoyed their coffee and chatted. Sheila thanked him again for the new table, and he seemed proud of himself. Sheila thought to herself, *It's now or never*, and she just told him. "Jack, I want to get a job and my driver's license."

Jack put his coffee cup down and looked at her angrily. He was just about to say something when Keegan came into the kitchen, calling his mother. Sheila went to him, picked him up, and got him some orange juice. Jack put his coat on and left, telling Sheila they would finish their conversation that night.

Sheila knew it was going to be tough to convince him. Then she remembered—it was time for her experiment. Sheila took the boys for a long walk that morning. Jesse walked most of the way, while Keegan rode in the wagon. Sheila went to the local mall and bought something sexy for that evening. Then she went to the grocery store to buy something nice for dinner. They stopped at a toy store, and Sheila bought the boys each a little something.

Sheila had only spent forty-two dollars on the weekend. Everyone had been buying most of her drinks, and Rick had paid for dinner. Sheila hadn't given Jack his change. Just having a little money in her pocket made her feel good. Sheila thought it would be nice to have her own money, to do things like this on the spur of the moment. Normally, she had to get money from Jack, and he would only give it to her if he felt it was something necessary.

When Sheila and the boys got home, they were exhausted from all the fresh air and the long walk. She fed the boys lunch, and Jesse asked to go for his nap early. Keegan agreed. Sheila put them down for their nap, went to the bathroom, and locked the door. Sheila was tired as well, but she wanted to start on the prep for dinner. Sheila was going to make one of Jack's favorite meals: stuffed pork tenderloin with roasted potatoes and glazed carrots.

Jesse and Keegan were still sleeping at 4:30 PM. Sheila didn't want them to be up too late that night, so she woke them and made them an early dinner. She let them play outside until 6:00 PM, and then gave them their baths and got them ready for bed. Just as they were coming down the stairs, Sheila heard the door open. Jack was home. Jesse and Keegan heard the door as well, and ran to greet their father. Sheila followed.

Sheila got the boys watching cartoons. She checked on dinner in the oven and got Jack a beer. Sheila walked up to Jack and handed him his beer. She kissed him on the cheek. She smiled at him, and he smiled back. They each hoped the other had changed their minds. Sheila told Jack they were going to be having a late dinner alone once the boys had gone to bed. Jack thought it was a great idea, and he went snooping

*Behind the Drapes*

in the oven. When he saw the pork tenderloin, he knew Sheila was buttering him up and had not changed her mind.

Jesse and Keegan went to bed without a problem. Sheila set the table and opened a bottle of wine. Jack helped Sheila serve the plates, and they sat down to eat. Sheila purposely kept the conversation light during dinner, and Jack was grateful. He'd had a long day and needed a little time to unwind. When they were finished with their dinner, Sheila started to clear the table, but Jack suggested she go to the garage for a joint, and he would clear the table.

Sheila thanked him and went into the garage. She sat there thinking of her strategies and enjoyed her smoke. When Sheila was finished, she went into the kitchen and told Jack to leave the dishes; she would take care of them in the morning. Sheila picked up the wine bottle and their glasses, and went into the living room. Jack followed.

They sat there on the sofa, and Jack started, speaking softly. "Sheila, I've been thinking. I think it would be a good idea for you to get your driver's license, and we could start shopping for a second vehicle. It would give you a little independence, and that's a good thing." His voice rose, and he continued. "However, Sheila, I think going to work would be a bad thing for you to do. The boys and I need you here."

"Jack, what about what I need?" Sheila asked him. Jack was just about to speak, but Sheila gently placed her finger over his mouth to silence him. "Let's talk about it later," Sheila instructed. Sheila told Jack she would be back and went to the bathroom, locking the door. Sheila did a few lines of cocaine and changed into the sexy lingerie she had bought that day.

Sheila went back into the living room. She had a sexy smile on her face and a very see-through teddy barely covering her body. When Jack saw her, he couldn't believe Sheila was his; she was so beautiful and luscious. Sheila walked over to him and climbed on top of him, straddling her legs around him. With her eyes wide open, she started to kiss Jack and tell him how much she wanted him.

They had an erotic experience that Jack would never forget. Again, Sheila stayed in control, and she enjoyed herself a little. The cocaine helped her to concentrate on the here and now. When they were finished, Sheila went to get a blanket to cover them up; she filled their wine glasses and snuggled close to Jack. He was feeling so satisfied and content when Sheila asked again.

"Jack, I need to get a job for my peace of mind. I am lonely all the time, and miserable. I love you and the boys. I'm sorry, but I need more. Please let me get just a part-time job, and I'll only work when you are here with the boys," Sheila pleaded. Jack looked at her, and at that moment could not say no to her, even though he believed it to be a terrible mistake. Against his better judgment, Jack nodded yes. Sheila squealed with delight and jumped on top of him. Again, she took control.

The next morning, Jack kissed Sheila and told her he would go and put coffee on. Sheila lay there in bed with a huge smile on her face. She thought to herself she had been taught a valuable lesson. Her experiment had turned out positive. She could have anything she wanted from men. Sheila knew what it was that mattered to them most, and she knew how to manipulate them with it, how to stay in control. Bobby and Marty had taught her their desires, and Jack had just confirmed what she had suspected.

Sheila went into the bathroom and locked the door. As she snorted the coke, she told herself she liked this stuff a lot. Whenever she had it, she couldn't stop doing it until it was gone. Before, she had been using it to make her forget, but now she just wanted it. Sheila never even thought of getting help or stopping. She only thought of when she could get some more. Yes, she needed a car. Sheila got up and went downstairs for coffee.

Sheila went into the kitchen, and Jack handed her a coffee. She sat down with him at the table. She was just about to remind Jack about his agreeing she could look for work, but before Sheila could say a word, Jack informed her that he would pick up a newspaper for her on the way home, so she could look for a job. He said he would start teaching her how to drive that evening after dinner, and he would also start looking for a second car. It was precisely what Sheila wanted to hear.

Later that morning, when Jack had left and the boys had eaten their breakfast, Sheila decided to take the kids for another long walk. First, Sheila finished all the dishes. It took quite a while, there being so many from the night before, plus the ones from this morning. The entire time she washed them, Sheila was singing to the radio. Things were looking

*Behind the Drapes*

up, and she felt happier than she had since they have moved from the city.

Sheila changed and asked the boys if they wanted to go for a walk. They both yelled yes, and she helped them change their clothes. Sheila told them she just had to go to the bathroom, and after doing a few more lines, she was ready to go. The boys put on their coats, and Jesse got the wagon from the garage. Then they left.

Sheila wanted to pick up a local newspaper. She knew that Jack would bring her one from the city, but she didn't feel there would be any ads that would be close enough for her. Sheila didn't want to drive all the way into the city to work. She wanted to meet new people in her town she could socialize with. Sheila and Jesse started to pull Keegan on the wagon, and as they reached the end of the driveway and turned, Sheila felt an excitement build in her.

She only took them half as far as the day before. Instead of going to the mall, she just went to the corner store. She let the boys pick out a treat for after lunch, and Sheila got a local newspaper. The man who owned the store was very sweet. He really enjoyed when Sheila came in with the boys. He gave them a free sucker every time they went in, and Sheila was always proud of the way the boys thanked him, so sincerely.

After lunch, Sheila tucked the boys in for their nap and made herself a cup of tea. While her tea was steeping, she went upstairs. Both the boys were sound asleep, so she took the opportunity to go out to the garage for a smoke. Sheila came in and drank her tea while she read the paper. She became very excited when she saw an ad for a part-time hostess at Barnabee's, the restaurant in town by the river.

She and Jack had only been there once, on the day they had bought their house. Sheila had really liked the restaurant. It was in a small hotel, and she thought she would love to work there. Rick worked in a restaurant, and he loved it. Sheila knew there was no comparing Rick's hotel to this one, but Sheila thought she wouldn't enjoy working in that formal atmosphere, while she did like the atmosphere of this place.

The ad stated to apply in person anytime after 5:00 PM. Sheila thought she would go and apply that night when Jack took her driving. Sheila ran to the bathroom and locked the door. As she snorted her lines, Sheila fantasized about getting the job. She happily went to her room and started looking through her clothes to see what she would wear. Sheila was so excited at the prospect of working, she would have taken a job scrubbing out horse stalls, just to get out and meet people.

That night after dinner, Jack drove her over to the restaurant. Sheila looked very pretty. She wore the new outfit she had bought the week before. She was so excited that she wasn't even nervous. When they pulled up, Sheila looked at Jack and the boys, and smiled. They wished her luck, and she got out and looked back, waving as she approached the front doors.

Sheila opened the doors and walked into Barnabee's Bar and Grill. The interior was all wood with huge windows overlooking the river. The place was fairly full, but Sheila didn't see anyone in a uniform, so she climbed up a couple of steps to the bar area. It was raised on a platform, with a half wall running all around it. There had to be thirty bar stools, Sheila thought. She looked around and noticed a little area down at the end of the bar. Two people in uniforms stood there talking.

Sheila walked over and waited quietly for one of them to notice her. Finally, the waitress saw Sheila and came right over. Sheila gave her a big smile and told her she was there to apply for the hostess job. The waitress told Sheila to have a seat, and she would go get the manager. Sheila sat at the bar, and the bartender came over to chat with her while she waited. He introduced himself as Parker. He was very friendly and funny, and he told Sheila dirty jokes until the manager arrived.

The manager came over and said hi to Sheila. He asked her to come with him to the office. Sheila followed him. As she watched him walking before her, she started to feel nervous. They arrived at the office, and he pointed to a chair for Sheila. He sat across from her and smiled. Sheila started to relax. They chatted for a few minutes, and he didn't even ask her any questions about the job, just talked to her about the weather and trivial things.

Finally, he introduced himself. As Sheila reached over to shake his hand, she saw him looking at her chest. His name was Jerry, and he managed the hotel as well as the restaurant. He was young, Sheila guessed about two or three years older than she was. He was tall, chubby, and, Sheila thought, a little sleazy.

Jerry told Sheila the job was hers if she wanted it. Sheila smiled and told him she really wanted the job, thanking him. He told her to come

*Behind the Drapes*

back at 5:00 PM the next day to start her training, and gave her an application to fill out. Sheila took the paper from him and started to fill it out as he leaned back in his chair. Sheila could feel him staring at her, and it made her uncomfortable, but she wanted this job. She thought she could put up with him, as long as he didn't touch her.

When Sheila was finished filling out the application, they walked back to the restaurant together. This time, however, Jerry followed Sheila, enjoying the view. Sheila asked Jerry what he wanted her to wear the next day, and he told her he would give her a uniform, but she should wear black pants. Sheila thanked him again and waved to Parker as she left.

Sheila walked up to the car, and when Jack saw her face, he knew she had gotten the job. Sheila climbed into the car and said she got the job; she started the next day. The boys were pleased for their mother because she was happy, and that made them happy. Jack had a feeling of doom he couldn't explain. He didn't say anything to Sheila. Jack reached over and gave her a kiss. He told her, "Congratulations," and they drove home.

# Chapter 22

Sheila paced the floor in her uniform—black skirt, tight white blouse, and black heels—as she waiting for Jack. She was going to be late for work if he didn't get home soon. She hated to be late. Sheila had been working for two months now, and she had been promoted to a waitress after one week of working there. She loved her job. She was consistently making over one hundred dollars in tips per shift, and she was working at least four shifts a week, but usually more, which infuriated Jack. He had agreed to part-time. Jack thought this was too much.

Sheila worked Thursday, Friday, Saturday, and Sunday nights. However, Jerry would phone Sheila often to cover other shifts, and she always said yes. Jack felt like he never saw her, and her response to that was now he knew what Sheila had felt like before she started work. Sheila just loved working. She felt needed and wanted, and she had friends now. One girl in particular, Natasha, had a lot in common with Sheila. They got along very well, especially considering Natasha was eleven years older.

Natasha was a tiny girl with dark black eyes, dark skin, and beautiful long curly jet -black hair. Like Sheila, Natasha had two sons, only slightly older than Jesse and Keegan, although Natasha's boys lived in the city with their father. Natasha had been divorced for a few years but she saw her boys often, and the four boys played together well. Sheila and Natasha had become instant friends. They both liked to party, and they liked their drugs. They worked all the same shifts, and for Sheila, work had become her social life.

Sheila, still pacing, picked up the phone and called work. Natasha answered and told Sheila not to worry, she would cover for her. Sheila checked on Jesse and Keegan. They were quietly watching cartoons. She went to the bathroom and locked the door. Just as Sheila was finished snorting the cocaine, she heard Jesse holler, "Daddy!" and with a smile, she ran from the bathroom. Sheila came into the kitchen, grabbed her purse, and gave both the boys a kiss. Then she gave Jack a peck on the lips and grabbed for the door.

"Wait a minute, Sheila! You can't even spare five minutes to talk to me?" Jack screamed as he grabbed hold of Sheila's arm tightly. "All we do is pass each other lately, and I don't like it. Things have to change," Jack continued in a calmer voice. Sheila looked at him angrily and pulled her arm from his grip.

"Jack, look at the time. I'm going to be late for work. I don't have time to argue about this now," Sheila said. She was always annoyed with him lately.

"I don't care if you're late! I want you to quit your job!" Jack demanded, yelling at the top of his lungs.

Sheila looked at him and saw her father screaming at her, and at that moment, everything changed. Sheila heard Keegan crying, and all of a sudden Sheila realized Jesse and Keegan were standing there, staring. She bent down and told them everything was fine in a soft voice. She brought them back to their cartoons. She gave them both a kiss and told them she had to go to work, and she would see them in the morning.

Sheila walked back into the kitchen and stood directly in front of Jack. She stared at him, and her eyes were ice as she quietly whispered, "Don't you ever take that tone with me again, especially in front of Jesse and Keegan. Do you hear me Jack? I will not put up with it." Sheila realized she was clenching her teeth as she spoke and knew it was time to leave. Without another word, Sheila went out and climbed into the car.

Sheila had her license now, although it had only been two weeks. She pulled out of the driveway much too fast, spraying gravel everywhere. Jack stood in the window of the porch and watched her leave; he felt her slipping away from him, and he didn't know what to do. Sheila had given Jack a look tonight that frightened him; it was almost like she hated him. He went back into the kitchen, got himself a beer, and watched cartoons with his boys.

Sheila pulled into the parking lot and looked at the time; she was five minutes late. She jumped out of the car, ran, and pulled open the large wooden door. Sheila hurried to the staff room behind the bar area, opened her locker, and put on her apron. She put her coat and purse in her locker and checked her makeup and hair; she quickly ran to the bathroom and did a quick line.

Sheila went through the kitchen and yelled hello to the boys working. They turned and yelled hello back. They loved Sheila and would do anything for her. She was beautiful and always nice to them, even when they were busy. Sheila came out from the kitchen and looked around. She didn't see Jerry anywhere, and she was relieved. Sheila came around the corner and climbed the few stairs to the bar area. Natasha and Parker were there, and they both gave her a big smile.

"Hey sexy," Parker yelled out, and a few boys sitting at the bar yelled hello to Sheila when they saw her. Sheila waved at them with a big smile and asked Natasha where Jerry was.

"Don't worry, sweetie. Jerry won't be here until six. We have two dinner reservations, and the tables are set. You take the nook, and I'll take the floor," Natasha said with that soft voice. Sheila always thought she sounded like a five-year-old. The dining room was split in two sections. Half was raised up three feet with a thick wooden railing all around; it overlooked the rest of the dining room and bar. They called this section the nook and the lower one the floor.

"Sheila, everything is done and ready to go. I'm just going to run to the bathroom and powder my nose," Natasha whispered with a smile. Sheila gave her a smile and nodded. Sheila checked the reservation book, and then checked her section to make sure everything was ready to go.

Sheila started to think of her fight with Jack. She couldn't believe the way he had acted earlier. He had reminded Sheila of her father and it scared her. Sheila would rather be single for the rest of her life than to put up with Jack acting like Bobby. Sheila was starting to get angry as she thought about it. Then she noticed some people coming into the restaurant and pushed the thoughts from her mind. Sheila immediately got into work mode, and, with a huge smile on her face, she went to greet them.

Sheila ran up to the service bar to pick up a couple of brandies. It had been a crazy dinner. Sheila and Natasha had been running for the last few hours, and things were just starting to slow down. Sheila whistled to get Parker's attention, and he quickly came over to the service bar. "What do you need, my love?" Parker inquired, and it made Sheila laugh. He was the biggest flirt. It didn't matter which girl it was. He treated every female like she was a god. He always made Sheila laugh, because she knew he was harmless.

Parker was a small thin man with a charming personality. Sheila had liked him from the first day she'd met him. Actually, there was not a person Sheila had met through work whom she didn't like. Everyone had been so friendly with Sheila, especially the men. Even Jerry had won her over. Jerry was still creepy, but he had never crossed the line with Sheila, and he had a funny side that she enjoyed.

Sheila delivered her brandy, and then told Natasha she was going to do a line before they stripped the room. Thursday, Friday, and Saturday nights they had a DJ at 8:30, so they had to take everything off the tables. Tablecloths, cutlery, candles, and the salt and pepper shakers had to be removed. By 9:30, the place would be packed. This was when the job really became fun for Sheila. After nine, it wasn't a restaurant. It was a bar with loud music and people partying.

When Sheila returned from the bathroom, Natasha said it was her turn, and she went to do a line. When Natasha got back, they cleared the tables together and chatted. Sheila told her friend about the fight she'd had with Jack, and how he wanted her to quit her job. Sheila assured Natasha she had no intentions of quitting. Sheila was making excellent money and having so much fun. This was the first time in Sheila's life she was building a little self-esteem.

People were constantly telling Sheila she was a great waitress. Even Jerry, who was tight with the compliments, had told her she was doing a great job. Sheila loved being good at something; it made her feel significant. Men were always telling Sheila how beautiful and sexy she was, and Sheila would play the game and play it well. She was aware her tips would reflect how she responded to them.

Sheila had been shocked at how the men came on to her, but it was a small town, and she was a fresh new face. They all wanted a piece of her. Natasha had warned Sheila to be careful and explained how they only wanted one thing. Natasha didn't have to warn Sheila. She knew exactly what the pigs wanted. Nobody had to explain it to her.

The music started blaring, and Sheila and Natasha smiled at each other. The DJ had arrived. His name was Matt. He was short chubby guy with dark brown hair, blue eyes, and a sweet personality. Matt was twenty-two, loved music, and had a very desperate crush on Natasha. Natasha thought he was fun, but she didn't want a man in her life. Still, he was not giving up, and was always bringing Natasha little gifts.

The place started to fill up. Sheila and Natasha were running and having so much fun, but the best part was they were making a fortune. Sheila ran up to the service bar around eleven, and as she stood there waiting for Parker to get her drinks, she felt arms go around her waist. She turned to see Vic standing there. Her face became hot as she blushed a deep red, and Sheila felt her legs wobble.

Vic was one of the doormen. He was thirty-nine, tall, very muscular and handsome, with mesmerizing blue eyes and graying hair. Sheila and Vic had terrible crushes on each other, and everyone knew about it. It was so obvious. Sheila was very uncomfortable with her feelings. She had never felt this way about a man before. In the past, she had found some men attractive, like Kim's boyfriend Steve, but Sheila had never felt this intense burning in her before. She didn't know how to react; but it didn't matter. Sheila was married, and Vic was divorced, but had a girlfriend.

"How are you tonight, sexy lady?" Vic asked as he brushed a piece of hair out of Sheila's eyes.

"Fine, but busy," Sheila responded shyly. She grabbed her drinks, thanked Parker, and rushed away from Vic just like she always did. Vic stood there and watched her walk away. He enjoyed observing her as she talked to the customers. Vic kept his eye on her and watched as she arrived at the table to deliver her drinks. She was smiling and laughing with them. Vic wanted her, and he wasn't giving up so easily. Suddenly,

*Behind the Drapes*

Vic heard Parker yelling. He looked down the bar and saw two men starting to get rough with each other, so he went back to work.

Finally, Sheila heard Matt announcing last call, and she knew her shift would soon be over. They had been so busy that she and Natasha hadn't had time to go do a line for a few hours, and they both wanted one desperately. It took the girls twenty-five minutes to do last call, and then, when they were finished, they went downstairs together into the public bathroom near the weight rooms. Sheila and Natasha did a few lines each, then went back to the bar to put in their orders.

It usually took Vic about an hour to get all the customers out. Then they would lock the doors, clean the place, and party. Sheila reset the nook with tablecloths and set the tables for breakfast, while Natasha cleaned the floor. The floor was always the dirtiest. It was closer to the dance floor, and more people sat down there at night. Vic helped them by picking up beer bottles and empty glasses around the dance floor.

Sheila finished the nook, went to the kitchen, and rolled a couple of joints. Natasha came in and told Sheila everything was finished, so they went to the bathroom and did a few more lines. When they came out, Vic, Jerry, Matt, and Parker were sitting at the bar, and the music was playing softly. When Parker saw the girls, he jumped up and got their drinks for them—rum and coke for Sheila, and a screwdriver for Natasha. Jerry told Parker to make a B52 for everyone. Then he pulled out a joint and lit it.

They sat there talking and laughing. They all had a story of something that happened during their evening: the rude customer, the fights, the drunks, and the idiots. They all had their own perspective, Sheila and Natasha getting hit on, Vic having every guy want to fight with him to impress a girl, or Parker being treated rudely by customers. Parker was so sweet, but because he was so small and kind, people took advantage of him. Men could be so mean when they were drunk.

Sheila listened to Parker's story and thought how she hated men. Ninety-nine percent of them were evil. She lit another joint, and everybody drank until they were drunk. Vic made eye contact with Sheila; as he held her stare, he slowly stood up and walked over to her. He stood in front of her and grabbed her hand. He gently pulled her off her stool, and she didn't protest. Sheila just stared into his eyes and couldn't pull away. Vic walked her to the dance floor and held her close. They swayed to the music.

Ten songs had passed, and they were still there with their bodies locked. Neither of them had said a word when Vic lifted her head from his shoulder and kissed her. It was magic. No one had ever kissed Sheila like that before, so softly and passionately. It made her feel loved. Sheila couldn't pull away, and then she felt herself kissing him back. All of a sudden, Sheila felt someone pulling her away, and she turned to see Natasha giving her a disapproving look.

"Sheila, come with me. We have to have a little talk," Natasha said, still pulling Sheila off the dance floor. Sheila was filled instantly with guilt and shame. She looked up, and realized everyone had seen them kissing from the bar. Sheila followed Natasha to the bathroom, and Natasha chopped a few lines while scolding Sheila. She reminded her she was married, and Vic had a girlfriend. It was too big a risk for a little fun. Sheila was so embarrassed; she didn't need to be scolded. She vowed never to let something like this happen again.

Natasha and Sheila talked for a while, and when Sheila looked down at her watch, she was shocked to see it was just after 5:00 AM. With a little screech, Sheila showed Natasha the time, and they both ran from the bathroom. The restaurant would be opening in fifty minutes, and the day staff would be arriving for work in twenty minutes. They found that Jerry and Parker had already tidied up the bar where they had been sitting, and sprayed air freshener to cover the smell of the drugs.

Everyone was gulping the last of their drinks. Sheila and Natasha picked up their glasses, winked, toasted, and then they drank the rest. Sheila put all the glasses through the dishwasher, and they left. Jerry and Parker got into their cars and drove away. Vic stood there waiting to speak with Sheila. Sheila knew she had to get away from Vic, so she climbed into her car and drove off with a casual wave.

When Sheila pulled into the driveway, she saw lights on in the living room. She felt guilty, knowing that Jack was waiting up for her. Sheila was a little drunk, but the cocaine made her feel alert, and she thought she was sober as she walked quietly into the house. The moment she closed the door, she stubbed her toe on the corner of the dishwasher. The pain caused her to fall back, and she landed on her bottom.

Sheila lay on the floor giggling. She felt pain, but she was more intoxicated than she realized, and at the moment, it was more comical than painful. Sheila composed herself, and reached for the dishwasher to steady herself, so she could stand. Sheila looked up and saw Jack standing there in the doorway, arms crossed with an angry stare. He turned and walked away.

# Chapter 23

Sheila lay in bed, enjoying the peace and quiet, knowing it wouldn't last long. Sheila and Jack had done nothing but argue for the last six months. It was Saturday morning, and she had the next two days off work. Jack had insisted she take a week off, and they had compromised on a weekend. The night before, Jack had gotten home from work at five; he was drunk by eight and in bed at nine. Lately, he had been drinking a lot, and it wasn't beer he was drinking anymore, but hard liquor.

Sheila couldn't really complain. She was doing at least a couple of grams of cocaine and about eight grams of marijuana per week. They were both miserable; Jack felt his family slipping through his fingers, and Sheila hated to be around him. All they did was argue, and lately he had been getting a little rough with Sheila. Every day, Jack seemed to remind her more of Bobby, and she hated him for making her remember.

She knew she couldn't stall anymore, so she climbed out of bed. Sheila walked into the kitchen and Jack was sitting at the table, drinking a coffee. His eyes were bloodshot, and he looked awful. Sheila felt great. She hadn't drunk or done any coke the night before, just a joint after the boys had gone to bed. Sheila was out of cocaine, and Joann was coming up for a visit today. She was bringing Sheila a fresh supply. Sheila, Jesse, and Keegan were very happy she was coming. They hadn't seen her for a few months.

Joann was coming up with her boyfriend Luc. She was still dating him, and Rick still had no idea what was going on. They were coming up for the afternoon and a late lunch. Luc had to work that night, and Joann always went to his bar Saturday nights. Sheila wished she could go back with Joann for a visit to the city, but she knew even the thought would send Jack into an absolute flip-out. Sheila just hoped for a pleasant afternoon with no fighting.

Sheila poured herself a cup of coffee and sat beside Jack. She gave him a kiss on the cheek and a smile. Jack grinned and pounced on her. He had his hand down her pants in two seconds. Sheila jumped back and pulled his hand out. She looked up at Jack; the last thing she wanted to do was have sex with him. Sheila had always hated having sex in the morning with no drugs or alcohol in her system, and ever since Sheila had shared the kiss with Vic, Jack had repulsed her. Being with Jack made Sheila feel like she was being molested by Bobby all over again. There was no passion, only Jack groping her.

Jack got very angry about being rejected and pushed Sheila away roughly. Sheila was relieved when she heard one of the boys coming down the stairs. She got out of her chair and went to see who it was. There was Keegan, standing and rubbing his eyes, still half asleep. When he saw his mother, he seemed to become quite alert, and he ran into her arms. Sheila picked him up and gave him a big kiss. She asked what he wanted for breakfast.

Sheila walked into the kitchen with Keegan in her arms to see Jack pouring brandy into his coffee. She looked at the clock. It was only a little after eight. Sheila put Keegan into his high chair and got him some apple juice from the fridge. She told Keegan she would make him pancakes. Sheila walked up to Jack, who was standing in front of the pantry. She looked deep into his eyes and kissed him softly on the lips.

"Jack, please let's not start fighting. Can't we try to have a nice day? I have the whole weekend off, and I want to enjoy Joann's visit. I promise to take care of you tonight," Sheila said. Jack hugged Sheila and agreed to try and have a pleasant day. Sheila started to make apple pancakes for Keegan, and was disappointed to see Jack pour himself another coffee with brandy.

Joann and Luc arrived just after noon, and Sheila was so happy to see her sister. Sheila hadn't realized how much she missed Joann until she saw her. They talked every few days. Sheila was working, and she paid the phone bill, which ensured that she didn't have to listen to Jack bitch about the phone bill. Sheila gave her a hug and said hi to Luc. The boys were pulling on Joann's legs, demanding attention.

Jack came out of the house with a drink in his hand. He sauntered over to Luc and introduced himself. He offered everyone a drink, and Luc and Joann accepted. Sheila asked for water. Jack went into the house to get the beverages, and they sat outside at the patio table. It was a sunny, warm afternoon. Jesse and Keegan began to play with their Tonka trucks quietly, once they were sure Joann was staying for a while.

Jack came out with rum and coke for him and Luc, beer for Joann, and nothing for Sheila. Jack always forgot a drink order if there was no alcohol in it. Sheila looked at him, annoyed, and went into the kitchen to get a drink for her and the boys. When she came back outside, Jack and Luc were engrossed in a conversation. Sheila tapped Joann on the shoulder gently and motioned with her head for Joann to follow her.

Joann got up and grabbed her purse, telling Luc she would be right back. Sheila reminded Jack to keep his eye on the boys for a few minutes, and told Jesse and Keegan she would be right back. Once in the house, the girls ran up to Sheila's bedroom, closed the door, and locked it. Joann reached into her purse and pulled out a large bag of cocaine. She started cutting up a few lines for her and Sheila

About a month earlier, Sheila had phoned Rick to arrange to come to the city to pick up some coke. Sheila and Jack had purchased a second car. It was nothing special—a rusted old white Oldsmobile—but Sheila loved it. Sheila had freedom. She could come and go as she pleased, and she treasured it. Sheila had been shocked when Rick started to give her a lecture about the evils of drugs.

Rick told her he was concerned Sheila and Joann were doing too much coke, and he felt he had no choice but to cut them off. Sheila offered to pay for it, and Rick told her it wasn't about the money; he felt it was a dangerous drug and he wanted them to stop using. Sheila almost laughed. He had introduced Sheila and Joann to cocaine, and now, after all this time, he thought it wasn't healthy for them. What a joke.

Sheila had phoned Joann, and they had laughed about it. Joann told Sheila that Rick had been talking about cutting them off for a few weeks. Rick would sit Joann down, and, while he was snorting lines, he would preach to her about the evils of drugs, saying it wasn't good for her. Later he would offer her a line and tell her, "One won't hurt." Joann told Sheila not to worry; she could get it from lots of people. Rick had introduced her to everyone, and she even knew who supplied Rick. They would have no problems selling it to Joann and Sheila.

Sheila bought enough for at least a few weeks and paid Joann from a large roll of bills. Tips had been very good lately. It seemed the more Sheila flirted with the customers, the more money she made. Sheila paid attention, and she was learning; she even flirted with the ladies. Flirting, to Sheila, was the ability to make people feel good about themselves. She had discovered that compliments made people happy and self-confident. Whether it was a man or a woman, Sheila played the game like an expert, and she was making a fortune.

Sheila rolled a joint and happily informed Joann that Natasha was dropping by to bring Sheila some pot. She was so happy for them to finally meet. Natasha had filled the void in Sheila's life that had been left when Joann moved back to the city. Nobody could ever replace Joann, but Sheila needed someone to talk with and do her drugs with. It made life so much more enjoyable, and Natasha was a great friend.

Sheila heard someone coming up the stairs. Quickly, she hid her drugs and unlocked the door. Sheila opened the door and saw Jesse standing there. Sheila started to chase him, and when Sheila caught him, she and Joann wrestled him to the ground, tickling him until he yelled uncle. They went back downstairs laughing. Sheila felt better now that she had her stash of coke safely upstairs.

They had just finished lunch and were sitting back outside when Natasha pulled in. The boys ran to the gate—they loved Natasha. Natasha got out of her car a walked over to the gate, waving at the boys. Sheila noticed Luc's face turn white. He had a horrified look on his face, but she didn't pay any attention. She went to greet her friend.

Natasha gave the boys a little treat from her purse. She always had something for Jesse and Keegan, today, a chocolate bar for each of them.

They thanked Natasha and looked at Sheila for permission to eat them. Sheila told them it was fine since they had just finished their lunch, and they ran off. Sheila grabbed Natasha by the arm and brought her over to the patio table. Before she was able to start the introductions, she heard Natasha squeal with delight as she ran over to Luc and hugged him.

Sheila and Joann looked at each other, confused. Then Natasha said, "Luc, what are you doing here? I haven't seen you since I moved from the city. I guess it's been quite a few years now. How's Sandra doing?"

"Fine. Good to see you, Natasha," Luc responded, looking very uncomfortable. Natasha turned to Joann then, and told her how long she had wanted to meet her; she had heard so much about Joann from Sheila. She said Joann was obviously very important to Sheila. She was aware from her late-night talks with Sheila that Jesse, Keegan, and Joann meant everything to her friend.

Sheila went to get everyone a drink, and Natasha came to help her. The moment they were in the house, they ran up to Sheila's room and locked the door. Natasha gave Sheila a bag of pot, and Sheila paid her. Sheila quickly chopped a few lines for them, and within a few minutes they were back in the kitchen, getting drinks for everyone. As Sheila opened the porch door, she saw Luc and Joann walking toward the gate. *They can't be leaving*, Sheila thought. She ran outside.

"Sheila, we have to get going. Luc has to work tonight, and he wants to try and get a little nap in. I had him up pretty late last night," Joann informed her sister with a wink. Joann told Natasha it was nice to meet her, and she told Sheila she would talk to her in a few days. Without a word to anyone, Luc climbed into the car and beeped for Joann to hurry. The second Joann was in, he pulled down the driveway, and he was gone. Sheila, Natasha, and Jack stared at each other. Sheila and Jack were confused about the sudden departure, but Natasha knew the reason for Luc's quick exit.

"Sheila, how does your sister know Luc?" Natasha inquired. Sheila explained he was a friend of Rick's, and Joann had been dating him since she had moved to the city. Natasha shook her head and told Sheila and Jack the unfortunate news: Luc was married and had three children. Natasha and Luc's wife, Sandra, had been friends since grade school. She told them that his wife was a lovely, kind woman who didn't deserve to be treated like this.

Sheila questioned Natasha about a possible separation. Maybe they weren't even together anymore, and Natasha wasn't aware of it? Natasha told Sheila she had just spoken to Sandra the week before. Sandra was planning a surprise party for her loving husband's birthday, and she had called to invite Natasha. Sheila was disappointed by the news. She knew she had to tell her sister, but how? Joann would be crushed, and Sheila didn't want to be the one to inflict pain of any kind on her sister.

That evening, after dinner, Sheila hesitantly picked up the receiver and phoned her sister. Rick answered and told Sheila he was about to call her. Joann had been locked in her room since she had returned from Sheila's that afternoon. Sheila asked to speak with Joann. Rick put the phone down and was back on the line a few moments later. He said she wouldn't come out of her room. Sheila hung up the phone and told Jack she had to leave.

"What the hell are you talking about, Sheila?" Jack shouted. There was no doubt, he was furious. Sheila had taken the weekend off to spend with him, and now she was going to the city. Sheila pleaded with him. Joann was in pain and needed her sister. Jack knew there was no way he could stop Sheila, so he agreed she could go see her sister on one condition: he wanted her home by midnight.

Sheila looked at the clock. It was 7:15. It would be two hours traveling time, which left almost three hours with Joann. She ran up to her room, grabbed a little coke, and threw on a sweatshirt and jeans. Sheila grabbed her purse and keys. She gave Jack and the boys a kiss as she ran out the door. She made good time and pulled onto Rick's street in fifty-two minutes.

Sheila walked into Joann's room and was met with a sad sight. Joann lay there with puffy red eyes and a steady stream of tears falling down her face. Joann couldn't help thinking it was ironic. She wondered how many times she had found Sheila in this state after a run-in with Bobby. She looked up at Sheila and pulled the covers over her head. She began to cry even harder. Sheila looked down at the bed. There was tissue thrown everywhere. She cleaned an area and sat down beside her sister. Sheila sat there for a few minutes patiently, and let her sister cry. Slowly, the blanket began to slide down off Joann's tear-stained face.

"When you're ready, you can tell me what happened. Until then, I brought you a joint, and I'll cut you a couple of lines," Sheila told Joann softly. They sat there silently and smoked the joint. Once Joann had consumed the coke, she started to open up. Through her sobs, Joann told her sister that on the drive home with Luc, totally out of the blue, he'd told her he couldn't see her anymore. Luc had dumped Joann, and she was completely destroyed. She had fallen in love with him. He was her first love, and he had broken her heart.

Sheila didn't say a word. She just let her sister get everything off her chest. An hour later, Joann had calmed and stopped crying. Sheila thought anger was the best way to heal, and decided to tell Joann the real reason Luc broke it off with her. As gently as she could, Sheila told Joann everything.

Joann was shocked. She'd had no idea he was married. Rick probably knew, but he wasn't aware of the relationship between Luc and Joann, so to him the information was irrelevant, and he'd never told his sister. Joann sat there and absorbed what Sheila was telling her. Joann felt used, foolish, and, worst of all, she felt incredibly stupid for not suspecting something sooner. The signs were there, now that she thought about it.

Sheila checked the time. It was 11:20. Sheila was not going to be home by midnight, and she didn't feel like having another fight with Jack. Sheila told Joann she had to get going home, and she invited her to come along. Joann refused, saying she needed to be alone. Sheila reminded her to call if she needed anything. Joann felt much better and thanked Sheila for coming. Sheila cut a few more lines, and then left.

On her way out, Sheila popped into the kitchen and talked to Rick. She told him Joann would be fine in a couple of days; it was just girl stuff. Rick told her to sit down and do a couple of lines with him. Sheila almost laughed. One day he wanted to cut off her supply, and the next he wanted her to get high with him. Sheila still could not figure her brother out.

Sheila thanked him for the offer, but said she was running late. She ran down the stairs and raced to the car. She climbed into the car and turned the ignition. The lights came on, and Sheila looked at the clock. It was now 11:34. Jack would be having a fit by the time she got there. Sheila peeled out of the driveway. She was on the highway soon, and she lit a joint, leaning back to enjoy the ride. The music played softly, and the peace was calming. She knew it wouldn't be lasting too long. She was on her way to a screaming match with Jack.

Sheila opened the door to the porch. It was twenty-four minutes past midnight, and Jack sat at the kitchen table with an almost empty bottle of rum in front of him. Sheila could tell before he said a word that he was extremely drunk, and furious. Sheila put down her purse, gave Jack a kiss, and told him she just had to use the bathroom. Jack didn't answer. He just stared at her. Sheila told him she would be back shortly and asked him to pour her a glass of wine.

Sheila quickly climbed the stairs. She put on her pajamas. She made the time to do a few lines, then checked on Jesse and Keegan. The boys were sound asleep. Sheila was back in the kitchen within a few minutes—not quick enough for Jack. He hadn't moved from his chair, nor had he poured Sheila some wine. He was still sitting there, fuming. Sheila didn't comment on the wine. She simply walked to the counter and poured herself a glass. She didn't want to upset him further.

Sheila sat across from Jack and told him about the evening. She told him how upset Joann had been and tried to make him understand why she had not been home by midnight. After all, she wasn't that late. It was only twenty-four minutes, not hours. She smiled, trying to get some response from Jack, but there was nothing, just a blank stare. Sheila apologized several times, and soon she gave up. She figured it was probably better to let him cool off.

Sheila picked up her wine and took a sip. She looked up at Jack and told him when he was ready to talk to let her know. Sheila walked to the sink, filled it with hot soapy water, and started the dinner dishes, which were still sitting on the counter. Sheila stood with her back to Jack while she washed the dishes. He finally started talking, but Sheila could not understand what he was saying. Jack was slurring his words, and he was not making any sense, but he was mad. There was no mistaking the tone of his mumbling.

Jack stood up and stumbled over to Sheila. He landed hard against her back and held on so he didn't fall over. Sheila was disgusted when he started roughly grabbing at her breasts and rubbing himself up against her. He smelled awful. All Sheila could smell was stale alcohol, and it repulsed her. She tried to push him away, but Jack became very angry when Sheila rejected his advances. He started to scream at her, "You little bitch! you told me you would be home by midnight. Where were you? Who were you with?"

Before Sheila knew what was happening, Jack leaned on her back with all his weight and pushed her head into the dishwater. Sheila found herself fighting for breath, submerged underwater. Terrified, she struggled to get free. She could still hear Jack hollering, but it was muffled. She was kicking and punching him, trying to get loose of his grip, but it was difficult. He was dead drunk weight. Sheila knew she was running out of time, and panic was setting in. Frantically, she kicked her legs back with all her might.

Sheila made contact with Jack's knee. It was a hard blow, and he fell to the floor. Sheila pulled her head out of the sink and gasped for air. Her head was spinning, and she was trying to take in deep breaths. Her hair was soaked, and soapy water was dripping down her face, into her eyes. Sheila looked around the kitchen frantically through her burning eyes, trying to take in what had just happened. She was shocked, scared, and confused. Sheila looked down at the floor and saw Jack. She couldn't even trust *Jack* not to hurt her. She burst into tears as she tried to steady her breath.

Sheila grabbed a butcher knife and ran up the stairs to her room. She locked the bedroom door, and sat on the bed sobbing with the knife beside her. What was happing to her life? Who did she marry, someone like Bobby? Were they all really like her father on the inside? Sheila was so confused. The one thing Sheila had always believed and counted on was that Jack loved her, and he would always take care of her. Now that security was gone, and she felt deserted.

Sheila had always assumed that if they had trouble in their marriage down the road, it would be due to Sheila not loving Jack enough. She never imagined he would hurt her, or try and drown her! Sheila wondered if Hugette and Bobby had been happy in the beginning, before they had so many kids. But it didn't matter; she would never treat her children the way her mother treated her. Sheila pushed the memory of her parents from her mind and focused on the present.

Sheila cut a couple of lines to calm herself. She listened at the door to see if she could hear Jack, but everything was quiet. She slowly opened the bedroom door and looked down the hall. Sheila tiptoed to check on the boys, and then, as quietly as she could, she went down the

*Behind the Drapes*

stairs. She was pleased to see Jack passed out on the sofa, snoring. Sheila knew from experience he would be out until the morning.

Sheila went into the kitchen and filled her glass of wine. She took a large mouthful as she leaned against the counter and surveyed the mess. Chairs were tumbled over, there was water all over the floor and counters, and Jack had spilled his rum everywhere. Sheila realized the floor had to be washed, and the table, chairs, and all the counters had to be cleaned. She went into the garage and smoked a joint, then returned to the kitchen and got right to work. She had everything finished in an hour.

The next morning, Sheila could smell the coffee brewing when she opened the bedroom door. *Jack must be sucking up to make up for last night*, Sheila thought. She checked in, and Jesse was still sleeping, but Keegan's bed was empty. Sheila was relieved. She knew things would be calm with him already up. She wasn't in the mood for another round of fighting and screaming.

Sheila went downstairs and found Keegan watching cartoons. She quietly snuck up behind him and started to tickle him. Keegan squealed with delight as he begged his mother to stop. Sheila giggled as she watched him squirm and laugh hysterically. Sheila looked up and saw Jack watching them from the doorway of the kitchen. Feeling his eyes on her made her uncomfortable, and the realization saddened Sheila. Things were never going to be the same between Sheila and Jack, and she knew it.

Sheila let Keegan go and asked him what he wanted for breakfast, he informed his mother that his dad had already made him pancakes. The television grabbed his attention, and Keegan went right back to watching his cartoons. Sheila got up and went into the kitchen to get some coffee. Jack was sitting at the table, and he watched her silently. Sheila leaned on the counter and looked at the man she had married. He was looking rough with his bloodshot eyes. She hoped he was suffering with a bad hangover.

Jack rose from his chair and strolled innocently over to Sheila. He tried to kiss her. Sheila pushed him away, recoiling with disgust at the thought. She asked him quietly, "Are you insane, Jack? After what happened last night, you have the nerve to think you have the right to kiss me?"

Jack stopped and looked at her with a blank stare. He didn't remember much from the night before. However, he was sure they had argued. Jack had woken up on the sofa, not sure why he was sleeping there. He'd had to go look out the window to see Sheila's car to be sure she was home. He tried to think about what had happened when Sheila got home, but he couldn't remember much. He had little flashes of memory, but nothing that explained Sheila's anger. Sheila seemed much too upset for it to be a simple argument. "Sheila can we talk about it over breakfast?" Jack pleaded.

Sheila looked at his eyes, and she saw no sorrow or regret, so what could they possibly have to talk about? Jack had some explaining and apologizing to do, but Sheila didn't think Jack trying to drown her was something she wanted to relive at the moment, especially with Keegan in the next room. Sheila sat down with her coffee and waited for an apology. It didn't come. Sheila noticed the confused look in Jack's eyes and it hit her: Jack couldn't remember.

Jack had been blacking out frequently for the last few months. Sheila demanded that he tell her what had transpired the night before. When he couldn't, Sheila became enraged. She grabbed the front of his sweatshirt, pulling him close. She stared directly into his eyes and whispered, "You tried to drown me last night, Jack. You came close to killing me. The fact that you can't even remember doing it is more scary to me than the experience itself." Sheila let go of his shirt and threw him back. She told him she and the boys were going out for the day; she needed some space away from him to think.

Jack stood in the window and watched his family drive away. As Sheila's car left the driveway, a feeling of doom come over him. He walked away from the window and opened the liquor cabinet. He grabbed a bottle of rum, poured himself a shot, and downed it. Jack was about to put the bottle back, and then he thought better of it. He brought it into the living room and sat down. Jack looked down at the rum, his trusted friend, and poured himself another drink.

# Chapter 24

Sheila and the boys pulled into Joann and Rick's driveway. Sheila noticed that Rick's car was not there. Sheila and the boys started up the stairs to the front door and heard someone calling them. They turned to see Joann walking up the street. Jesse and Keegan bolted from their mother and ran into Joann's waiting arms. Sheila sat on the step and watched her sister with the boys. Joann was looking better than she had the night before. Sheila hoped she was over the shock of finding out Luc was married, and feeling better about things.

Joann and the boys reached the house, and Joann told Sheila she had gone to the store to pick up some juice for the boys. Sheila grabbed the grocery bag from Joann, and they entered the main door. When they reached their front door, Sheila and Joann looked at the door, then at each other. There in large letters, carved into the wood, was a message for Rick from one of his cocaine suppliers. The message read: *You are late with your payment, not a good idea to keep us waiting. Call very soon or I will be back.* It was signed Charlie.

They entered the house, and Joann locked the door behind them. They climbed the stairs silently, both girls uneasy and a little scared about Charlie's message. Joann got the boys a glass of juice while Sheila found some cartoons on the television for them. Once the boys were quietly watching television, Sheila asked Joann what was going on with Rick.

"Sheila, he hasn't been himself lately. He's been grumpy, paranoid, and acting just weird. He's been doing way too much partying and not enough sleeping," Joann said. Joann wasn't aware of him owing money to Charlie, but that didn't mean he didn't. Rick wasn't in the habit of informing his little sister of his personal business. However, if he did owe money and didn't have it, Charlie was not the sort of person you would want to mess with. Charlie and his buddies were scary people. They'd certainly scared Joann when she had met them.

Sheila was nervous about being there, so she suggested they go to the park for a picnic. Joann and the boys thought it was a great plan. Jesse and Keegan found a Frisbee and football to play with, and Joann found a large blanket, while Sheila made a list of things they would have to pick up at the store. They packed into the car. Then as Sheila started backing up, she noticed a man sitting in a car across the street. When she pointed it out to Joann, she told Sheila it was Charlie.

Sheila quickly locked her door and told Joann to do the same. She drove on, still watching him in her rearview mirror. Sheila almost burst out crying when she saw the car following them. She didn't have to say anything to Joann, who noticed as well. Sheila very calmly drove to the store a couple of blocks away. Everyone got out and went inside. They bought what they needed and left. As they were leaving the parking lot, Sheila noticed the car parked at the corner. He was definitely following them.

Sheila drove to the park and laid the blanket close to an area that was full of other people. She felt a little safer that way. The boys ran to the play structure and started to have a great time with all the kids that were there. Sheila kept her eye on Jesse and instructed Joann not to take her eyes off Keegan. Sheila let the boys play for a while, and then she noticed Charlie leaning against a tree. Sheila walked up to the play structure and told Jesse and Keegan it was time for lunch, promising they could go right back to play after they ate something.

Sheila sat the boys on the blanket and looked back at the tree. Charlie was gone. She couldn't see him anywhere. Once the boys were eating safely on the blanket, Sheila told Joann to watch them, and she

*Behind the Drapes*

walked to the parking lot to see if Charlie or his car were still there. Much to Sheila's surprise and relief, his car was gone. It wasn't in the parking lot. Sheila walked the outer perimeter of the lot to see if he was parked on the street, but there was no sign of him. She breathed a big sigh of relief.

Sheila walked to the car and did a few lines, then went back to Joann and the boys. Sheila handed Joann her car keys and told her it was all clear. Joann left, and Sheila began to relax. The boys finished their lunch, and their mother told them they could go back to play with the children at the play structure. Jesse and Keegan loved to play with other kids, but the opportunity didn't always present itself. Except for Natasha's boys, they really didn't have any children living close by.

Joann returned and dropped on the blanket. "That was scary, Sheila. Why do you think he was following us?" she whispered. "You don't think he would hurt us, do you?" Joann said, raising her voice slightly. Sheila shook her head no. She wasn't really sure why he had been watching them. If Charlie had wanted to hurt them, he'd probably had the opportunity while they were in the house alone. Sheila wasn't sure how long Charlie had been parked outside Rick's house, but she told herself he had seen the car in the driveway and known someone was there, yet he had done nothing.

"Maybe he just followed us to see if we were meeting Rick. He obviously wants to talk to him. He probably just stayed for a while to see if Rick would show up. I'm sure there is nothing to worry about," Sheila told Joann, trying to reassure her. Sheila wasn't so sure, and she tried to convince Joann to come home with her, just in case, but Joann refused. She had to work in the morning, and she didn't want to get up extra early so Sheila could drive her in.

They stretched out on the blanket together, watching the boys play. Sheila told Joann all about her fight with Jack the night before. Joann was surprised by Jack's violence, but she told Sheila she had noticed Jack's heavy drinking for some time now. Sheila explained Jack was the kind of drunk who was a totally different person under the influence, and it was not an attractive side of him. In fact, Sheila found it repulsive. Sheila told her sister she was seriously thinking of leaving Jack, and Joann was disappointed, but she did understand. The last thing either of them needed was to be married to someone like Bobby.

Sheila and the boys dropped Joann off at home at 3:00 PM. Sheila tried again to convince Joann to come home with her, but Joann wasn't budging. When Joann refused, Sheila insisted they go in the house with her; just to be sure everything was fine. Rick's car still wasn't there, and Charlie didn't appear to be around, but Sheila needed to be sure before she left. They went upstairs, and everything was just as they'd left it. Sheila told Joann to call if she needed anything, and they left.

When Sheila pulled up to her house, she noticed a strange car in the driveway. She didn't recognize it, and after the day she'd just had, she was consumed with fear. Sheila was quite relieved when they got closer, and she noticed Jack and Tony sitting outside, having a beer. Jesse and Keegan got out of the car and ran over to their father and Tony. At the same time, they both told them about their day at the park with all the kids. Jack and Tony listened to them and couldn't help sharing their enthusiasm; Jack found himself sad he had missed the outing.

"Well hello, stranger. How have you been?" Sheila asked. As she bent to give Tony a kiss on the cheek, Sheila noticed Tony pull away. He gave her an unenthusiastic half smile. Sheila instantly felt uncomfortable in her own house. What had she done for Tony to be so cold towards her? She wondered what Jack had been telling him. At that moment, she felt a strong need to get away. Sheila said hi to Jack and quickly went into the house, mentioning she would go and start dinner.

Sheila entered the house, ran up the stairs to her bedroom, and locked the door. After a few lines, she felt a little better. She changed her clothes and went to the kitchen to start dinner. It wasn't long before Jack came in, looking for more beer. Jack walked up to Sheila and asked her for a kiss. She reluctantly gave him a peck on the cheek. He told her Tony was having one more beer, and then he had to get going back to the city. Sheila hoped he'd drink it fast.

Sheila went to get the boys to wash up for dinner. When she got outside, Sheila realized Tony had left. She was hurt that he had left without saying bye to her. Tony was Jack's friend, and Sheila knew at that moment that if she and Jack broke up, she would not have any support from their mutual friends. Mutual they were not; they were Jack's friends. It didn't matter, Sheila thought. She had Joann, Natasha, and her boys, and that was the only support she needed.

Dinner was a quiet affair that evening. The boys were exhausted from their day at the park, and Sheila and Jack were lost in their own thoughts. Sheila thought about the relationship she and Jack once had. She missed his friendship. On the drive home from the city that day, Sheila had wanted nothing more than to come home and talk to her husband about her fears for Joann, their marriage, Rick, and Charlie. But when she got home, hostility from Tony and early drunkenness from Jack had been all that awaited her.

Jesse and Keegan were in bed early that night, and sound asleep long before their usual bedtime. Sheila took a long hot bath, and when she came out of the bathroom, the house was eerily quiet. She went to her bedroom to see if maybe Jack had gone to bed early. The bed was empty, so she locked the door and did a few lines. Sheila went downstairs and found Jack passed out, sitting at the kitchen table. Sheila walked past him, went into the garage, and smoked a joint.

Sheila sat down to read the newspaper, enjoying the peace and quiet. It didn't last long; Sheila heard a smash in the kitchen. She jumped up and ran to the kitchen to find that Jack had knocked his glass of rum on the floor. Sheila bent down to clean up the glass and noticed Jack watching her. The breaking glass must have woken him. He got up and went to fix himself another drink.

"Don't you think you have had enough for today?" Sheila pleaded. Jack ignored her and took his drink with him into the living room. Sheila finished cleaning up the mess, and with Jack awake, she decided to go to bed and finish reading the paper. Sheila said goodnight to Jack and climbed the stairs. Sheila curled up into bed and started to read the paper, but soon she heard Jack coming up the stairs, so she quickly turned off the light and pretended to be asleep. Sheila had had enough excitement for one day, and she didn't want to end it fighting with Jack.

Jack came into the bedroom and closed the door behind him. He turned on the light, and Sheila could feel him staring at her. It made her nervous. Jack stripped and jumped into bed. He reached over and started to grope at Sheila's breasts. She pushed away his hand and moved closer to her side of the bed as she told him to go to sleep. Jack became enraged and jumped out of bed. He ran to her side of the bed and grabbed on to Sheila's ankle roughly.

"Why don't you want to have sex? Is there someone else?" Jack accused. Sheila tried to pull her leg free as he screamed at her, but Jack had a firm grip, and she couldn't get free. "It has been months since we have had sex. You are a bitch, and I want you to take care of me," Jack demanded. With this, he pulled Sheila violently from the bed and onto the floor, where he jumped on her.

Sheila had had enough, and she fought for her life. She started to bite, scratch, kick, and punch with all her might, and finally, she broke free. She jumped up and ran to the bathroom, locking the door. Sheila sat on the side of the tub and trembled. She had hit her head on the floor when Jack pulled her off the bed, and now she was feeling the pain. Jack was at the door in minutes, banging, just as her head was pounding.

"Please, Jack. You are going to wake the kids. I promise we will talk about this tomorrow, but I'm not coming out until you calm down," Sheila informed him. Jack gave up shortly, and Sheila heard him going down the stairs. She tiptoed out of the bathroom and checked on the boys. They were still sleeping soundly. Sheila went into the bedroom and got a pillow, a blanket, and some coke. She was back in the bathroom quickly with the door locked, and she waited there for Jack to go to bed.

Sheila never slept a wink that night. She left the bathroom at two in the morning, having written Jack a nine-page letter. In the letter, she explained that she wanted a divorce and nothing he could say could change her mind. Sheila had been miserable for some time, and it was apparent Jack wasn't any happier. She would not tolerate being mistreated by him, and the abuse was going to stop now.

She told Jack she would be contacting a lawyer to find out her options, and then they could discuss it that evening. Sheila wrote down everything he had done to her in the last few months, especially the times he couldn't remember because he was drunk. She mentioned that she thought Jack had a drinking problem that he had to work out. Sheila told him they could tell the kids together, when he was ready.

Sheila devoted a page to telling him how sorry she was that things didn't work out. Jack was the first person other than Joann whom she trusted, or at least she had at one time. They did have some good memories, and she hoped they could both be happy on their own. It was definitely time for both of them to move on. It wasn't healthy to be living the way they were, and she didn't want the boys growing up in that atmosphere.

Sheila heard Jack's alarm clock going off upstairs, and she walked to the kitchen to put some coffee on. She did a few more lines to calm herself, and then she sat down at the table, waiting for Jack. The coffee maker beeped, and she poured two cups, placing them on the table across from each other. Sheila retrieved the sugar bowl and milk from the fridge, and put them between the cups. She placed the letter in an envelope and leaned it up against one cup. She sat in the chair in front of the other.

Jack came walking into the kitchen, looking like a truck had hit him. Sheila pointed to the coffee, and he sat down. Jack moved the envelope and grabbed for the cup; after he prepared his coffee, Sheila pushed the envelope back in front of him. Jack picked it up and looked at Sheila. "Read it," was all she said as she left the room and went upstairs for her shower.

When Jack got home that evening, he was early, and he seemed quiet remorseful. Sheila was putting dinner on the table for her and the boys, and when Jack arrived, she added another setting. They sat down to dinner and chatted with the boys about their days. It almost seemed like old times. Jack drank a pop with his dinner. When dinner was finished, Jack offered to give the boys their bath while Sheila cleaned the kitchen. Sheila gratefully accepted, and Jack and the boys headed upstairs.

Sheila was finished before Jack, and she gathered her notes from the lawyer. She had been astonished to discover what she was entitled to. The lawyer was someone she knew from work, and he had been a tremendous help. She felt a little empowered with all the information she had learned. Sheila was so tired. She had not slept the night before, but she felt like the weight of the world was being lifted off her shoulders, and she had her bag of cocaine to keep her going.

The phone rang. Sheila grabbed for it, and it was Joann. Sheila had phoned her earlier and left a message, and Joann was returning her call. Sheila had started to tell her what was happening between her and Jack when Keegan came running into the room. Sheila quickly changed the subject and asked if Charlie had been back. She was relieved when Joann told her no. Keegan started to grab at his mother, demanding her attention. Sheila told Joann she would call her back when the kids were in bed, and she hung up.

Jack came into the kitchen and poured himself a glass of wine. He asked Sheila if she wanted one; she accepted. Jack told the boys to go watch television, and he sat at the table. He asked Sheila if they could have a talk. Sheila knew the time had come. They had to talk about the logistics of the divorce. Sheila suggested waiting until the kids had gone to bed, but Jack insisted it was not necessary, so she sat down at the table with him.

They were silent for a moment, and it was Jack who broke the silence. He told Sheila he had read her note, and he had to agree with most of it. He knew things had gotten way out of hand between them. Maybe Sheila was right that they needed some time apart to figure things out, but he totally disagreed with a divorce as an answer to the problem. Sheila was about to object when he asked her to let him finish—he had a suggestion.

Jack thought they should separate for a month. He didn't feel that they should involve lawyers just yet. They could try a separation and see if they felt any differently at the end. He had made arrangements to stay at Tony's, and he would take the kids on the weekends while Sheila worked. That way, they would only have to find a babysitter on Thursday nights. Jack promised that at the end of the month, if Sheila still wanted a divorce, he would not stand in the way.

Sheila thought about it. She knew she wouldn't change her mind. She was positive she wanted a divorce. If doing it Jack's way made him feel better, then Sheila knew she owed it to Jack for everything he had done for her in the past, to at least give it a try. He had thought of everything except what to tell the kids. Sheila brought it up, and Jack told her they could handle it any way she wanted. There was really nothing Sheila could object to, so she agreed to a one-month trial separation without lawyers.

They decided that Jack would take that week to get organized. They would explain it gradually to Jesse and Keegan as the week went on. Sheila hoped the boys were young enough to adapt to the separation easily. She felt anything was better than growing up in a violent and angry home. Friday, when Sheila left for work, Jack would move a few things out and bring the kids with him to Tony's for the weekend. He would bring them back on Sunday evening after he knew Sheila would be gone to work.

Sheila told him she would stay at Natasha's on Sunday nights and be home in plenty of time for him to leave for work on Monday mornings. With everything agreed on, Jack poured them both another glass of wine. Sheila took a sip and thanked him. She thanked him for the wine, for being so understanding, and for making the arrangement process so easy. Sheila picked up her glass and went to join her sons watching television. Jack followed.

# Chapter 25

It was Saturday night and the boys were with Jack for the weekend. Sheila was in a fantastic mood as she pushed her way through the crowd, holding a tray of empty glasses high over her head and pushing people gently out of her way. She had just finished last call. It had been a busy night. Sheila finally made it up to the bar and started unloading her full tray. She thought about ordering her drinks for after-hours, but Parker was still very busy, so she started to run the glasses through the glass washer for him.

The music was pounding, and Sheila was singing and dancing while she worked. Sheila loved her new freedom. This was the first time she had felt totally in control of her life. Sheila had been so at peace with life the last four weeks since Jack had moved out. Everyone at work had been commenting about Sheila's great mood, saying it was fun to be around her. She loved the peace and quiet in the house. Sheila had even stopped using cocaine during the week, although she still used at work, and when the boys were with Jack.

Keegan didn't even seem to notice his father had moved out, and he was flourishing in Sheila's new relaxed and upbeat attitude. Jesse was asking a lot of questions, but overall he seemed like he was adjusting

*Behind the Drapes*

to the changes. Sheila tried as best as she could to answer his questions honestly, without being too harsh. Sheila had found them a babysitter, and the boys adored her. Her name was Mandy. She was sixteen—fun and bubbly. Mandy lived a couple of doors from them, and Sheila felt safe knowing her mother would be close by if something happened.

Parker came over and handed Sheila a shooter. He told her it was from Vic. Sheila looked down the bar, where Vic was standing, also holding a shooter. He smiled at her and drank his, and Sheila followed suit, then waved a thank you to him. Sheila gave Parker her and Natasha's order for after-hours, and then, as an afterthought, she ordered two rounds of shooters for everyone. Sheila grabbed her tray and went back out on the floor to pick up more empty bottles and glasses.

Natasha was just coming back with a full tray, and she winked at Sheila. She knew what Natasha was winking about. It meant Natasha had a few lines waiting for her. Sheila smiled at her friend and put her tray down. She went to do her lines. Sheila was coming out of the downstairs bathroom when this girl came running in, and ran right into her. Sheila hit the floor with a thud. She looked up and saw Becky, one of her customers from the bar. Becky bent down and helped Sheila up as she apologized to her.

Sheila mentioned to Becky that these washrooms were just for staff. Becky told Sheila she'd worked at Barnabee's before, and she knew what these bathroom were used for. Becky grabbed Sheila by the hand and led her back into the bathroom. Sheila was surprised when Becky pulled out some coke and started to cut a few lines. They both started to laugh, and Sheila and Becky became friends at that moment. Becky grabbed Sheila's hand and introduced herself, and Sheila did the same.

Becky was a beautiful girl with dark hair, smoky brown eyes, and a lovely figure. She was the same age as Sheila, but she was single with no children. Sheila discovered Becky was originally from the city and had hated this small town when she first arrived, something the two girls had in common. The girls did their lines and chatted like they had known each other for years. Sheila looked at her watch and realized she had been down in the bathroom for fifteen minutes. She told Becky she had to get back to work. They walked back upstairs to the bar, talking and laughing.

As Sheila opened the door of the bar, she heard Matt announce last song. Sheila ran and picked up her tray. She got right to work cleaning up. The last song ended, and people started to leave. Some took longer than others, and that's when Vic got to work encouraging people to leave. Becky came over and said bye to Sheila. They exchanged phone numbers, and Sheila promised to call her the next day. Sheila really liked Becky and hoped maybe they could get together the next day, before Sheila had to go to work. Sheila said bye to Becky, picked up her full tray, and headed for the bar.

Natasha was standing behind the bar, cleaning glasses. When Sheila put her tray down, Natasha had a little advice for Sheila. "Sheila, that girl you were talking to, do you know her well?" Natasha inquired. Sheila shook her head no; Sheila had been serving her for months, but they had never really spoken until tonight. "Becky is very well known in this town. She has a very bad reputation. Word is she is a real tramp, and Sheila, if you start to hang around with her, you will get the same reputation." Sheila thanked her for the information and went to get more glasses.

Sheila felt protective of Becky immediately. As she filled her tray, she found herself feeling sorry for Becky, and at the same time, a little upset with Natasha for being so stuck up. Sheila had been called a tramp and slut so many times, and she didn't feel like she was, so who was to say if Becky was? Whether or not Becky was a tramp, Sheila really didn't care. She liked her and wanted to get to know her, and people could say whatever they wanted. Sheila would form her own opinion of Becky rather than listen to other people's opinions.

Finally, Sheila and Natasha were finished cleaning up, and they set the nook for breakfast. The place had been such a mess that it had taken them almost an hour. The girls sat down and did their cash-outs. Sheila counted twice. She couldn't believe it, but she had made $247 in tips. The last few weeks, Sheila had been making incredible tips. The happier she was, the more money she seemed to make.

Parker yelled for them to hurry; everyone else was finished, and they wanted to start partying. They drank and laughed, and it was three thirty when Sheila decided it was time to go home. Sheila was going home earlier all the time. She was actually glad to go home now that she always knew what to expect when she got there. She didn't have to

*Behind the Drapes*

worry about Jack being up drunk waiting for her. Vic tried to convince her to stay, but Sheila didn't want to sleep too late the next day. She was hoping to see Becky. So she left.

Sheila woke up feeling great. She looked over at the clock, and it was only eleven. She jumped out of bed and went down to put the coffee on. She sat in the garage and had a coffee and a joint. Sheila went back into the house and picked up the phone. She called Joann. No one answered. She left a message that she was thinking of coming into the city for lunch, and she told her sister to call back. Next, she called Becky. They discussed going into the city for lunch, and Sheila told her she would pick her up at noon. She raced up the stairs to shower.

Just as Sheila was about to leave, the phone rang, it was Joann. She was up for lunch; Sheila told her she would pick her up at one o'clock. Sheila arrived at Becky's apartment building, where she was waiting on the front steps. When she saw Sheila, she smiled and ran to the car. Becky offered to cut them some lines, but Sheila insisted it was her turn. After they did a few lines, they were on their way. Sheila and Becky drove into the city, laughing the whole time. The two girls got along so well. They had very similar personalities.

Joann enjoyed Becky's company, and the three of them had a great afternoon. After lunch, they went back to Joann's place to smoke a joint. Joann told Sheila she had to talk to her in private. Sheila told Becky they would be right back, and went into Joann's room. Joann was very upset. She told Sheila that Rick's partying had gotten totally out of control. He hadn't been to work in over a month, and sometimes Rick and his friends would party nonstop for days at a time with no sleep.

The week before, Rick had come home, and he had obviously been beaten up. Then, the night before, he had come home with a broken arm. Joann told her sister the house was always full of creepy people, and she didn't feel safe there anymore. Sheila and Joann both agreed it was time for her to leave. Sheila made a suggestion she was sure her sister would hate. Sheila thought she could move back in with her. Sheila could get Joann a job at Barnabee's. Sheila knew she would not be getting back together with Jack, and it would help her to have someone share in the expenses.

To Sheila's surprise, Joann was excited at the proposition. "When could I move in?" she said. Sheila was thrilled with the thought of Joann moving back in with her. She said she would talk to Jerry that night and call her in the morning. Sheila and Joann decided that, as soon as Joann found a job, she could move. They agreed not to say anything to Rick until the day she was leaving. Sheila told her sister that, until she moved, she was to call Sheila immediately if she felt in danger at any time.

Sheila and Joann walked back to the living room, and there was Rick, coming on strong with Becky. Sheila slapped him and told him to leave her friend alone. Her brother looked awful. He looked like he had aged years in the last month since Sheila had seen him. His skin was gray, and he had lost weight. Sheila apologized to Becky, and they went into Joann's bedroom to smoke the joint.

They stayed in Joann's room, away from Rick, and chatted for a while. Then Sheila reluctantly told Joann and Becky she had to go, or she would be late for work. Sheila and Becky left, and Sheila made a point of avoiding Rick on their way out. Sheila told Joann she would call her first thing in the morning. Sheila dropped Becky off and raced home to get ready for work. Sheila pulled in the driveway at 3:50, and was surprised to see Jack's vehicle. She thought something might have happened, and she ran into the house.

Sheila opened the door, and Jack was sitting at the table, having a beer. "Where have you been? I've been waiting for you," he said. Sheila looked into the living room, and she didn't see the boys. She was just about to ask for them when Jack told her they were having a nap. Sheila was getting angry. He was not supposed to show up until he knew Sheila was gone to work, and here he was, sitting there, waiting for her.

"Jack, what are you doing here? We made an agreement." Sheila demanded an explanation, and Jack could see she was upset. He reminded her of the arrangement they had made. It had been four weeks, and now he wanted to talk. Sheila told him she had to get ready for work and didn't have the time. "You should have called, Jack. I didn't know you were coming," Sheila pointed out to him, and she went to her room to get ready. Jack watched her go, and the anger started to build in him. He decided he was not going to leave until they had spoken.

Sheila came back downstairs and grabbed her keys and purse. She told Jack she was leaving. He grabbed her tightly by the arm. "I'll be here when you get back. We are going to talk tonight," Jack informed her with an angry look in his eyes. Sheila pulled free and ran out the

*Behind the Drapes*

door. She got into her car, and she peeled out of the driveway, spraying gravel behind her. Sheila knew her four weeks of peace had just ended, and she had a feeling the next talk they had about divorce would not go as smoothly as the first.

Sheila sat in her car after work with the keys in her hand. She couldn't bring herself to start the car and go home. She was so full of mixed emotions. Jerry had told Sheila he would give Joann a job as soon as she moved. She was so happy about her sister moving back. Then there was Jack waiting at home for her, and she was terrified of what might happen when she told him she wanted a divorce now more than ever. Sheila vowed to herself that she would be strong. She knew the way she wanted to live her life, and she would just have to stand up to Jack.

She smoked a joint and did a few lines, and finally, knowing she couldn't put it off forever, she put the key in the ignition and started the car. Sheila saw her street approaching. She reached it. With a feeling of dread, she turned and headed for her house. As she pulled in, she noticed the lights were all on. She prayed that Jack would be passed out, but when she opened the door, he was sitting at the kitchen table, waiting for her.

Sheila put down her purse, but she kept her car keys in her hand as she sat down at the table across from Jack. She looked at him and she knew he had been drinking all night, waiting for her, but he seemed strangely calm and in control. Sheila was instantly frightened. There were two glasses on the table and an open bottle of wine. Jack reached over, picked up the bottle, and filled his glass. He went to fill Sheila's glass, and then he stopped and looked her straight in the eye, and asked her the magic question.

"Sheila, are you ready to try and make this marriage work, or are you just going to throw our family away?" Jack asked her calmly. Sheila stared into his eyes, and she was truly scared. She knew she had to tell him, but she was terrified of his reaction. When she didn't answer him right away, Jack asked her another question: "Do you still want to get a divorce?" This time, Jack's voice was not calm, but harsh and deep.

Sheila stared at her hand and replied, "Yes, Jack. I want a divorce." She said it in a soft whisper, but loud enough that he heard her. Jack put the wine bottle down, picked up his full glass of wine, and he drank every drop. Sheila sat there without making a sound, still staring down at her trembling hands. She slowly raised her head and saw him filling his glass. Jack stood up with the half-full bottle of red wine and threw it at the wall with all his might. It shattered.

Sheila jumped out of her chair as shards of glass flew through the air. The chair fell to the floor as she tried to make it to the door. Jack grabbed her by the back of the hair and pulled her back. He threw her down into a pool of red wine on the floor. He picked up Sheila's chair and told her to sit down, and when she didn't move fast enough, he grabbed her by the arm and helped her along, roughly.

"I played it your way! Now we are going to play it my way, Sheila!" Jacked screamed at her. Jack kept her there for the next two hours as he tried his best to bully and intimidate her. Jack told her he had spoken to Julie, Joseph, and his parents, and they all knew about Sheila's drug habits. He said Julie was willing to testify that Sheila had locked Jesse and Keegan out of the house while she was smoking drugs with Joann and Rick. Sheila knew there was no way Julie had ever seen them doing drugs, and she had never locked the boys out of the house, but who would people believe.

Jack told Sheila that he would fight her for custody of the kids and win. He also informed her that his parents were moving in to help him with the children for a while. They would be arriving in two weeks. He reminded Sheila that she didn't have family, just a drug dealer for a brother, which, he assured her, would come out in court. Jack told Sheila not to forget about his family. They had money and a judge. He told her he would keep the house and the kids, and there was nothing she could do about it, but she was welcome to fight him in court. Jack told her he hoped she did fight him. He would enjoy seeing her humiliated in front of all those people. The judge would probably be so horrified by Sheila's drug habits and family, he wouldn't give her any visitation with Jesse and Keegan.

Sheila sat there listening to him. She felt beaten and overwhelmed. Sheila didn't think she had the strength to fight Jack and his family. She also didn't think she had a chance of winning against them. If Julie, Joseph, and his parents testified, she would be doomed. Sheila couldn't imagine living without Jesse and Keegan. She began to cry. She received no sympathy from Jack. Finally, Jack rose from the table and started to leave the room, but he stopped in the doorway and added one more thing for Sheila to think about.

"Sheila, I'm willing to give this marriage another try if you're willing. You have one week to make up your mind. Either you try to make this marriage work and quit your job, or you move out. It's your choice," Jack said firmly, and he went up to bed. Sheila sat there and cried. She kept going over everything that Jack had said to her, and she didn't know what to do. She didn't want to leave the kids, but she didn't want to spend her life with Jack. Most of all, she didn't want Jesse and Keegan growing up in an unhappy environment.

Sheila needed someone to talk to. She picked up the phone and called Natasha. She answered on the second ring. Sheila couldn't speak. She burst into tears and tried to explain to Natasha that her world had just crumbled. Natasha told her to come right over to her house so they could talk. Sheila managed through her tears, "I just have to clean up the broken glass and wine, and then I'll come right over."

Sheila walked into Natasha's apartment and directly into her waiting arms. She cried nonstop for an hour. Natasha suggested Sheila sit on the sofa, and she brought her a cup of tea. They talked all night. Natasha knew exactly the way Sheila was feeling. A few years back, she had been faced with the same decision, albeit with completely different circumstances. It had been tremendously painful, but in her heart, Natasha had made the only decision she could. She'd needed to do what was best for herself and her children, and she explained it to Sheila now.

Eventually, Sheila looked down at her watch, and realized she had to get home to the kids; Jack had to leave for work. They did a couple of lines, and Natasha told her she would come by that afternoon to check on her. She reminded Sheila to think about what they had talked about. Sheila felt much better leaving than when she had arrived at her friend's. She was glad she had come. Natasha was the one person who understood what she was going through.

As Sheila climbed into her car, she knew what she had to do. She turned the key, and drove home. Sheila took a deep breath before she went into the house. She opened the door and walked into the kitchen. Jack was sitting there having coffee, and he said hello. Sheila walked past him and looked into the living room. The kids were still in bed.

She went to the coffee pot and poured herself a cup. She picked it up and went to sit beside Jack.

"I'll be out by Friday. I'm not walking away with nothing, Jack. I have spoke to a lawyer, and I know I own half this house. I don't want to go to court. Let's try and figure this out without lawyers, Jack," Sheila pleaded. Jack got up. Without a word, he grabbed his keys and left, slamming the door on his way out. Sheila went up the stairs and watched her children sleep as tears flowed down her cheeks. *Will Jesse and Keegan ever forgive me for what I'm about to do?* Sheila wondered.

# Chapter 26

When Joann woke up, the first sounds she heard were music and Sheila's distinct laughter. She couldn't believe Sheila and Becky were still up partying. It was eight thirty in the morning. Joann had gone to bed at midnight, and she had to work at ten. She didn't want to be late. Joann loved her job. She was the day bartender at Barnabee's, and had been now for six months. Sheila was now the night bartender. Parker and Jerry had gotten into a fight, and Parker had quit. Everyone had been surprised when Jerry offered the job to Sheila, but she had quickly accepted.

Joann climbed out of bed. She reached for her robe and went down to the kitchen. Sheila and Joann were renting a cute little house. It was small. There were two bedrooms and one bath upstairs, and a large kitchen and living room downstairs. It was like a little cottage in the middle of town, and they all loved it. There was even a large backyard, a basement, and a park at the end of the street where the boys could play with other children. The rent was even cheap. It cost Sheila and Joann $500 a month.

Joann walked into the kitchen, and there they were—Sheila, Becky, and two guys Joann didn't know. Joann never paid any attention to the men Sheila brought home. They never stayed around long. Sheila's pattern was to get what she could from them, chew them up, and spit them out. She always made sure she hurt them during the dumping process. Sheila would intuitively figure out their soft spots, and the moment they told her they loved her, she would end the relationship, showing them the exit, and saying something to hurt them deeply as they left.

They were men, and Sheila hated all of them, but she was masterful at playing the game. Sheila could be charming and sexy when it suited her purpose, but when Sheila was angry, she could be cruel and vicious. The angry side of Sheila was something that scared everyone who observed it, even those close to her, like Joann.

Sheila enjoyed the chase of getting men to fall for her, but she only wanted them to care for her for the sole purpose of breaking their hearts. Over the last six months, there had been over a dozen men. Sheila had changed so much since Jack had taken the boys from her. All she did was party with Becky and men. Sheila had become quite promiscuous with all the freedom, alcohol, and drug abuse. Quite frankly, Sheila Parks was out of control. She was consuming more and more drugs, and her habit was costing about as much as she was making.

Natasha was very concerned about Sheila's behavior. It was rumored that Sheila was responsible for breaking up two marriages in town. Natasha and Joann felt that Becky was a terrible influence on Sheila, but Sheila thought Becky was perfect. Becky was the only person who was capable of helping Sheila forget. As far as Becky was concerned, life was only about men, beer, lines, and a good time; she was the perfect distraction for Sheila.

Sheila was having a rough time adjusting to life without her boys. The pain was unbearable. Jesse and Keegan came every second weekend for a visit, and Sheila always stayed clean while they were there. The problem was, she partied so hard during the two weeks that she would crash and dry out while the boys were there, and that meant a lot of sleep. Sheila would start to be herself by Sunday afternoon, just in time to take Jesse and Keegan back to Jack.

It was Sheila's day off from work, and she planned to party all day. She was doing a line when Joann entered the kitchen. "Here honey, do you want one before you go to work?" Sheila asked as she passed Joann the straw and mirror. Joann picked up the straw, bent down, and did two lines. She thanked Sheila and grabbed a coffee. Now Joann was ready to start her day, and she went back upstairs to have her shower and get ready for work. One of the guys complained that Sheila had given his lines to Joann, and on came the wrath of Sheila.

"This is my house, and I will do what I want, when I want. Get the fuck out of my house now, you piece of shit," Sheila said in a firm, loud voice. The guy didn't move fast enough for Sheila, so she repeated what she had said, this time throwing a beer bottle at him and screaming. His friend tried to plead his case, so Sheila threw him out as well. The two guys left very disappointed. They'd had a different end to the evening planned. Sheila and Becky sat there alone at the table, giggling. Sheila cut some more lines while Becky rolled a joint.

Joann got home from work at seven. She brought Chinese food home, knowing Sheila probably had not eaten all day. She barely ate while she was doing cocaine. Sheila had lost a lot of weight in the last few months as her habit spiraled out of control. Sheila and Becky were still sitting at the table playing cards when Joann came into the kitchen. Sheila and Becky looked a mess. Neither of them had showered, slept, or eaten all day. Joann fixed three plates of food and tried to get them to eat.

Sheila picked at it, and she tried to eat a few bites. The phone rang and Joann went to get it. "I just paged Dude for more coke. It's probably for me," Becky yelled after her. Sheila got up and opened the fridge to get herself some more wine; she filled her glass full and retuned the bottle to the fridge.

Joann came back into the kitchen. "Sheila, the phone is for you. It's Jack," she said. Sheila felt herself sober at a fast pace. What was wrong? she wondered. She and Jack rarely spoke, even when Sheila was picking up or dropping off the boys.

Sheila picked up the phone and placed the receiver to her ear. "Jack, is something wrong?" Sheila asked nervously.

"Kids are fine." Jack paused for a brief moment and then continued. "The boys and I are moving back to the city in three weeks, Sheila. I sold the house. I'll have your money ready for you when you pick up the boys. Certified check, just like we agreed. Sheila, you are still responsible for transportation when the boys visit you," Jack told his wife, flatly devoid of any emotion. Then, he hung up the phone before Sheila could respond.

Sheila hung up the phone; it rang immediately, causing her to jump. She picked it up, and it was for Becky. Sheila yelled for her and placed the receiver on the arm of the sofa. She yelled to Joann for her to put a pot of coffee on, and climbed the stairs. Sheila grabbed her robe and went into the bathroom. She turned on the taps. Sheila needed a long, hot shower. She needed to sober up and absorb what Jack had just told her.

When the water started to run cold, Sheila turned off the taps and climbed out of the shower. Sheila felt hungry; it had been a while since she had felt a hunger pain. She changed into sweatpants, a T-shirt, and big fuzzy wool socks, then went down to the kitchen. She poured herself a big cup of coffee. She pulled the Chinese leftovers out of the fridge, got herself a big plate, and put it in the microwave.

Sheila ate every morsel of food on her plate. She was going for more coffee when Becky offered her a line. Sheila looked at the cut lines in front of her and shook her head. "No thanks, Becky. I need to speak to Joann in private. How about you take off now and call me later?" Sheila gently suggested to her friend. Becky and Joann where both surprised when Sheila refused the coke, but Joann was absolutely shocked that she would ask Becky to leave.

Becky was obviously a little hurt, but she knew she and Sheila had been together constantly for the last six months; Sheila would be calling soon to party. Becky called herself a cab and got her stuff together. As she left, she told Sheila she would call her later that evening. Sheila closed the door behind her. She locked every lock on the door and told Joann to roll a joint; they had some talking to do. Sheila poured herself another coffee and sat with her sister. She told her all about Jack's call.

They sat together, two sisters, talking like they hadn't in a long time. Joann was thankful to Jack for upsetting Sheila and giving her a reason to be sober, even if it was just for tonight. Joann missed her sister. "Can you believe it, Joann? He is moving back to the city. All I ever wanted to do was go back, and now that we break up, he is moving back. Jack always told me to wait five years and he would bring me home. It's only been two years, and now they're going without me. He's just doing it to piss me off. I know it," Sheila complained.

*Behind the Drapes*

Sheila was angry. Jack was moving the boys away from her. Every time she picked them up or dropped them off, it would be at least a two-hour drive. What would she do if she had car trouble? Sheila's car was old, and it would not last forever. All of a sudden, Sheila jumped up and started to cheer. She reached over, pulled Joann up off the sofa, and spun her around. Sheila was giggling loudly. It had just occurred to her: if the boys were not here anymore, there was no reason for her to stay. She could move any time she wanted.

"I'm moving back to the city!" Sheila announced with a screech. The phone started to ring. Sheila picked it up, and Joann heard her excitedly telling Becky about her new plans. Becky wasn't too pleased Sheila was moving away. Who would she party with? Joann wasn't too excited with the news, either. She loved her job, and she had no intention of leaving. Joann had grown to appreciate Cedar Falls. She would have to get a new roommate, but she was not moving.

That next weekend, Sheila had the kids. Saturday afternoon, Sheila and Joann brought the boys to the city for lunch. On their drive in, Sheila stopped at a dozen bars and dropped off résumés. Sheila had a lot of experience from Barnabee's; Natasha had helped her do up a résumé, and she had some great references. She was encouraged that she would find something. On the way home, they stopped at the park. For the first time in months, Jesse and Keegan really enjoyed their time with their mother.

By Monday afternoon, Sheila had three interviews set up. After each one, she looked for apartments in the area of the bar. Sheila accepted a bartending job in a sports bar called Third Base. It was owned by two Italian brothers, Gus and Nick. Sheila was giving two weeks' notice at Barnabee's, and she would commute to the new job until she moved. She had found a nice apartment—two bedrooms. She wanted the boys to have their own bedroom. Jesse and Keegan always slept in Sheila's bed when they visited, but she wanted them to feel more at home when they were over. She wanted it to be more than a visit.

It was Friday afternoon, and Sheila had been out shopping. She had been looking for some things for the new apartment. As she entered the house, the phone was ringing. Sheila struggled with her bags, trying to get to the phone. As she reached it, it stopped ringing. Sheila looked at the clock. She had two hours before she had to be at work. Only three more shifts, and she would be finished at Barnabee's. Sheila had taken a few days off between jobs; she started at the new place the following Friday night.

Sheila reached for the kettle to make herself a cup of tea, but before she could pick it up, the phone started to ring again. Sheila answered it, and it was Natasha; there had been an accident. Jerry and Joann had gone to the liquor store to pick up a few things for the bar, and on their way back there was a car accident. Natasha was at the hospital, and she told Sheila to stay there. She would come and get her right away.

Sheila was paralyzed with fear. Was Joann hurt? When Natasha arrived a few minutes later, Sheila was standing there holding the receiver with tears streaming from her face. She said nothing as Natasha took the phone and hung it up. "Sheila, we have to hurry. Come on, honey," Natasha said in a soothing voice. Natasha walked Sheila out to the car, and they drove in silence to the hospital.

Sheila and Natasha walked through the door of the emergency room at the small country hospital. Natasha told Sheila to sit down, and she would find the doctor. Sheila sat there and prayed Joann was okay. The doctor came over with Natasha. Sheila noticed that Natasha had tears in her eyes, and she panicked. Sheila stood up and started to back away from him. Soon, she felt the wall behind her. There was nowhere left to run. Natasha held her tight as the doctor introduced himself, looking directly into her eyes.

"Mrs. Currin, I'm so sorry. We did everything we could. Miss Parks' injuries were too severe. There was nothing anyone could do. She passed away a few moments ago," the doctor said as gently as possible.

"No, no!" Sheila screamed as she fell to the floor.

# Chapter 27

The music was so loud, Sheila was reading lips to take people's orders at the bar. The place was packed. It was Tuesday, Karaoke night, one of the busiest nights at Third Base. Sheila was running; she had been for hours, and she couldn't wait to get to the bathroom for a line. The disc jockey got on the microphone and announced it was Sheila's fifth anniversary of working at Third Base. Everyone at the bar started to clap and holler.

It had been a long five years for Sheila. It had taken her two years to somewhat heal from Joann's death. Sheila had never been the same. She was cold and mean to most people, especially men. Her drugs had gotten her through the pain. In the first two months after Joann's death, Sheila had lost eight thousand dollars to cocaine. All the money she had left from the house, gone. Sheila still used cocaine, alcohol, and marijuana often, but she had never returned to the dark days, like when she had first lost the boys. She partied after work, but not until the sun came up. Sheila spent most weekends with Jesse and Keegan. Jack was being more civil and allowing her more access to the kids recently.

Gus and Nick came behind the bar and handed Sheila a shooter. They both gave her a kiss on the cheek. Gus had his hand firmly on

Sheila's ass. "Five years already. We will celebrate after work. Now go make me more money," Gus whispered in her ear. He tapped her gently on the butt, smiled, and left. Nick told her to make two more shooters for them when she had some time. There were three waitresses waiting for drinks at the service bar, and people everywhere. Sheila flew around the bar and got herself caught up in no time.

Gus stood back and watched Sheila work. She was the fastest bartender he had ever seen. Sheila was his star. She kept the staff and customers in line. Sheila had a rough exterior for such a beautiful woman. The entire staff was terrified of her; she would rip them apart for the smallest infraction. Sheila was more relaxed with the customers. Tips were what paid her bills. However, they knew not to piss her off. Sheila certainly had a reputation as a hard ass. She had an excellent rapport with her employers. They really understood each other. Sheila made them money, and they liked and respected each other.

Gus had been trying to seduce Sheila since the day he met her, with no success. Gus was a slimy but sweet man in his late thirties. He had huge black eyes, a thin mustache, and receding jet black hair. He was short for a man, but he was rich. Gus felt the most important thing about a man was the amount in his bank account, and he thought he was the sexiest man alive. Why shouldn't he? He had slept with every waitress and most of the female clientele of the bar.

Although his brother was older and looked just like him, Nick was a little taller, and overweight. Gus and Nick's personalities could not have been more different. Nick was a family man. He had a beautiful wife and child whom Sheila had never seen, only in a picture. Nick didn't feel that a bar was any place for a lady or children. Nick was tough like Sheila with the staff, although Sheila and Nick never had any problems. Sheila worked hard and was good at her job, and that was all Nick cared about.

Gus and Nick were hands-on owners; one of them was always there. Usually, it was Nick during the day, and Gus at night. They would only step out if Sheila was working. Nick came back behind the bar and poured two shooters. As Sheila ran by, he stopped her and told her to have a drink with him. Sheila looked at the waitresses waiting at the service bar. She quickly gulped the shooter, and kept going.

*Behind the Drapes*

"I have to go. The wife is waiting," Nick said. "Sorry I can't stay and party. Here, Sheila. This is for you, just a little bonus," Nick said as he stuffed something in her tip jar. She thanked him and was waving bye when Sheila's attention was brought back to work. The new waitresses had spilled a drink on the service bar. Sheila started to scream at her as it rolled toward her. Sheila reached for a rag, but it was too late. It rolled down and off, into the ice sink underneath the counter. The entire sink had to be emptied and refilled with fresh ice. Sheila was about to blow when Jennifer, a girl who had worked there for a while, offered to clean it up.

Sheila went back to serving her customers. Finally, last call was over. Sheila handed Gus her cash drawer and went right to the bathroom to do a few lines. Sheila came out full of energy. She went back behind the bar, poured herself a drink, and picked up her tip jar. Nick had slipped two crisp hundred dollars bills in her jar. Sheila smiled; he was so good to her. Just then, one of the cooks came up to the bar. "Do you need any help, Sheila?" he asked hopefully.

Sheila looked at Darrel. He had a huge crush on Sheila, and she was well aware of it. Sheila thought he was such a nerd—tall, thin, and awkward with thick glasses—but he was harmless, and he sure came in handy at closing time. "Sure, stock the beer fridge," Sheila said. "When you're done, you can run the dirty glasses through the dishwasher," Sheila smiled as she looked at the full bus bins of glasses on the bar. There were more still to come. Darrel was thrilled to help Sheila, and he ran to the beer fridge, almost tripping on the way. Gus came around the corner just in time to witness the scene.

"You sure have them whipped, honey. Your cash balanced as usual. Come get me in the office when everyone is gone," Gus told her as he copped a feel of her ass and went back down the hall. Sheila yelled at the bouncers to get to work and get everyone out. They immediately started to move people along. Craig came up and asked Sheila if she wanted to smoke a joint. Craig was a waiter at Third Base, the only waiter they had ever had, and Sheila was sure he would be the last. Sheila thought Gus kept him around just so he could have a man to bully around. Gus was always picking on Craig.

Sheila and Craig had become the best of friends. In so many ways, he reminded her of Bill, except for the fact Craig was gay, although he had not come out of the closet yet. Craig was tall and thin, with white skin, bright orange hair, and soft blue eyes. He was very sweet and a little feminine. Guys always gave him a hard time. Even Jesse and Keegan were rough on him, although they really liked him. Sheila always stuck up for him. She felt a little protective toward him, and he seemed to fill a void left by Joann's death. Sheila had been renting a house for the last few years, and about a year earlier, Craig had started renting the basement from Sheila. It had been a wonderful arrangement for both of them.

"Just wait until most of the people are gone. You want something to drink?" Sheila asked her friend with a smile. "Why don't you help me count the beer. Then we can slip out to my car, and I'll cut us a few," Sheila continued. Craig nodded and grabbed the clipboard. He and Sheila went to the beer fridge. Darrel was just coming out; he was finished stocking. Sheila told him to get started on the glasses, and she would be out in a few minutes.

They got out of Sheila's car, and a cloud of smoke emerged with them. Craig and Sheila were giggling, and Sheila started to bang on the back door. Gus opened it and gave Sheila a disapproving grin. Gus hated Sheila using drugs, but he was not about to upset her, so he kept his mouth shut. Sheila and Craig walked by Gus, back to the bar. Darrel and Jennifer were sitting at the bar; everything was spotless.

"Thanks buddy," Sheila said, punching Darrel in the shoulder.

"I helped, too," Jennifer offered, hoping to be included in Sheila's kind words. She tried so hard to be Sheila's friend, but Sheila tolerated her, and that was all. Jennifer was young, nineteen, with soft pretty features. She was from a rich family and was always talking about what Daddy had just bought her. She had no idea what real life was about, and it infuriated Sheila. She thought Jennifer was an immature, naive idiot. It never stopped Jennifer from trying to get on Sheila's good side.

"Thanks," Sheila said coldly as she walked down the hall to get Gus out of the office. Sheila returned a few minutes later with Gus, and they all had a few drinks and chatted. Gus gave Craig and Darrel a hard time as usual, and treated the girls like queens. They were all having fun. Sheila even laughed with Jennifer about the new girl's face when Sheila started to scream at her. There was banging at the back door, and Gus went to see who it was. He returned a few minutes later and told Sheila there was someone at the door for her. By the look on his face, Sheila knew it was a guy.

Sheila still hated and used men. The moment they started to care, she cut them loose. She opened the back door. There stood Simon. He had announced his undying love for Sheila a few nights before when he had taken her out for a nice dinner. Sheila had gotten up from the table, said goodnight, and walked out of the restaurant. She had not answered, taken, or returned any of his many phone calls, and he, like the rest, was devastated.

"What do you want, Simon? I've said all that needs to be said," Sheila asked aggressively.

"Please, Sheila. I just need to know what I did wrong? Please give me the chance to fix whatever I did," Simon begged her.

"It's over because I said it was over. I don't want any more calls or visits!" Sheila screamed and slammed the door in his face. She was being mean and cold, and she didn't care. He was a man. Sheila walked back to the bar like she had just talked to an old friend, and sat down. She looked over and saw Simon crying, watching her through the window. Sheila brought her attention back to her audience and began telling everyone a new joke that she had heard that day. When they all laughed at the punch line, Sheila laughed harder than anyone, looking directly at the window to make sure Simon saw her joy.

Later, Sheila and Craig walked into the house, and Sheila went upstairs to put on her pajamas. Craig sat down, turned the television on, and cut a few lines for them. He saw the answering machine blinking, but, knowing it would be for Sheila, he left it alone and found something to watch on TV. Sheila came back with her flannel pajamas and fuzzy slippers, carrying a bottle of wine. She poured a glass and offered one to Craig. Sheila picked up the straw and snorted her lines. She looked over and saw the flashing light. Sheila reached over and hit the button. "You have seven new messages," the machine told them.

The first three were from Simon. Sheila and Craig listened to them and laughed. The next one was from Jesse, telling his mother about a field trip at school he wanted her to go on. Keegan had gotten on the line and told her he loved her. Sheila listened with a big smile, and she saved it. The next was from Natasha; she was confirming lunch for that weekend. The next one was from Simon, and Sheila just erased it without listening to the whole thing. When Sheila heard the last one, she almost dropped her glass of wine. Craig and Sheila looked at each other, and she played it again.

"Hi, Sheila. I hope you're keeping well. I know you are probably surprised to hear my voice. I've been thinking of you a lot lately, and I wanted to take you to lunch sometime this week. Call me at the office tomorrow. Sheila, I hope I hear from you," she heard Jack's voice saying. She listened to it a dozen times and just couldn't believe it. After all these years, why would he want to take her to lunch? But more importantly, why was she feeling so excited at the prospect? Sheila couldn't wait to call him the next day.

Sheila heard knocking at the door. She checked herself in the mirror. She looked lovely. Her figure had not changed one bit. She wore a light blue sundress that brought out her eyes, and tan heels that showed off her striking tanned legs. She had her hair pinned in the back with little whips falling around her face. It made Sheila look soft and gentle, not the way most people saw her.

Jack was wearing a dark blue pinstriped suit, and he looked at her with a smile, then handed her a lovely bunch of long-stem roses. He reached over and kissed her cheek, and they were both surprised when she didn't pull away. Sheila invited Jack in, and she put the flowers in water. Jack told her she looked beautiful, and she thanked him, feeling shy and a little nervous. He asked if she was ready to go, and she nodded yes. Jack grabbed her by the arm and led her to the truck lovingly.

He took her to a small, romantic Italian restaurant. It was dimly lit, and the food was wonderful. They chatted about Jesse and Keegan. Jack was so charming, and he kept Sheila laughing throughout the afternoon. Sheila had ordered wine, and she noticed Jack was not drinking. When she commented on it, he informed her he had been on the wagon for the last ten months, but he had no problem with Sheila drinking. Sheila was duly impressed. She told him she was proud of him, and he seemed pleased with her comment, as well as himself.

Jack explained to her that his last live-in girlfriend—he had had three over the years—was an alcoholic, and it had turned him off alcohol. She had turned into a raving lunatic near the end, and it had scared Jack. Sheila had heard all about her. The kids had hated her, especially Jesse.

For the first time, Jack apologized to Sheila about the things he had done to her in the past, while he was under the influence.

Sheila told him it was in the past and forgotten. He reached across the table and touched her hand, and Sheila felt an exciting shiver run down her body. The wine, the room, the lighting, the familiar friend, the delicious food—it was all so warm and inviting. Sheila was having the time of her life, and she didn't want it to end. Eventually, Jack looked down at his watch and told Sheila he had a meeting to go to. Jack had done quite well for himself. His business had really taken off in the last few years, and he had made a small fortune.

They walked back to his big, luxurious truck. He opened the door for Sheila, and she climbed in. She watched him as he walked around to his side and jumped in. He looked handsome, Sheila thought. He was wearing contacts now, and he looked very professional. Sheila liked it. Jack bent over and kissed her softly on the lips, and Sheila felt herself kissing him back. He pulled away and told her, "I've been wanting to do that since I picked you up. You look so irresistible."

Sheila giggled like a little schoolgirl, and Jack noticed she was blushing. He kissed Sheila again, softly, and then started the truck. Jack held her hand as he drove her home, and they chatted casually. When they reached her house, he paused before getting out of the truck. Then he invited her out to dinner on Saturday night. Sheila reluctantly told him she had to work. Jack suggested he would cook her a late dinner at his house; 3:00 AM, he offered. Sheila worried about the boys, but Jack assured her the house was big enough that the kids would never see her.

He was right. Sheila had never really seen Jack's house before, and it was huge. She'd never pulled all the way down the driveway, because Sheila had never wanted to run into any of Jack's former girlfriends, especially the ones that had given the boys a hard time. She was always worried about how she might react. Sheila got out of her car and looked around. There were trees everywhere, and she loved trees. She closed the car door softly and went to the back of the house, as Jack had suggested.

Sheila came around the corner and saw a large deck. She could see light coming from that direction, so she climbed the steps. She reached the top, and the first thing she noticed was candles everywhere. The deck was huge, and it completely surrounded a pool, which was dimly lit. To one side were patio doors leading into the house; on the other side there was a table beautifully set for two. There was a bottle of wine, and one glass.

Sheila walked to the table and picked up the bottle. She was just about to pour it when she heard the patio door open. She turned to see Jack standing there. He looked so attractive with his dark tan. He wore cream shorts, a deep green golf shirt, and sandals. Sheila was looking a little more dressed in a sexy little black dress; it was backless, with a plunging neckline.

Jack smiled and walked over to her. He grabbed the bottled. "Allow me. You are my guest. Sheila, you look lovely," Jack whispered into her ear. Sheila told Jack how exquisite his yard was, and he said he would show her the house after dinner, which would be ready in twenty minutes. They chatted comfortably about their day. Sheila sat on the side of the pool with her feet dangling in the water, sipping her wine. Sheila couldn't help being impressed by her surroundings; it was all so luxurious and classy.

Jack made them a wonderful dinner. He made some joke about having to learn how to cook after she left. They both laughed. After they ate and Sheila consumed more wine, Jack suggested she smoke a joint, and they could take a swim together. Sheila thought a moonlit swim would be a perfect way to end her day. She told Jack she would just like to go to the ladies' room first. He brought her in and showed her the rest of the house.

They walked through the patio door into an enormous living room with a large stone fireplace. To one side was a beautifully furnished dining room, and on the other side was a door that led down a long hall. The first door off the hall led to a big country kitchen, and the next was one of the bathrooms. Sheila went to go in, but Jack stopped her and brought her up the stairs. They climbed them silently.

They stopped at Jesse and Keegan's rooms. They were peacefully sleeping in their big rooms. They passed another bathroom, and Sheila went to go in, but Jack insisted she keep following him. They walked into his room, and he closed the door behind them. Jack walked to the bed, reached down, and handed Sheila a sexy black bikini. "I bought this for you today. I hope you like it," Jack whispered.

Sheila kissed him softly. "I love it. Thank you. I'll change and be right down," Sheila said. There was a bathroom inside the master bedroom, and when Sheila went in, she noticed that there was a large Jacuzzi tub off to the side. The house was magnificent. She loved it, and she was happy for Jack. She was pleased to know Jesse and Keegan were growing up in this luxury. Sheila was about to do a few lines, then realized she didn't want to. She happily placed it back in her purse and changed into the bikini. It fit like a glove. When she came out, Jack was gone, so she quietly tiptoed back down the stairs to find her way back to the yard.

Just as she was about to open the patio door, she heard Jack whistle and she turned to see him standing in the dinning room doorway. "Let me show you the downstairs," Jack offered. He grabbed her hand and led her through the kitchen, down a long flight of stairs. Sheila looked around, and it was beautiful. There was a large television, an impressive stereo, a few large deep sofas, and a lovely cherrywood bar. Sheila looked behind the bar and was surprised to see it was fully equipped—fridge, sink, glasses, and alcohol. "I'm looking for a bartender. Do you know anyone?" Jack asked, and they both laughed.

He chased her back to the yard. Sheila picked up the joint while he poured her some more wine. Sheila looked at Jack, and without putting the joint to her lips, she put it back down. Jack smiled. He picked up her hand and gently pulled her off the lawn chair she had been sitting on. He wrapped his arms around her, and kissed her long and soft. There was music playing in the background, so they held each other close and danced. It was the most romantic, magical evening Sheila had ever experienced. She melted in Jack's arms.

Jack picked Sheila up into his arms and brought her over to the pool. Gently, he stared into her eyes as he peeled away the bikini. He looked down at Sheila's naked body; she was breathtaking. Jack wanted her then and now, but he knew he had to be patient and soft with her. Jack removed his clothes and jumped into the pool. He reached his arms out to Sheila, and without any reservation, she plunged into the water and his waiting arms.